W9-AJW-489

ISTHMUS

ISTHMUS

GERARD LASALLE

Isthmus is a work of historical fiction. Apart from some well-known actual people, events, and locales that are part of this narrative, all names, characters, businesses, organizations, places, events, and incidents are either a product of this author's imagination or are used fictitiously. Any resemblance to current events, locales, or to living persons is entirely coincidental.

ISBN-13: 978-1503183339
ISBN-10: 1503183335

Published by Avasta Press
Seattle, WA
www.AvastaPress.com

Copyright 2015 Solipsis Publishing

Editor and interior: Sherry Roberts (The Roberts Group)
Design: Maps and Isthmus Medallion—Randy Mott (Mott Graphics)
Cover Design: Neil Gonzalez (Greenleaf Book Group)
Distribution and Production Direction: Kelsye Nelson
Social Media: Archana Murthy (Writerly)
Web design: Tony Roberts (The Roberts Group), Kelsye Nelson
Audio Book Production: Mike McAuliffe, Tom McGurk, Wendy Wills (Bad Animals, Inc.)

To los discapacitados

CONTENTS

MAP ONE: THE ISTHMUS OF PANAMA

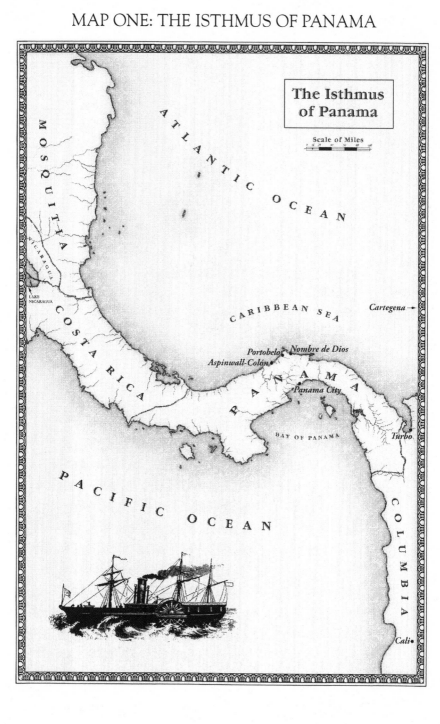

The Isthmus
of Panama

Scale of Miles

MOSQUITIA

ATLANTIC OCEAN

NICARAGUA

LAKE
NICARAGUA

COSTA RICA

CARIBBEAN SEA

Cartegena →

Portobelo
Aspinwall-Colón

Nombre de Dios

PANAMA

Panama City

BAY OF PANAMA

Turbo

PACIFIC OCEAN

COLUMBIA

Cali

DRAMATIS PERSONAE

The Customers

Emmy Evers, Sarah Evers, Jacob Evers, and Napen'tjo "Jojo"

Emilio Gattopardi, nephew of
Bourbon Duke Alphonso Gattopardi

Antonio "Ari" Scarpello, valet of Emilio Gattopardi and
follower of General Giuseppe Garibaldi; Artemesia "Lita"
Perdellaño-Scarpello and their two sons, Jonny and Falco

Tomas Bossman Gonsalves, his adult son, and Tomas's
companion, Gabriella "Gabi" LaFleur, and
their bodyguard "Big Bob" Dorn

Lieutenant Rory Brett, US Army assistant surgeon

Other passengers, including
the Reverend John "Plump Jack" Otis

The Company

J. Abbot Foil, president and CEO of Foil Transport

Carlos Quitero, captain of the Isthmus Guards

Ran Runnels (a.k.a. "El Verdugo")

The Competitors

Rafael Gianakos (a.k.a. "Bocamalo") and "Los Descapacitados"

Nick Deacy, Apolonio Haut (a.k.a. "Pallino Haut)
and the "Deriénni"

The Cimaroons

MAP TWO: THE PANAMA RAILROAD

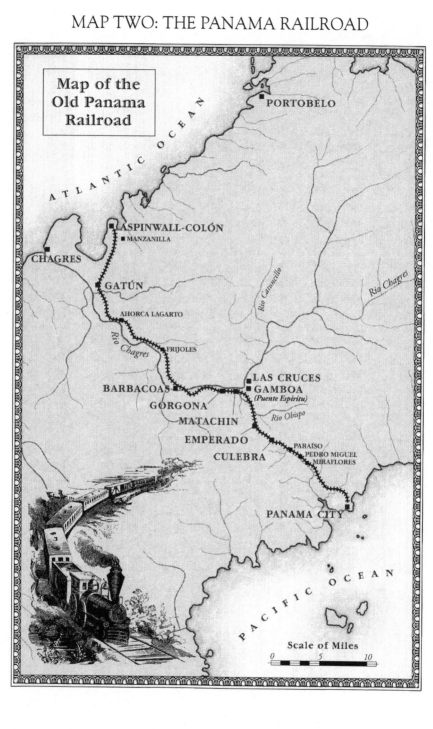

Map of the
Old Panama
Railroad

ATLANTIC OCEAN

PORTOBELO

ASPINWALL-COLÓN

MANZANILLA

CHAGRES

GATÚN

AHORCA LAGARTO

Rio Caruncillo

Rio Chagres

Rio Chagres

FRIJOLES

LAS CRUCES

BARBACOAS

GAMBOA

(Puente Espiritu)

GORGONA

Rio Obispo

MATACHIN

EMPERADO

PARAÍSO

PEDRO MIGUEL

CULEBRA

MIRAFLORES

PANAMA CITY

PACIFIC OCEAN

Scale of Miles

0   5   10

PART ONE

⬦⬦⬦⬦⬦⬦⬦⬦⬦⬦⬦⬦⬦⬦⬦⬦

ON THE TRACK

Travelers of the early and mid-nineteenth century pathways across the Isthmus of Panama aptly called the routes "murderous." The density and unpredictability of its lush terrain, vicious banditry, and an assortment of deadly diseases killed many who dared to trek the overgrown remnants of the old Spanish Camino Real, a four-foot-wide, seventy-mile trail from Las Cruces to the Caribbean ports of Portobelo and Nombre de Dios. "Bungo" boat travel to Panama City via the Chagres River and then overland via the Real Las Cruces was no better, and promised the gold-rush voyager a high probability of illness and death over the ten arduous, perilous days it took to navigate that sinuous route. It wasn't until 1855, when officials of the American Panama Railroad Company drove the final spike in their trans-isthmus railroad, that a truly efficient, relatively safe means of transport for cargo and passengers from one ocean to the other permanently prevailed. On that day, all other routes—including the Camino Real, ship travel across Lake Nicaragua, and the forty-seven-day circumnavigation around the Horn of South America—became comparatively more expensive and impractical.

The oceanic transport efficiency afforded by this route favored trade with the rapidly emerging trade centers of the southern and eastern United States, and with it the eventual dominance of the world's economy by the young, aggressive Yankee nation. From 1855 to 1860, more than 190,000 passengers traveled on the new railroad, the majority westbound to California and the Oregon territory. Within five years, the railroad company's stock value soared to over $350 per share. Profits from passenger and freight transport returned the $7.5 million initial investment to stockholders in less than three years, and annual dividends during the first eight years of its operation exceeded 15 percent. Until the Panama Canal was opened in 1914, the isthmus railroad was one of the most profitable entrepreneurial investments in history. To those fortunate enough to afford the usurious cost of travel and transport across the isthmus, it was the most wondrous experience in the modern world.

Many men died constructing the railway. Many men died protecting it.

CHAPTER ONE

◇◇◇◇◇◇◇◇◇◇◇◇◇◇◇◇◇◇◇◇

BOCAMALO

The reports came to him on time and, to his deep satisfaction, told him exactly what he needed to hear. The first report, relayed in breathless detail by an inside observer who would be hanged if his betrayal was ever discovered, was the most important of all the ones Rafael would receive that morning: he learned that by four A.M., in the light of lanterns trimmed to offer only a dim light, eight burly, quiet men had completed the quiet transfer of the cargo he had anticipated for months. While several other armed men looked out into the dark, attempting to guard the railroad station from whatever they likely had been told might be lurking in its jungle periphery, one by one the big men lugged more than one hundred padlocked containers from carriages, up a stout plank, and into a plainly painted, oddly trimmed rectangular boxcar. In that freight car, a huge man had wrestled each of the metal containers across the metal floor to massive, thick-walled gray safes, one in each corner. Three broad-shouldered black men then hoisted each box onto neat stacks, the numbers of each sequentially ordered container turned outwards. Standing in the center of the boxcar two men had supervised the operation. The taller of the two, wearing black overalls and a dirty, beige leather coat, cradled a double-barreled ten gauge in his folded left arm and silently watched the workmen. The other, dressed in tweeds like a business dandy, closely watched the cargo boxes while checking and rechecking a long manifesto. When the last of the steel boxes were berthed, the man in the tweeds signed the document and nodded slightly. On that signal, the three blacks pushed the massive safe doors shut. The short man in tweeds walked over to each safe and, with a ceremonial flourish, spun its dial. When he finished his task, he tucked the manifesto into his breast pocket, raised his chin, and lit a cigar in a display of official satisfaction.

"Den de big man, he points his gun at us and says 'now get your black asses outta here.' De little man . . . after he spin de dials on the safes . . . he clicks his heels together, like he is real happy," said Rafael's insider.

Rafael smiled on hearing that last detail from his informant. The man in the beige leather coat had to be Quitero, the foreman of the railroad's henchmen. The dandy in tweeds who had clicked his heels had to be the one and only J. Abbot Foil. The prize was in position, and despite several delays that had threatened his entire operation, Rafael knew they were back on schedule.

The next information Rafael wanted came less than thirty minutes later. Another insider, a kitchen worker at the posh Enterprise Hotel, reported that by five in the morning the entire executive staff of Winfield Scott, the most decorated United States military hero in modern history, had partaken in a lavish breakfast. Afterwards, as his staff began final preparations for the general's brief rail trip to Aspinwall-Colón, the old general had slowly waddled down to his room, with two aides following a step behind. One wrote notes while the other reached forward with orders for the commander's approval and signature. Most importantly to Rafael's plans for the day, the worker told him that everyone had eaten an ample breakfast.

The next report Rafael received told him about the *norteamericanos*' security for the notorious general. By five fifteen, outside in the alley next to the hotel, five armed but shirtless dragoons wearing suspenders, dress blue pants, and polished boots had led strings of horses to the rails in front of the expensive hotel. A sixth shirtless soldier had followed behind with their coats and pressed blouses, as if they were preserving their uniforms to keep them neat. Rafael thought about what that meant. Indeed, the heat from the scorching previous day had dissipated little during the languid night and what little cool air crept in from the waterfront had certainly increased the humidity and would thus increase the stickiness of the escorts' starched uniforms. Everyone knew about this particular *norteamericano* general's insistence on decorum. Because his escort dragoons would be expected to be proper, prim, and neat for their security escort to the train, none likely would want to provoke the inevitable reprimand for a less than crisp appearance. Rafael smiled again. He loved benefiting from the ironic consequences of such impractical etiquette.

Having heard the last of several other reports, by six thirty that morning, Rafael was ready to place himself unobtrusively in a large group of smartly dressed people, each holding passenger tickets, umbrellas, and various handbags, all queued in a neat line that wrapped half-way around the yellow stucco train station's office. He wondered who would be in his car and observed which amongst them were armed. He watched carriages arrive with late-comers who anxiously reached out to busy porters to negotiate the transfer of their baggage.

He became alarmed when he saw twenty-four New Grenada soldiers arrive on horseback, but relaxed when he realized they were armed with only drums, coronets, and piccolos. They almost certainly were a local military band dispatched to honor Winfield Scott's departure from Panama City. The soldiers marched through the gates with their instruments onto the platform and disappeared out of sight.

The hubbub increased. Vendors, some of them Rafael's own men, moved up and down offering the travelers trinkets, bright orange and red flowers, and street food—fried plantains, mango juice, coconut rice, and an assortment of colored meats wrapped in blue corn tortillas. Few of the people in the line purchased the food, he noted, but several bought the souvenirs, little tin and ribbon mementos of the railroad adventure. He listened carefully as several ticket holders in line attempted conversation, raising their voices to be heard over the vibrating metallic sounds of steam engines that moved back and forth coupling the last cargo and flat cars to the plush passenger compartments. He watched dark-skinned attendants in white uniforms push wagons to the open baggage compartments and briskly transfer the remaining steamer trunks, crates, and bags into the hands of the porters waiting in the cars. The ambient hum and buzz of the station increased in intensity as the engine's flywheels whirred a steady counterpoint to the clarinets' and piccolos' practice ditties. Then the gates opened and the passengers, eager to begin their grand trip on the most luxurious and expensive transport in the world, surged forward to their assigned coaches.

Trailing a few steps behind the throng, Rafael looked down at his passenger ticket. Coach number four. He noted the time on the station clock. Seven. It was the ninth of February 1860. He fingered the cylinders on one of the pistols he concealed in his waistband, and as he did so, he laughed quietly to himself. It would be an auspicious trip indeed.

CHAPTER TWO

<><><><><><><><><><><><><><><><>

SARAH

She watched as she always liked to do, in the brazen sort of way she knew. It was her private game, one that she had always kept to herself. She knew it discomfited some, but she also was amused that most people dismissed it, likely because of her age. And she had become good at it, taking in each person's dress, posture, and accouterments then guessing their background story. Based on her deductions, she guessed, as well, a destiny for each soul's life. Past events assured her that she was correct often enough. She wondered what the passengers would have thought about that ability. "Prescient" was the word Emmy, her mother, used to describe it.

Outside on the platform to the right of the cars, a military band was playing brassy versions of songs she had heard a few times in the Northwest, and off to the left she heard the shout-barking of vendors reaching out to the travelers, guessing their nationalities and trying out languages, beckoning them with street food and drink for the trip. The noise amplified her excitement, and she played *her* game, guessing about each of the passengers as they took their seats in the coach.

There was an obese man with a red face that resembled the plump apples she had seen when they had stayed in San Francisco. Wearing a stiff preacher's collar and a large, flat, shiny but simple gold cross on his chest, he was perspiring heavily, the sweat soaking through his shirt and white coat. He fanned himself with his straw fedora—so uncomfortable, not long for this world, she thought and wondered where he was headed, why he needed so much heft around his soul if he really had Jesus to care for him.

Two elderly women, pale and frail, wilting like delicate, fading flowers laden by the heaviness of the warm, wet air, wore matching white linen petticoats with a fine, delicate lace trim; they held on to each other closely, perhaps spinster twins no longer identical, taking the journey of their lifetimes, she guessed.

A broad-shouldered, black bushy bearded man with big, beautiful, peacock-blue cat-like eyes, had his face turned down, only glancing up and around periodically, careful not to make eye contact with anyone. Wearing a brown plain sombrero, thin cotton striped serape, and a light blue kerchief, which made his eyes stand out dramatically, he concentrated intently on the playing cards spread out on the seat beside him in a silent game of Patience—a lonely loner most likely, she guessed. A native of this country? she wondered.

Sarah noted that every person who boarded their car carried a different type of grip, each built for a different purpose, and each with its own set of distinct weathered scars. The most elegant person to enter the car that morning was a tall, narrow-shouldered man, wearing a red cambric tunic beneath a dapper, black silk long coat. He clasped a finely stitched teal-blue leather valise. The thin veneer on the bulging bag had started to peel back from its latches betraying a mismatch between its intended show of elegance and travel practicalities. When he handed it to his valet, he used both hands as if holding the satchel together lest it spill open and embarrass him. As he did so, he saw Sarah's mother, and his expression changed. Then, he noticed Sarah watching him. Her curious stare made him fumble a bit. He made a slight nod to her and, with a gentle, apologetic grin, placed himself in a row further down the aisle. He had lingered too long in his glance at her mother, Emmy, Sarah surmised, and had been caught. He looked out the window, feigning no further interest in Emmy. But Sarah was not fooled.

The gentleman's valet was an older, sturdier man in his forties and almost as tall as his employer. He had the strong, rough hands that reminded her of the farmers who had worked for her late father. He was also wearing a bright red shirt, but his was cut from a coarse flannel. He gave quiet instructions in a gentle tone to a woman carrying an infant and holding the hand of a little boy—his wife, Sarah guessed. The woman and her children sat behind the gentleman. The valet then dismounted a sturdy, tan canvas knapsack covered with repairs completed in many different colored threads embroidering it. As he sat down beside his employer, he let out a slight sigh. When he saw Sarah watching him intently, he cocked his head, reached up, and twisted his bushy mustache. Then he winked at her. He reached into the sack and pulled out a tattered pamphlet and began thumbing through it. The title on the cover read "Revolutione e Risorgimento." Italian, her mother told her later. When settled in, his frock coat opened, and she saw a two-barreled hammer-percussion pistol tucked into his waistband.

A few minutes later two black-skinned men and a tan-white woman boarded followed by a large, burly fellow. Sarah easily surmised by the jaw and brow features of the two black men that they were related. The older of the two, short and power-fully built, carried a small carpetbag. Like the tall, genteel man with the blue valise, he was dressed somewhat formally for the short rail trip, wearing an elegantly cut, white linen jacket and sharply pressed trousers. He wore thick, heavy gold chains around his neck and on both wrists and diamond and ruby rings with big, shiny stones on the small fingers of both hands. For a small man, he carried himself with a determined air of authority and a poorly concealed impatient condescension.

The second man, who appeared to be his son, stooped slightly and seemed meek, Sarah thought. "Deferential" was the word she had learned from her mother's copy of Dr. Roget's *Thesaurus*. He was deferential to everyone around him. He looked broken and depressed. She tried to make eye contact, but he avoided the gesture. The woman, dressed in a white silk taffeta long dress with a red silk crochet edging, was attractive but hard-faced. She also wore the trappings of wealth, with multiple strands of shiny pearls around her neck and dangling gold earrings. The set of her jaw was forced and determined as that of her companion, the older man. She wore many rings with big stones, but no wedding band.

As the threesome settled into their seats, two beleaguered and poorly dressed, shoeless attendants, one black and one mulatto-white, entered. Each carried additional baggage, carpetbags that matched the others. In their struggle to mount the pieces in the overhead travel rack, the white attendant stumbled and bumped the carpet satchel out of his master's hands and onto the coach floor. At the slip, the short, dark man quickly reached down and, snarling a command in a Spanish accent that Sarah had never heard, snatched it up and placed it squarely onto his lap. Protecting something, Sarah thought. He barked again, sending the two attendants meekly bowing and backing their way out of the cabin. He glanced at Emmy and then stared angrily at Sarah. The stare was defiant and intense. She did not back down from her study of him, however; so he gave up and turned his attention to the bustle outside.

She turned her attention to the large, burly, white man who sat in the seat next to the black man's son. What was his relationship to that group? she wondered. Was he what they called a "bodyguard"? He had a scarred, ruddy, weather-beaten face; large hands with swollen knuckles; and wore a silk suit that certainly didn't fit very well; it was too small at the middle, as if he had gained weight and had impatiently stuffed himself into it. He didn't seem happy and looked sleepy. Was he a drinker and a brawling man, she thought, like many of the ones she had seen working the docks at home on Whidbey? She wondered where he had been. She tried to make eye contact with him, but he ignored her stare and looked straight ahead.

"Mrs. Evers! How wonderful to see you again! What a pleasant surprise!" she heard a voice call from behind her. Turning, Sarah saw two men in blue military uniforms walking down the aisle approaching her mother. Their buttons were polished, and they toted black leather bags that looked like the one that Dr. Edwards carried back home on Whidbey Island. Sarah recognized the men—had seen them a few times when she, her mother, Jacob, and Jojo had stayed in San Francisco a few weeks before. The younger of the two, she remembered, had stared at her mother in a way that the other soldiers, the ones who had done all of the showing off that day, had not. He was very handsome, compared to the rest, she thought. "Captivated," she had decided was the right word to describe the attention he gave to her mother. He was handsome . . . and captivated. That was a funny condition to be in, Sarah thought. She didn't understand it.

"Captain Letterman! Lieutenant Brett! What a surprise to see you as well!" she heard her mother say. But their banter was interrupted by a loud peal of thunder, followed almost immediately by a downpour of rain that created a deafening drumbeat on the roof and windows of their car. And when it let up briefly, a flash of lightning and more thunder came. For almost a minute, no one spoke, everyone listening to the pounding roar and watching the flooding display. And then, just as it let up, Sarah saw the short, dark man stand and peer through the open window at a commotion building outside their car. His laughter turned into a snorting cackle as he spoke to the woman beside him.

Sarah turned to see. Eight nearly naked, yellow-skinned men, Chinese or isthmus natives, had mounted the platform and were struggling with a slowly writhing mass—the biggest snake she had ever seen—perhaps sixteen feet long and as thick as a fat man's leg. They were holding it up to the passengers in the car. Behind them stood a weathered, toothless woman, topless and wrapped in only a loincloth holding up four thick-bodied snakes: one dark black, two bright green, and one gray. They appeared to be dead, but as the downpour came on again, the gray snake—it was as long as the woman— began whipping its tail, coiling itself around her small waist. The little woman grinned and held it up higher to the car.

The dark-skinned man in the train car brayed a deep, sonorous laugh that raised in pitch as he turned to the woman and young man next to him and commented loudly, "He he! *Nos vamos comer muito bom esta noite! Eh?*" Then, to some of the other passengers who appeared to be Panamanians, "*Una comida grande e mucho seta noche! Eh? Una comida grande!* Ha, ha!" Sarah had learned enough Spanish from the farmhands on Whidbey to have a sense of what that meant. She shuddered. Were they really going to eat that thing? She wondered if Jojo and her brother, Jacob, who were riding in the car ahead of them, had seen the spectacle—and wondered how Jacob, who now showed little reaction to anything after the ordeal he had endured in the Pacific Northwest, would respond. She looked over at her mother's reaction for some guidance. Emmy simply smiled and shook her head very slightly. Another "admonition," Sarah realized.

CHAPTER THREE

◇◇◇◇◇◇◇◇◇◇◇◇◇◇◇◇◇◇◇◇

BOCAMALO

Rafael drew a red ten of diamonds and placed it on a black jack of clubs, the Yankee version of "La Sota," the peasant knave. He was becoming very good at this game of Solitaire, "Patience" as the English liked to call it. Each card turned gave him new hope for a neat, ordered solution, and he had to neither concede failure nor share the winnings with anyone else. He had all of the aces in their place now. It was easier, he thought, than the Baraja he had played for so long—with each card bearing its own story. This Yankee game was simple by comparison, just like them. The simple strategies he employed while playing tested him while allowing him to keep alert to his surroundings. And each hand reinforced his sense of brilliance and luck, for he was certain he seldom missed the solution, if indeed, one was to be found.

It would be a well-coordinated move. He had been known for that among the few who really knew, the other *pantera* who preyed on those fat ones who were foolish enough to traverse the isthmus jungles. That admiration from his brothers had always been so very important to him, he realized. But, unlike his previous hunts, this one also would be bold as well as precise. And, because he always quietly kept to himself, like the jaguar crouched in the underbrush of the night waiting for the larded traveler, the ambush would be unexpected and, to those who survived, would seem to have come from out of nowhere.

He knew he was shy, so unlike the other highwaymen, and that distinction, as much as it often had been a painful badge, had kept him alive, he realized. So many of them loved to chatter like howler monkeys in the dark canopy and, gamblers that they all were, boast about themselves and their exploits—how lucrative they had been and that bragging had gotten them on the famous "list of el Verdugo," which did not serve them well at all. Unlike them, his exploits were unsung, perfect but modest raids—precise stings that hurt the Yankee investors but not as much as did the big, sloppy hijackings, of which his competitors bragged. By comparison, his thefts were subtle and never overreaching. They were discrete in their planning, execution, and aftermath—first hitting the mule trains and then the early crossings of the new railroad, usually timed to coincide with other larger raids by the Deriéni, who could never keep a secret. Using artifice and distraction, learned from the lessons of cutpurse pursuits, he kept the prospectors and New York investors confused with their attention to the big mouths and big spenders of Aspinwall and Panama City. And long ago he had moved himself outside of the larger coastal towns to the countryside, stayed away from their bars and cantinas, kept to himself with his most trusted allies, all of whom he had known for many years.

And if anyone outside of his allies ever had really watched him, they all forgot about him. Everyone. Because he had stopped the raids; stopped surprising everyone with his quick, little strikes. They forgot about him because anyone who knew of him assumed he too must have been among those chosen to so prominently be executed in Panama City and Aspinwall, hanging and rotting with all the rest, all in a line on the ramparts of the old fortresses.

But, he smiled to himself, he had not been among the stupid, unlucky ones. He had escaped—was away in Cali when the railroad company's hired assassin, Ran Runnels, "El Verdugo," had killed so many of the other Deriéni, the highwaymen of the region. So when word about the deaths of seventy-five of the Deriéni reached him in Colombia, he stayed away and quietly waited.

And now Runnels, the intrepid dogged one, was gone, his butchery work completed. He had, with all of the hangings and whippings, beaten the desperadoes of the region into submission. And although Rafael knew that Ran Runnels's reputation still lingered like a retributive spirit over the newly completed railways, he instinctively knew that a quick, coordinated attack against a treasure train like this—which secretly carried the gold dust and nuggets of two hundred lucky miners from the Pacific Northwest's Fraser River—certainly would be easier to carry off than it ever had been. Because the miners and security company and railroad owners assumed their secrets were well kept. And everyone thought he, if they knew of him at all, was dead and buried—with all the rest in two big, common, unmarked graves. The unexpected strike would be widely acknowledged as masterful and swift, and that was as important to Rafael as was the treasure itself. And then he would go away again, far to the south perhaps. He moved a six of hearts to the seven of clubs, exposing a ten of hearts.

Rafael Bocaro-Gianakos, later to be called "Bocamalo," was the bastard son of a very popular fair-haired, blue-eyed Colombian woman who called herself Ava, although she was called by many "Boca Caro" or simply "Bocaro." Kidnapped from somewhere in the north as a young, white adolescent and sold into servitude by a Portuguese slaver, Ava no longer knew her real name and, as part of her journey, had been moved as an indentured young prostitute through various South American Pacific seaport towns. Because she was clever and resourceful, she survived that long, terrible ordeal, and by the time she was sixteen, she had secreted away enough gold to purchase her freedom from the mean but aging brothel owner in Cali. She moved across the neck of Colombia to Cartegena, a decadent and prosperous town that was favored by the Spanish crown. It was also the seat of the Church's Inquisition in the New World, and Ava had heard correctly that discrete services in such a repressed society paid well. She had the chance to marry, but after a luckless first year, because she had no other marketable survival skills, she purchased a room in an upscale and well-disguised bordello that serviced the Cartegena upper class.

Over the next few years, having developed a reputation for exotic favors and also because she was considered beautiful and had somehow escaped the external manifestations of the diseases that plague the women in her trade, she became highly sought after by many wealthy and influential men. She also became the covert obsession of the royal family's regional confessor, an older, brilliant monsignor named Xavier Maria Quintarosa, whose interest in her developed from the territorial governor's confidential divulgences to him in the cathedral's private shriving pew. After hearing similar confessions about Ava from the penitent voices of other prominent men, every one of whom he recognized in the cool darkness of his private booth, Quintarosa's curiosity pushed him past the boundaries that governed sin. At first, while taking an early dinner in a small trattoria nearby, he simply observed the men coming and going from the bordello. But when he finally had a glimpse of Ava passing by as she made her way to the market, the temptations of a liaison kept Quintarosa in a frenzied passion for her. Unable to contain himself any longer, he crossed over, falling headlong into the addiction of the sins of the flesh.

He devised several ways to satisfy it. For months, disguising himself as a wealthy French merchant or a Portuguese minor diplomat, he paid his way into the bordello to see her, and because she was discrete, he knew his secret was well kept. A half-year later, when the possibility of discovery nevertheless became too great, he arranged for Ava to visit him in his rectory after the Monday and Wednesday masses, when the attendance for the services would be at its nadir. When they sensed that the housekeeper assigned to clean the rectory was becoming suspicious, they pushed themselves deeper into sacrilege and taboo. The back entrance to the confessional led into a resting room that was kept well stocked with wine and housed a small bedroom. The profanity of that forbidden liaison was as exciting for Ava as it was for Quintarosa. Her own lust brought her to the church every day. But it could not last.

Unfortunately for Ava, she had fallen in love with her intense, fervent lover, who had increasingly, in the aftermath of each encounter, when they had the time and privacy to talk to each other, spoken to her about his hopes and fears. He described his home in Spain and, on occasion, told her that he might someday take her there, to see the fine buildings in Madrid and Barcelona, to show her Paris or Rome or the countryside and mountaintops of Andorra. She allowed herself to dream about a life away from Colombia, where she could live in peace with her lover for the rest of her life. She did not understand or appreciate the depths of his torment, however.

Initially, Quintarosa's lust was overpowering and his desires were insatiable. But over the next year, the intensity of his guilt and repeatedly confessed sins, detailed in increasingly elaborate detail at the request of his own confessor, overwhelmed all else, and he forced himself to begin distancing himself from her—to save both their souls, he told himself. Ava, sensing that she might lose him to his guilty remorse and fearing the pain of this loss, allowed herself to become pregnant by him. It was the worst of dilemmas for both of them. The monsignor, having participated as a condemning Inquisitor judge in similar circumstances involving other Spanish clergy, understood all too well the consequences of discovery. To protect them both from a scandal that would have resulted in torture and probable death, for his confessor had deduced her identity, Quintarosa disavowed any association with her and had her sent away to the countryside. Ava, who neither understood nor cared for the gravity of this problem, was heartbroken at this rejection. In her secluded confinement, broken by the horror and insecurity of an uncertain future and loss of her first-ever love, she foreswore the risk of such enraptured feelings forever. In the fifth month of her pregnancy, she tried to kill herself with a deadly abortive concoction she had purchased from a local Wounaan tribal shaman. She failed in her abortion and suicide and, after a tumultuous recovery, carried her pregnancy to full term.

Tormented by guilt after her sins, Ava baptized her newborn as "Rafael" because the one Cartegena priest who was willing to take a prostitute's confessions told her that devotion to the archangel of healing graces would help her son survive somehow, with all that he had going against him—he had been born with a severe cleft lip but also a strong constitution that likely would keep him alive to suffer all the physical discomfort and mental anguish so inevitably implied by that deformity. Each time she looked at the baby's facial disfigurement or felt his lips at her breast, Ava was saddened, convinced that the abortive concoction she had taken had caused the defect in her child.

She tried to love him, saw a resemblance to her in his eyes, but found that she could not, for she also saw in him his father's determined jaw and demeanor, felt it when she fed him at her breast. Although she tried to protect her son, quietly she wished to herself that he might become ill and die as did so many infants in the coastal towns. When her confessor asked her to reflect on this selfishness, her guilt deepened as did her inability to be a mother to the child. She turned to her bastard son's father, but the monsignor, summoned to imminently return to Spain after the decline of Napoleon's family's influence on his country, simply and coldly gave her a small purse and refused any more help. When the financial supplement was exhausted, Ava in desperation again returned to the only trade she knew and rented a room near the same bordello where she had previously worked.

Because no one else would care for her baby, she kept him in her room behind a curtain, seldom taking him out or having anyone else care for him, even when she was entertaining one of her many frequent visitors. He grew stronger despite her repressed hopes for him to die, perhaps, she thought, because the infant boy was protected by the archangel for whom he was named.

Rafael drew a red jack of diamonds and placed it on the queen of clubs. The queen of clubs, the commoner's mother—"Madre de los plebeyos"—would mate with "Suerte Rey," the king of diamonds, if he could be found, he thought. She would be less interested in the love of a more powerful but dallying king than the security of a lesser nobleman's wealth, he was certain. Where was this king hiding, he wondered?

As he watched the passengers select their seats, Rafael observed the men and remembered what he had learned about behavior when he lived in the room with his mother in the bordello. The tall, round-faced, genteel-appearing, well-dressed one was an Italian, he surmised. He looked at the man's hands and saw that they were, despite his height, small, soft, and well manicured. He looked down at the Italian's shoes—beautiful, highly buffed, alligator leather on the man's small feet. Aristocracy? Rafael had been told once that their class could be distinguished by the refinement in their features. Small women and tall men with small hands and feet. Perhaps, he mused to himself, the man was trying to travel inconspicuously and without fanfare. He knew the type. He was the type of man who, when visiting Ava, would speak softly, pay well, prop himself up on his elbows, and keep most of his clothing on during the encounter—and almost always finish immediately. Satisfied at the ease of taking their money, his mother would always hum a little song to herself after men like this one left her bedroom.

Rafael would watch this Italian aristocrat closely. A possible valuable hostage?

CHAPTER FOUR

◇◇◇◇◇◇◇◇◇◇◇◇◇◇◇◇◇◇◇◇

GATTOPARDI

Emilio Gattopardi glanced at Scarpello to see if he was alarmed, but his valet only raised his eyebrows and nodded. As the little men outside struggled with the writhing giant reptile, he wondered whether there was an equivalent for it anywhere in Europe. He had seen vipers in Sicily, broad-headed, coal black, and deadly, but they were small, no longer than his outstretched arm. The bulge in the middle of this huge snake's body was as large as a small animal, perhaps a goat, he thought to himself—or perhaps a small child. He wondered if these aborigines were savage enough to use a child for such purposes. He tried to peer into the black eyes of the old woman holding up the four snakes to see if she had ever done evil, dark things. He knew about the vodou he had heard existed in some of the remote parts of this region. If black magic existed in his Sicily, it certainly had to be practiced here as well. She was singing something to herself, doing a little circle jig, smiling through a cracked, tattooed face that told him nothing. But he wondered.

He looked over the other passengers on the coach, caught himself again lingering on the beautiful woman sitting with her daughter, and wondered what she was thinking about the spectacle. He reached up to be certain his hair was pushed back and in order. Then looked back outside at the slick, spotted, giant reptile and its swollen mid-girth. That was how they must have caught the creature, he realized! They baited it with some type of prey, waited for it to gorge itself, and then, as it was close to bursting in the middle, caught it as it struggled to escape into its nest's door. Or maybe, as it became lethargic after swallowing its prey, it just had decided to nap in the sun, reflecting on the beauty and fairness of this full-bellied moment in its life. An "Abodanza," the peasant's heaven. He smiled to himself. Or maybe the snake wasn't really digesting anything at all but, rather, was showing a pregnancy, burdened with a terrible fecund load of viper eggs that when hatched, would be scattered throughout the region, a brood of predators that would clean out the forest's small mammals and birds for fifty kilometers around. He definitely would have to ask Scarpello. The fellow knew about this sort of thing.

So much was in turmoil. He was settled onto a comfortable seat now, anticipating a pleasant ride again as he had enjoyed several months ago traveling west across the isthmus. The North Americans had done a good job keeping the rails clean from garbage and safe from the beggars. He wasn't looking forward to the passage across the ocean, despite his booking into an ample berth on a fast ship, for he knew that as he came closer to his homeland, his anxiety would only increase and his apprehension would make the luxury of his travel irrelevant. He didn't know what he would find upon his return.

He looked down at his tattered valise, bulging with letters of introduction, correspondences depicting hopes and conveying rejections in the most polite and diplomatic manner. It was the symbol his failed "mission," if that is what it could truly be called. His eight months in South America—this break-back, humid, rotten, six-month trek, from which he was now returning to Italy empty-handed and exhausted—had left him more confused than he had ever been before about what his purpose in life really was. He was already thirty-one and had nothing to show for his efforts. "You are a failure," he heard it from many voices, the loudest of which was that from the ghost of his father.

This mission had started out with some promise, albeit with some mixed purpose and blurry goals, he had to admit. After a good amount of earnest effort, continuing his publicly avowed distaste for the excesses of the noble class into which he had been born, he had agreed to leave his home and accompany old comrades from his past far beyond the borders of Europe to spread the word about human rights.

It wasn't that long ago, he recalled, that he had been swept up, inspired by the passionate orations he heard at the academies in France and Italy on "social justice," as they called it. It had started in a way that he suspected was the way it began for many—at first to impress the young women (whose names he could not remember now) and compete for their affection—daring to speak up in meetings, then at rallies in Milano, Torino, and Bologna. As his popularity grew and he achieved approving nods from colleagues—and coy, welcoming smiles from the more "progressive" of the women—he authored pamphlets that, he learned later, were distributed widely in Paris and Rome and even here in South America. In a few short years, he had been befriended and had won the sufficient trust of enough liberal elements in Italy, all outspoken advocates of exporting revolution throughout the world. He had even been arrested once and briefly held, although he had also been released very quickly via the quiet influence of his family, a convenient secret that he cleverly kept to himself. Using the episode as a badge, he was given the blessings of wealthy liberals and ultimately, a few years later, their financial support to explore South America for revolutionary opportunities. Everyone knew that slavery continued in Brazil, Paraguay, and North America. Everyone knew that inequality and poverty existed in every country in the "new" world. "Go west with the apostles of change and see if there is opportunity for social upheaval," they had encouraged. "You will be remembered!" He actually believed in those causes as a younger man, he reflected.

But things had changed. He was older now and, with the death of his father and the economic impact of the potential loss of financial security that had always been a quiet, private reassurance to him, with his inherited assumption of responsibilities that he be the steward of his family's dwindling fortune, he began to understand certain realities. He had become frightened, he admitted to himself reluctantly.

It wasn't that social causes were frivolous; he had seen the living conditions of families in Torino. It was just that he was beginning to understand what his father had repeatedly told him when he was growing up and, later in different ways, again on his deathbed—that all men in reality were victims of the human condition. Everyone suffered and died in his or her own way. A family's survival was entirely dependent upon whatever means it could master, be it title, force, or cleverness, to preserve the cushions of privilege. Family, not friends, mattered. It was family that bribed the jailers and judges, not friends. It was family that kept the hearth fire warm. Friends and lovers drifted away.

After his father passed, and he was draped with the head-of-household mantle, Emilio found himself lost in a tunnel of doubt. Notices of accrued delinquencies frequently arrived on the same day as letters from his revolutionary cronies in Milano. He found it almost impossible to keep his priorities. He wanted to be faithful to a noble purpose—but he had to care for what was left. He learned that the debts on his father's estate, built up over generations, were enormous. The payouts for extravagances of the past, for indulgences in which he had partaken but had not initiated, were coming due all at once and had fallen into his lap. The cushion that had always been there, the assurance that had been given and which he had easily assumed, was as thin as sheets of paper in his father's ledger. He would be bankrupt. He would be poor, not by choice, but by happenstance. And the letters from colleagues from his carefree past kept coming.

It wasn't fair.

So he was caught. Trying simply to find a safe beach-hold

as he was carried along in the continued, admittedly heady momentum of a reputation he had so ably created for himself during his days as a student, and tossing in the bewilderment of now having to manage the crumbling remains of his family's fortune, he began reaching out in several directions. He kept up his correspondences with old friends, for they were tied to a time when he was celebrated and popular. The women, the passion, he smiled to himself as he thought of the trysts. But he also had started quietly communicating with men of his father's generation—the men who he knew were connected to the old ways, the very men who represented all that he had railed against in the past. It wasn't sinful to have done so, he reminded himself.

Could he again sleep on the floor as he had as a student?

Was his a carefree past or a careless one?

Who had the wherewithal to help him find firmament?

It wasn't fair.

Over the next year, he began comparing himself to student colleagues with whom he had marched arm-in-arm in the student riots in '52 in Paris and then in Rome in '54. He started to resent them. None of them had his pedigree. None of them had his responsibilities. None of them were giving up something as they cried out to burn down trappings of social order that had endured for so long. Perhaps the social order had endured successfully for a reason, he heard himself say. He began to see many of his colleagues from the past—no most of them—as feckless and envious rock throwers.

He came to the conclusion that men needed to look out for themselves. He heard his father's voice again. "God, if there really is a God, allows men to decide their own fates in this

29

life. . . . The next life will even things up perhaps." But Emilio had been born into *this* life! He decided that it was impossible to help men help themselves. He needed to help *himself* and his family first, then worry about fixing the rest of the world.

As the year passed, Emilio kept those opinions to himself. Thus, his liberal associates continued to correspond. And for reasons he still did not understand, perhaps because he couldn't stand the embarrassment of failure in maintaining the Gattopardi family estates, perhaps because he needed to find some adventure and break away from the doldrums of the ancient Sicilian lands that had been bequeathed to his great-grandfather, he took leave from it all. He agreed to travel with other colleagues—comrades—who were spreading out through the new world to find opportunities for revolution. His family was stunned.

He realized that by his own bourgeoisie actions over the past eighteen months, he might be perceived as deceptive by some of the very people with whom he had once shared many youthful ideals. For at the same time as he was taking the money of his wealthiest friends in Bologna and Paris, all social liberals, he had also covertly begun accepting the beneficent support of Bourbon and papal benefactors. Certain debts would be forgiven—substantial debts—if he did what they wanted. And all they wanted was for him to simply find a way to seduce away from their Italy the most famous revolutionary leader in the world, Giuseppe Garibaldi, and all of his damned mischief. "Let them take their revolution elsewhere," his benefactors said. "That's all we ask." Emilio understood the sentiments of the patrician class in which he had been raised, and although he did not completely agree with all of what they promulgated, he did appreciate that there would be much less unnecessary violence if the likes of Garibaldi could be diverted from provoking even more dissent on the Italian mainland. This solution seemed simple and, to his own mind, evolved and wise.

But it was all too complicated. He had nothing to show for his time. None of the diplomatic or revolutionary contacts he had made while visiting Uruguay, or Ecuador, provided any opportunity. He had visited Paraguay thinking *that* might hold promise because slavery still flourished there and so many liberals had beseeched him to persuade Garibaldi to lead their miscellaneous causes in an armed upheaval of the country's dictator. But Garibaldi had shown no interest. He was too clever to go back to South America again without certainty of success and ample financial support.

And then, two weeks ago, Emilio had received a coded dispatch from his Bourbon contact with news that Garibaldi was about to begin another campaign, bypassing Rome this time and heading to southern Italy with a small army—"a thousand men" to "liberate" the region from the royal families that controlled the local governments. The Bourbon and papal benefactors were withdrawing their support. His mission was terminated. He had been "summoned" home to receive different instructions.

Thinking about what that meant, Emilio cursed to himself. He had tried—he couldn't blame himself. In his last few months, desperate for success and anticipating everyone's displeasure and without the help of his valet, Antonio Scarpello, who had taken leave to travel to Quito to retrieve his Ecuadorian wife and child, he had intensified his efforts on his own. Using an assortment of Spanish and Italian noble class connections, he discretely had made ambassadorial visits to Italian contacts in Chile and Peru, looking for *anything* that might help him accomplish his task to find a way to get Garibaldi to return to South America. But those efforts were also complete failures, and in Santiago all he had accomplished was the acquisition of a festering genital rash after a brief dalliance with someone, a supposed naive virgin, he had foolishly convinced himself would be an easy conquest.

And so he was here, crossing back across the center of the American continents, wondering what would be done with him, author of the disappointing information he had sent back home. Could he keep the trust of the liberals? Would the Bourbons and papal contacts honor their promises? Would they ask him to do more—be bolder and go to Caprera, the Goat Island, Garibaldi's refuge off of the coast of Sardinia, to feed lies to him anyway; to attempt to dissuade the hero from his latest adventure for revolution in southern Italy and Sicily? And if he so improbably were to be successful, might they ask him to also send emissaries ahead of Garibaldi to negotiate a clever, quiet kill in South America, far away from the Italian peninsula? Or believing that he might not win "the hero of the people's" trust, would he be asked perhaps to arrange an even bolder action? Lace the man's imported food with arsenic? Arrange to poison him slowly as he had heard the English had done with Napoleon? Or dashing it all, simply tell him to send in a team of suicidal assassins and attempt to overwhelm the man's loyal guards? He did not know what he would be asked to do upon his return to Rome. But could he ever attain the charismatic zealot's *real* trust, even accompanied by Scarpello, one of the leader's most loyal followers? He doubted it. Garibaldi was a clever man.

Emilio had only met Garibaldi on a few occasions. He thought about those events. Emilio certainly had been taken with him, just as most people were. To him, the man was actually larger in spirit and physical presence than the way he had been depicted by fawning journalists, the romantic writers such as Dumas and Victor Hugo and the many women who swooned in his wake. His hair was as fiery red, although a few gray hairs were showing in his beard and long, braided mane. He was wiry and broad shouldered and carried himself with so much flair that it was just impossible to not turn and try to take it all in. A *contadino*'s king, he thought to himself. Or perhaps he was the embodiment of that which his own royal ancestors had manifested when they had fought for their kingdoms.

Emilio wondered how much he was being used by both sides in this struggle. He was coming to understand that he was not in control of anything.

Emilio sighed. He looked at his own reflection in the window. He knew he was handsome, but to what purpose? He wondered if the vigorous élan and physicality that had been present in his own family's line centuries ago had been bred out over the generations by indolence and lust, the disease and rot of the noble classes of Europe. He shook his head as he thought about the damning inanition and presumptuousness of his own family, which had allowed the caretakers of the Sicilian estates they managed to progressively take over and push the patrician owners out, slowly but surely, and as effectively as would have been a bloodier solution, like the ones promulgated by the followers of the troublemakers like Marx, Mazzini, and this common sailor pretending to be a liberator, another Simon Bolivar.

He shook his head as he thought about his young and ignorant sisters and frail mother, dependent on but increasingly unprotected by a social order that was crumbling all around them, vulnerable to the very people they had trusted to assist them—the *padrino* estate managers, those sullen, dark characters deeply ensconced in superstition and vendetta, carrying out his orders with a transparent and resentful subservience. Certainly, they bowed as they were expected to do, but in their every gesture, he felt that they barely pretended to follow even a shabby version of appropriate decorum or respect for their superiors.

What difference would it make if his patrician secret benefactors murdered the likes of Garibaldi, Marx, and Mazzini—made them dead saints instead of living, unpredictable, and unmanageable heroes? It was all over. Within Emilio's own lifetime likely, his family's estates, the grand facades of an economy that was being challenged everywhere, had become unsustainable burdens, dilapidated and embarrassing reminders of overextended, diminished aristocratic power. And, like the frescos that once, when fresh, had brought delight to its owners, but now were mildewed and peeling, his family's fortunes would dry up and fall away as well.

He wondered how it would all end.

He turned to glance again at the beautiful woman sitting with her daughter. A North American, perhaps? She was wearing black. A young, unattached widow with her daughter? What would she think about all of this? There was a composed stateliness about her. He liked that. Wondered, as he watched her discrete movements, what she would be like as an intimate companion. Perhaps there would be the occasion, some pretense to engage, to compare her with the baronesses and student lovers with whom he had dallied only a few years ago. There would be enough time on this train ride to catch her attention—turn her head enough that she would be taken with the softness of his eyes—then he would keep that attention with the subtle mention of his family name, his title, and its implied power. It had worked well so many times.

The thunder outside opened the sky, blurring everything, but the vendors on the platform remained and he watched the gray snake in the little woman's left hand come alive. He realized he knew nothing about snakes. He would have to ask Scarpello about that one also.

CHAPTER FIVE

EMMY

That morning, she had pushed herself out of bed as she always had done. It was a hard habit and, as much as it always seemed to hurt, she had gotten accustomed to that pain long ago and the ache always faded quickly.

The breeze coming in from the Pacific had helped diminish the pervasive stench of the town. The malodor was present with every breath, and to mask it somewhat, she had purchased tincture of violet and doused kerchiefs for herself, Jacob, Sarah, and Jojo. They had smelled Panama long before their ship had come in close enough for docking at the long wharf. It was as if its streets, churches, hotels, shops, and houses had all been built on a heap of detritus mixed with sweat, raw sewage, and locomotive oil.

After the ship set anchor and they landed at the pier, while riding in the carriage from the dock into town, Emmy realized that she had been prudent to make arrangements ahead of time for accommodations at one of the better of the town's thirteen hotels, the Casca Viejo de la Panama. Although it was exorbitantly expensive, ten dollars per person per night, the ship's captain had promised that its accommodations would be comfortable, but more importantly, its security would be robust. In the short ride to the hotel, she saw many vagrants and thugs hanging about, eyeing them as they passed by, and couples—dandies and whores—copulating in the filthy alleyway behind one of the churches. Brazen beggars approached their carriage and tapped on its sides. One tried to open the door but was slapped down by the driver who wielded a long stick. It was discomfiting, and she was relieved that Jojo, observing the same, did a good job distracting her children from these sights.

Making their way into the old town, they passed the saloons and store fronts, the ruins of Spanish villas, and the fortifications that over the years had been destroyed, rebuilt, and destroyed again, and she wondered how this ancient town had come to its present state of disrepair.

It was all built around greed and convenience, she realized. As a portal and passageway, at first for gold and silver being moved along trails through the jungle by the Spanish from Peru to Europe, and now serving trains for the hopeful and newly rich, souls passing in the night in opposite directions, it was a convenient whore of a town. Looking about, the degree of desperation she felt from everything and everyone she saw along the route, outweighed the ambitious hopefulness she perceived in the spirit of other cities she had visited like Boston, Victoria, or San Francisco. This wasn't a place to settle; it was a place to use and leave. That ambience of functional expediency was pervasive and left a humid patina of decay on everything that attempted permanence. And it seemed to cling to everything and everyone here. One should not linger in Panama, she concluded. She knew she would need to keep her family indoors for the balance of the day and then depart as quickly as possible on the first train in the morning.

She was relieved to see that the hotel employed uniformed guards at each entrance and at the base of its alley fire escape, but she was disappointed to find that the interior was run down and far from comfortable. She found bed bugs in all of the linen, and the largest cockroaches she had ever seen crawled on every surface. Two were larger than her fist. The sound of the street below, shouting vendors during the day replaced by hollering drunken men and women at sundown, only abated during the many downpours throughout the day. The cacophony kept her from relaxing at all. She shared a room with Sarah and Jacob and taught them about bedbugs and roaches, neither of which they had experienced in the Pacific Northwest. They would have to fumigate their belongings when they finally got to Boston.

A distant calliope, its bright sounds muffled, droned on in the midst of it all, even during the rainy lulls late into the night. Despite the wet heat and the buzzing of flies and mosquitoes that somehow found their way through the screened windows of the hotel, she had slept for a few hours, waking sooner than she had wanted. She found herself waning a bit while running through an inventory of everything that had to happen before sunup—so much to do, to get Jacob and Sarah ready for this leg of the trip. So many details to make them respectably presentable; to send all of the luggage, trunks, and packages ahead. She kept checking her list. What was missing?

And then she had drifted off while fighting it. Quiet, it seemed for a few deep breaths . . . and then she was running again and her feet were torn and she was in rags on a hot beach. Something was trying to wrap itself around her left ankle, and she didn't know whether she was running toward something she needed desperately or away from something fearful and loathsome. She heard pounding. Sharp reports. Gunshots? Pounding and then the screaming—a little child's voice—bam, bam, bam; pounding and hollering. Men's voices. Angry men's voices. More pounding. More men's shouts and a few women's voices now. Calling out. Bam bam bam bam bam! Then the small voice, a familiar one, and she turned because she knew it was Jacob calling out again. And then Sarah calling out. Then Jacob again. And he was there at their bedside, screaming again. Three A.M. The screaming, startling her awake. Jacob crawling into bed with her and Sarah. Sobbing. She would not get back to sleep she knew, and the soreness of that rubbed deeply.

CHAPTER SIX

◇◇◇◇◇◇◇◇◇◇◇◇◇◇◇◇◇◇◇◇

BOCAMALO

When Rafael was five, Ava then twenty-five and very tired of her trade, found a gullible customer—a small-shouldered, quite homely but passionate red-headed man, who was vulnerable to his insecurity and arrogance—and was able to seduce him into falling in love with her. The customer, Savas Michaelis Gianakos, whom she and the other women had always called "the Greek man," promised to leave his wife and take Ava and Rafael away from the brothel in Cartegena. Using much of his modest savings from his official duties as a solicitor for the region, he had purchased a small rancho near the new military port of Turbo, when the republican president granted one thousand "fanegadas" of uncultivated land to men who were willing to relocate. In Turbo, the Greek man told Ava, they would build a new life, carve out a coffee plantation from the lush and fertile jungle mountainside, and perhaps become rich by supplying a growing Yankee addiction to this new drug. She would be his queen, he told her. She could forget her past and all of the pain she had suffered.

Savas Gianakos, who also was an earnest and protective man, adored the clever Ava, who plied the art of flattery and lying on insecure men like him. She told Savas that she was afraid that her former lover, the monsignor, who had recently returned to the New World from Spain, would reappear in her life and try to hurt her. She promised Savas every form of pleasure and told him he was the greatest of lovers and her love of loves. So beguiled, and feeling powerful in a way that he had never known before, Gianakos took on the demeanor of a protector. In return for her favors and the security of her love, he doted on her and promised as best he could that he would provide for her boy. He promised to teach her to fly high above her fears. Perhaps because he was so emboldened by his newfound sense of invulnerability and with renewed energy and enterprise, he changed in a way that all of his associates noticed. He improved his posture, purchased concoctions for virility, consciously deepened the timbre of his voice, and stepped forward with a heady confidence that he had not previously boasted. His business ventures and influence flourished. He became an exceptionally generous benefactor to the Church and to the community, and was extolled for his accomplishments and brilliance, which helped silence the clucking of the town's more conservative gossips.

But Ava's fears about the return of her past lover became a reality. Less than a fortnight after his return to Cartegena, assigned there to reestablish the Inquisition in the New World, Xavier Maria Quintarosa began sending cryptic messages to her asking for a quiet, private meeting. At first the messages were civil but soon turned pleading and then threatening. When she did not respond, he called her a "coward." Sickened by the thought of renewed obligations to a man whom she had decided to hate, and terrified by the possibility that Quintarosa might harm her, Ava conveyed her fears to her Greek lover.

Having met the mercurial Quintarosa on more than one occasion, the Greek man understood the validity of her fears. Because Savas was well-connected, he was able to make several appointments with influential clergy in Cartegena, Cali, and Turbo. He asked Ava to ignore the missives. One week later, after prominently contributing large public purses to the Colombian Church and arranging lucrative, private annuities for its most influential hierarchy, Savas brought Ava to the periphery of the town, where he had hired a hot air balloon from a visiting French circus. Aloft over the forests and on to Cartegena, peering down at the towers of the cathedral and the rectory of her previous lover, he held her hand and boasted to her that she was now well protected. With the dramatic, dizzying perspective so gained, the church seemed small and insignificant. Savas reassured Ava that all men, except perhaps for pilots like himself, were small in spirit.

And his clever ploys worked. After their move to Turbo, and then, after investing his increasing fortune in a vast plantation above San Isbel in the Gulf of San Blas in the lush foothills above the mouth of the Rio Cuango, even farther away from Cartagena, they seemed to escape all the past. The memory of Quintarosa just faded away. The Greek man's business flourished on the plantation that was high in the hills overlooking the ocean. Ava grew plump and comfortable.

For a few years, they enjoyed the security of prosperity, and Ava felt a peace that she had not known before. At her urging, the Greek man gave to Rafael his family name and, when he was in a generous mood, taught the boy to play card games. He conducted lessons in speaking English and reading in Spanish and Greek. To please Ava, he generously also paid an aging Irish barber, a self-proclaimed surgeon, to perform a difficult cosmetic procedure on the little boy's deformed, gaping upper lip. Unfortunately, the barber, as skillful as he was, had poor judgment and failing eyes. Operating in poor light and without magnification, he succeeded in closing the boy's grotesque cleft, just as he recalled seeing it done once before by a skillful physician in London. But the barber did not understand facial anatomy very well and did not appreciate that the closure of the lip would only partially correct the underlying deformity, a partial cleft in Rafael's hard palate that would push the boy's palate, teeth, and scar apart as his skull matured. And, because he used no form of anesthetic, he approximated the lip edges poorly as the boy writhed in pain during the procedure. The wound healed poorly, leaving a visibly thick scarification. As he grew older, Rafael tried to hide the botched lip for he saw that people seemed to immediately focus on that part of his face when meeting him for the first time. When he looked into a mirror, an infrequent conceit, he complimented himself for the beauty of his widely spaced blue eyes and when he forced himself to look at his lower face he fantasized that the deep fissured deformity running vertically from the cupid's bow of his upper lip up to the base of his nose made him resemble a jungle panther.

The surgery had been meant to help, as well, the boy's speech defect. However, although Rafael's enunciation was more intelligible after the procedure, in his self-consciousness he soon developed a stutter that drew more attention to his problems. His teeth grew further apart and drainage from his sinuses kept his breath fetid, only partially masked by the wild mint leaves he found in the forest. The Greek man, who believed he had done his duty by paying for the expensive operation, teased Rafael as did others. Shunned by everyone on the hacienda, Rafael learned to keep to himself, and his loneliness grew more intolerable.

Sometimes, at the worst of times, he left home, hiding for several days at a time, hoping he would be missed by Ava and the Greek man. In the forest and on the riverbanks, he encountered the native Kuna and Embera Indians of the Darién who left him alone, but allowed him to watch their activities from a distance. Thus, he taught himself to live in the wild. When he had the opportunity to interact with the Kuna, he listened carefully and learned their Chibcha language well enough that they accepted him. Following their habits, he smeared his skin with the paste of ground Azteca ants to repel the mosquitoes and the sicknesses they were believed to bring. He watched the animals, learned to distinguish the vipers from the harmless snakes, find their lairs, and snatch their eggs. He found the holes of the tarantula and learned how to tease it out using a soft, bent grass reed. He learned to spear hunt for javelina and roast its meat over small fires. He caught the yellow frog and used its skin as a potent poison concoction for his dart tips. He built cozy homes for himself in the treetops and in one of the caves and stayed up in his fortresses at night, high above the forest, away from the big cats.

And he tried to teach himself the ways of the educated. During the day in the filtered light of the lush forest's canopy and in the evening in his cave, he attempted to read books that he had stolen from the Greek man's hacienda library. To overcome his speech impairment, he occasionally travelled through the jungle to the seaside and put stones in his mouth and practiced enunciating dramatically in Spanish, English, and Greek over the pounding surf, as had the famous ancient stuttering Athenian orator, Demosthenes, whom the Greek man had once described. But despite his absences and what he hoped was an improvement in his speech, his mother gave him little attention. To his disappointment, she never professed missing him. The Greek man, whose insecurities more and more frequently provoked him to take advantage and show cruelty, only teased Rafael all the more and started calling him "Pico Demotenes." Rafael, intensely lonely and bitter, found himself beginning to hate the man.

He put the eight of spades on the nine of hearts, moved the pair to the ten of diamonds, and listened to the dialogue between the well-dressed Italian man and his valet. He watched the valet speak to the woman behind them. She nodded and handed the infant in her arms to him. The valet hoisted the fussing baby above his head, singing a gentle little song, and it calmed immediately. Commoners attending a wealthy aristocrat, Rafael thought. He was impressed with the placidity and confidence of the valet and wondered whether the valet would put up a fuss when his men snatched the hostages.

Twenty miles away, just outside of the town of Barbacoas, near the tall bridge that spanned the Chagres, four men emerged from the jungle, took sledges and pick axes from their mules, and sat down in the morning shade next to the track. They looked at their timepieces.

Just outside of Gorgona, as the line reached the plateau before reaching the river, four more men did the same.

CHAPTER SEVEN

◇◇◇◇◇◇◇◇◇◇◇◇◇◇◇◇◇◇◇◇◇◇

SCARPELLO
AND LITA

He traded his infant son for Jonny, who was squirming. Lita needed to feed the baby before he also became fussy again and disturbed the other passengers. He looked over the coach's riders, noticed a young girl, perhaps ten or eleven, watching him intently, closely examining his actions and that of every other person who boarded. That made him smile. He looked at the woman dressed in black who sat beside her. He assumed it was the girl's mother. They had the same facial characteristics, but her eyes, also widely spaced, were brown whereas her daughter's eyes were a pale blue. The two of them were intelligent, he sensed—and fierce, but in a different way. The girl was curious and bold. The woman was calm and contained. Kind but tired, he sensed. Grieving.

He had traveled on this train once before in the other direction. The brief journey would take four or five hours, if there were no mudslides or washouts. He was excited to get to Aspinwall and then to the ship that would carry him and his family across the ocean and home to Italy. Much was happening there, and he wanted to be part of it. And he wanted his children and Lita to meet his large family in Rome. It would be safe if he quietly slipped into the city up from Naples and kept the visit brief. Perhaps he could leave Lita and his children with his parents for a while.

Antonio Scarpello was born to a family of hard-working, honest, agnostic cobblers who lived on the periphery of the Jewish Quarter of Rome. The durable workman's boots handmade by Antonio's grandfather lasted a lifetime, and the fine leather gloves made by Antonio's father fetched a price ten times that of the commoner's shoes. As a result, his family prospered by its steadfastness in the turbulent ten years after the Bonaparte family's exit from Italy.

During his first seven years, the Jewish and Christian communities had coexisted peacefully. For in the early years of his reign, Napoleon Bonaparte had advocated inclusion of Jews into his new, enlightened Europe, cynically placating Christian critics by announcing that his liberalization was calculated to help the Jews "abandon their usurious ways" and assimilate with society. The scheme, designed in part to co-opt and employ coveted wealth to help finance his expansionist ambitions, was dependent on political stability and wide-spread martial success. It did not succeed. The peace did not last. After his defeat at Waterloo, many of the reforms that Bonaparte's liberal regime had instituted were abandoned or reversed—the exiled pope returned to control his papal states, the Inquisition was reinstated in many parts of Europe and the New World, and aristocratic families that had been displaced by the Corsican reclaimed titles and expanded their own privilege. They exacted revenge on anyone with whom they had issue, including many apolitical bystanders. Widespread bloody civil conflict erupted again, and coinciding with the pendulum's swing back to royal hegemony, the Jews of Europe experienced yet another series of pogroms, outright takeovers, and lesser assaults, conveniently rationalized in a variety of ways, legal and religious, by the perpetrators. Antonio's family kept to its quiet, unassuming ways, servicing the rich and poor alike with its reputable work.

During the weeks of the Passover and Easter celebrations, when Antonio was only seven, bands of thugs ransacked the Jewish Quarter, torched several homes, and beat to death an elderly couple who happened to be caught outside as they returned from tending to an ill daughter. The next day, else-where in the ancient city, as long processions of reverent, white-clad celebrants moved along the corridors in honor of the risen Christ, gangs of urchins descended into the area look-ing for loot in the burned-out community. Antonio, who had been kept safely inside during the violence, watched events from the second-story window of his grandmother's home and saw a group of five Roman teens begin violently harassing three small Jewish children who were attempting to salvage possessions from the debris of their destroyed homes. He did not know the children personally but had seen them in passing, and their discourse had always been civil and respectful. The bullying he witnessed was so disturbing to him that, without stopping to put on a shirt or shoes, he ran down the staircase, picked up a brickbat in the courtyard, and jumped into the fray to defend the smaller children. Crouching low and roaring in a way that surprised everyone including himself, he struck hard, crisp blows with the brickbat to the shins of each of the older assailants. They ran away, howling in pain. After they left, he conducted the children to safety and then returned home without revealing to his family what had transpired. But the event did not go unnoticed. One old Jewish bystander watching from behind a curtain in his home later relayed the vision of seeing a small "crouching angel" descending onto the scene, routing a large crowd of teenaged bandits. It was, he said, "as if a small lion had been sent by God." Despite Antonio's embarrassment by the sobriquet, thereafter he was called "Ari," or "God's Lion," by the Jewish and Christian children in the community.

Fifteen years later, at the age of twenty-three, he read the social justice works of Mazzini and then became captivated by the exploits of a flamboyant, patriotic, red-haired sailor, Giuseppe Garibaldi, who knew how to stir men into fighting with passionate disregard for personal safety. Antonio had found a cause, the "Risorgimento," into which he could invest his passion. It put him in the company of other young student idealists, all of whom were aching for change in a society that prominently displayed its disparities and injustice.

In 1848, after reading Alexandre Dumas's accounts of

Garibaldi's exploits, he traveled to join the firebrand in South America, fought by his side in Argentina, escaped repeated assassination attempts by the landed gentry in Uruguay, and then, when the zealot was sent away from that country, he returned with Garibaldi to Italy with ambitions to again march on Rome to depose the pope and help rid his country of the French, Austrian, and Spanish interference into his emerging nation's sovereignty. As the revolution written about by intellectual agitators like Mazzini took hold in the hearts of men, the Romantic Movement's most influential writers became its leading proponents. Dumas, Hugo, and Sand extolled the virtues and built the myth of Giuseppe Garibaldi, the revolution's most visible and charismatic character.

During those famous exploits, Antonio "Ari" Scarpello won the trust of Garibaldi and others in his entourage, for he repeatedly proved himself to be dependable, competent, and loyal with a passionate but careful advocacy for the rights of all men.

And in the course of this journey through numerous countries, including Ecuador, Chile, Peru, China, and the United States, following a famous leader whose ego made him vulnerable to manipulation by clever politicians such as Count Emilio Cavour and the future Italian king, Prince Victor Emmanuel, Ari Scarpello was diverted by his heart. He fell in love with a young Ecuadoran student, Artemesia Maria Perdellaño.

Artemesia, called "Pistolita" by her father and known as "Lita" by everyone in Quito, was an anomaly in Ecuadorian high society. The youngest daughter of a prominent physician who had been trained in Madrid, she had insisted, with her father's blessing, on attending an academy that had been created by Jesuits for the exclusive education of young wealthy men. Because she was intelligent and tenacious, the Jesuits made an exception for her but insisted she dress in men's clothing during her attendance. In all of her studies, including fencing and shooting lessons, she bested most of her classmates. She was fervent in her studies and had great difficulty restraining her liberal opinions during the philosophy, theology, and political lessons. She became easily provoked when speaking of the ineptitude of the Ecuadorian government in addressing inequality in her country, which had endured repeated power shifts and twelve different presidents in less than ten years. She dressed in peasant's clothing, disowned her dowry and contributed it instead to a mission orphanage. She disavowed what would have been a considerable future inheritance. And then one week before completing her studies, she abruptly quit the academy. She was pregnant.

Her lover, as she later explained to her father, was a young man named Ari Scarpello, one of the ardent followers of the Italian revolutionary, Giuseppe Garibaldi, who had been invited by her father to stay as a guest at his estate. The young man had flirted shyly at first, then began sending her little gentle poems, in Italian, English, Spanish, and French, each of which she had committed to heart. The one written in both Italian and English, which she had always kept close to her, read:

"Su fra gli alti alberi,
da un triste sonno
Questa fragranza mi risveglia
Nella notte focoso,
Scivola via e mi dice che sei lì, Amore
Ancora lì, Amore mio,
nelle profondità e al di sopra
di questo bosco rigoglioso e fecondo."

"Up into the long trees,
from a sad slumber
This fragrance wakens me
Out into the torrid night,
It drifts above and tells me you are there, Love
Still there, my Love,
deep in and high above
this lush and fertile forest."

It was the poem she had read on the first night she had come to his room.

She was passionately in love with Ari.

She kept her pregnancy to herself—and wept in private. She knew the scandal would jeopardize his safety and ruin Garibaldi's trust in him. On the day of Ari's departure with Garibaldi, she hid a letter in Ari's possessions announcing her condition and promising him her everlasting love. He did not discover it until he arrived in Italy fifty days later. He wrote a long letter to her every week thereafter.

In 1858, after Emilio Gattopardi, the nephew of one of Sicily's most wealthy Bourbon aristocrats, approached the

Garibaldi insiders with a scheme to have the hero return to South America to lead a revolution in Paraguay, an opportunity arose for Ari to return to Quito and retrieve Lita and his son. Garibaldi, who was increasingly frustrated in his exile in Sardinia, was intrigued by Gattopardi's overture. He assigned Ari to accompany the young nobleman, with instructions to serve as his valet but, because of the man's family ties, also to carefully watch his activities. Ari, who had become active in a number of abolitionist causes in both the United States and South America, eagerly accepted the assignment. He penned his thoughts in a letter every day as the opportunity for their reunion approached.

Ari met his little boy, Giovanni Perdellaño-Scarpello, or "Jonny," for the first time on the steps of the cathedral in Quito on the morning of his baptism. Lita became pregnant again within a few days of his return. The trip across the isthmus would take them to Italy, where she was prepared to follow him with Garibaldi's One Thousand Red Shirts into yet another region of that peninsula, a famous adventure that likely would be watched by the entire world.

CHAPTER EIGHT

<><><><><><><><><><><><><><><><>

BOCAMALO

By the time Rafael was nine, he understood that the plantation was not far enough away from the bordello he remembered from the Cartegena days. It was too close to Portobelo and Colón, where many merchant ships anchored. Ava's reputation had followed them. On successive warm nights during the torrid, dry season, when the Greek man was away on one of his many business trading ventures, the boy saw men riding up to the hacienda, led from the town below on mules by an enterprising town waif. Remembering the bordello and all he had witnessed as a small boy, Rafael realized that the visitors sought joy from his mother, the woman who, in years past, had given pleasure to many. On the first encounter, Ava, seeing the danger to her security in this, was embarrassed and sent the men away. But she had been found, and despite her protest and refusal to be with them, they kept coming nevertheless, singing ribald love songs to Ava as they neared the rancho, always when the Greek man was away in Turbo or Cartegena. Within a few months, gossip reached the trading house in Colón where the Greek man made many of his business transactions.

At first, the Greek man refused to believe the stories, but the deep-seated sense of inadequacy he had always carried with him—insecurities that had been so skillfully suppressed by Ava's reassurances—seeped through. He did not confront her directly about the rumors but spoke to his ranch foreman who said that he had seen men coming from the hacienda. At the beginning of October, he cancelled his trip to New Orleans, an important annual business journey that was always his most profitable but one that would have kept him away for almost two months. Suspicious of every man who stepped off of the ferry from Cartegena or Colón, on one occasion, he convinced himself that one of them, a priest, was Ava's former lover, Quintarosa, returning to find her. He followed the man to the inn where he had lodged. The next day, after waiting outside all night, he realized that the cleric really bore no resemblance to the man he knew she had once loved.

This foolishness did not mitigate the Greek man's obsession. Despite Ava's protests of innocence, he began spying on her. As the weeks passed, he became increasingly sullen, jealous, and then, indulging in a vice that he had always avoided, he began drinking. Reading the smiles of associates in town as smirks and hearing derision in their voices, his fears overwhelmed him. His accusations increased, and he became abusive, first in private and then in public to the woman he loved and also to the boy.

On the fifth day of December in 1821, Rafael, knowing the truth to the circumstances his mother had attempted to explain, dared to advocate for her innocence. The Greek man, who had never before been violent, set off into a drunken rage and beat Rafael with his fists for interfering.

Ava showed little concern for Rafael or the punishment she saw him sustain on her behalf. But after that incident, she withdrew her affections from the Greek man and refused to let him into her bedroom. That only made matters worse. Over the next several days, in his darkening fears, the man's verbal abuse became more and more explosive and violent. Then he slapped her. Ava, who never had been struck before, fought back in the manner she knew would wound him deeply. She told him that she had never loved him and that he was a little fool. Everyone knew it, and she had known it from the beginning.

Rafael saw that exchange. Not comprehending the depth of Ava's insult to his stepfather, he again attempted to intervene. As Savas Gianakos, now thoroughly inebriated, prepared his mount to ride down to San Isbel, Rafael approached him, intending to stand up for his mother. But Gianakos, hurt and furious, chased him through the stables, beating him this time with a thick bamboo shoot, and sent him running away into the forest.

Rafael stayed in his cave high in the foothills overlooking the mouth of the river. He brooded over the events, still wondering how he might resolve the conflict, convinced that his own loathsome appearance had somehow brought on the events. A few days later, during the most vulnerable moment in his mother's existence and unbeknownst to him, further events changed Rafael's life forever.

Disguised as a French merchant in the same clothing he had worn ten years earlier, and guided by the urchin who had in the past brought other men up the foothills to the plantation, Quintarosa reappeared.

Ava heard them approach as the guide hollered out the same ribald song he had sung when bringing men in the past. She stepped outside, waiting to chastise the boy for bringing yet another suitor whom she would have to send away unfulfilled. From the kitchen of the hacienda, as she peered down the valley pass at the approach of the two riders a half-mile away, she recognized her former lover. While she waited, her stomach turned in anger and disgust, for she had long ago closed her heart to the man and wanted nothing he could give her. When the two were within fifty yards, holding up a bloody poultry axe, she stopped them and began screaming loudly for them to leave.

Quintarosa, who had rationalized his entire journey as some private mission for the salvation of Ava's soul, was so stunned and embarrassed by the vehemence of her rebuke, that he pulled off his disguise and looked to her beseechingly to see if she recognized him. When he did this, Ava laughed and quietly said to him in contempt, "Hippocrite! *Enganador!*" He was shamed. After a long pause, he turned his mule to head back down the mountain. Unfortunately for Ava, the monsignor passed Gianakos, who was making his way back home. They recognized each other, and in the awkward pause,

Quintarosa sneered, then reached into his vest and threw a pouch of gold coins in front of Gianakos's mule and rode on, laughing as he made his way down the mountain. Gianakos said nothing to Ava on his return but went into his study and began drinking again.

The next day, on a warm New Year's Eve, five years after moving to the hills outside of San Isbel, in a fugue from the bleak despair and hopelessness that is found when one believes one's deepest fears have been confirmed, the Greek man dismissed the hacienda's house servants and rancho hired hands. He released the horses and livestock. Early the next morning, after watching the dawn come up over the estate he had created, he forced his way into the bedroom that for all those years had been his private heaven and strangled Ava. As he did so, he told her that he would always love her. Then he set fire to the hacienda and hung himself in the orchard on the first avocado tree he had planted. It had just started to bear fruit.

A few days later, when the welts and cuts had healed from the beating he had sustained by the Greek man, Rafael came home from his small haven in the forest. As he walked up the road, he saw two of his stepfather's horses and a cow wandering and untethered and Gianakos's two black dogs bound at the gate. A few minutes later, he found what was left of Ava in the cold ashes of the hacienda. As best as he could manage and in the bewilderment of the cruel surprise, he retrieved a nearly melted gold locket that she had always worn on her neck, one that she had given to herself before moving to the rancho, and then covered her charred remains. He left the body of the Greek man hanging and tethered the dogs beneath the corpse's feet. After gathering up whatever surviving possessions he could carry, he walked down the mountainside to the coast, bypassing San Isbel, and trekked west along the beaches all the way to Portobelo. There he found respite in the protection of the Franciscan missionaries who maintained a small parish that served both the poor and the wealthy on the town's highlands. For a short time, they let him attend their school where they taught him to serve mass for the priests and act as an acolyte for their numerous processions. Unfortunately for him, the one priest who had reached out and provided some solace and guidance died of yellow fever shortly after Rafael was taken into the parish.

Rafael drew two red jacks in a row. No vacant place to put them, so he drew again and added a diamond queen to his one exposed black king, the king of clubs. Still no other king in sight.

He watched the threesome speaking Portuguese fuss over the dirt on their carpetbags from the train seats and saw their two meek attendants back their way off the car. Their attendants behaved like slaves, he thought, fear and anger mixed together in their faces. Almost certainly that was what they were, he surmised, bound for Brazil because slavery was legal there, even though it had been outlawed almost everywhere else in South America. The loud, short, black man in the white linen suit was a Brazilian and had been a slave himself at one time, Rafael thought to himself. The man carried the anger in his shoulders and belly, but without the fear. He was on top of the heap now, he thought, and wore his pride of wealth prominently.

Rafael thought it was interesting how tightly the man held the small carpetbag.

The huge man who sat next to them most certainly was his bodyguard, Rafael knew. By his stiff posture and lack of engagement, he knew the man was on duty. But judging from the man's oversized belly, red face, and bulbous, misshapen nose, he was also a beer drinker and most certainly let himself go during his off hours. He saw the man touch the bulge in his suit on the left side of his chest. Three times in the course of a few minutes. That's where he kept one of his pistols, most certainly. The man had been hired because he was mean and big. But he was an amateur, and despite his size, he had been bested more than once. Thus, he was likely somewhat desperate. Holding on. Drinking himself to death. That would make him less predictable, driven by impulse and fear. More dangerous than the professionals, Rafael knew, unless you could read their emotions, which they always tried to hide. He glanced at the big man's ruddy face and posture. He was holding his head straight up on a rigid neck, eyes fixed forward, taking in as much as he could without looking about. But, if Rafael was correct in his assessment of him, he surmised that the man had clouded his consciousness, and was gamely trying to maintain a practiced method of taking in everything without letting on what he had seen. He was struggling because he was hung over—an impulsive lout in a tight suit. Dangerous, he mused, like a sleeping dog.

Lifting the black seven of clubs to the red eight of hearts exposed a red diamond king. Rafael moved it to the open space.

The torrent of rain outside pounded the car's roof. The thunder rattled its windows and then abruptly, the rain stopped as quickly as it had started. The guards on the roof would be miserable, he thought. He smiled at the passengers' reactions to the commotion outside. He watched the two servants of the Brazilians walk down the platform and join a waiting contingent of black and a few white men, all bound together in chains, heading to the rear, open boxcars. A large group of yellow men and women, unfettered, carrying supplies and personal effects, followed. Slaves and indentured Chinese, likely bound for Cuba's sugar and coffee plantations or Brazil's mines. They all belonged to the loud, swaggering black man up the aisle.

CHAPTER NINE

◇◇◇◇◇◇◇◇◇◇◇◇◇◇◇◇◇◇

TOMAS

He had been called "Tomas" for the first fifteen years he could remember of his life, enslaved as he was. He did not remember much of the journey, for he had been a small child when he was taken. All he could remember was that he never saw his sister or brothers or mother again. He had tried at times to remember their faces, dream about what they had looked like and how they had sounded, but when he did, they were simply tall shadows with kind voices.

Somehow he had escaped. It had been an accident, really, and he knew that if the cart carrying the master and the fore-man had not overturned and pinned them down, he would have likely died like so many others he had watched perish in the jungle and on the rubber tree plantation. But the cart *had* overturned, taking all of the men chained to it down the bank to the river as well, and while the fools struggled to get the two white men out before they drowned, he had found a sharp, heavy rock and broke the weakest link holding him to the rest of them. It wasn't hard to hide in the dense jungle, but he took no chances and ran for hours, stopping only to catch his breath. He ran through streams and up onto their banks for a few feet into the thick underbrush, then back into the stream and down it, over and over again. To fool the dogs if they came. Spoil the master's sport.

He had watched one such hunt on the plantation—out through the fields where he was working and up into the hills. The foreman had left them to chase the runaway, and as he was leaving he was speaking loudly so that everyone could hear him, saying that he was going to break every square inch of that runaway man's skin when they caught him—make him regret running for the rest of his wretched life . . . that he would hunt down any of *them* who tried to escape while he was gone. So Tomas didn't try to escape then. Instead, he had taken his shovel and moved quietly behind the foreman, far enough behind so that he could not be seen. And then he heard the dogs and followed them all and watch them gathered at the base of a tall balsa tree, all looking up, and heard the foreman and the master calling to the fool to come down and get back to work . . . how they wouldn't hurt him because he was too valuable and they would treat him better from now on and, then, when the fool came down, Tomas watched as they pulled the dogs off and started beating the man—beating him and beating him until he stopped crying and then they dragged him back through the fields so everyone could see him and threw the man into the pig shack where he slept for three days. No one had attempted to escape during the episode, and no one did over the next five years. Until now when the cart slipped off the path.

As Tomas ran, he wondered if the white bastards had been rescued. If they died, who would take care of the land and what would the fools do without someone arranging things for them? He didn't care. He was free for now, and he would live every second of that without fear, he had decided. And if he ever got the chance, he would find a way to live wealthy, like the men who had enslaved him along with the fools.

He'd gone south, following the river for several miles and had hidden in the forest for five weeks, avoiding as best he could contact with all but the indigenous people he encountered. From a boatman on a small tributary of a large river, he learned several weeks later that the master, Ricardo Gonsalves, and his foreman, who was called "Bossman Mick," had died in that accident along with several of the slaves who had been pulled under the wagon and also drowned. Tomas was certain that, in the chaos, only a few had noticed him striking his chain with the big rock. Likely he had not been missed, he reasoned, because so many others had been killed. A few weeks after that, he learned that no one had come to claim control of the slaves on the plantation, and many people simply had wandered off. A few of the others stayed and were working out a meager subsistence. He thought about the mess that had been left behind by the accident. The man who had owned them all had done a good job of punishing or selling off anyone who took any interest in learning. He had broken up families so that little knowledge had been passed down. But Tomas had been given an advantage by his curiosity. He had watched and learned, always keeping his observations to himself, and by testing himself, by comparing what he saw to what he predicted, he had developed confidence in his observational skills. He had sharpened his intuition and deductive reasoning.

A few months later, without knowing he had done so, Tomas crossed over the border from Brazil into Paraguay's fertile Rio de la Plata, and rested himself in a small village called Vara Quebrado, nestled on a tributary stream to the Rio Paraguay. It was a fortunate happenstance for him, for the countryside was in disjointed turmoil over fighting that had erupted over border disputes between Paraguay and both Brazil and Argentina. Although Paraguay continued to promote slavery, unlike Uruguay, its eastern neighbor, there were no slavers in the region, and no one cared for the raised scars and numbers burned into Tomas's right arm. No one cared that he was an escaped slave. Many of the people he met in the other villages along the big, broad river had fled from the fighting, and he realized that all the inhabitants had once been slaves like him. They were leaderless and frightened. He, on the other hand, had not only freed himself, but he was clever and driven.

As he watched them, he realized that it would only be a matter of time before they would again be victimized by their own confusion and loss of territorial perspective. Most had not heard that Uruguay had abolished slavery a few years before, in the year 1830, and those who had could not migrate there for one reason or another. He soon realized that his proclivity to imitate what he had seen the Bossman Mick do to push the slaves on the Gonsalves plantation gave him an advantage over the confused refugees. He had also learned to hold his actions until a clear declaration of intent had been spoken. When arguments erupted, he listened to all emotional positions and, careful to avoid taking sides, spoke calmly and with authority. And he always spoke loudly. Within a short time, he had a following of younger men and women. A few of the older men began to call him "Petrao." Although it was meant to be a term of derision, events a few months later turned that title into one of respect.

On a June afternoon, as the entire village slumbered in a stupor from the jungle's unrelenting heat, when it seemed that neither the tepid water of the slowly moving waterway nor languid inactivity could provide any relief, a Brazilian dragoon armed with two cutlasses and a whip rode across the shallow stream and into the village and asked to speak with the village's leader.

The old men withdrew into their huts. Tomas looked at the white man. His uniform, that of an officer with gold-trimmed epaulettes and a red sash across his belly, was filthy and torn. His mount, gulping fresh water from the stream, was heavily lathered, steaming hot, and seemed to be favoring its right leg. He saw desperation in the soldier's eyes. The soldier dismounted and pulled up the hoof of the lame leg and sighed. Sensing an opportunity, Tomas stepped forward and introduced himself confidently to the soldier. As he fussed with the hoof, the soldier asked Tomas if there was a way to bypass the small stream to reach the large Paraguay River that he said ran through Brazil into the Paraguay countryside.

Although Tomas did not know for certain, for he had never seen any of the mighty rivers in that region and knew little about the geography of the area, he lied to the man and told him he knew a way to reach it without following the tributary downstream. At that, the soldier pulled a small single-shot musket from his vest, pointed it at Tomas, and told Tomas to show him the way. The villagers all backed away, and Tomas saw some of the old men watching from their huts, smirking at him and his foolish boldness.

So Tomas began traipsing along a path he knew ran a long distance parallel to the river, moving slowly so the dismounted dragoon and his lame horse could keep up with him, but far enough ahead so that he could escape if the opportunity presented itself. They travelled for several miles, and each time the path seemed to move toward the river, Tomas stopped and looked for an alternate route out of sight of the waterway. On the third hour, it began to rain heavily, then it stopped abruptly, and in the quiet, they heard hoof beats, felt the ground rumble, and heard men shouting. The dragoon began breathing quickly, and as the voices grew louder, he became more agitated. He swung himself onto the horse and dug his spurs into its flanks, but the animal, suddenly again forced to put weight onto its right front quarter, stumbled then tumbled over into the brush throwing the soldier chest-first into a protruding stump of a guayaba tree.

Tomas saw the fall, heard the dull thud, and knew that the soldier would be hurt. He moved past the horse, which had regained its footing and was standing calmly in the tall grass, and found the soldier, breathing in short grunts, attempting to pull himself into a sitting position against a mangrove tree.

Fumbling in his vest pocket, he again pulled out his pistol and aimed it at Tomas. Tomas looked at the broken man. His uniform was torn and stained from the ripe fruit of the guava. He closed his eyes and then, through a mouth and jaw that was bloody and broken, his respirations became loud and stertorous in the way that Tomas had seen some of the older slaves breathe just before they stopped breathing altogether. His pistol drifted downward and then jerked up as the man regained his consciousness. But Tomas saw that the pistol was not cocked, its hammer and flint resting against a wet powder pan. So Tomas calmly walked over to the soldier, pushed the musket away, and then put his hands around the man's neck and squeezed. The soldier put up no resistance.

Tomas listened for the sounds of the horsemen they had heard just a few minutes before, but he could hear nothing. The sounds of the creatures in the forest had subsided as well, as if all of them were waiting, watching his actions. He began stripping the dead man, first his boots and spurs. For the first time, he could remember in his nineteen years, Tomas compared his feet to another man's. His were wider but a bit longer than those of the dead man. His own great toe was longer than his others, whereas the soldier's second toe was much longer than all the rest. Was this how white men's feet were?

Tomas sat down and pulled the boot onto his right foot. When he put on the second boot, he stood up and looked down at himself. He was taller and felt powerful. He walked a few steps. First, the right then the left boot pinched at his toenails and chafed at his ankles. But it didn't matter, he thought, he had never worn shoes before so it made no difference that they pinched his toes. He assumed that was what most boots felt like. But if he were rich, he would have boots made that felt like cotton cushions around his feet. And he would have his own slaves to polish them. White slaves, perhaps.

Next, he pulled off the man's coat. As filthy as it was, it was pretty, an azure blue with black trim and braiding. What rank was this man? The rips on the sleeves and on the back could be repaired. If Tomas wore it, how would it look? He tried to put it on, but it was much too long and tight for him—so he would sell it, perhaps keep the gold epaulettes. He untied the bright red sash and slid it away from the man's trousers—he would keep that, perhaps make a kerchief from it as well. Then he tried to lift the body to take off the riding breeches—but the body was heavier than he expected and he saw that the man had soiled himself so he worked instead on unbuttoning the man's vest. He would wash the pants and sell them because the man was much thinner than Tomas and would never fit anyway.

When he unbuttoned the last button of the vest, he saw that there was a cord attached that went down into the man's groin—and that was when he found the little yellow leather pouch. He tried to pull the pouch away from the dead body, and as he tugged, he realized it was strapped by a short string to the man's shrunken yam! He held his breath from the stink and freed the pouch by biting down on the string. He lifted the little pouch and examined it. It was not heavy, just a few coins perhaps? He opened the pouch, and in it, he found a piece of paper wrapped around a big, unpolished stone. He recognized the stone from descriptions he had heard—it was what the Portuguese called *o brilhante pedra* or *um diamonte*, a diamond. *Um grande diamonte*—it was almost twice as big as his fifth toe.

And when Tomas unfolded the wrapping paper, he saw that it had a map and diagrams and writing in dark red ink.

The whistle shrieked, and Tomas decided it was time to sit down and control himself, not that he cared that the other people in the car were watching him. He didn't care, he told himself. He could buy this entire railroad enterprise if he wanted and then the Anglos and Yankees would be paying him and his investors to take a ride with him. He pulled the small carpetbag closer to him and pushed his lower lip into a satisfied smile as he watched his slaves and workers being led to the flatcars at the end of the train.

CHAPTER TEN

BOCAMALO

During his two years there, Rafael discovered that Portobelo, overlooking the ancient harbor used by the Spanish to conceal their gold galleons and long-displaced by Colón as an important seaport, was not a kind town. Its population had been decimated by cholera over the previous years, and many believed God was punishing the town for the voodoo practices and observance of Dios de Diablos, which was celebrated in the ghetto by the population's black and white ex-slaves. Many of the parishioners who had survived the cholera outbreak assumed that their health was due in some way to divine intervention for their fastidious attention to propriety with the added reassurances of well-placed indulgences. Some of these same people presumed that the horrible events that had befallen Rafael on the remote hacienda were some form of providential disapproval, just as was his infirmity. Giving no pity to Rafael's plight or his facial deformity, the children and many adults in the Portobelo parish were cruel, calling him "Bocca Malo." When so taunted, believing he had no one to whom he could turn, he buried his feelings and, as in the past, became quietly resentful. When the jibes and ridicule worsened, his anger increased. He swore at the cruel ones in his broken speech, which only made them laugh all the more in their derision. That was too much for the child, and it set in motion a pattern of actions that subsequently defined much of his reputation.

Although he never was observed by any witnesses to be violent, it was rumored that he devised severe retributions for the worst of his tormentors. At first, they were simply mischievous. Two haughty women who gossiped about the tragic circumstances involving Ava and the Greek man found their purses filled with cockroaches, which spilled out onto their laps during their communion. One week after mocking Rafael at the Palm Sunday Mass procession, five adults who had participated in the taunting suffered severe diarrhea immediately after the Easter vigil's midnight feast. No one else became ill. Rafael had been their server.

The happenings worsened. A visiting elderly Dominican priest, who cursed and slapped Rafael in front of the entire congregation when the boy stumbled and dropped the silver tiara during the ceremonial crowning of the Virgin, later broke his hip in a tumble down a dark stairwell when he tripped over a wine cask on the steps. The candle on the rectory's steps was missing from its berth, and Rafael had been seen the night before delivering wine for the morning mass. And then one boy simply vanished, the disappearance occurring a few weeks after he had repeatedly abused Rafael with particularly cruel and sneering derision. The only trace was the purported sighting of a dog carrying what appeared to be the femur bone of a child. Although every one of the various incidents appeared to be natural and coincidental, rumors took hold. Rafael "Demotenes" Bocca-Malo Gianakos was left alone after that. He was also isolated, more so than when he had been left homeless after the murder of his mother.

Rafael drew a red three and placed it on a four of clubs, moved that to the diamond five, exposing the five of clubs. No twos or sevens yet.

He heard heavy footsteps above him on the metal roof of the car and noticed a young girl down the aisle staring at him. Two Yankee soldiers stood talking to someone next to her, blocking his view of the windows to his left outside. His other men were getting on the passenger cars. Off to his right as he looked out the window, he saw three more he had assigned standing on the platform checking their pocket watches. They were keeping dry under plain brown umbrellas. One looked up at him and then held up his hands showing five fingers—five armed men on the roof. The second man held up both hands—nine armed men with rifles total, and, he thought to himself, likely an armed brakeman every third car. The two Yankee soldiers in front of him had no weapons, and neither of them looked like a fighter. Good odds, overall, and he knew the rest of the Yankee soldiers would be staying in Panama City this morning.

CHAPTER ELEVEN

◇◇◇◇◇◇◇◇◇◇◇◇◇◇◇◇

BRETT

All he could think about as he and Captain John Letterman mounted the steps into the train was that he had worn the wrong uniform for this blasted heat. He wanted to be out of uniform once and for all. The collar had become tight and was cutting into his neck. He realized he had gained a few pounds in San Francisco during the numerous banquets held in honor of Winfield Scott and had not been able to trim down because traveling with the Hero usually meant that there would be a bountiful table set for the morning, noon, and evening meals, and it would be impertinent, he had been told, to push himself away before the commander had consumed his own ample portions of bread, meat—sausages especially, wine, and frequently, an assorted array of sweets. The weight gain was a nuisance but worth it, he rationalized , for ever since he had been asked to accompany Captain Letterman from San Francisco to Washington DC, as part of the entourage for Scott, the country's most famous warrior, he had had several opportunities to listen to Letterman's ideas for solutions to a variety of field medical management problems. Many of them, he was certain, would soon be tested, given the high probability of a brief, bloody conflict that would ensue if the slave-holding states did, in fact, resort to a forceful withdrawal from the Union.

On a few occasions, he had discussed the consequences of such a mess with Letterman. As he entered the car, he thought about how much he hated the prospect of any war and the disorganization and avoidable mayhem that always was part of battles. He had seen it in Mexico and regretted that he could not have done more for his fellow soldiers in that fight. He remembered seeing a young cavalry officer, Rice was his name, who broke his femur bone when his horse was shot out from under him. The boy was very much alive right after the fall, howling and cursing at the pain, but very dead by the time he arrived at the medical tent only a few minutes later. No bullet wounds. Judging by the size of his swollen thigh, he likely had simply been internally drained from a leaking femoral artery, lacerated by the sharp spiral-fractured bone. Brett had heard that Welsh bone-setters had developed some form of a splinting device that prevented such a loss. Perhaps something similar could be offered to the troops for this condition.

And there were other opportunities. In Texas, while fighting the Apache, Brett had studied the corpses of soldiers who died from simple flesh wounds. They were senseless deaths in which, had he been present or had there been someone present with a modicum of common sense, the application of a tourniquet might have saved the man. Havoc. Ignorant bravado of young men rushing headlong into the mouths of cannons for pieces of ribbon. He hated it, he realized, as he walked down the aisle. And then he saw Emmy Evers.

Seeing Emmy again was a gift from God—and he remembered at that very moment how truly he was taken by her when they met in San Francisco a few weeks ago. By happenstance, he and Letterman had made her acquaintance when she had been seated at the table next to theirs in the gilded San Francisco Grand Palace Hotel's restaurant. They were waiting, as they often had to do, for the general's entourage to arrive that morning. Such a sturdy, lovely woman, each of them had remarked afterwards! She was bound for Boston, he remembered, and was bringing her two children and an aborigine from the Northwest with her—to meet her parents, she had said. She mentioned that she had become acquainted with a Captain George Pickett, a West Point graduate, and knew quite a bit about General Winfield Scott's mission to settle a boundary dispute in Washington Territory with the British.

He would pursue her, Brett had decided! He had intended to present his calling card to her the day after meeting her, but had found that she and her family had checked out of the hotel early that morning and had left no forwarding address.

He thought about the lengthy discussion they had enjoyed. She seemed sad but resolute, he had noticed, and her children were a study in contrasts. The young girl, eleven or twelve— Sarah was her name—was precocious. She had a fierce, almost rude way about her, and seemed intensely protective of her mother and brother. The boy, about five or six, was quite withdrawn. At first, Brett thought the child might be a victim of the catatonia condition, similar to what he had observed as a young medical apprentice assisting in the treatment of the insane in the poor houses of Philadelphia. Letterman had a different opinion, though, comparing the boy's odd behavior to what each of them had seen in the aftermath of battle—men just staring blankly, barely responding to auditory or visual stimuli, going through the motions. Letterman believed the boy was recovering from some terrible event rather than suffering from an untreatable malady of the insane. As Brett thought about it, he recalled that he had not seen the catatonia in children as young as this boy, so possibly Letterman was correct.

Brett looked about but did not see the child, was about to gently inquire of Emmy about her boy, but before he could do so, they were interrupted by a sergeant who handed Letterman a message from the general's aide-de-camp. Letterman opened the envelope and read orders that the two of them were to leave the train immediately and report back to the general's headquarters—which apparently had not left the hotel in Panama City this morning as had been planned. Letterman apologized to Mrs. Evers for their abrupt departure.

As he dismounted from the railroad car, Letterman turned to Brett and shook his head in disgust. "We will not be heading to the Atlantic Coast today after all, Lieutenant," he said. "Old Fuss and Feathers is incapacitated." Letterman knew he could trust Brett with that irreverent, unbecoming comment. Both of them knew the delay was almost certainly the result of Scott's proclivity to excessive self-indulgence. It likely was either a flare-up of the general's dropsy or his gout. Letterman predicted they would be stuck in Panama City, that infected, sweat hole for at least another day or two in any case. That made Brett furious; he would lose the opportunity to spend time with Emmy. This morning it seemed that God had listened to his prayer, but damned if the devil had not just intervened once more.

As they walked down the platform past the military band that was packing up its instruments, Letterman must have noticed Brett's disappointment. He reminded Brett that he had wanted to study the malaria and yellow fever problem in this region more closely. The rainy season had just finished a few weeks earlier, and Brett had wanted to see the efficacy of the Panamanian quarantine process in combating the spread of that strange disease, did he not? The stultifying, torpid heat had to have an effect on the miasma that he was certain contributed to the condition—some as yet undetectable airborne effluvia was likely the etiology, he had theorized. So perhaps, Letterman suggested, the tropical conditions of the area might have an effect in either limiting or expanding the disease. Letterman noted that Brett certainly would need time to study the conditions more closely.

As military surgeons who had seen more men die from malaria, yellow fever, and dysentery than by bullets and gangrene, they also wanted to see if the quinine-specific remedy given in large doses had any effect at all on the yellow fever in its rapid, deadly presentation. Perhaps this stay-over would give him time to make that observation as well, Letterman said. Brett thought about that. That reasoning provided no comfort to him.

As they walked past the railroad car behind the one they had just exited, Brett looked up and saw the Evers boy, "Jacob" was his name he recalled, looking out of the window, watching the spectacle of the snake handlers. He had a vacant stare, even with all that was happening on the platform. The lieutenant regretted not having the chance to observe the boy again and was now certain that Letterman had been right. The boy was recovering from some terrible event.

Brett hesitated and looked back, then fumbled for something in his pocket. He was tremendously disappointed in this dashing of opportunity, for he knew that he might never have the chance to speak to Emmy Evers again. Suddenly, he excused himself to Letterman and turned back to the car, mounted the steps, took a deep breath, and walked down the aisle to where Emmy was sitting with her daughter. He was perspiring heavily and stammered, "Mrs. Evers—I would like to present my calling card." Then he tried to say, "I must depart—but if you do not mind, I would like to correspond with you, perhaps visit you in Boston—after I resign my commission with the army . . ." but the train whistle shrieked and blocked most of what he said. By her expression, he realized that she had heard only his first few words. Others were looking at him, listening. He reddened and realized he was dripping wet, with his perspiration falling onto the card he handed her, and in his embarrassment, he found that he could only repeat, "I must depart." Emmy smiled gently. He nodded and then turned and left, chagrinned at his shy loss of nerve and this opportunity. He knew the devil had pulled that whistle cord.

CHAPTER TWELVE

◇◇◇◇◇◇◇◇◇◇◇◇◇◇◇◇◇◇◇◇

JACOB AND JOJO

J acob had to open the window. It was so sticky hot, but when he saw the bustle on the platform below, heard the hollering, smelled the smoke from the coal and wood burning from the engine, all mixing in with the ripeness of the surrounding jungle, the odor of the town and the bay, Jacob pulled back in his seat and decided to wait. He looked over at the other passengers in the car—all of them, the thin and the fat ones, but especially the fat ones, seemed to be suffering, all fanning themselves, sweating wet stains into their armpits and their backs. The longer the train took to depart—he thought it should have left by now, as hurried as his mother and Jojo had been to get them down to the surrey and onto the car—the more anxious he became. But he did not know why. And then they had just sat there. One by one, the men had taken off their coats, but none of them seemed any less uncomfortable.

He watched two large groups outside—about forty black, brown, and white men in chains, and another thirty or so, small Chinese men and women, none of whom wore chains— all moving in the same direction along the dirt track below the platform. Every one of the Chinese men and all of the women who were not carrying children were toting huge bundles, some as large as themselves, strapped to their backs. The women carrying children also balanced huge bundles on their heads. He wondered what was in the bundles. Were they carrying their homes? Did they ever find a place to unwrap them and spread their possessions out? The men in chains were slaves, he knew. He hadn't seen many black or Chinese back north, just a few on the ships that stopped to purchase goods from his father on Whidbey, but he had seen a lot of Chinese in San Francisco. The slaves always looked grim and tired, he thought. He knew the look; he had seen it when he was in captivity himself during his ordeal in Vancouver last year. He felt himself breathing anxiously, rapidly. The sounds and colors all became louder.

He heard heavy footsteps above him—it startled him, a man's walk, lumbering slowly, stopping for a moment, and then moving in the opposite direction. Then he saw the dark men on the platform looking up at where he believed the sound was emanating and then making some gestures to someone in the car ahead of them where his mother and Sarah were riding. He wondered whether Jojo had seen the same thing. "Subtle," he thought, remembering that word Sarah had taught him. But each of the men had some type of deformity. One was missing an arm and was accompanied by another man, without legs, who was scooting himself along on the ground. A third man walked with a pronounced limp on a club foot. He wondered what their signals were all about and who in the coach ahead of him might be signaling back. They weren't officials. No uniforms.

Jacob saw two blue-uniformed soldiers walking along the platform away from the train. Neither of them seemed to notice the signaling that was going on. He remembered the soldiers; they had been with a group who had conversed with his mother at breakfast in the hotel in San Francisco. The taller of the two was confident and had twisted his beard repeatedly during that conversation with his mother. He had leaned forward and seemed to boast a lot. The second soldier was the same height as his father, Isaac had been; had the same square, broad shoulders; and when he had stood up, his resemblance to Isaac made Jacob catch his breath and feel a desperate twist in his stomach. For a moment, he thought it *was* his father, come alive again, here to hold him as he had when they were together on Whidbey. Before the murder. Before the captivity. Before he had been beaten repeatedly. Beaten down. He moved closer to Jojo and held onto his arm. He needed to find Sarah and his mother.

Jojo looked down at the small boy and put his arm around him. Jacob had survived, but the brutal ordeal had almost killed him. He was a strong, little boy, Jojo thought—few other children could have endured the abuse to which he had been subjected. His rescue from the Northerners—including the final battle in which Emmy contended with the infamous Anah Nawitka Haloshem, the man called "Black Wind" by all of the native tribes along the inland coast of Vancouver Island—seemed to put an abrupt end to the slaving raids. The British had brought in two steamer gunboats later that spring, and if there were any surviving predators, they were keeping away from the straits and inland waterways. They would prey on some of the coastal tribes, most likely, or desist from the slaving and predation altogether. They would adapt, he surmised, and then forget about that history. And the most enterprising slavers like Anah were no longer a threat up there.

Jojo felt odd in the clothing he wore, pants and coat fitted for him up north and then refitted by a more competent tailor in San Francisco. The cloth was stiff. He wondered what would happen to it if he climbed or ran in it, stayed out in the rain or snow in it, swam in it. He knew it would not give much back to him because it was made by strangers, and they did not know him. But, with all of that, even with the ridiculous derby cap Mrs. Evers purchased for him that had replaced the even more ridiculous hat from Port Townsend, his new clothes had helped a bit to reduce the number of stares he received from the whites in San Francisco. Emmy paid no attention to the turning of heads and simply went about her business with her little band in tow. He really didn't mind either.

Jojo watched and listened, quietly making his careful observations to Jacob and Sarah, both of whom asked few questions in public but unloaded a bevy of their own observations in private. "Why did the man in the store spit on the floor when he saw you with us? What did the soldier mean when he told Mother he had seen all the Indians he needed to see for a lifetime? Why did the railroad clerk tell Mother you might have to ride in the flatcar instead of the coach?" He answered quickly and tried to make them laugh. "Because the poor man had a mouthful of hate, and it was burning his little tongue." "He meant that he had seen so much beauty that he was now becoming blind and unable to see any more." "The flatcar is open to the air and reserved for those waiting to be kings." And because he spoke so many languages, he was able overhear conversations and, thus, gain insights that helped him guide Emmy away from a few swindles as she negotiated her fare for the shipping and passage across the isthmus and onto the ships that would take them to New Orleans and then on to Boston.

He listened to the banter in the car, to the syncopation and rhythmic patterns, and realized few passengers were speaking English. He recognized Spanish, of course, which was the prevailing language in the New Grenada territory, but he heard no French, Russian, or Scandinavian, all with which he was familiar from his days as a translator for the Pacific Northwest territorial traders.

He watched four men and two women sitting together at the far end of the coach, conversing and gesturing in a somewhat animated, agitated manner and, after listening, wondered if they were Italian. He had only met a few Italians—Jesuit missionaries who passed through his homeland—but had not observed them long enough to pick up the lilting, dancing inflection and pronunciation of the words that sounded very much like Spanish, but lighter, rounder, and more playful. He could mimic it, but not understand it well when it was spoken fast. This group's mannerisms were exaggerated, almost bold in an amusing, somewhat grandiose way. They reminded him of the poster he had seen in the hotel announcing something called a "Grande Opera. Rigoletto." with colored drawings of a hunchbacked man in a colorful striped costume and two men and two women. Then he realized that these were the same performers from the poster—singers or dramatists, like the ones he had seen on the stage in what was called a "dramatic play" during his brief visit to San Francisco. These people were unhappy, and it seemed that they wanted everyone around them to know it. But it didn't matter what nationality their gestures typified, he thought, because everyone on the coach seemed to be equally affected by the stultifying heat. The intermittent deluges of warm rain seemed to bring little relief. So different from the freezing drizzle-rain of his home.

This was such a big, strange adventure for Jojo, a gift Emmy Evers had decided to make to him as a reward for his help in rescuing her son, Jacob, from the Northerner captors. All he had wanted as recompense was to be taught to read, but after he had repeatedly risked his life in that almost suicidal quest, she told him that she wanted to do more for him. So she would bring him back home to Boston with her and enroll him in a fine academy. And she told him that she also had come to realize that Jacob's recovery from his horrible ordeal would require more than she herself, as a widowed mother, could offer. She had watched Jojo, with his wry but gentle observations, reach out and help nurse the boy back to some semblance of sanity. Her son had taken to Jojo, just as had her daughter, Sarah—and the boy would need a competent, savvy male figure in his life, at least temporarily, who could be there during difficult times, Emmy had told him, when she and Sarah could not help. And Jojo understood that she was far from ready to take on a new husband who could act as a male influence for the boy.

So he, Jojo, would have to do. She and Sarah would attend to his nightmares, but he would have to be there for Jacob during the day. Show him that he could be a boy again. Laugh. Help him see the world through the eyes of a stronger, older male who, as it turned out, also was a friendly "aborigine." So here he was, caring for a frightened, energetic, damaged six-year-old boy, on a train ride en-route across the Isthmus of Panama. Jojo thought about the serendipity of this responsibility. He would help as best as he could and then, perhaps, find a new life. Perhaps he would learn to sail a tall Yankee ship someday after all.

As he listened and observed the opera troupe for a few minutes, he turned to Jacob and whispered a perfect rendition of the group's lively dialogue. Jacob's eyes widened, and the right corner of his mouth turned upward.

◇◇◇◇◇◇◇◇◇◇◇◇◇◇◇◇◇◇◇◇

CHAPTER THIRTEEN

BOCAMALO

At the age of eleven, Rafael left Portobelo and, trekking through a wild and dangerous terrain, hiked his way further west to Colón to find a new beginning. The town was booming and had the same great disparities between the rich and the poor that he had seen in Portobelo. He was homeless and the people he encountered on the way there seemed rude and uncaring. Still, he hoped to find some better days.

As he entered the city, he asked a shopkeeper for food. The man refused him but, seeing the boy's facial scars and malformed lower face, referred him to a small mission in the ghetto called Iglesia de Los Niños con Discapacidad, The

Church for the Children with Disabilities. Rafael found the church, but it had been abandoned and its ruins stood instead as the quarters for a gang of homeless beggars, all shepherded and mothered by a loquacious and affable sixteen-year-old street waif named Ira Abrigada. Each of the children in the ragtag group had a much worse disability than Rafael, which gave him some comfort. Abrigada, who had been born with a functionless stump instead of a hand on her right wrist, was a talented pickpocket. In the growing ghetto of the thriving seaport town, homeless street children survived by burglarizing the churches and homes of the wealthy, pickpocketing travelers, and rolling drunken sailors. Children with disabilities were perfect distractions for the most nimble of the cutpurses.

Abrigada, viewing Rafael's disfigurement, immediately saw the benefit of befriending him and symbolically welcomed him into her cadre by returning to Rafael something she had skillfully and immediately snatched from the boy's pocket—Ava's melted gold locket. The gesture instantly created a bond between the two, and Rafael became an ardent student of her tricks. It was not difficult for Rafael to learn the trade, and he quickly realized that although he was one of the youngest in the gang, he was more clever than all the rest, including Abrigada, whom he admired, nevertheless. As the weeks went by, he became enraptured with her, just like all the other small boys in the gang. He could refuse no request from her and competed with all the other homeless children for her favor and affection. Two months after joining *los discapacitados*, in a quiet corner of the ruined *iglesia* where he kept his meager bed, when all the other children slept, he was visited by Abrigada. It was his first such encounter, and he frequently forced his thoughts to return to that isolated event, keeping those memories encased with a reverence that would endure for years to come.

Six months later, a bungled heist of one of the shipping company's offices, poorly planned by Abrigada, set the *polizia* onto her and her ragtags. Converging onto the church and rousting the urchins out of their beds, the *polizia* chased them to the outskirts of the town. The jungle was Rafael's friend, and he led his friends away into its darkness, quickly leaving the pursuers mired in the dark swamp at the southern part of the city, one that he easily had navigated many times. In the confusion of darkness, however, Abrigada and one of the smallest of the waifs, a boy with two club feet, were apprehended before they could escape. The police chief, a man known for cruel tricks and pious displays, and frustrated by the disappearance of all of the others, stood the two up, hollered into the darkness after the escapees, then shot the two children dead on the spot. The sudden, brutal executions stunned and infuriated Rafael and other young desperadoes, who had watched from their hidden perches in the trees of the forest. All of the children wept at the loss, but no one more than Rafael, who was certain he had been in love.

In the two weeks they stayed in the forest, Rafael kept them safe, found food and cover for all, and promised that they would have their revenge. When they emerged unobserved from the forest several days later, he had fortified his reputation for resourcefulness and careful planning. He had become their leader, and he kept them bound to him with his plans for revenge and survival in a world controlled by those more fortunate than themselves.

By the time he was thirteen, he had achieved prominence as the bold child boss of an increasingly dangerous group of young street thugs, preying on sailors and hapless travelers seeking pleasure in the back-street bordellos. They killed many victims, at first unintentionally, then out of necessity, and finally for pleasure. Six months later, he organized an ambush with explosives that killed several police, but the chief who had shot Abrigada survived. So Rafael arranged to have the man and his entire household poisoned. All of them—the chief, his wife, and three children—died painfully and slowly. Rafael felt no emotion or remorse. Over the course of several weeks before the revenge killings, his gang had painted black graffiti threats on the whitewashed walls of the police chief's hacienda. After the assassinations, their night-graffiti boasted of the feat. Thereafter, the police avoided the ghetto. They knew Rafael's name only as "Demotenes Bocamalo," and the few who had seen him could only describe his beautiful piercing blue eyes and fair complexion. Rafael, as proud as he was of his accomplishments, kept in the shadows and, until he could grow a thick beard, always wore a bandana to cover his lower face. His teeth grew further apart and he knew from the way women responded to his attempts at amorous attention, despite the mint leaves he chewed, that his breath was fetid.

He had enough lined up for two kings' courts and had filled the column to the fives for one other. His jack of hearts led the column to the one that would complete the exposed red diamond king. Where was his queen of spades?

The two soldiers blocking his view down the aisle turned to another Yankee soldier, a subordinate, who saluted them and handed the captain an envelope. They read the message and then tipped their caps and departed. It was then that Rafael saw the person with whom they had been conversing, a woman, the young girl's mother. Staring at her, he lost track of his card count and absently reached to his neck for his medal.

There was something about her.

CHAPTER FOURTEEN

◇◇◇◇◇◇◇◇◇◇◇◇◇◇◇◇◇◇

EMMY

She watched Letterman passing on the platform out-side the window and realized that she was relieved at his sudden departure. As polite and gallant as he had attempted to be, it simply wasn't a good time for pleasant-ries, for she was still grieving and in recovery. Her stomach, so irritable over the past two days, had settled a bit, but the thought of an extended conversation with the two soldiers over the four-hour ride from Panama City to Aspinwall had started a weariness and nausea that she had been fighting ever since settling the events up north. She just wasn't ready.

When the young Lieutenant Brett had returned and fum-bled in front of everyone, so self-conscious in his shyness, handing her a hasty request to call upon her in the future, she was amused—touched actually, as it reminded her of when Isaac, her slain husband, had introduced himself seven years ago. And remembering the sweetness of that, his gift of white roses, started an aching deep down inside that she knew she would have to outlive somehow. Friends had said it would take time, but a few who had lost husbands said it might take—a lifetime.

She wondered whether Brett was like Isaac in other ways. And that frightened her because if she decided to favor his attentions—what would he be like? Would he stand on his head showing off in the same manner as had her husband? Attempt to dominate her and, if unsuccessful, feign power and control? Would there arise painful comparisons that she might not be able to endure? Were the men to whom she found herself attracted all alike? It made her appreciate the convention of the black she wore. Black absorbed everything. Black hid it all. Black allowed a dignified retreat, giving her time to decide how to respond, or whether to respond at all. It spoke with a calm, civil equanimity, and by its pervasiveness, its deep power as a place within which to park her soul, it substituted itself conveniently into everything and gave respite for the diverse energies necessary to manage the other colors of life that she remembered were out there. She might choose some color sometime again. Later. But not now.

She surveyed the people in the car. Looked at the women seated in the rows ahead. Of the four in her view, only one, the one tending to the infant and small child was a mother that she could tell. The elderly twins were holding on to each other too tightly, as if they had never been separated. One struggled to stay awake, leaning her head on her sister's shoulder, while the sturdier of the two looked out the window absently. She estimated that neither had ever raised a child.

If the hard-looking, well-dressed mulatto woman had ever been a mother, there were no vestiges left anywhere in her demeanor. She was much too young to be the mother of the loud man's meek son. Her countenance, as beautiful as it was, was baked on hard, and Emmy wondered what she had experienced in her past to make it so. She wondered if the woman, if any of them, had suffered what she and her family had endured. None of them wore any black. Practical or by aversion, she wondered? She bet that the expensively dressed mulatto woman was accustomed to suppressing pain, so she would be unlikely to ever show mourning or hide in it as Emmy felt at times she was.

Much of the mourning pain she herself felt was a manifestation of guilt, she had surmised, related to an overpowering sense of failure in so many ways that she knew she did not yet truly understand. Was it from being a survivor of a massacre that should have taken her as well? Or was it guilt over feeling angry at being in the shadow again, painted now irreparably as the "fortunate" widow of a man who was depicted by so many as a hero and a martyr, but whose weaknesses and failures she knew all too well? Or was it that Isaac's murder had set in motion officially condoned horrible acts of retribution by the white settlers up north—outright theft and widespread violence against many innocent Pacific Northwest aborigines?

She had fought down the anger that would have let her run with those who used the brutal events, the massacre and abduction, to justify their extermination of aboriginal tribes. She focused her anger, instead, on what she believed was the viciousness that lurks in all men—and held that down as well, so that she could attend to the mending of what remained. She was proud of that at least. But it was pride tempered with guilt—for she knew she had not spoken out.

She also knew her son, Jacob, had been bent by his experiences in captivity. She saw it especially when everything else was quiet, at rest—in his new, nervous little repetitive movements; his mutterings; and his careful, secretive rituals. Was he crazy now? So many nights had passed—at their house and during their trip, where he been awakened by his terrors, running to her bed, panting and screaming, waiting for "him" to break his way into their room. "He's taking me back! He's taking me back!" he cried. Each time, Sarah and she hugged him and held him, reassuring him until he fell into a sweaty, exhausted sleep. She feared she had failed her son, despite trying to take the right steps, whatever they were, to let him heal. Her little boy had come back as a stranger.

She drifted and for a moment dozed . . . She was on the ship again looking off the portside for anything that looked like land. The swell and roll pitched her toward the rail. The skies off to starboard were getting darker and darker; the wind was picking up. She was cold but didn't want to go down below— not just yet. She heard the sailor on the big mast calling out, saw a few sailors looking out in the aft direction he was point-ing. What were they seeing? She moved up closer to the stern, peering into the waves that were getting bigger. She felt herself rising on a huge surge and then turned and felt the whole ship sink down, sliding into the trough of a huge wave, then rise up its shoulder and then sink again. She needed to throw up but would have to do it down below because if she stayed up on the deck, she knew she would be extinguished, swept aside and overboard. She pulled herself to the hold's entrance. Held onto the portal's horizontal overhead beam. Should she go down there to the stench of the cabins, perhaps perish below, trapped in a capsized wreck, or stay up here and be swept away in an instant? No recovery. Jacob, Sarah, and Jojo were below. If she were to die, she would be with them at least. A wave's salute flew across the deck and wet her back as she closed the portal's door behind her.

The trip from Port Townsend had been much more tumultu-ous than she had anticipated. They almost foundered twice, once off of the Oregon coast and then again right outside of the entrance to San Francisco Bay, and her tolerance for the constant nausea and vomiting had reached its limit by the time they disembarked onto the teeming wharves of the boom town. The color and bustle of the town had perked her up for a bit. Sarah and Jojo were fascinated. Jacob kept close to Jojo.

In San Francisco, safe on its streets, she thought again how much she hated sailing, had never taken to it when she was a young girl in Boston, despite the urging of her father who loved to bully the family out on his little schooner . . . "salty jaunts," as he liked to call them. Her journey to the Northwest with her first husband several years before—around the Horn in South America had been so very difficult—two young men disappeared right overboard, and she watched an elderly couple turn their insides out and simply die, exhausted, in front of the helpless physician on board. She swore to never attempt that again.

Her thirteen years in the Oregon Territory had diminished that memory—enough that she had booked passage for herself, Jojo, and her two children. But the journey down the northern coast had provoked enough of a reminder that when the opportunity for a quick passage to the Atlantic by rail across the Panamanian isthmus of New Grenada presented itself—she dug deep into her limited reserves and altered her course. It would be an expensive luxury—twenty-five dollars in US gold, one way, for each of them; three dollars for each pound of their luggage—but it would reduce their discomfort and peril considerably. And it would save seventy days or more of travel. She had to get home before her mother passed.

She watched the soldier doctor Brett walking away beside Letterman and smiled to herself. He walked with his shoulders thrown forward as if he were headed into the wind, just as Isaac had on most occasions. But there was a spring in this young man's step that spoke of an energy deep inside him that she remembered had disappeared from Isaac a few years into their marriage. That loss had pulled her toward Isaac and made her keen for intimacy. But he had not responded. She wondered if the young soldier had experienced suffering yet. She had seen no scars on his face or hands, no sadness in his eyes—simply an earnest idealism fringed with frustration. Their conversation in San Francisco had not given her enough information to glean much about him, except that he clearly was passionate about returning to his home on the Chicahominy River in Virginia. He had explained his worries about the probability of a political storm that would arise if the radical abolitionist Republicans won the election in November. "Mrs. Evers, you have no idea how much unrest there is all throughout my Virginia, since John Brown raided Harper's Ferry." He had said that many men in the army had expressed the same concerns. She wondered whether he was a slave owner.

Like her, he wanted, needed, to get home—in his case, before his ailing father passed. Emmy had been impressed with the intensity and seriousness of his presentation. He was a passionate man, she had decided, unexpectedly so, given his profession. Was he perhaps the type that blindly charged into situations, overcome by some things he could not really control? She wondered if that was a desirable trait in a soldier. And what were the desirable qualities that a trained military physician was to have? Would he be less sanguine in his professional demeanor?

She looked at the card he had given her, it read, "Lieutenant Rory Charles Brett, MD, Assistant Surgeon, US Army." Written in small block letters on its other side it read, "Mrs. Evers, please indulge this earnest man's tender quest." His stiff fumbling was so different from the ornate way Captain George Pickett had presented himself to her back on Whidbey Island.

She wondered how Pickett was doing. She did that often, she realized—wonder about tender, gallant, plucky George Pickett.

She tucked the card away in her purse. Heard the conductor calling for the doors to close, saw him waving at someone up ahead, maybe the man who ran the big black engine. The ride across the isthmus was about to begin.

CHAPTER FIFTEEN

FOIL

He was a tight, little man, and, like many arrogant persons who drape themselves in the perceptions they create about themselves, he had chosen to ignore the denotations and connotations of insulting descriptors and instead think of them as high and attractive compliments. He had convinced himself that he was a powerful package; a compact, indispensable threat of organizational prowess. Thus, he carried himself with a cocksure and condescending bravado, and exaggerated the attention he prominently gave to detail. For the many who had grown to detest him, it seemed as if his every step was trimmed in swagger. He dressed in a fashionable, modern cut with specially crafted boots that added a full two inches to his heels. He lifted gymnasium weights to build up his slender physique and constantly reassured himself by quietly flexing his biceps, which were adorned with tattoos of tall ships he had sailed on only a few times. As his business fortunes expanded, he convinced himself and many others in his organization that his emergence into prominence was due to his brilliance and underlying wiry, masculine appeal. As a single man, he took full advantage of that reputation and played the women who were foolish enough to be swayed by his smug confidence.

On rare moments when he bothered to be self-reflective and modest, he realized that it was the rush of events that followed the gold discovery in California that had changed his fate forever, rather than by any bold action of his own or his distinguished prowess and sagacity. As it had for so many others who happened to be present near Sutter's Creek in March of '49, J. Abbot Foil had been at the right place at the right time—although he would never admit such to anyone. For indeed, he rationalized that, with an almost inimitable self-congratulatory selfishness, he had started his small fortune by being one of the first to realize the profits from the immodest and rapacious pricing of simple goods sold to hungry and desperate men and women who came to the region in search of wealth. During the early days of the rush, he had been able to successfully charge the equivalent in gold of twenty dollars for a single egg, one hundred dollars for a pound of coffee, and thousands of dollars for simple tools like wheelbarrows. He condoned no charity to any soul, for he firmly believed that all men made their own decisions and had to live and die with the consequences that invariably ensued. He detested people who trusted in undirected chance or who enabled self-pity.

One year later, in 1851, when burgeoning competition for supplying dry and durable goods dramatically reduced his profits, he shifted his attention to the safe transport for processing of the precious and coveted metal. In the summer of '53, two years before the completion of the trans-Panamanian railroad, J. Abbot Foil had arranged for the passage of several million dollars of gold dust and nuggets, first by ship to Panama City and then by mule trains across the New Grenada Isthmus to hired, well-armed fast clippers and on to the mints in New Orleans and Charlotte. None of his mule convoys had been successfully raided by any of the numerous desperadoes, the Deriéni, who preyed on travelers from the jungle cover the of the Darién Gap.

As a result, J. Abbot Foil and his company's name, Foil Cargo, became associated with the secure transport of precious commodities. His business flourished, and even as the gold supply from the California Sierras diminished and the gold fever in California defervesced, gold discoveries elsewhere, including Peru and British Columbia, placed a premium on secure transport. Foil Cargo and its investors additionally enjoyed a steady profit by servicing customers with other expensive cargo, including Chinese workers and slaves, which he categorized and charged as livestock. He became a significant investor in the Panama Railroad Company, and it was he who had suggested the usurious one-way passenger fare of twenty-five dollars in gold and the equally exorbitant per pound prices that governed the cargo. He had been the instigator that pushed to combine freight-heavy transports coupled to passenger trains to increase the efficiency of the trips. Although he had not been able to invest in the first offerings of the railroad's stock, he had been able to quadruple his personal wealth in less than nine months with the substantial growth of its stock value.

Gold frenzy again emerged after discoveries on the Fraser River in British Columbia. But by 1860, although the federal government had finally established a US Mint in San Francisco, many miners, particularly those with sympathies for a potential new government for southern states, began looking for private mints that could service their needs for easily transportable gold bullion or coinage. The most reputable mints with the best transaction prices were all on the southeastern coast of North America. Smaller discoveries of gold within reworked Inca Peruvian mines brought additional opportunity. Thus, in February, when quantities of gold ore had been accumulated by collectives of Vancouver and Cajamarca miners, sufficiently large enough to pay the steep price of secure transport, Foil Cargo again benefited. For this covert transport, to add to his margin, Foil purchased the gold of thirty of the miners who did not want to leave their claims, thus assuring himself of a good margin on the exchange. For the balance, he and several of his colleagues provided a personal insurance bond at a large additional expense to the collectives. His profits would be handsome.

He was certain that his arrangements were secure. It would be a heavily guarded operation, but, conducted in the same manner as had previously been successful for him, bypassing most of the regular stops, it would run on the regular schedule on a routine express passenger and cargo run, to reduce outsider speculation about any special arrangements. Fortuitously, he had decided to have the transport quietly coincide with the crossing of a well-advertised, important US military entourage, the prominently festooned escort and camp of none other than General Winfield Scott, who had arrived in Panama City a few days before—after he had famously conducted sensitive negotiations in the Pacific Northwest to avoid war with the British. The town's gossips, drawn to the hoopla of the events surrounding the general's stay in Panama City, would assume the fuss was over his departure that morning and thus would be distracted from Foil's business. In addition to Scott's armed military presence, the entire train would have an abundance of well-positioned Isthmus Guards who knew their business. And J. Abbot Foil himself would oversee the project. His investors were pleased with the plan. A few even boasted about it, confidentially, to envious friends.

CHAPTER SIXTEEN

<><><><><><><><><><><><><><><><><>

SARAH

The piercing shriek was irritating, unlike the loud, deep, sonorous whistles she had heard on the ships all along their passage south and in the harbors at Port Townsend, Bellingham, and San Francisco. Its dissonant intrusion brought her back to her observations. She had been lost for a bit, thinking of days when she had been a child, although she knew that everyone considered her still to be one. But Sarah knew otherwise. She had for a long time considered herself an old soul. It was as if her bones and spirit had endured for centuries and simply redressed themselves periodically in fresh, less durable external trappings. There was little new, she thought, and often after the excitement of some adventure, she asked herself if that was all there was. And now she was here—predicting again, a predestination for each event and person in it. She wondered if that was a sin, her presumptuousness, as her mother had called it.

She went back to watching, noting that the whistle had prompted several of the men to reach into their pockets to consult their watches. A few wound them. One listened to his clock ticking. Her mother and the women in the car straightened up, as if readying themselves to sing in a choir, waiting for the conductor's baton to move. Two seats away, the dark-skinned man sat down and tilted his chin forward and upwards, ignoring his wife and son and bodyguard. Smug man. She looked at the burly man next to him, was amused at the word "bodyguard." It seemed like such a funny term for bullies hired by rich people. She wondered if there was such a thing as a "soul guard." That might be much more important, she thought. Did people really believe in angels? She wondered if she still did. That thought made her turn to look over at the fat preacher across the aisle. He twisted in his seat slightly and put his much too small hat back on his head. Awkward, unaware, and self-absorbed, she thought.

She listened to a conversation that had started up between the twins and the obese preacher. The women said they were from a little town in New Jersey. "A small community near West Point," they said, "near the military academy." They claimed to be descendants of George Washington himself. They had decided to travel after Edith, who said she was five minutes older than her sister Teresa, had begun having fainting spells. Edith's late husband had left her a sizable estate, and her physicians, Drs. Elizabeth and Emily Blackwell from

New York, had told her that she might not have that much time left to live. She had reconnected with her younger sister, Teresa—they both giggled demurely at that old joke, which Sarah suspected they told repeatedly—and had taken a clipper ship to Paris and then a few months later traveled all the way to Patagonia. They were returning home now because the fainting spells had become more frequent, and Edith was becoming very tired after walking even short distances. Edith knew she needed to get back home. Teresa said very little and nodded approvingly at everything that Edith said. Sarah noticed that the preacher seemed disinterested, kept looking out of the window. She wondered if he was bored with the content of the discussion or irritated at having to converse in the hot weather.

Sarah watched the bushy-mustachioed Italian man pull his boy close to him and point outside to the action on the platform, which had changed in character with the signal. Gentle. Loved his children, she thought. His wife, nursing the baby, had covered herself. The black bearded man in the sombrero glanced around and continued his game of cards. Every time he turned a card and placed it in a stack, she thought she saw him smile, although it was difficult because his black beard was so thick. There was more to him that she would need to learn. He stopped his play and looked outside. Everyone was paying attention to this moment, waiting for the first tug from the big black engine up front that would pull them forward. A change to the show was about to begin.

Sarah noticed that the dapper, tall Italian man had again glanced at her mother. Four times now, she had counted. She knew what that meant. She expected that he soon would stand, probably after the train was moving, and make his way over to Emmy, introduce himself. She had seen other men do that, and it always started this way. There would be a bit of an exchange and usually the man would ask to join them, perhaps after making a comment to her or to Jacob, always ignoring Jojo if he were near. Her mother would always be polite, respectful, and careful. She would say far fewer words than the man, weigh the content of his words, and measure her response. Sarah mused that her mother gently would equal the intellectual content of the other person's comments, but noted that she seldom had seen her mother descend into a loss of her composure or competition. Her mother was steely in that way, and Sarah wondered if she herself had the same wherewithal. As ancient as she had decided she was herself, frustrated to be encumbered as she was as an eleven-year-old girl, she thought that form of control was the result of something much more ancient. That was why she listened to her mother.

The train lurched slightly, gave a loud deep groan, and the cars began shaking, rattling the windows, like the earthquake she had felt in San Francisco.

CHAPTER SEVENTEEN

✧✧✧✧✧✧✧✧✧✧✧✧✧✧✧✧✧✧

FOIL

J Abbot Foil checked his pocket watch—7:17 in the morning. The military band that had assembled to see Winfield Scott had disbursed with the news that the man was indisposed. That was an inconvenient disappointment for this transport but not disastrous, Foil decided, because he knew that the US military entourage would have taken up as much of his attention as did the security details for a cargo that he considered infinitely more precious and valuable than the bloated general. And he realized he needed to pay attention to detail. After sending a note to Quitero to wire ahead to his Isthmus Guard captains in Gorgona to arrange for more armed men to join the train, he stepped as far back away as he could from the huge French locomotive to get a perspective again—six passenger cars including the one up front that had been specially outfitted for Winfield Scott, two flatcars carrying human cargo, and three boxcars trailing behind the heavy armored car he personally had designed.

As he looked down the boardwalk, he saw that the bustle of predeparture had transformed the entire area into a loud, animated assortment of colors and cacophony with vendors crowding the platform's passengers with their trinkets, refreshments, and souvenirs. As much as he hated that disorganization and the shove of native barkers, Foil knew he could not control more than a fair share of it, so he concentrated on his covert project. One by one, Quitero's Isthmus Guards had mounted the cars, a guard on every passenger and cargo car, nine in all. Most were simply sitting quietly, as he had instructed, but a few were pacing, unfortunately, drawing attention to themselves. He shook his head and looked for Carlos Quitero, his foreman. An hour earlier the man was to have issued to each of his crew, a double-barrel ten-gauge shotgun and a copy of the 1851 Colt percussion pistol, the lot purchased at a very reasonable discount from a small Japanese manufacturer in Hiroshima. If all went as planned, it would be a short and uneventful crossing. Inexpensive. He looked at the closest of the mounted sentries and saw that he had his long barreled shotgun slung over his shoulder. He looked at the space between the cars and then up at the engine. Quitero had armed the railroad company's brakemen riding behind every other car and had positioned an Isthmus Guard to ride with the engineer and the two wood tenders.

The horizon to the north was black, so more torrential rain

would certainly pour down onto the train, soaking his guards on the roofs, and all the slaves and the Chinese workers on the open flatcars. As he walked back to the closed boxcar that contained his cargo and five more men, he was relieved that the weapons he had issued were of the new and more dependable breach-loader type that used percussion cartridges rather than open powder barrels. He had calculated that the mid-February weather would have changed by now into the more unpredictable rain of dry season characterized by substantially fewer of the constant, warm, heavy showers. But it had not this year, so he had his man distribute rubberized parkas. The closest guard, pacing back and forth on top wasn't wearing his. Too hot likely.

The first whistle from the engine surprised him. It seemed too early. He again pulled his pocket watch from his corduroy red vest and looked for the conductor. Three minutes sooner than usual. Was it his clock or that of the engineer? He shook his head again. If the whistle was correct, the train would leave in no more than ten minutes. Where the hell was Quitero?

CHAPTER EIGHTEEN

◇◇◇◇◇◇◇◇◇◇◇◇◇◇◇◇◇◇

BOCAMALO

He watched Foil outside consulting his watch, impatiently prancing about. He knew that man—not personally, but as an observer from his days working the isthmus trails, guiding passengers and pack trains and, periodically, surreptitiously arranging for the robbery of them. He also had watched Foil and many other men increase their fortunes after the railroad was completed. For many reasons, Rafael really did not like J. Abbot Foil. He had seen him on one occasion, standing on a railroad flatcar that had derailed, while forty men and a few horses attempted to lift it up back onto the rail. He was boasting about how he had never been ill during all of his travels on the isthmus and how twenty of the men lifting him and his associates would be dead within a month because their "constitution" was weak and their habits predestined them to die before they were thirty. The cocky way he walked reminded Rafael of the man who had killed his mother. "*Pene Pequeno*," he thought to himself.

During those pack train days, Rafael had been careful to stay out of view, to never engage, sometimes playing the role of the deaf mute, sometimes just ignoring questions. He read the papers and intercepted telegraph dispatches, secretly copied to him by friends he had acquired over the years.

And he knew the railroad well. Realizing that if it succeeded, the railroad would change everything—bring much greater opportunity for some, more people, more silver and gold crossing over from one ocean to the other—Rafael had watched the railroad's construction patiently and unobserved. He knew the faces and had logged the routines of almost all of the attendants at the twenty-six stations along its route. He knew the meeting places for the Isthmus Guard, where its captains lived and how their shifts were scheduled. For many months, he had simply and unobtrusively ridden the cars back and forth along its entire length. And, several times, for the privilege afforded to the locals who could not afford the exorbitant one-way price of riding the train, he had paid the railroad company its excessive toll of four-and-one-half dollars for the privilege to walk the rails along its forty-seven mile stretch. Every time he did so, he observed and took careful notes. Long lists. Details. Preparing.

In all of this deliberate, meticulous work, Rafael understood the importance of patience, quiet timing, and the supreme value of being alert for opportunity. Unlike so many others, the great majority of whom had been caught, tortured, and hung, he had modestly saved most of the booty from his small heists before the railroad had been completed. Remaining conservative with his proceeds, he had set it aside in a safe place where no one would ever think to go. He even had invested a small amount in railroad stock so that he might understand the greedy ones and their grand scheme of egregious returns on investments.

Over the course of the years, he also had learned to be a competent, careful cabecilla. He identified with each of them, every one of them recruited from the huge pool of "*los discapacitados*," the damaged refuse of society. he took care of his men and women, wisely never commanding more than a fair share of the spoils and avoiding the jealousies that always developed when one allowed oneself to become greedy, ostentatious, or power hungry. He was smart enough to stay away from other men's women, as much as he liked women, because he knew very well how easily provoked jealous men could become over their possessions.

He kept to himself, mostly. And although he might have admitted to a deep loneliness at times, he had disciplined himself over the years with an appreciation for the splendor of solitude. In so doing, he had refused to ever allow himself to be in love with anyone, especially a woman, or ever accept a woman's love, no matter how often it was offered, because he told himself he did not believe in it. Love had always proven to be a destroyer of the foolish, in his estimation. And why should he long for something that likely was beyond his reach anyway? Or didn't really exist?

What was it—about this love, or the ownership of a special

woman, that he had seen drive men crazy? It was as if one of the cards laying face down on his lap, like the queen of spades, held more magic than did all the others. And just what was the allure of the queen of spades? More magic? Power? Security? Did men think that owning her gave *them* more power? Make them live for even a half-second longer? Was that rational? Was that what love really was? And in the game of life, if a man bet on turning his cards over and finding her, the special one, and then took the chance to play the other cards to win, giving up so much to get it—that "love"—would the magic really be there after all? And if it were, this strange thing, would it be as powerful and durable as he wanted it to be? Would it solve the deep ache he always felt inside? And if it did act as a powerful salve for all that was raw and painful, what would happen to him if love petered out or, worse, walked away from him? And then what would it feel like, knowing he had been a fool all along, placing hopes on one card?

No. He did not believe in love of a woman. As fascinated as he was with women, all of the ones he had taken over the years—he seldom had to work for it, as clever and handsome as he was—he did not believe in the love of queens. And with every woman he had taken, held, watched, dissected—the sexual playthings, commoners, purported nobility, self-appointed queens and all—every one of them had disappointed him. They were lying, all of them. He always saw it in their faces when they used those words, looking up at him. And they always turned away the more he looked at them, unwavering.

He had enough to live very comfortably now, but he wanted and needed more, much more. He did not know what it was, perhaps to find someplace befitting his potential, far beyond simple comfort. It wasn't love, he knew.

So here he was now, culminating his patiently constructed plans based on research he had collected over the past six years, waiting for the right opportunity, and hoping for something that he could not yet place. Maybe then he would let everyone know who he was. Maybe. He sensed that would take more than what he had accumulated. Many games of Patience might help him sort it out.

The engine whistle shrieked its chords, and he glanced outside at his men, waiting for their signal that the military had departed. It came. He saw Foil hollering at someone outside. He smiled as he turned over the next card.

The railroad had taken more than five years to complete, and it was gratifying to know that the stops and starts of the enterprise had driven investors like Foil into a daily frenzy. Each delay, related to one form of disaster or another, from loss of equipment or human capital, cost the North Americans a fortune. Their first fodder, the Irish, wouldn't work, he remembered. They, like the Scottish in 1848, had perished by the hundreds after several disastrous attempts at establishing domicile in this region. When construction of the railroad by the North Americans began, they came in big ships by the hundreds. He talked with many of them. The Panama Railroad Company had recruited them from the immigrant masses in New York and Boston that were pouring in from Europe, particularly Ireland and eastern Europe, with contracts that assured free passage from Panama City to San Francisco in return for six months of labor in the jungles. Everyone wanted to go to San Francisco to be rich. Because the work was brutally hard and dangerous, and the allure of opportunity in California was so great, few lasted the requisite length of their contracts. Many simply abandoned work and made their way to Panama City by the old trails, and then north by whatever means they could to get themselves to the Sierra gold fields.

Then he watched as the railroad company next resorted to importing African slaves, accompanied by their Arab slave drivers who whipped and punished them. They died just as easily as did the whites, proving even more susceptible to the many diseases of the tropics. He had heard that one of the physicians attending the camps, agreeing with Foil, opined that the blacks died easily because of their "inferior constitution, which was composed of excessive amounts of nitrogen and less oxidized tissue." The railroad company then turned to Chinese labor and black slaves from Barbados who were more accustomed to the tropical heat. To the slaves, they promised freedom, and to the Chinese, a high wage and ample supplies of opium. He spit, perhaps in disgust, perhaps in envy, he didn't know which, when he thought of how the railroad people had used addiction and slavery to push their way through the jungle.

Judging from the cemetery on Mount Hope, which expanded daily with the bodies of white laborers, he estimated that cutting across the challenging terrain to complete the rail lines had killed at least six thousand. However, and he spit again when he thought about this, slaves and Chinese dead bodies were seldom counted in the tally. Nor were the bodies that were pickled in formaldehyde and packed off in barrels to American and European medical schools for dissection. The Panama Railroad Company made a neat profit on those, and some accused the company of hastening the death of some afflicted individuals because intact rather than decomposed cadavers brought much higher prices. And there was never an accounting of those lost in sink holes, or the bodies of those who simply collapsed in the heat and died off of the trails. If left for a day, the carcasses would just disappear, consumed by the carrion eaters and vermin.

He remembered Mount Hope, outside of Colón. Before the Panama railroad construction had started, he had known the wooded ridge as "Monkey Hill" because so many small howlers lived there in the trees. The whites in the cemetery had replaced them.

Rafael could tell when bodies were piling up by looking in the sky for the black and white vultures and crows. Before the railroad was constructed, every day that he traveled the ancient Gold Road he found bodies of travelers who likely had set out on their own to get to the Pacific Coast and make their way north. They were freshly dead; he knew that the bodies wouldn't last more than a day because of the ants and crabs.

There were many ways to perish, he knew, but the fairest of the whites were particularly susceptible to the shaking chills disease, from the bloody diarrhea or from the "*vomito-negro*," that always occurred after the afflicted's skin turned yellow. On two occasions, early on, he had watched the bodies of Chinese and Irish pile up so high that the builders couldn't get anyone to volunteer or work for a week, even at the promise of exorbitant wages. The black slaves brought up from Cuba, Guinea, and Brazil died so quickly that the slavers couldn't resupply them. And the ground would not accept them. The water table was so high that after a burial it was a common occurrence to see the bodies belched from their shallow graves within a few days of the burial. The slave handlers tried disposing of the bodies by dumping them into the Chagres in Manzanilla, but the lazy river would just give them back, depositing them along the shore of the town. During that time, he remembered that the cockroaches crunched under his feet on the cobblestones in Colón and flies hung like a quickly moving diseased cloud over the river's mouth. The stench from decomposing bodies and raw sewage pouring in from the streets of the town made him vomit every time he visited. He estimated that the enterprise had cost a bloody terrible fortune, and only the money investors who sat in their gilded North American mansions profited, not the ones who invested with their lives.

Rafael knew all of the routes, for he had travelled the foot paths as a mule skinner when he was a young man. Seeing the doctor-soldiers who had spoken to the pretty woman in black across the aisle reminded him of one experience in 1852 with US military officers whom he had helped guide. He had advised the medical doctor on that journey, a stubborn man named Tripler, to reconsider their isthmus crossing and wait until the rainy season ended. His advice had been ignored, and more than one hundred travelers in that party had perished from disease, desertions, and disappearances.

There were other disasters he had watched as well.

When abundant quantities of gold had been mined from California and the packing of fortunes began again, the Deriéni and Cimaroons had re-emerged, attacking and plundering. He had quietly visited every one of the places where they had attacked the mule trains on the Gold Trail, on the Chagres to Colón, and on the Camino Real to Portobelo and Nombre de Dios, discerning how they had made their entrances and the routes by which they had escaped. After a while, simply by hearing where a recent robbery had taken place, he was able to predict which of the bandit crews would be caught by pursuers. There were too many places with pitfalls and dead-ends. He also knew how well the terrain could easily provide cover and disappearance to those seeking to vanish. None of the Isthmus Guard would have that same knowledge, particularly since Runnels had retired. They were afraid of the forest.

And he knew the weaknesses and strengths of the railroad's pathway and rail bedding design. The path being cut for the rails bordered closely to the Chagres, and he had counted more than one hundred and seventy different dry gullies, wide and narrow streams, that it crossed over. While acting as a transporter for supplies to the cooking camps, he had listened to the gossip, knew exactly where the engineers and architects had chosen to place stone and boulder fill to bridge the long stretches cutting through mangrove bogs and deep swampland. He kept a list of where the trestles had been built with mahogany timbers that would rot in less than six months from the constant rain and heat, and which bridges had been fortified with the Lignum vitae timbers or concrete pillars. He knew where the railroad had hidden its redundant telegraph wires. He knew the place on the bogs of Matachin where an entire locomotive, wood tender, and six cars were left standing idle while its crew went into the forest to pick plums and mangos and that it quietly had tipped over in the soft ground and sank, disappearing completely in less than a half-hour. The men of the crew, emerging from their early lunch, saw only the tip of the last coach car before it was covered. The engine and cars were still there, rusting their way deeper and deeper on their way to hell, he mused.

And the Rio Chagres was his friend. For seven years, he had travelled up and down it and its main tributaries, the Obispo and Gatuncillo, transporting supplies and passengers with Embera tribal pole men in their short, carved-out guayacan tree bungo boats and the longer dugout piragua boats of the Kuna. He had poled small rafts that carried pack mules and heavier objects, like the printing press that an enterprising *norteamericano* had shipped to Panama City. He knew where the many openings of trails at the riverbanks slipped off into a torpid jungle that enveloped everything. Some of the trails were well-worn because they led to crossroads that provided pathways to forks that, if one knew the correct choice, might lead to one coastal town or another, or to a copper mining town with decent whorehouses and cantinas. He knew that deep viper pits, carved out of the mud and rock by flash floods and torrential rains, ran the entire length of the trails. The rest of trails might last only for a few miles, particularly if they were not well travelled.

He knew that if one became lost or took the wrong direction at the fork, it would mean death, for during the dry season, the jungle lianas could grow six feet in a day, completely obliterating a passage way, and during the wet season, the mango, zapote, and gourd trees; the fragrant violet, orange, and crimson garlands of flowers; and the long sinuous creepers running up and down the tallest of trees, spilling into the rivers and narrower streams, would quickly crowd in behind the swath of a machete and erase all trace of one's passage. He wondered how many of the gold-hungry travelers on route to

California had disappeared that way. Their bones would never be found. A different form of compost, he laughed to himself. This was *his* jungle. It had a heartbeat of its own, and he knew how to read and respect its pulse. It defied the conquering spirit of arrogance and simply overwhelmed the ambitions of enterprising men.

And, most importantly, he knew the tree homes used by the Wounaa and the caves that had been left vacant by the Old Ones after the Spanish had hunted and killed them all. He knew their secrets and had added to them some of his own. Dark secrets. He thought about some of those secrets and, although he knew they were unconfessed sins that would send him to the darkest part of Hell, right beneath the Evil One's heel, unless he confessed himself some day, he brought them forward for a moment and realized that they still stirred him after all these years.

The train lurched. He looked down at his men outside and saw them grinning, opening and closing their brown umbrellas. It was all ready. He looked for Quitero, Foil's henchman. He hoped the bastard was feeling well enough to make this trip.

CHAPTER NINETEEN

◇◇◇◇◇◇◇◇◇◇◇◇◇◇◇◇◇◇◇◇◇◇

QUITERO

When the whistle blew, he reached over for his overalls hanging on the nail in the privy's door. Had his watch stopped? It was still running. Could it be that far off the right time? He started to get up, but another twisting spasm pushed him right back down onto the john. The diarrhea had started last evening a few hours after eating, recurring episodes every forty minutes or so, doubling him over. His mouth was dry and he felt lightheaded, but he dismissed that. He had suffered through and survived an episode of cholera during one of the outbreaks in Aspinwall-Colón a few years ago. It had killed hundreds, and this was nothing like that. The cholera and yellow fever illnesses came on fast, and either one killed you within a few days. This was just an inconvenient distraction. He would get past it. Where was the military escort for Scott, he wondered? They were late.

He had been up all night, would have been in any case, checking and rechecking all of the details for the security of the shipment, including the two American cargo ships, sent to accompany each other for security and rescue if necessary. The guards and several nervous gold miners had arrived safely from Bellingham in the Oregon Territory after a brief stop for resupply in San Francisco. He had kept them safely anchored off of the long wharf and had placed two boats with armed men next to each. At three A.M., the crew had loaded one hundred and four small, hundred-pound sealed boxes, each carrying, he calculated, twenty-five to thirty-five thousand dollars in raw gold ore—dust and nuggets—into eight ship-to-shore craft. They then transported them down the wharf to an inconspicuous boxcar, bearing only the letters "FC" eighteen inches high, on each side's sliding door.

Foil had designed the car himself and was proud of it. Quitero thought about how he had argued with the man about its numerous shortcomings as he had watched it being built, hoping to convince Foil that it might be just as useful to simply double up on the number of men guarding this shipment. But Foil had dismissed his objections, angrily noting that as additional shipments were arranged in the future, the reuse of the car would keep future costs down and reduce the number of persons privy to the cargos.

Certainly, it was sturdily constructed. Lead panels lined the ceiling, floor, and side walls. Hidden slots, placed eight inches and four feet above the reinforced floor, could be accessed by shootists standing up or lying on their bellies. Quitero had concerns that the inside of the boxcar would become very hot during the sunny days, and Foil at least had allowed for the car to be equipped with a built-in water dispenser and several hidden, slotted vents in the roof for ventilation. It had four thick-walled safes, one in each corner—three for the gold and an open one to house extra weapons, powder, and ammunition.

Up until yesterday, Quitero had been quite certain none of the ammunition would be needed. But he was feeling a queasiness today and was concerned that it might be more than this damned bout of dyspepsia. It wasn't from any sense of unpreparedness or experience. Ever since Señor Ran Runnels had retired a few years back to marry a wealthy woman, Quitero had competently managed the western section of the Isthmus Guard as well as all of Foil Cargo's security operations. He knew his men and kept a regular and precise routine. He knew he was feared, perhaps as much as Runnels had been. Seven years ago, he had been with Runnels at both of the mass executions of the denizen Deriéni desperados. Like Runnels, he was a harsh taskmaster, well known for decisive justice. He had flogged native trespassers on the railroad thoroughfare— shot more than a few of the more scurrilous ones. He was a good hunter of men, slaves, or bandits. He was given respect for that. It wasn't from any sense of inadequacy that he felt this way this morning.

It was something else. He had an uneasy feeling, starting last night as he walked through the "Mingello," the native ghetto market, even before he became ill with the craps. It was like the feeling he had a few years ago, just before the episode that they now called the "Watermelon War," he realized.

He thought about that fiasco. Were the conditions similar now? He, like the Americans who had hired him, had enormous contempt for the riffraff and native slackers. He hated the Negroes almost as much as the Chinese, all of them crowded into the Aspinwall and Panama City ghettos. They were insolent and ungrateful. Although they had been displaced from work by the railroad, they should have appreciated that they had been given their freedom in return for their work when it had been available. It was their problem, not his, that most of the work had disappeared when the railway was complete. All the old jobs were gone: guide work, boat transport, mule-skinning and carrying supplies to the old Gold Road that was now overgrown and obsolete with the railroad line's monopoly. That the blacks and Chinese had the misfortune to have no other skills than the breaking of their backs with manual labor, which, he was convinced, they did in a lackluster, indolent manner, was not his problem. None of that had changed really since the railway had been opened four years ago. They all just had gotten poorer, if that was possible.

But recently, just over the past few months, the inhabitants in the ghettos had become restive again, and he wondered why that was. Was it that the railroad, attempting to control overhead costs for the Isthmus Guard and the rail maintenance, had made the prudent decision that isthmus natives now had to pay a fee to walk the forty-seven mile right-of-way? Was it resentment? Was that it? Surely not.

He remembered Jack Olmer, the drunken *norteamericano* lout who had started that Watermelon War mess. Quitero had seen him briefly that fatal evening after the massacre, saw him refuse to pay a nigger vendor in the Mingello for a piece of melon as he and his *vagabundos bêbados* had staggered their way through the barrio that night. He remembered how Olmer had spit seeds at the man and then shoved him, drew a pistol, and in the tussle shot an onlooker. A deadly mess ensued. The night then had been hot, still over one hundred degrees at nine o'clock. Like last night, he thought.

When the scrap had started up, a crowd gathered, for it had been too hot for people to stay in their quarters that week. Olmer's shooting of the black bystander sparked an enormous explosion of violence. Within minutes, the ghetto, normally languid and dormant during humid, hot spells, erupted into a ferocious maelstrom. Niggers brandishing machetes rushed amok and attacked every nonblack person they could find, running through the hotels and breaking down doors in the upper floors, dragging people by the hair into the hallways, stripping, beating, and killing them. Twenty-seven terrified *norteamericanos* managed to escape from the burning hotels and made their way to the train station, where they barricaded themselves inside behind its thick brick walls and massive doors. The growing crowd caught a few of them who did not get through the closing doors in time and literally tore the victims to pieces.

From the second floor windows of the inner compound that looked over the tall outer wall, a few of the whites tried disbursing the crowd by firing pistols into the crowd, wounding three and killing two, including a small boy who was riding on the shoulders of his father who had come to watch the spectacle. That provoked an even wilder frenzy, the enraged mass shouting in angry concert. The din of the furor could be heard over a mile away on the outskirts of the town. More mayhem followed as the blacks in the crowd, frustrated at the escape of the white Americans into the station, started turning on the Chinese merchant shops in the area, tipping over carts, breaking windows, and looting.

As the rioters tried to break into the armory down the street to seize weapons and powder, the New Grenada military police, rousted from their barracks, finally arrived and attempted to put themselves between the North Americans and the rioters. But one of the besieged Americans fired his pistol again, this time killing one of the police. When that happened, the police captain told his men to step aside and watched as the rioters brought a telegraph pole forward to use as at battering ram against the station's thick, metal doors. Some of the police, enraged at the loss of one of their own, turned their rifles against the station, firing at the upstairs windows. With each thud of the ram against the courtyard's tall doors, the crowd's screaming, cacophonous rage intensified. The right door broke first, falling off its hinges into the courtyard onto three of the hapless, wounded *Americanos*.

The crowd poured in, and when they came through the opening, some tripped and were trampled by those behind pushing their way in. A few seconds later, a large explosion shook the building when the stationmaster discharged a cannon, a makeshift weapon from an old Spanish mortar he had filled with gunpowder, nails, and bolts, into the mob. Fifteen rioters, the stationmaster, and his assistant were killed instantly. The crowd surged forward over the fallen bodies, pushing its way in, pounding on the heavy inner door and shuttered windows of the compound. The Americans inside desperately began firing into the crowd. As six rioters rolled two large barrels of oil from the engine yard toward the station, the women in the crowd started yelling "*Quemelos! Quemelos!*" Burn them!

That's when they heard the harsh, steady whistle of a rapidly oncoming train. The shouting and screaming abruptly diminished as the insistent crowing of the engine whistle grew louder. A hush came over the crowd. The blacks and Chinese in the crowd knew what that meant. Word must have gotten out to Ran Runnels and his vicious Isthmus Guard before the telegraph wires had been cut. The rioters disbursed quickly. The *norteamericanos* were saved.

As Runnels's first captain, Quitero had been on that rescue train with the Isthmus Guard. By the time they got to the station, he found that only the bodies of the rioters and the Americans killed in the courtyard remained. The cleanup of the mess and fire-gutted hotels took months, he remembered, and the ghetto still bore the marks of the riot six years later. Jack Olmer, unscathed by the events, had somehow departed for San Francisco the next day and had never been located.

As Quitero walked briskly to the train, surveying the disposition of his men on the roofs of the passenger cars and the closed boxcars, he felt some relief. The train would be out of the town quickly, running full steam through the center of the Mingello. Once underway, the traverse through the ghetto would take less than ten minutes, and then, when finally en route through the isthmus countryside and jungle, he would feel safer. The Isthmus Guards, their small barracks quartered at every other stopping point, were well disciplined and trained to be mean—vicious if necessary. A few managers with a need to know had been alerted that an important train was coming through this morning. All had assumed it was for the four-hour express crossing of the famous General Winfield Scott and that their mission was to be available to protect the detested *norteamericano* hero, the one who had defeated Santa Anna in the Mexican War that had given California and the Southwest to the *yanquis*. He and Foil had allowed them to continue thinking that.

He doubled over again with a sharp spasm and had the feeling he was about to lose control and soil himself. He wondered if he should turn back and run to the privy shack? Couldn't. Foil would be unforgiving. What he had eaten the night before? Damned embarrassing inconvenience.

Coincidentally, in Barbacoas, Gorgona, and Matachin, the stationmasters and Isthmus Guard captains and several of their key men all were similarly inconvenienced. Because their symptoms were relatively mild, none had bothered to report their illness. They simply had stayed at home that morning, each assuming that his duties would be picked up by assistants.

CHAPTER TWENTY

EMMY

ama!" she heard. Turning, she saw that Jacob and Jojo had left their car to join her and Sarah. Jacob squeezed himself in between her and his sister. She put her arm around him and looked up at Jojo, who shrugged and gave her a mildly exasperated smile. It had been at her suggestion that Jacob travel with Jojo in a separate car for this short, safe train ride adventure—a little test to see if he might be ready to start being his old self again, the fierce little boy she remembered, filled with a staunch bravado and unrelenting curiosity. But as her son snuggled close, she realized he probably wasn't ready yet. He was still too frightened to venture out very far away from her. She wondered when and if that would ever change again.

Looking up, she saw across the aisle the black-bearded man with peacock-blue eyes. He was staring at Jacob. And then he looked at her, searching for something, it seemed. His unblinking stare was intense and piercing. After a pause, she nodded to the man. Was he reading them? Did he understand something? He reached up and tipped his sombrero at her then gathered up his cards and put them under his serape. The steam whistle called out again. Because there were no available seats, Jojo excused himself and returned to the other car. The train began shaking and started to move forward.

Although this long ride across the isthmus would be a wonderful adventure, and she wanted to see it as if through her children's eyes, she was weary. She ached and fought to stay awake. As the train started picking up speed, shudder-lumbering slowly at first, she thought about her return to the East Coast after living for so many years in the Pacific Northwest Territory. The letters from her father had arrived a week apart, four months after she had retrieved her son from his captivity with the Haida slavers and returned him to the safety of her Whidbey home. The first letter hastened her decision to leave the fertile homestead she and her husband had developed on that island. In that message, her father said that her mother was very ill and Emmy should plan on returning very soon, if only for a visit, because the sugar disease was consuming her quickly. She might not last long, he wrote, "She was melting away."

On the day of her departure, Emmy visited her husband's grave site to say good-bye to Isaac. She knew she would need to leave. Staying there, carrying on, would give her little comfort, and bringing her children back to meet their grandparents had always been one of her hopes. Her life, all that she had built with Isaac, had been destroyed on that one fatal, devastating night. So perhaps the opportunity to start anew, see how Boston might have changed over the past thirteen years, get her children into a decent school, give them a chance to refine themselves before they would have to go out and make a life for themselves on their own—all of that made the decision much easier.

Judging by the different shades of ink, her father had penned his second, longer letter over an extended time. By the entry dates on each page, he had started it well over eighteen months before he had sent his first letter. In the first entry of the second letter, her father mostly complained about his frustration with expenses and tightening financial times and the sparsity of financially responsible legal clients. In the second entry, he said he was debating whether to accept recommendations that he run for political office; in the third, he said he had decided to do so; and in the last entry, he mentioned that Senator Benjamin Butler himself, a former law partner, was promoting his candidacy. And Butler had inquired after her.

She found that odd, and for a moment, it made her question her decision to go back. Ben Butler was married. He was almost forty years older than she. She remembered that he also was an obese, arrogant braggart, who seemed to fill almost every conversation with references to himself and his accomplishments. He never used the pronouns "I" or "us" or "we," but preferred instead to speak of himself as if he were referring to a third, highly respected friend with whom he was very familiar. She remembered him approaching her just before she moved away to the Oregon Territory with her first husband. She was only a few weeks past her sixteenth birthday and very excited about the future. At the going-away party, Butler stooped down, interposing himself between her and the woman seated to her left, and in front of a small group at the table said loudly, "Ah, Emmy, lovely Emmy, Ben Butler wishes you all the best in this grand adventure of yours. The Butlers are certain you will become rich and make your father proud." And as he did so, he touched the top of her folded hands, put his other hand on the back of her upper arm and squeezed, palpating and lingering a bit as he did so. She blushed, kept her composure, but felt compelled afterwards to wash her hands and rub away the feeling of the man's hand on her arm. Her father had smiled proudly at his senior partner's compliment.

Her mother did not miss that gesture, but as Emmy reflected later, all she had said was that she was pleased that Emmy was being afforded the opportunity to leave Boston for better things. Her mother was an astute woman, Emmy knew, but she was meek and needlessly deferential to her husband, who Emmy realized to her embarrassment, was an insecure man, almost always allowing his pride to obscure his better judgment. She had watched her mother stand by him as he gambled on professional relationships and took ridiculous financial chances that had nearly bankrupted the family's security, which had been endowed primarily by her mother's considerable dowry. Emmy had already decided she would never allow a man to own her, and that incident with Butler made her angry with her mother for not standing up for her.

She wondered what she would find when she returned to

Boston, wondered what her father meant. She knew that she had the wherewithal to resist unwanted advances. If she had the nerve to contend with a criminal monster as she had done on a beach in British Columbia, the likes of an ambitious, conniving letch like Butler would not be daunting. But she wondered what her father had in store for her.

She put that aside.

When they were breaking free of dirty Panama City, the sound of the squealing and skidding of the train raised to a high whine, holding, holding, holding, then breaking in a rapid decrescendo to a steady rumble as it picked up its pace with the new sounds of rail tie-ribbons rhythmically tapping beneath the steel wheels. Emmy forgot about Boston and Whidbey for a few minutes. The town started rushing by—clack clack, clack clack—and its colors, the buildings, and the people in the streets blurred into a red-brown jumble. The sounds quickly mesmerized her, and she drifted and stopped seeing outside. Clack clack, clack clack, clack clack, clack clack. She would find a new life, she told herself—go up to the Maine coast and buy lobster from the fishermen on their little skiffs beached on the seashore. Cook them on the beach and break their red tails open, pull their white flesh out with her fingers. Have churned butter on fresh bread and walk the shoals as she and her sisters had done with her family when she was a young girl. Show Jacob a different coast. Let him run on a shore that was already tamed and free of killers.

She heard tapping from across the aisle, like the sound she remembered when crows pecked at her upstairs window when she lived on Whidbey. She looked across and caught the flutter of black wings but missed whatever being they belonged to.

A raven, she wondered? She saw that the man with the black beard and the blue kerchief was gone. That was when the window right next to her suddenly cracked in several places, a spider pattern running up to the top of the pane. It made no noise. It just happened. Strange. It was as if some violent spirit had pushed its heavy finger into it, putting a punctuation on her last thought, bringing her back to the present. She watched the verdant countryside rushing by.

CHAPTER TWENTY-ONE

◇◇◇◇◇◇◇◇◇◇◇◇◇◇◇◇◇◇

JACOB

When is the train going to leave?" he had heard Sarah ask his mother. And just as she said that, the car had jolted and creaked and then lurched forward, and when he looked out the window, he saw the station start moving slowly past their window. They were leaving, and he forgot about the black-bearded man across the aisle with the fierce blue eyes.

But he had seen it. After the man tipped his hat at his mother, he had briefly looked back down, briefly peeking at the face-down cards, then up again, staring at Jacob directly in his eyes. That's when Jacob saw it. A cold chill then . . . he felt himself getting warm all over and he began to perspire.

He felt faint and as if something was pushing into his belly. This man knew him, and he knew the man. Even though Jacob was sure he had never seen the man before. It was just a brief glance, but it went right into him. Jacob knew him from someplace. He knew him. He pulled himself close to his mother and looked out the window.

He listened to the fat man, the preacher, who was talking, boasting to two old women. The man said he was "the Reverend John Otis, but my parishioners call me 'Reverend Plumpjack,'" and laughed. He said he was a "well-worn bishop of a well-heeled community." Jacob watched the two women's polite reactions to the preacher, who went on about himself and his wife. "We lived very well. My flock is very large and my congregation . . . is quite generous. One must suffer a flock's beneficence, of course." The cleric laughed again at his smug little joke.

Jacob looked at a boy a few years younger than him, short with big, brown eyes, sitting a few seats away with a man in a red shirt who he assumed was his father. The little boy was fidgeting and didn't seem interested in what his father was pointing to inside the car or on the streets of the town as they were pulling away.

Jacob turned his attention to the tall, well-dressed man who had left his seat and was leaning over to address his mother. "Madame," he said to Emmy, "may I introduce myself? I am Emilio Gattopardi. I was wondering whether you would grant me the honor to ride with you and your family, for some company for a little while." His mother was gracious, as always. The man sat down and immediately started to talk about himself. Jacob decided he didn't like the man. He wasn't honest. He knew his mother would dismiss the man soon enough.

Within minutes of the train passing through the sleepy town of Pedro Miguel and then Paraíso, men waiting a thousand yards beyond the stations climbed both sets of poles and cut the telegraph lines. Others did the same twenty-five miles ahead at Frijoles and Ahorca Lagarto.

Two work crews, four men in each, pried the spikes and pulled off both the rails in Gorgona and Mila Flores. They dropped the rails in gullies in the forest and covered them with dirt.

PART TWO

◇◇◇◇◇◇◇◇◇◇◇◇◇◇◇◇◇◇◇◇◇

ON TO THE
CHAGRES

Distinctive because it alone of all rivers drains into
two oceans, the Rio Chagres is still called Rio
Lagartos by some because of the giant lizards who
prey on the slower creatures that brave the waters there. The
Spanish preferred trekking their Camino Real rather than
navigating the difficult Chagres waters. In 1671, however, the
English privateer Henry Morgan ascended its sinuous pathway
to circumvent the Camino Real route to sack Panama City.

In 1860, the headwaters of the Gatuncillo (also known as
the "Boqueron") and Chagres Rivers ran through canyons and

tall gorges. Travelers in the piraguas, cayuco canoes, and bungo boats had to navigate over waters that included numerous rapids and waterfalls. During the rainy season, the height of the river in some of the gorges could rise forty to eighty feet during a heavy downpour. All of the rivers are wed to their mother, the Darién, and it to them, in a fertile, defiant cycle of life and death—a commensal dance that has not changed in eons.

CHAPTER TWENTY-TWO

FOIL

He eased back into the cushioned seat as they moved beyond the slums of the city and the train picked up speed, starting its gradual ascent, sixty feet a mile, up the ten-mile incline toward the railroad's crest, the continental divide at Culebra. As the train passed Mount Ancon and then entered the beautiful valley of Paraíso, he watched the morning sun glistening on the tributaries to the Isthmus Rio Grande. Pretty, like the Chesapeake, but hotter. And he owned a good piece of it. Needed to figure out the best way to use its resources. He smiled. It was all going well.

J. Abbot Foil loved what had been accomplished over the past five years. The New Grenada Panamanian countryside now lay spread open to him and his fellow entrepreneurs, as if it were a wild and resistant mistress, now forced into accommodation by the overwhelming preponderance of American will, brilliance of organization, and ingenuity. Proudly, that forbearance and skill had bested even the most accomplished of national rival enterprises—the sultry French and arrogant Brits. And he was a beneficiary of his own distinct and aggressive contribution to this marvel, a rail line cut through the most inhospitable of terrains, cleverly engineered with the loss of only a few, irrelevant lives. The enormous initial expense, more than seven million dollars—or about one hundred and fifty thousand per mile—had been recovered within the first year. In just a few years, it had become a hugely profitable enterprise that was the envy of entrepreneurs around the world. The Panama Railroad stock that he had purchased at thirty dollars a share was now worth hundreds, and the dividends he had received exceeded 40 percent for each of the past three years. No one, not even the ones down in their luck, was selling his stock. And Foil knew that the return on this shrewd investment would go on indefinitely, because no one had been able to find a viable shipping alternative. He knew about several failed expeditions to map a water canal route. Vanderbilt and the others had abandoned their route across Lake Nicaragua. They all had conceded. This was proof of a God-given manifest destiny to his country and to him, as one of its loyal citizens.

Foil had invited two of his partner investors to ride with him right behind the engine and tender, in the special private parlor car that had been prepared for Winfield Scott and his staff. He had arranged for the railroad company to stock Scott's car with ample amounts of food and great rum, Yellow Dant Bourbon and several bottles of James Crow's specially brewed "Old 1776" Bourbon, straight from the Pepper Distillery itself. As a result of Scott's trip over to the Pacific side several months earlier, the company also had equipped it with sturdy, reinforced furniture to accommodate the big man's massive three-hundred-and-eighty-pound frame, for he had broken the one chair in which he was able to fit on the trip westward. Scott was accustomed to royal berths, and his staff devoured the luxuries lavished upon him. And now that he was indisposed, why waste it? The food would have to be replaced anyway, Foil reasoned, so he and his colleagues helped themselves to the pastels and petit fours. He looked over at the bottles of Amontillado and a new fine Kentucky bourbon refined from the continuous still process, and, despite reminding himself that his own heavy drinking days were behind him, he opened a bottle of cooled French Champagne and poured his colleagues a toast in a tall crystal flute. No need to give a libation to the gods, and why waste something like this to superstition? A few sips of a fine brew. A fine cigar. A fine, plump, blonde woman waiting for his bidding in Aspinwall. Foil looked out the window. It was all his.

The first ten miles of the trip, the train's exit from Panama City on a fertile plain through plantain, sugar cane, and coffee plantations, took forty-four minutes. Foil's express train slowed as it bypassed its first station at Culebra, and Foil thought it strange that the stationmaster did not appear as was his custom for the passing of the morning's first express. After the peak at Culebra, the train picked up speed again, moving down a 2 percent grade and was at full speed as it rapidly passed through Emperado and the narrow valley of the Obispo, past Matachin, "The Dead Chinamen" town, where hundreds of coolies had killed themselves when their opium had run out, having been cut from the budget by the railroad construction accountants. After Matachin, it sped on toward Gorgona, a crossroads town where the old Gold Road, a tortuous pathway traversable only by foot and mule trains that had been used for three centuries by the Spanish, and forked north five miles to the filthy town of Las Cruces. Three miles outside of Gorgona near the village of Gamboa, the train picked up even more speed on a descent and then entered the first of three tunnels, each built with high arches to accommodate oversized freight and the railroad company's four powerful French- and Belgian-made engines that had been constructed with high smokestacks that would lessen the amount of funnel soot falling on the trailing passenger cars. Going through the tunnels, the Isthmus Guards knew they would not have to duck down, but every one of them had turned facing backwards to avoid the smoke issuing from the engine's stack.

It was at the second tunnels' exit that Rafael Demotenes Bocamalo had ordered his men to drop and tighten two cables, barbed-wire twisted around rawhide rope, the moment after the engine's high vertical stack had passed through. When the train emerged from the third tunnel, all but one of the guards had been neatly peeled off, every one of them killed outright or dismembered by the taut cables. The remaining Isthmus Guard, spared from the garroting because he was on the car closest to the stack, had been temporarily blinded by the smoke and had not noticed the action behind him. A hundred yards beyond the tunnels, as the train slowed for its approach to Puente Espiritu, a long trestle bridge that passed over a deep gully, he was shot from his perch by one of Bocamalo's marksmen. In the darkness of the tunnels, none of the brakemen and no one in the passenger cars had seen the slaughter. The Chinese laborers on the first flatcar were screaming loudly, however—for the bloody upper torso of one of the Isthmus Guards had fallen into their midst.

CHAPTER TWENTY-THREE

◇◇◇◇◇◇◇◇◇◇◇◇◇◇◇◇◇◇◇◇

QUITERO

Quitero had joined Foil ten minutes before to give him the report that, as ordered, he had sent off the telegram to his captain in Gorgona, but the train had departed before he had received confirmation that the order had been acknowledged. Because Foil had ordered the forward doors of the six passenger cars to be locked with chains as a security precaution, Quitero had been forced to make his way forward from the guarded cargo car, the flatcars and then along the roofs of the six passenger cars to Foil's car, which was coupled immediately behind the tender. He missed being decapitated in the tunnels by only a few minutes.

Foil was not happy with Quitero and berated him in a

cruel way in front of the other men, using long, show-off words. Quitero's intestines started up again as he listened to the pompous bastard's insults, turned his eyes away, and was briefly distracted by the sight of yet another group of mule skinners whipping a long-tethered pack of mules forward in the same direction of the slowing train. They carried no baggage. "Are you listening to me, Quitero, you incompetent?" He heard Foil slur a few words and, seeing the open bottles of whiskey in the car, Quitero realized that in the short ride from Panama City, his employer had gotten himself slightly inebriated. He had only seen Foil like this once before, and then as now, he had behaved in a similar manner. He was a mean, little drunk.

Quitero had expected the train to slow, as it always did, when it emerged from the third tunnel. But he did not expect the whistle to blow three short and one long blast, signaling it to come to a halt as it did abruptly, its brakes screeching loudly. Interrupting Foil's stream of insults, Quitero pushed up the window and saw that the engine, tender, and three of the passenger cars, including this one, were halfway across the trestle bridge, which spanned the deep, wet, foggy river gully below. The rest of the train's trailing cars which were not sitting on the trestle, were obscured by smoke and steam from the engine and a fog wafting up from the valley. "Stay here!" he said to the men in such an angry, commanding tone that it halted his employer's tirade.

Unholstering his pistol, he stepped out of the rear door. "Lock this door!" he said to Foil and made his way along the trestle past the tender car to the engine, its boilers loudly bubbling and steam escaping in a slow rhythm as the pressure valves released it from the vents. Up ahead of the engine, he saw what appeared to be a "snake head"—a rail curved upwards when the metal tie fastening the steel to the timbers broke. He realized that the engineer had slowed the train for the trestle crossing and then had braked it to a full stop when he saw what would have caused a disastrous derailment on the bridge. Quitero pushed his pistol back into its holster, waved to Foil and to the conductor who were leaning out of the windows of their cars, and climbed up into the engine compartment where he found his cab guard and the engine crew holding their hands high over their heads. Their fearful expressions registered suddenly, just as he felt the two barrels of a shotgun pushed into the side of his neck. He was disarmed. From the other side, two other men climbed up into the engine compartment. Despite the bandanas across their lower faces, he thought he recognized them both. He tried to place them.

"Señor Quitero! Thank you so much for stopping by. Please follow us," said one of them, pulling down his mask. He was a tall, toothless, thin man wearing a tattered tan felt hat and filthy checkered shirt. Quitero noticed that the man had no thumb and only the remnant of a fifth finger on his right hand; he had likely been a railroad brakeman in the past—the train car links, which had no bumpers or cushions, invariably caused that form of injury. And if he had been a brakeman, the man almost certainly had been discharged by the Panama Railroad Company since his injuries would have made him of no further use to the organization. He noted that the man had no trouble balancing the side-by-side double-barreled ten-gauge shotgun, however. Its hammers were cocked. The smiling man had his left index and middle fingers poised on the triggers. So, with his hands tied behind his back, Quitero was helped down from the cab and followed the man along the rail. He looked back, saw that none of his men were riding on the cars, heard the deep clang as the engine and three cars on the trestle were being uncoupled from the rest of the train.

Walking the trestle, he realized that what appeared to be the broken rail up ahead was simply a piece of steel placed on the track to mimic a curved snakehead. Cursing, he gave up trying to contain himself. Letting go, he soiled himself, shook his head, and waited while, one by one, the four disarmed brakemen, the conductor, and the guard from the engine compartment were led to the middle of the trestle with him.

He remembered the crippled guy's name now: "Haut." Apolonio "Pallino" Haut. A mean-angry-whining-never-happy bastard. Turned petty thief after he left the railroad company. He felt Haut's fingerless right hand on the small of his back. The last words Quitero heard were, "Now jump, gentlemen."

CHAPTER TWENTY-FOUR

<><><><><><><><><><><><><><><><><>

JOJO

Because there were no open seats remaining in the car where Emmy, Sarah, and now Jacob sat, the conductor insisted over Emmy, Sarah, and Jacob's protests that Jojo return to his seat in the other coach. He acquiesced without objection, for he noted that Jacob seemed comfortable and secure, and it gave him the chance to observe and listen, as he had always loved to do, without having to interpret everything for Jacob. He had noticed that his young charge seemed to be brightening somewhat and was much more responsive to the banter that Jojo kept up as a stimulant for him. He knew it would take time for the boy to recover from the brutality he had endured. Jojo was pleased that his efforts might be paying off.

As much as his journey south on the big sail ship had been a great, albeit uncomfortable adventure, and as much as the bountiful experience of San Francisco had been a continuously engaging series of new interactions with all kinds of people, he was even more fascinated by the huge train. Like most of the passengers on this ride, had never been on such a marvelous contraption. He had counted everything that the iron steam engine would pull behind it—six passenger cars, followed by two flatcars filled with riders, and then three closed box cars. He wondered how many horses and men it would take to pull so much weight. In his translation work for the Bella Coola and Bella Bella in the Pacific Northwest, he had boarded the big sailing ships of the Americans, Spanish, and Russians and in Esquimalt had seen the machines on one of the British steam-powered gunboats. He understood that the same principles were being used to make this iron horse do its work. It was like when a pot boiled and pushed up the lid. As a small boy, he had often wondered if that power could be harnessed somehow. The whites had figured out how to contain the steam and let the force from it push other devices that would make the wheels turn.

But the overwhelming realization for him, as he thought about it, was how many other things were in place—the metal rails laid out flat and evenly on rectangular ties in measured regular intervals, the tracks that he knew would have to run over or through carved-out stone hills. How would the thing cross over rivers? On big bridges, he presumed—and it all worked so consistently to make it all happen predictably, things for which no one person was the creator. The people responsible for all of this must have cooperated, shared, and learned from each other in a way that he had rarely seen in the tribes he knew up north. Now that Mrs. Evers was teaching him to read, he found that a door had opened for him that he knew would give him the same advantage. She had told him that he was smart, but he already knew that. He would need to learn how to make people work together so that what he learned in school would add up to more than what he could do all by himself.

A few minutes after the train had passed through the slums of Panama City and entered the countryside, Jojo looked about and realized the mood of the passengers had improved. The temperature in the compartment had cooled, for as the train picked up speed, the morning air flowed through one of the windows that had been pushed open by the man across the aisle, a sweat-drenched, portly traveler. He recognized the language. By the man's conversation with the woman next to him, Jojo thought the man was a Swede. Both the man and the woman were fanning themselves with palm leaf fans. The miserable man seemed to prefer inhaling smoke from the engine up ahead rather than suffering from the humid heat. When the train slowed as it started up the grade to Culebra, the smoke, fleas, and various flying insects filled the car until the man's companion persuaded him to close the window. The train accelerated five times on reaching the various plateaus up to the Culebra peak, and each time the man reopened the window briefly and then closed it at his companion's insistence. Within forty minutes, most of the passengers in the car were covered with a fine soot.

Although Jojo saw that many of the travelers were quite irritated by this, he noticed that the Italian Rigoletto singers at the end of the car were not. Their mood had completely changed, and they seemed to be enjoying themselves immensely as they shared a breakfast picnic. They were amused at the man's folly, he realized, and were discussing, predicting amongst themselves, when he would reach up to unlatch the window again. "Ah, we are picking up speed again," he heard the youngest of the group say in broken English.

"Time for more flies," Jojo said loudly in response. The Italian translated that to the others, and they all began laughing. They raised their cups to him and started singing. They had pretty voices and sang in a beautiful harmony some song that made them all happier. The singing brightened up everyone in the car.

When the train had slowed to a stop after emerging from the tunnels, Jojo, like all of the passengers in the car, had tried to see outside. The smoke from the engine cleared for an instant, and he realized that the car was stopped on a bridge and he was looking down into a valley. He couldn't see how far down, but it appeared to be very deep. The foggy morning mist rising up over the lip of the trestle combined with the steam from the engine, and its soft, wispy grayness crawled toward the rear along the length of the train and obscured all but what was happening close to the train itself. He heard the heavy, brisk footsteps of several men running on the roof of his car, and then there was pounding and the deep clang and groan of metal grinding on metal from behind his coach. Then he saw several men take shape, one by one emerging like phantoms, walking slowly along the narrow trestle, tenuously forward toward the engine up ahead. Four of them were carrying two unholstered pistols. The tenth man to pass by his window was the conductor. He was no longer wearing his yellow conductor's hat or his blue coat. He was followed by a clubfoot carrying a shotgun. He seemed to be pointing the shotgun in the direction of the conductor.

Jojo knew something was wrong. His hand went to his side to unsheathe his knife, but then he remembered that, at Emmy's request, he had placed it out of sight in the tote he carried for him and Jacob. He looked about and realized that no one else in the car understood the possible danger. He spoke to the man across the aisle. "Did you see that?" But the man, looking out the opposite window, fanning himself furiously, ignored him.

Jojo stood up and reached for the tote buried beneath other luggage in the overhead rack. As he brought it down, the train lurched and threw him off balance for a moment. Then the train began moving again, and he watched as it passed by four armed men standing on the side of the trestle. One of the men waved at the passengers as the car passed by, and the other men were laughing. He did not see the conductor or the other men who had passed and wondered if they were in one of the other coaches ahead or in the engine compartment.

The train, now freed of eight of its cars, picked up speed quickly after it crossed the trestle and moved down the side of the pass, faster than he had ever traveled before. Its cars swayed back and forth from side to side, and as it accelerated, the frequency of the rhythmic clacking beneath the steel wheels increased until the sound merged into an indistinct hum. The Swede opened the window again, but this time, perhaps because the train was moving much faster now and swaying in a way it had not before, the passengers had quieted, their banter subdued and muffled by the sound of the short train rushing over the rails.

Thirty seconds later, less than a mile away from Gorgona, the engine's right front wheels struck the spot where twenty minutes before, on a prearranged schedule, Rafael's men had removed two rail sections. The engine slipped off the track, twisted and careened down onto its right side as it plowed forward and fell over a five-foot embankment into a shallow stream running along the built-up track. Their momentum propelling them forward, the three trailing passenger cars stacked into a crushed broken pile on top of the tender car. The last compartment, carrying forty passengers burst in the middle, spewing Jojo and the other victims into the stream and surrounding jungle. Steam from the cracked boilers poured out over the wreckage.

Because the primary and redundant telegraph wires had been cut in four locations thirty minutes before the derailment, no message about why the eastbound train was late went out from Gorgona for over ninety minutes. It would have been longer had a rail tender not been patrolling in the vicinity. The distraction of the accident kept the railroad rescue efforts occupied, just as had been planned.

CHAPTER TWENTY-FIVE

◇◇◇◇◇◇◇◇◇◇◇◇◇◇◇◇◇◇◇◇

SARAH

Somehow, somewhere, she had been here before. Perhaps in a dream, she wondered? When the train had stopped, through the cracked window next to her mother, she saw Chinese men and women, some with packs, scurrying back and forth and away from the train into the fog. They looked bewildered, she realized. She and Jacob moved over to look out the window from the seat across the aisle where the bearded man with blue eyes and kerchief had sat. On that side of the train, she saw several figures moving in and out of the fog and steam. In contrast to the Chinese on the other side, they were moving purposefully. One of them, dismounting from a mule, was wearing a blue kerchief. The man walked up to their car, shouted out some instructions to three men who then moved off in different directions, then looked up briefly at their window. It was him—the black-bearded man who had been playing Patience. He saw them and fixed a stare for a moment on both of them. Sarah sensed Jacob tensing up, heard him gasp. He moved back across the aisle and pushed himself up close to Emmy. She followed Jacob and sandwiched him between herself and their mother. Others were peering out of their windows. Something was very wrong, she knew. An accident? What was happening?

A few moments passed and then the rear door to the coach burst open and a man wearing a train conductor's hat walked in. The hat was yellow and had "PRC" in red letters stitched into its brim. But unlike the conductor for the train, this man wore no uniform and kept his hands beneath a dirty, tan rain poncho. He was smiling through brown, ragged teeth. Had he taken the conductor's hat? she wondered. He was followed into the car by three other men—two Negroes and one pale white-skinned man, all wearing kerchiefs over their lower faces. Each man was carrying a double-barreled scattergun, like the one that her stepfather, Isaac had kept by his bed at their home in Washington. The men were filthy and seemed desperate but determined, she thought. They spread out down the aisle of the car, carefully watching the passengers who sat quietly. They were joined by two other passengers who stood up from their seats. Everyone watched these men. She held her breath.

"Ladies and gents, Señora, Signorina," the leader nodded, smiling at her and her mother and the twin spinsters across the aisle then scanning the faces of the men. "And caballeros . . ." The man with the yellow hat carefully enunciated his words in a thick Irish accent, "Me name's Deacy, Nicky Deacy, and I'm yer new conductor. We need to have you all be steppin' outside of dis 'ere coach." She saw the man look directly at the two red-shirted Italian men and then push up and point what appeared to be pistols under his poncho. "Please, per fervor." When the Italian man holding the baby hesitated, the man with the pistols nodded at his accomplice, who pointed the short-barreled shotgun at the infant's head. "Don' break ar' 'earts, Señor." The man's companion stepped over and took the two-barreled hammer pistol from the bushy mustachioed Italian's belt.

Deacy then walked over to the large, burly man sitting beside the loud Negro man and his son and wife. "Hey, you, Bob Dorn. You—stand up!" and then, "Come on, Big Bob— *levantate!*" The man he called "Bob Dorn" stood slowly. He was a huge man, over a foot and a half taller than Deacy. Sarah saw Dorn's eyes narrow as his mouth closed and his jaw clenched. The two men knew each other, she realized. Dorn was angry—and afraid, she thought. She sucked in her breath, wondering what he would do.

"Bugger you, Deacy, ya little shit," the big man said. The man called Deacy didn't like that response. His nostrils flared, and his face reddened. He pulled two big nickel-plated pistols from under his poncho and pointed them at Dorn's burly chest.

"Let's not be makin' a mess in 'ere, Bobber!" His accomplice searched the big man and retrieved two pistols and a folded razor. Deacy then shoved the pistols into the big man's belly and nodded for him to move to the open door.

Turning back to the rest of the passengers, Deacy said, "Now . . . God, it's so hot in here. Everyone please step outside of this stuffy car. I be promisin' to treat yer well and with utmost respect." He laughed, as he emphasized his last two words. He pointed the pistol in his left hand at the short Negro man in the white linen jacket. Only a few minutes before, the man had been telling crude jokes to anyone who would listen. As he pulled the rings from the black man's fingers and jerked off his gold chains from his wrist and neck, Deacy said, "Señor, I bin asked by my boss to tell yer: please not to be forgettin' all ya been holding on to so damned tightly—yer carpetbags."

Sarah watched the expressions on the faces of the black man and his wife. They were surprised and angry. They cursed the man named Dorn, their bodyguard, who was exiting, and she realized they were mad at him for not putting up a fight to protect them.

Sarah looked up at Emmy. Her mother's face looked calm, but Sara felt her mother's hand—it was tightly and firmly gripping hers as she and Jacob were guided out of the rear door and down the steps onto the sod below the tracks. "Cooperate" was all that Emmy said quietly and squeezed her hand hard to emphasize that command.

When they stepped off the train, steam enveloped them for a moment and then cleared again. It smelled like burnt wood and greasy metal. Sarah looked to the right. The two other passenger cars behind theirs were being evacuated at the same time by more men. The Chinese had all disappeared, but a large group of black men and a few whites and mulattos in chains—slaves—milled about in one big clot to the rear. No one was guarding them. Further back, Sarah saw several men surrounding one of the closed cargo cars. Through the fog, she saw glimpses of a bright blue kerchief, and for a moment, when a patch of clearing opened up, she again saw the black-bearded man who wore it. Men came up to him, and he seemed to be directing everything, giving them orders. Then the fog covered them all again. Sarah heard the engine start up and looked to her left. The front part of the train with three cars had been unhitched and was starting to pull away across the trestle. "Jojo was in that car!" she heard Jacob gasp out. "He's going away!" She pulled Jacob close to her. She felt him straighten up, breathing fast. "I'm on my own again," he said quietly.

Then the man called Deacy reappeared. He spoke to everyone in Spanish and then in English: "Now, you all, please pay attention! We respectfully are askin' each of you to remove your pants and skirts. It will soon be hot. Some of you are comin' with us, and we want youse all to be comfortable for a long ride. And please, knowin' what yer thinkin' put yer purses, pocket watches, necklaces, doodads, and billfolds out in front of yer clothing so we won't be haven' to search yer personal spaces." He snickered, leering at them all, "Not that it would be displeasurable to us." He laughed again.

"So please, beggin' yer haste here." He reached into the linen vest pocket of the short, black Spanish man and pulled out his pocket watch, yanked it from the man's vest, and looked at it. "We really don't have much time." Sara looked up at the windows of the coach. Inside the cars, masked men were tearing through the luggage, emptying out suitcases and valises. Down the line, some robbers were throwing trunks and steamer cases from the baggage cars, and others, mostly women, were rummaging through the contents.

"This is disgraceful! We will not take off our pants!" Sarah heard the portly preacher shout out to the two spinsters and then to big Bob Dorn who stood next to him, as if appealing to him for help. Sarah wondered whether they would do anything to stop this.

Deacy, who had overheard the remark, walked up to the preacher and Bob Dorn, pushed his yellow conductor's hat back on his head, smiled, and put his pistol to Bob Dorn's neck, cocking the hammer. "Yes, you will, Señor Padre." Then he fired the pistol upward into Dorn's throat. She saw the back of the man's head explode outward as he crumpled backwards into a disheveled heap. His body convulsed for a few moments and then become still. Twenty yards down the line in front of the third car, another shot rang out, and she saw another man fall backwards. At this, the stunned preacher and everyone along the line began disrobing down to their underwear and pantaloons. Rain started pounding down. A few of the robbers opened umbrellas and laughed as they watched the passengers struggling in their soaked undergarments.

Jacob was shaking, and Sarah and Emmy pulled him close while they took off their skirts and helped him pull down his pants. Deacy moved down the line hollering at other people who were struggling with their breeches.

Sarah heard a loud "Thwump" down the line where the closed boxcars had trailed the flatcars. The explosion cracked all of the windows behind her and shook the entire train. Several people shrieked and fell to the ground in terror. Dust and debris swept over everyone.

This was much worse than what had happened to them up north in the Washington Territory. They were going to die, she thought. Then she felt a firm but gentle hand on her shoulder. "*Venga*—come, come, little ones," she heard in a loud whisper.

CHAPTER TWENTY-SIX

◇◇◇◇◇◇◇◇◇◇◇◇◇◇◇◇◇◇◇◇◇

EMMY

Make yourself small," she said to herself. She pulled Jacob and Sarah close to her. "Quiet. Keep your heads down. Don't look in their eyes."

Up and down the line, several men and a few scruffy women were pushing people, shaking out their clothing for billfolds and watches, screaming orders in several languages, mostly Spanish. When the man who called himself Deacy murdered the man he had called "Bob Dorn," she knew how she and her children behaved during the next few minutes would determine whether they survived this outrage. The robbers would leave. Let them have their money. Don't provoke them. And then down the line, she heard women's voices screaming and heard three more shots. Executions? She glanced sideways and saw two women, one with a small child, being pulled out from the line. Another woman was being pulled out of the line by the hair. She felt herself breathing fast and shallow and felt dizzy. She couldn't allow herself to faint. She had to keep control. Hold on to the kids!

"Mama?" Jacob called. Emmy turned and saw that the broad-shouldered Italian man with the bushy mustache was crouched down and was attempting to pull Jacob and Sarah away. He looked her directly in the eyes and put his finger to his lips. "Shh, lady, let me," he whispered. She turned and saw that he was pointing to the narrow undercarriage behind the wheels of the railroad car. He had hidden his little boy and baby there. She looked over and saw their mother nodding to her. She understood immediately.

"Do it!" She pushed Jacob and Sarah together and said, "Go with this man!" When they started to protest, she squeezed their hands tightly. "Do as I say!" She looked down the line and saw that the bandits were occupied, slapping a man and his wife, who were both screaming, resisting in terror. Another shot! Then another! Then another from further down the line! The man called Deacy had shot them, too, and others were being murdered! Jacob and Sarah left her side, and the crouching mustachioed man pulled them away, tucked them into the darkness under the large carriage wheel. Emmy tried to keep her composure, and as the fog cleared, she saw the man in the blue kerchief sitting on a white mule, watching her children escape.

CHAPTER TWENTY-SEVEN

BOCAMALO

R afael was somewhat surprised but not disappointed that they found four of the five guards already dead in the armored boxcar. Less trouble for him and an important time-saving gain, he thought. The opiate he had arranged to be spiked into their water supply had been meant simply to make them sluggish and more easily overcome when the time was right. Not arouse suspicion. But by 8:15, the heat inside Foil's car likely had reached a high enough temperature that the men started drinking much more water than he had expected. They had grown drowsy and then stopped breathing altogether, he reasoned. That was how he had seen it work before.

But all the time saved by not having to fight with the guards was wasted, for when his men entered Foil's boxcar fortress, they found all of the enormous, identical safes were locked and thick-walled.

He was becoming anxious at the time delay, and he was angry at himself, for he realized it was a serious error on his part for him to have assumed his lieutenants would be smart enough to precisely follow his orders. He hated Pallino Haut because he was sloppy, and Nick Deacy because he was an insolent, stupid bully. But he knew he needed them, couldn't accomplish this without them and their gangs. Rafael, who had calculated the risks of including them in this strike, knew they would cause trouble and was furious at them, for they had disposed of Quitero and let Foil escape before they had acquired the safe combinations from either of the men, despite his admonitions.

To make matters worse, the demolition explosion that had blown down the heavy sliding compartment door also blew out the eardrums of the one surviving guard. In the wretched man's groggy, deaf stupor, he was of no use to them to identify which of the safes contained the gold and which one contained ammunition. That meant it would be extremely hazardous— and unwise—to use explosives to retrieve the gold. He did not want to damage the gold containers, which would spill the gold dust and nuggets and make the transport impossible. Unnecessary, avoidable delays.

Then he saw Haut walking back from the bridge. He was wearing Quitero's tan leather coat, likely stripped from the man before they had decided to push him off of the trestle. They found the combinations in the dead man's right breast pocket.

When they opened the safes, they found the sealed containers neatly stacked and numbered. He instructed his men to gather from the fourth safe whatever ammunition fit their pistols and rifles. He expected interference at some point.

Disarming the miners, all of them riding in the sixth passenger car, the one closest to Foil's armored boxcar, had been the most dangerous trick he had accomplished that morning. He had them watched in Panama City. They were, to the man, an anxious lot, and he knew that while accompanying their pan riches to the New Orleans mint they would likely all be armed. Thus, he simply had overwhelmed them by placing several of his own men in their coach. When the train emerged from the last tunnel, each of them had found a pistol pointed at his head. No shots had to be fired.

The timing was the most difficult challenge, however. He knew the regular schedules sent another train in each direction at four-hour intervals. The station office managers, accustomed to the electrical telegraph chatter of the morning's routine reports and intermittent news exchanged from Aspinwall and Panama City, would quickly note the silence resulting from the downed telegraph lines. The Panama Railroad Company had placed redundant lines to preclude the periodic and not infrequent weather-related downing of decaying telegraph poles. In the four years of operation of the rail lines, the communities all along the line had become dependent on the coast-to-coast communication. When one line went down, the redundant system kicked in. Thus, the extended interruption of the clicking banter would alert the stations all along the line that something was wrong. Although it would take time for them to locate the sites of the problems, he knew that the

Isthmus Guard would be alerted in all of their ten stations. Gandy dancers would be sent out by the station managers in each direction to look for trouble.

Anticipating this, Rafael had his men steal all of the wheel lugs on the nearest stations' hand cars and lame the mules at Matachin, Culebra, Gamboa, and Gorgona. He scheduled his men to take the rails off in four locations several miles apart on the tracks leading to and from the heist. His men cut the redundant wires in four other locations, including those to Las Cruces. It would take time, he expected several hours at least, for the railroad company to locate the site of the real problem at Puenta Espiritu. They almost certainly would be distracted by the derailment up ahead and would be confused at first, assuming that the entire train had been involved in that disaster. But despite the havoc he knew he had created, he also knew the Isthmus Guard would be on to him soon enough— four hours at the most. He had to get the cargo loaded on the mules and then down the steep path two hundred feet below to be loaded, mules and all, onto the long, dugout bungo boats and rafts strung out and waiting on the river.

While the tethered, distraught miners watched and bellowed out profanities in several languages, his men worked rapidly, unloading the heavy boxes of gold and strapping each mule with one on each flank. His skinners had lined up sixty mules—much of the available healthy transport stock in the region, and his boatmen had purchased every available bungo craft within a ten-mile stretch in each direction. He saw that they all quickened their rapid pace when they saw him ride up.

It was all working as he had planned. Pursuit by the decimated, leaderless Isthmus Guard would be disorganized and ultimately futile, burning furious but short-lived, he thought to himself with some satisfaction. And if the fools tried to follow, didn't give up quickly and pass on the losses to the railroad company's insurers, he would kill the hostages one by one to dissuade pursuit. If they persisted or the insurers sent in their thugs to prevent their losses, he would lose their posses on the river, in the dense jungle, or kill their men off as well. He knew the Darién wilderness. They did not.

Mounted on his big, white mule, Rafael rode up to the line of waiting, terrified passengers. They were a wealthy lot, he knew, because the cost of the passage kept poor people off the train, forcing them to pay a usurious tariff to walk the rail by foot or take their chances on the old trails. Most of the people lined up outside of the three remaining passenger cars would be British or North American, although he had overheard several other languages as he had sat waiting in the car before the train departed. No Greeks. And no soldiers, he smiled to himself. His men would have already disarmed or disposed of anyone who might be a threat. Now he just needed to pluck a few from the lot who might be of use to him. Hardy women would be of good use—one way or another. Maybe the Italian aristocrat and the loud Brazilian. He knew how to make best use of the fat preacher as well.

He told Haut to unshackle the slaves and use their brace-lets for the hostages. As he watched Haut unchaining them, he studied the faces in the motley, ill-fed group of blacks and mulattoes, saw a few white faces in the mix. No women. They just stood there confused, untrusting. "*Vamos, amigos! Vamos!*" Haut hollered out. "*Vamos!*" One by one, the men started to leave, wandering away in different directions. Each and every one of them stopped and looked back at their liberators, bewildered. Five of them in one group, however, remained and did not move, just stood watching. They seemed angry, which surprised him a bit. He looked at their eyes and determined who was the most likely leader in that group.

Rafael smiled to himself, considered the line of terrified, bewildered passengers, then rode over to the group he had observed while playing cards in the passenger car. He stopped in front of the loud Brazilian and his wife and son and saw that Deacy had already disposed of their clumsy lout of a bodyguard. Flies covered the mess of the man's blown head. He called out to Deacy, who was harassing some of the passengers, the Italian valet, and the widow in black, about their children. "Deacy, enough." Referring to some of the men who had started to rut on a few of the women, he said forcefully, "Get your men in line."

Motioning to the Brazilian threesome, he said to Deacy, "Put these ones in the shackles first and bring me this one's little valise." Deacy had the valise—turned it upside down, emptying a bunch of folded finely stitched white silk shirts, showed it to Rafael. Rafael took the empty carpetbag, looked at it briefly, and had Deacy put the silk shirts back in it then tied it to his saddle.

He rode up to the Brazilian who was watching him intently, leaned down as he was being shackled, said, "Welcome back, Señor, to where I think you rightfully belong. No?"

At this, the loud Brazilian man screamed out, "*Puta merda!*" and spat at him.

Rafael grinned, showing his widely spaced teeth, and said to Deacy, "Just take his woman."

Nodding at the loud Brazilian, he said, "Keep this one chained and give him to those ones over there." Laughing, he pointed to the remaining group of blacks, who only a few minutes before had been chained together. "He is now their property."

Rafael moved further up the line, looking over the passengers, then returned and rode over to the others who had been in the coach with him while he played his card game. He pointed to the tall, well-dressed Italian who looked less elegant than before with his breeches on the ground beside him, then to the two women—the young widow in black and the wife of the Italian's valet who, only a few minutes before had been protecting their children. "Take these three."

He looked at the Italian valet, whom he had watched hide the children beneath the carriage. As the valet's wife and his employer were chained together, and the valet's woman was pulled away from him, he looked directly at the red-shirted valet, then nodded over at the undercarriage of the passenger car, where he knew the children had been secreted. He flashed a wicked conspiratorial grin at the valet, then frowned with a pure, dark stare. Paused. "A gift, Señor." Then, nodding his head at the hostages, who were being manacled, he said to the valet, "Don't try to follow us. *Capisci?* These ones here, and your woman, are our . . . assurances that you will not do so. Maybe we will be kind, if you are as smart as you seem, and listen to what I am telling you." Rafael knew he would follow. It was a game, after all.

Rafael looked over at the young widow, who was being cinched in chains along with the others to walk in a line behind one of the mules. The woman's black blouse contrasted with her white pantaloons, and despite this insult, she stood up straight with her chin held high. To retain her dignity, he thought. She had been looking down at the ground, avoiding his eyes. He stopped his mule in front of her and studied her. But then she looked up at him and her contempt went right into him with a single, piercing stare. It was a fierce rebuke, one with such stern authority, that he could not dismiss it. He felt a sharp twist in his stomach, similar to one he knew he had felt before but could not place and not for a long, long time; an old, deep pain and he could not remember why it cut. He didn't have time to think about it now. But he would. He tucked it away then turned and rode off to supervise the packing of the remainder of the gold. As he did so, he said to Deacy, "Give the women back their skirts. We don't have time for frolic."

As his boss rode away down the line Deacy said, "Sí, sí, Señor!" then, when he was out of earshot, leering at the women, Deacy said loudly so that everyone could hear, "For now, mio capitán Bocamalo."

CHAPTER TWENTY-EIGHT

◇◇◇◇◇◇◇◇◇◇◇◇◇◇◇◇◇◇◇

BRETT

Lieutenant Rory Brett detested General Winfield Scott in a way that exceeded loathing, he thought, and wondered if that was possible. Certainly the man was a hero; he had been deservedly decorated for his leadership in two wars. He was brilliant, prescient, and forceful. But it was the man's arrogant, entitled behavior that provoked Brett's feelings about him. It diminished the importance of everything else. He had come to hate Scott's every gesture, the way he waddle-strutted, throwing his belly forward, behaving as if he were some God-ordained royalty. His attending staff promoted his expectation for private deference and public obeisance with lavish ceremonies in his honor conducted at the considerable expense of others. He had seen it the first day the general had arrived in San Francisco en route back to the East Coast from the de-escalation mission in the Pacific Northwest. Perhaps it was the dismissive way Scott had with everyone around him, the sycophants and parasites, throwing their meager petals before him. It was as if the man's body, and not just his head, had swollen up over the years in an exact proportion to that of his reputation. To overcome his own anger at the way Scott swaggered and intimidated underlings, Brett imagined what the hero must look like when he is naked. He laughed, shook his head at the thought, wondered if the bloat could even reach himself to clean his private parts, then shook his head again, shuddering at that thought.

He was through with the army. As he had attempted to tell Emmy Evers on the train, Brett's plan had been to tender his resignation as a US Army assistant surgeon, assigned in San Francisco to accompany Scott's extensive entourage, as soon as it was in sight of the East Coast's mainland, wherever that turned out to be. He would book a passage and, as a civilian, head home from there. While in Panama City, however, he had received another letter from home—he was too late. His father had already passed. Now, his return home would be for family business, to settle up debts, perhaps free the estate's slaves—it was time—and determine whether the family home on the Chicahominy River could be saved. He was angry with his military superiors for denying his request for a leave of absence after he received the first letter from Virginia. Couldn't be spared, he was told; the general's needs were greater. So he endured the five weeks of business and festivities in Scott's honor in San Francisco, the subsequent repetitive ornate and sumptuous ceremonies in Panama City. And then he received the second letter and, in his grief, had to wait several more days while waiting for Scott to finish meeting with numerous military dignitaries and various political schemers from Peru, Chile, Colombia, and Bolivia. The only bright moments over the past sixty days were the two occasions when he met the widow, Emmy Evers. He was overwhelmingly smitten with her, he realized.

When he returned to the hotel that had served as Scott's headquarters, he was surprised that the customary bustle of activity was absent. All of the baggage was still loaded on the carriages and the guard troopers lined the street outside, but they were in the process of standing down, and the escort dragoons were at rest beside their horses. Some of the troopers were taking off the saddles from their mounts. The departure of the entire military escort assigned to be certain Scott was safe in his travels in New Grenada apparently had been abruptly postponed. He was informed that not only Scott, but also his entire officer entourage had taken ill, almost simultaneously, after the early morning's breakfast, incapacitated by repeated bouts of projectile vomiting and watery diarrhea.

Captain Letterman, who like Brett had been excused from attending the final Panama City breakfast to make his own preparations for departure, had been consulted by the one physician in the entourage who had not also been taken ill, to determine whether to announce a new cholera outbreak. The hotel proprietor, however, well aware of the disaster for his business if word were to spread that the dreaded scourge might be originating in his establishment, was quick to point out that none of the other hotel guests and none of his own staff, except for two attendants who had cleaned up the food after the sumptuous breakfast, had taken ill. Letterman concurred that this inconvenient illness was inconsistent with the typical outbreak of cholera, which almost always was sporadic and widespread. Instead, he said, the corpulent general and his staff were almost certainly the victims of contaminated food. Brett agreed with that assessment.

That morning, three men were required to attend to the general who repeatedly had to rise from the bed and be helped down the hall to the indoor latrine. The entire floor, every room, reeked of sour excrement. Opening the windows to ventilate only made matters worse because it seemed as if every fly in Panama also had been invited to the scene. Brett was disgusted, witnessing the way all of the officers in the general's staff behaved with their infirmity. The disarray he observed in Scott's command only confirmed Brett's decision to resign from the US military.

And then word came in about the railway derailment.

Unlike the general's personal physician, who had commented that he was relieved he had avoided the railroad disaster, Brett's first thought was of Emmy Evers and her children. Were they spared? How could he help? Could he bring men, medical aid, and supplies to the disaster scene? Perhaps provide some martial order in what must certainly be a disorganized mess?

He made his way down the hall to the room of his immediate superior, James Jonathan Pincaire, MD, and requested a brief audience. Major Pincaire hollered for him to enter. The exhausted man lay spread-eagled on his bed, wearing only a pair of soiled gray underpants. Two filled chamber pots covered with black flies sat next to the bedstand. The room smelled terrible. Brett told him about the derailment and, although he had no details other than that the train had slipped its tracks and people were hurt, requested to be allowed to respond by leading a company of soldiers to the disaster. Pincaire, perspiring profusely, looked at Brett with a quizzical grimace. Shook his head.

"Don't you understand, Brett? We've been poisoned. The Colombians—we thought they were desperate—don't want us to negotiate with the Brits in Aspinwall tomorrow . . . over their support of what's going on south of 'em in Brazil . . . and Ecuador," he paused and started to retch into one of the chamber pots. "Excuse me, son—right now. It's a warning, I think." It seemed that the effort to speak made Pincaire diminish further. His face was as pale as the wet sheets on his bed. "Gotta stay here. Wait for 'em to come here next week. Gotta." He started to vomit again. "Dammit to hell, anyway." When Brett started to protest, Pincaire cut him off. "You heard me, Lieutenant."

At that, Brett told him he intended to resign his commission. Pincaire paused, and a stern sadness crossed his face. He said, "That'd be looked upon as desertion, son. Please leave this room now."

Brett saluted and excused himself, walked down the hall, saw the guards at the door of the presidential suite where Scott was berthed, and heard groaning and hollering emanating from inside. He paused, thought about what an accusation of desertion would mean to his life, to his budding career; thought about what obeying, staying in Panama would mean. Then he thought about whether he might find Emmy Evers hurt.

Or worse. He remembered how many times he had appealed to Pincaire for a leave to go home and square up things back there, maybe personally attend to his father or find another competent doctor. He had been refused repeatedly by this same intermediary. He listened to the sounds of men retching behind every door as he made his way back down the hall and entered Pincaire's room. "So be it. I resign. Scott's got enough medical assistance here. You don't need me. I'm leaving now. Not deserting, Jon. But if you choose to designate it as such, then let them find me."

CHAPTER TWENTY-NINE

SARAH

The screams and gunshots and cries of men and women, muffled somewhat by the dark covering of the train's undercarriage where she and her brother had been secreted by the strong, gentle man with the bushy mustache, shook her and then everything slowed down and she felt a calm alertness she had never experienced before. She felt the baby struggling in her arms. Saw the detail of every bit of grit on the steel of the undercarriage, smelled the steam and char, felt the wet greenness in every shade of the surrounding forest. As alert as she always had been, as much as she had always been a keen observer of everything around her, she felt as if she had suddenly been wakened from a deep, numbing sleep, called out of bed by something, slapped rudely. She looked over at Jacob who was rocking back and forth, breathing fast, hugging the little Italian boy. By the look on Jacob's face, she knew he was reliving terror, too.

She looked out from behind the big, greasy wheel and saw that the men with the pistols were forcing the people from the train to lie on their bellies, including the man who had hidden them, and were cinching their hands behind their backs. She heard a gunshot, saw the man wearing the yellow conductor's hat, Deacy. He was holding a smoking pistol a few inches away from a woman's head or what was left of it. She was not moving. He had shot her just like he had the big man who was riding in their car. Sarah heard another explosion; she looked to her left and saw that other men wearing kerchiefs on their faces were setting a fire to the train trestle up ahead. Then, to her right, she saw Deacy heading down the line in their direction, looking under the cars. Looking for them?

Sarah took Jacob's hand and crawled out the other side of the car. "Quick!" The little boy with Jacob understood immediately and followed them. She handed him the baby, who was crying loudly, and they ran for the bushes. Crouching down, she looked back and saw Deacy crawling out from under the carriage where they had hidden, turning in their direction. His pistol was still smoking. As he stood up, his hat fell off, and when he bent down to pick it up, she whispered, "Run, Jacob!" They ran deeper and deeper into the underbrush, down an embankment of thick, wet bushes. She heard three shots, "Pop, pop, pop" and saw a branch snap above her head. A bullet? They ran further down the embankment until they couldn't hear the hollering and the gunshot reports from the rail cars became faint. It started to rain. They stopped to rest when the baby finally quit crying for a few moments. Sarah started to rock it back and forth, and it fell asleep. It rained harder. They huddled together. She listened for movement, but the rain's loud patter against the foliage covered everything.

They waited for a long time for the loud rain to stop. She wasn't sure how long. When it did, she could hear nothing but the howling of some animals off behind them. The baby and the two boys had fallen asleep. All three of them slept with their mouths wide open. Thick vines twisted up the wide trunks of the trees and spilled back down the branches, rooting in places. She wondered whether the vines strangled the huge trees or nourished them. She stepped out a few steps, pulled down a large green palm leaf that was as big as her body, and drank some of the rain water that had pooled in its center, washed her face. She peered into the forest as far as she could—no more than ten feet in any direction—and looked for their tracks. None. She didn't know which way to go to find their way back, to look and see if the men had left. They had run a long way, down several embankments. It started to get hot. They were lost, she realized. She heard noise from off to her left. What was it? It stopped, and the birds stopped their chatter. Then she realized they were being watched.

CHAPTER THIRTY

RUNNELS

It didn't sit well, this demand. It didn't matter that William A. Nelson himself, his former patron, had conceded to one of his own business partners, J. Abbot Foil, that he, Runnels, should be called out. And it didn't matter that Nelson had procured from Foil an extravagant fee for Runnels's services. Ran Runnels was retired now, at the insistence of the wealthy Panamanian beauty he had married three years ago. And, even though most folks would have considered him lean and well muscled, he believed he had allowed himself to grow fat and lazy during that time away from the saddle. The calluses were gone; his hands were soft mitts now. Thus, he knew that the pursuit of these new Deriéni gangs would be much more difficult for him than it would have been just five short years ago. He didn't need the work. Didn't need the money. He had left that business, the vigilante work, behind him. He was abiding by the Lord and keeping his own peace now. And it didn't sit well, this demand and the way it had been presented to him.

But the stories that came in from Gorgona and Gamboa, the purposeful derailment that killed so many and the holdup at the Puente Espiritu—the kidnapping, rapes, and executions—turned his head. Nelson, who knew Runnels's reverent proclivities, told him the predation had to be stopped immediately lest it set a precedent and ruin the country. And, Nelson told him, his hard-won legacy was at stake—and no one else could respond competently or with the God-given decisiveness as well as he could. Quitero, his own protégé and successor, had been murdered along with sixteen men from the Isthmus Guard, many of whom he had hired and trained. He knew their families. Nelson told him the killers were more vicious than the ones he and Quitero had executed in Aspinwall and Panama City in '54 and '55. More vicious than he, himself. "El Verdugo." He had no choice.

When he arrived at the site of the heist, he knew he was in for a long ride. The Isthmus Guard hadn't moved any of the bodies—at his request, so the stench was overwhelming. He had to cover his mouth and nose to get close enough to view them. The passenger victims, hands tied behind their backs, lay on their faces, most with their brains blown out, shots fired at close range to the back of their heads from large-gauge pistols. A few had been shot with slugs from big barreled shotguns. All of the dead women, and a few of the men had been violated.

Three hundred yards away in the dark tunnels, his men had collected the body parts of the garroted Isthmus Guards, the ones who had been placed by Quitero and Foil atop the cars. His men had sorted them as best they could and covered them with tarps awaiting his inspection. The barbed-wire wrapped cables that had cut them down were still in place in the tunnels. Foil's armored car was destroyed. Runnels immediately recognized that it had been incompetently designed. "A damned rolling death trap," he commented out loud. Inside, the open safes were intact and empty, so somehow the Deriéni had gotten the combinations.

They followed the mule train tracks down to the river a mile away and found notes with Greek lettering tacked to trees along the way to the embarkation point where the Deriéni had loaded their mules, gold, and hostages onto their bungo boats and rafts. One of the railroad officials who had studied some Latin and Greek in Philadelphia said these notes were warnings, promising death if anyone followed. At the end of the path, they found the gutted remains of a very fat man who might have been a preacher, they surmised, because of the gold cross, twisted tightly around his neck. He looked ridiculous— the fat carcass, covered with ants and land crabs and wearing only undergarments and a cleric's collar, was nailed to a cross at the river's edge. Beneath the cross, another note hung from his neck. It was written in the man's own blood: "Τίποτα δεν υπερβαίνουν." The Philadelphia man said it meant "Nothing in excess."

Runnels was frustrated that he would have to delay the pursuit until the morning when more boats and mules arrived from Panama City and Aspinwall. He had already loaded three boats with supplies for what likely would be a short trek past the rapids upriver and a long, difficult, if almost impossible, pursuit up into one or more of the Derién's many possible jungle escape routes. Because the telegraph wires in all directions had been cut in several places, and because the killers were clever at traps, he had sent men up three of the remaining passable old trails to Las Cruces to learn if any of the raiding party had stopped there since the event earlier in the day. One of them might get through.

He estimated he had enough men—had decided to discourage disorganized pursuit by volunteers. The volunteers who came forward, many of whom had ridden into the camp from Panama City and Aspinwall, some fifty-five or so men and a few women, were unknowns. Most were simply out for the reward they assumed Foil Cargo and the Panama Railroad Company likely would offer. Several were angry survivors of the massacre, including all the miners, who, to a man, insisted on being part of the posse. So, after sifting through the lot, looking at their hands and eyes, he excluded all but a few—twenty of the secret society Isthmus Guards, five Kuna and Embera native guides, an ex-soldier doctor volunteer, and one survivor of the holdup who was a relative of the hostages. He knew he would have to contain and focus the wrath of the Isthmus Guards, most of whom had lost friends or relatives, and keep Foil, who had sent word and insisted on accompanying the posse, off of his back. Foil was an arrogant fool. He kept that thought to himself

He had spent the evening of his arrival late into the night questioning each one of the surviving passengers. What had they seen? The "Deriéni" bandits—how many of them were there? What did they look like? Were they "Cimaroons," the black descendants of escaped slaves who lived in the Darién, or were they white French-speaking descendants of the pirates who had migrated from the Caribbean to the eastern part of the jungle? As he had experienced with similar holdups in the past, the information he received from the survivors was inconsistent and exaggerated. Out of all of it, and after the reports had come in from Foil and the survivors of the wreck five miles up rail, he estimated that at least fifty men and a few women had been involved in the direct assault—mostly Spanish, a few English speakers, and, oddly, several with deformities or obvious handicaps. He had telegraphed to Aspinwall and Panama City descriptions of three of them: the leaders.

He expected most of the small-time thieves, the ones who had stripped the passengers of their jewelry and pocket books, and the rapists would disperse throughout the countryside. He would have to ignore them. Let God provide judgment in His own time; he didn't have the interest to go after the littlest of the scurrying rats. But he knew that a few of the most reliable ones in the pack, one or two for every five of the pack mules, would be necessary to transport the cargo. And he knew the leaders would stay with the gold. Sixty mules, he calculated, twenty to thirty riders, if he included the hostages—while they were alive. Twenty-five of his men to perhaps less than twenty of them. The men he selected were reliable and tough. Good odds. If they moved quickly and found the places on the river where the mules had come off the rafts, even if the rain started in this dry part of the year, their trails might not be too difficult to follow because of the mules. If they waited, or missed the spots, they would never find them.

He learned that one of the leaders—every one of the survivors remembered him—was a loudmouth named Nick Deacy who some called "Dosat," the native name for Beelzebub. The thug had a thick Irish accent and had made no effort at concealing his identity, as if he was daring, just aching, for someone to pursue him. He had behaved as if the notoriety from this holdup was as important to him as was the booty itself. Deacy was a relatively new arrival in the area. He had drifted south from California, had a small gang of mixed-breed cutthroats, and kept mostly to the Panama City terminal area working on travelers who were foolish enough to wander into the Mingello looking for whores or opium. Runnels knew that Deacy had never worked the railroad lines before or Quitero would have dispatched him before now.

The second one, recognized by a brakeman who had hidden himself in the undercarriage during the heist, was a guy named Apolonio Haut, whom everyone called "Pallino." He had a maimed hand. The brakeman said Haut was a ne'er-do-well complainer who had a reputation for unpredictable violence. Six months ago, he had killed a fool in a card game in the midst of a full saloon in Aspinwall, after the gambler, referring to the small stump of a finger on Haut's left hand, had derisively called him "Pinky." Haut turned over the table, stabbed him in the throat, and then twisted the knife as the stunned man was croaking. Haut had left Aspinwall after that, and since then no one had seen him, although many thought his family lived close to Las Cruces.

Runnels thought about these two. Both men were known killers, but as far as he could figure, neither of them were careful or big planners. As a matter of fact, they were stupid, like all the ones he and Carlos Quitero had lynched five years ago in Panama City and Aspinwall. Deacy was boastful, flamboyant, and vicious. According to the survivors, he had ordered or personally carried out most of the executions of the passengers. Haut sounded to be impulsive and foolish. They were small-time desperadoes, ignored and charmed-safe in their ways as a result of a lack of useful law enforcement in both Aspinwall and Panama City.

There was another person of interest, identified as a middle-aged, stuttering English speaker by one of the posse volunteers, but he was an unknown. The Italian volunteer he had chosen to be part of the posse, a passenger whose employer, wife, and two children had presumably been taken hostage, said that he had heard Deacy refer to that one as "Bocamalo." Another passenger described the man as "quiet" and in charge, but it was difficult to be certain because it was all so confusing.

As he watched his men cut the carcass of the fat preacher down from its cross by the river, Runnels shook his head. He wondered if the Comanches he had fought in the Panhandle sixteen years ago, just as viciously demonstrative as this, had ever studied Greek. They had always left warnings, he recollected—less schooled, much more direct. Except at one massacre scene at a mission twenty miles outside of San Antonio—where they had found the victims' charred bodies propped up side by side in a semi-circle, kneeling with their hands tied together in praying positions; eyelids peeled off by the fire; empty, popped-out dead eyes staring back at a melted crucifix—the Comanches never attempted to make humor in their use of the remains of the victims. They just abused the victims while alive and left grisly reminders scattered about or stuffed into unmentionable places. They were predictable in that way alone. But this was different. Unlike the Comanches, the joke these killers had displayed indicated that they were smart—and judgmental. And, unlike the Apaches and Comanches whose raids were sporadic and seldom scheduled, this heist had been carefully planned, by careful murderers. The planning and those who participated in it would come to light eventually, but that wasn't his responsibility. He was here for the hunt.

It was getting dark, and the light clouds rolling in from the west were catching part of the setting Pacific sun and showing red and orange on their crests and fringes. Some stars were already visible. He would have to sleep soon. Say his prayers. Get ready for tomorrow. Wondered if he was about to follow an even more dangerous set of killers. And who was this Bocamalo? Was he anything like the Comanche killer, Henry Black Rattle, whom he had tracked in '49? Just who was Bocamalo?

And he wondered whether he would find any of the hostages alive by the time he caught up with them all.

CHAPTER THIRTY-ONE

◇◇◇◇◇◇◇◇◇◇◇◇◇◇◇◇◇

EMMY

They had been pulled hard, walking in a line down a muddy steep path, and loaded onto water craft—ten-foot carve-outs lined up in a row on the river. They had shoved off immediately to make way for the cargo that was to follow. Looking back at the shore about twenty yards away, she saw Deacy pushing another of the hostages, the preacher who had put up the fuss during the holdup. She saw the poor man fall to the ground, pleading, crying. Deacy started to kick him.

She couldn't stand to watch it and turned away. Up front, a well-muscled little brown man, an aborigine, pushed the boat forward with a long pole in the water. He wore a skimpy leather belt and a dirty cloth slung from it covering his privates in front but nothing on the back side. One other man, chewing tobacco and spitting frequently, sat in the back of the boat, a shotgun lying across his lap, pointed forward. She looked down at her bindings, heavy iron. They had been ratcheted down tightly, and the bloody chafe on both wrists had already started to attract thick-bodied brown flies. Mosquitoes and gnats bit and moved. Black and white birds, large ones, circled high above their boats as they moved up the river. The other three hostages, two women and the Italian man, Emilio Gattopardi, sat facing forward. They were silent. She called up to them, exhausted. "Do you have any idea where they are taking us?"

Gattopardi, without turning, said, "I have spoken to one of them. Our captivity is a form of protection for them, he said, to discourage pursuit. I have offered a reward from my contacts in the Colombian government if they release . . . us." Emmy knew from the pause that the man had likely bartered only for himself. She knew his type.

Staring forward in the boat, traveling up river, she tried to sort the mean jumble of events of the morning, all wrapped in the holdup's shrill cacophony—the cries blending into and masked by the screeching of the metal wheels of the departing engine and cars on the rain-rusted-red tracks; the bellowing of angry men punctuated by gunshots, explosions followed by a brief silence, then a few birds calling out again from the surrounding jungle; and then the weeping of both men and women, up the line to her right and left. The chaos intensified—her children swept away into hiding; she forced face down onto the gravel and turf embankment, hands bound behind her back. She could still smell the grass and feel the ants crawling onto her chin and up her cheek. The sticky heat that drove itself into everything she wore burned hotter as her black blouse absorbed every degree. During that thirty minutes of the heist, she had repeated to Providence over and over again her silent plea, hoping, praying, that this mayhem would pass, and everything rushed past her in those minutes with the sun cutting through and dissipating the fog, men talking loudly then softly. She strained to remember whether she had heard Jacob's and Sarah's voices in the fray, amidst the gruff laughs of Deacy's men and that nasty bastard's cocksure growling and grunting. She had heard shots behind the coaches—Jacob? Sarah?—then loud pops, shots to her right. More executions? Another woman crying in terror, weeping out "Please! Please! No! No!" Crying and sobbing. More loud booms from pistols. Then, as the shouts subsided, the braying of mules and their mule skinners. Crows calling.

She thought about the morning's next set of events, when she had been pulled to her feet—when she regained her balance and stood upright, how the morning sun's light hurt in a way she had never known was possible. Her bonnet had been pulled off, and thus unprotected, she squinted through the burning of her tears. She had tried to not look back at the undercarriage where the Italian man had hidden Jacob and Sarah with his own children. She wondered whether *he* was still alive. She had stared ahead as she was being manacled into chains by order of the black-bearded man on the white mule. He was the same one who, earlier that morning, in the decency and excitement of those proper, peaceful moments, when they all seemed to be sharing in the hope of a contained, luxurious new adventure, when she finally had begun thinking about letting some color back into her life. He was the same one who had watched her children then tried to convey something quickly in a flick of a glance to her—some form of empathy she thought at first, then a second look, a beseeching plea almost. She had responded politely but without a hint of encouragement to his strange overture, and he had tipped his sombrero at her then looked away. And then later, in the murderous disorder of the pillage and rape outside, she knew he had watched her from the saddle of his mule, waiting again for some eye contact. How dare he? How dare he? she thought, reconstructing the events that morning as their boat moved up stream in silence.

She thought about what she had seen as they had shoved off that morning, Deacy and the preacher; about the conversation she had overheard in the coach between the fat preacher and the elderly twins. He had been leaning back in his seat, fanning himself uncomfortably, as he told them that his wife of forty years had just passed away, and he had buried her at their home in Charlotte. "Her name was Charlotte," Emmy heard him say, observing that the man's face was transformed, saddened when he said her name. "She always wanted to travel to California, but she passed away from the dropsy before she could do so. She was a large spirit, like me." For a moment, Emmy thought she saw the man stiffen up. A self-righteous, resolute expression replaced the sadness. He went on, "So after she died, I decided I would take the trip for us."

There had been a pause, an embarrassing lull in the conversation, Emmy had noted. She had wondered how the two elderly women were interpreting the preacher's declaration, which seemed to her to be a selfish, smug boast. Then he reached into his pocket and pulled out a pair of spectacles. Put them on. They were much too small for his plump face. The glass was very thick and made his eyes appear enormous.

"These were hers," he said, blinking, which emphasized the strange caricature it made of him—oversized eyes magnified by small spectacles on an oversized, flushed face. "She couldn't see very well in the last five years of her life. Cataracts, you know. Sugar disease blindness, we were told." Another long pause. "I put them on whenever I see something that she would have been interested in seeing." He blinked, and she remembered she could see them becoming moist. The conversation stopped then.

As Emmy thought about that now, she changed her opinion of the man, understood that he had been in the process of grieving and adapting in his sad way to his loneliness, wondering what to hold on to and what to leave behind. Like herself.

Far upstream, three hours after shoving off, they passed Las Cruces through a black cloud of flies, fleas and mosquitoes swarming, hovering over its wharves and riverfront. She had heard that for two centuries the town had been important to the gold trade, but within a very short time, less than seven years since the introduction of fast rail transport that bypassed the Chagres, the jungle had started to heave it up. The town's stone walls and towers were crumbling; already long obsolete by the invention of heavier assault cannon, disuse had broken the innards of the city into a dilapidated, rat-run ruin. Empty warehouses with slumping roofs dotted the entire length of the waterfront. The stench from the town's open sewers pouring into the Chagres was overwhelming, and she was relieved that they passed without stopping.

She thought about her children and repeated a prayer that they were safe . . . that when they had been hidden in the train car's undercarriage by the Italian man, they had been overlooked by the bandits and then were found by authorities afterwards. Maybe Jojo had come back to claim them and bring them to safety and return them to their parents. She thought her children must be waiting in Aspinwall, hoping for news of a rescue, or an exchange, or of her escape. She knew Jacob would be terrified but reassured herself that his sister, Sarah, was uncommonly intelligent and capable for a girl of eleven and would figure things out somehow. She also remembered how often she had given herself similar reassurances about Sarah's protective nature when she had journeyed up north to negotiate with the murderers who had kidnapped Jacob the year before. It was surprising that Sarah had proven to be younger than she pretended to be in that circumstance, and it was interesting that she had taken a bit of comfort in seeing Sarah's precocious headstrong tendencies daunted somewhat. But now, in this brutal assault, she was hoping that her daughter would be as bold as she knew she could be. Jacob would need that. So would the Italian man's two children. "Oh God! Please be fierce, Sarah!" Emmy prayed over and over again.

Two hours later, they found a sandy flat area, paused for a rest, and waited for the heavier boats to catch up. Sand fleas and mosquitoes swarmed over them as they beached the boats. After the guard scouted the area briefly for reptiles and large cats, he took off their manacles, and Emmy stretched alongside the other two women. Gattopardi, who had negotiated and retrieved his long pants, attempted to converse with the guards of the four boats that had beached on the shore. One of the women, Lita Perdellaño-Scarpello, the mother of the two infants and the wife of Gattopardi's valet, was an Ecuadorian from a wealthy family. She spoke English and translated the Portuguese of the third passenger, the mulatto woman who had ridden the train with the loud Brazilian man and his son. Emmy learned several things during the half-hour interlude and realized what would happen to each of them if they appealed to the good nature of their captors or trusted too much in the grace of Providence. The mulatto woman, who appeared to be a hard but intelligent young woman, said her father was Cajun. Her name was Gabriella but preferred to be called "LaFleur" or simply "Gabi." She said that she, like Tomas Bossman Gonsalves, the Brazilian man she had accompanied, had once been a slave. She said she knew how to run and she knew what would happen to her if she did not run again. She had no intention of waiting to see. The Ecuadorian woman listened and then nodded her head in agreement, looking to Emmy for her decision.

Emmy looked out at the water and saw the outlines of several huge reptiles floating, just breaking the surface of the river. She had only seen them in picture books when she was a child; they were much larger and more frightening than anything she had remembered back then. They were waiting, disguised as sunken logs. She looked back at the dense, deep green of the jungle behind them. When she turned back to the river, she saw that the first group of boats had caught up. At their lead in the first boat sat the man with the black beard in the blue kerchief and following only a boat-length behind sat Deacy, grinning and singing loudly. She looked back at the other two women. She nodded her head in assent. She understood and agreed. It would be foolhardy to expect anything short of pain and death from these murderers.

They would run as soon as the morning's light broke, or when they were preparing to shove off again—to take advantage of their captors' need to continue evading likely pursuers. She decided she would try to leave some signs along the way, wherever they were headed, to find her way back or to help guide rescuers, if God willing, any were following. Neither she nor either of the other two women were prepared to be separated from each other in a gambling bargain between the monsters who had captured them.

CHAPTER THIRTY-TWO

<<<<<<<<<<<<<<<<<<<<<<

SARAH

When the young aborigine stood up and stepped away from the large palm that had hidden him, Sarah turned her eyes down and away, almost out of embarrassment rather than fear, because, except for the black and red ornate patterns on his face and belly and a quiver of arrows strapped across his shoulder, he was completely naked. She found herself unable to move and stood stock-still. When she forced herself to look up again, she saw a second person, an older male, bald with a four-inch white bone protruding through his lower lip, standing behind the boy. Both of them carried bows, and strings of small monkey carcasses were tied to their wrists.

She tried to read the expression on their faces. Was it fear or anger? She decided it was neither, but rather curiosity. The bald man said something to his young companion then turned and walked away, disappearing immediately into the heavy foliage. The boy, she guessed he was about eight or nine years old and was likely the man's son, seemed hesitant for a moment, then he walked up to her and took her hand! He led her over to where Jacob, the little Italian boy, and his baby brother were sleeping, and motioned for her to bring them and follow him. It wasn't a forceful gesture. It was gentle, and the brief clasp of his hand to hers was soft but firm at the same time. Sarah looked at the dead monkeys tied to his wrist, then up at his calm face and realized she had no choice. She knew they couldn't go back to the train, as worried as she was for her mother and Jojo. The man in the yellow hat who had shot at them and the rest of the murderers were likely still there. She took a deep breath, picked up the infant who was crying again, put her other arm around Jacob who was holding the little boy's hand, and followed the aborigines deeper into the dense jungle.

They moved along a worn path and crossed under a water-fall, where they stopped for a few moments to drink and splash their faces with the warm water spray. The path led up and down the ridges of hills and through a vast broad shaggy field of tall soft grass that slapped at their chests as they passed through it. Chiggers bit at her ankles and all the way up her legs. Sarah held Jacob's hand tightly and tried to console the baby who was becoming more agitated. He had to be hungry, she thought, but she didn't know what to do about it.

The party descended to a river then followed it upstream for what seemed like an hour. She was surprised when they came upon a small, well-hidden village and a crowd of other savages, most of whom wore loincloths or nothing at all. Summoned by the bald aborigine with the bone in his lip, the people gathered around Sarah and her little entourage as they passed into the center of the village to a large open hut that had a roof thatched with what appeared to be dried fan palms. As they walked in, the bald man was speaking excitedly. She tried but couldn't understand one word. A painted woman wearing a short skirt made of palm leaves and carrying a painted baby infant at her breast, walked over; took the crying infant from Sarah; and put him to her other breast. He stopped crying immediately. The aborigine boy motioned for Sarah and the children to sit down. When they did, women put in front of them green palm leaves with some food—small roasted whole fish, fried yellow discs, and white mounds of cooked rice. One of the women stepped over and dipped her hand into the rice and ate a few bites. She said a word and then ate some more, repeating the word to them. Sarah understood. She was very hungry. The rice was sweet, and she recognized a coconut taste, like the pudding she had at the hotel in Panama City. She motioned to Jacob and the Italian boy to also eat, but Jacob held back and would not.

While she and the Italian boy ate hungrily, the bald aborigine man who had continued talking rapidly was interrupted by a pot-bellied man in the crowd, and the two of them began a conversation that increased in intensity and loudness. Although she couldn't understand what they were saying, she realized that both of them were angry. Sarah watched. What were they arguing about? She tried to understand the expressions on the faces of the people who were watching them and the argument between the two men. The heated discussion ended when the pot-bellied man said something in a very loud voice to everyone. It was an announcement, she realized. At that, the crowd of people disbanded, and she and the children were left there with the man and boy who had brought them to the village and two women. Sarah watched the face of the bald aborigine who had been arguing with the pot-bellied man. He was agitated, and she thought she read embarrassment on his face. He said something to the women, handed his string of monkey carcasses to them, and walked away.

After Sarah and the boys finished eating, the young woman with the infants at her breasts led them down a path past several huts sitting on stilts to a small empty hut at the edge of the village. The woman handed both of the babies to Sarah, climbed a stair notched from a thick log, reached down to Sarah and took both babies up into the hut, then waved for Sarah and the children to join her in the bare hut. Just as they entered the hut, a heavy rain started outside. By the time the rain stopped, both infants were sleeping and the young woman stood up and left, the infants still cradled in her arms. A few minutes later, it started to rain again.

Sarah looked over at Jacob, who was hunched in one of the corners of the square hut. He was trembling and crying softly, as he had from time to time since his ordeal one year ago in the Pacific Northwest. Sarah crawled over to him and put her arms around him, and he seemed to settle down a bit. She looked over at the Italian boy, "Jonny," he said was his name. He was weeping, too. They both were crying, "Mama."

She pulled on Jonny's shirt, and he came over and nestled in her other arm.

She rocked them back and forth, until they quieted down. As she did so, remembering what her mother said she always did every day, she tried to think about what she had observed and learned from the events. But it was all too confusing. Who was the man in the yellow hat, this Deacy? Why did he do what he did? Who were these people who had found them in the forest? She tried to compare them with what she had experienced in the Northwest, less than a year ago. Deacy and all of his men were killers like the ones they had endured when their home had been attacked last year. These aborigines had the same type of markings as the Northwest natives and also spoke a language that she couldn't understand at all. Were they killers, too?

She sensed there was difference between the aborigines here and Deacy, but she didn't know if she was correct about that, or whether she was missing something and they really were alike. She thought she saw the difference in the way the aborigines moved their eyes and how they smiled, how the people kept a distance from them and how the woman had held the baby.

Deacy's gang had no respect for others, she knew. When Deacy had smiled, his mouth turned up on the right and his eyes gleamed and looked up and away as if he were looking at something in the distance. When he talked, his speech was forceful and angry. He reminded her of a sick, smelly dog, like the one her stepfather had shot a few years ago. "Must have gotten into a rabid skunk," he had said. Sarah had never thought much about that dog until now.

And who were these aborigines? Did they have souls? She didn't know. If they did, what were their stories? What were their intentions? She would watch, if she were allowed to do so. And she wouldn't keep her eyes down.

CHAPTER THIRTY-THREE

◇◇◇◇◇◇◇◇◇◇◇◇◇◇◇◇◇◇◇

BOCAMALO

He had moved his flotilla of bungo and piragua boats and rafts carrying mules, gold, and hostages quickly upstream on the slow-moving Rio Chagres, ten miles up to the second fork where he stopped at the delta of the Rio Gatuncillo tributary. There, Deacy split off continuing northwest on the Gatuncillo with his seven piraguas and rafts carrying fifteen mules and two of the women hostages. Deacy had wanted all of the women as well as the Italian "genteelman," said he wanted to screw every one of them over and over again. Bugger them, too, then give them to his men until they were too tired to screw anymore and then, "if they had anything left worth screwing," sell the women to the whorehouse at the copper mining camp ten miles up on the next big fork of the river. Rafael smiled at Deacy's insane sexual rage, realized that the fool didn't really understand the value of the hostages, especially the Italian. But he didn't really want to fight with Deacy over it. So they drew straws and split their winnings.

Despite Rafael's warning noting that the pursuit would likely be rapid and aggressive, Haut had indicated he planned to stop briefly at Las Cruces, and then continue up the winding north fork onto the Gatuncillo like Deacy. Rafael had not protested when he heard Haut announce those plans, for he knew that Haut would likely take much longer releasing some of his men and throwing out shares of booty to the families of his loyal lieutenants. He would party and drink. He might even inadvertently linger in the little stink of a town long enough to give whomever would be hotly pursuing them an opportunity to catch up. Haut would squander his gains, and his disorganization would be his undoing. Rafael didn't wish the fool any harm but understood that such an event would provide a convenient rear-guard action to help his own escape. It might even dissuade further pursuit. So Rafael had just listened and did not protest at the risky plan.

He watched Deacy's boats move away up the Gatuncillo, waited for them to turn around the distant bend and disappear, and was relieved that he did not have to manage that lunatic or his men any longer. The Wounaa called a person like Deacy "Dosat," their version of a trickster Satan, but Rafael had been occasionally called that himself and he knew that Deacy wasn't smart enough to merit that status. He had allowed Deacy to play because he knew his tendencies. Deacy was mean and arrogant, and Rafael had predicted that the braggadocio would create a big, distracting profile for himself in the heist. He had done exactly that, and everyone would know Nick Deacy's name up and down the isthmus. He would enjoy notoriety for a while, but no matter how far upriver he went, Deacy would eventually need to spend his gold and would prance around as loudly as he lived. He would come out, likely sporting the yellow conductor's hat to which he had taken a fancy, and eventually would be caught—and then be prominently lynched by the Isthmus Guard. Deacy would dance prominently on the rope as well. Rafael wished he could watch that.

Rafael waited for a half-hour after Deacy's departure, then had his men follow Deacy's boats up the Gatuncillo a quarter mile and throw out garbage, including some of the hostages' personal belongings, strewn out close to the riverbank. The pursuers, at least some of them, would find those discards and continue up that fork. Deacy, unlike Haut, was smart enough to not tarry but, if cornered, would definitely take his own toll of the posses.

Rafael looked over the remaining boats and rafts as his waterborne entourage continued northeast on the Chagres. He had kept his fair share of the gold and two of the hostages, the young American widow in black and the tall Italian, whom he had learned, by reading his papers and listening to the man's pleas, was a well-connected Bourbon nobleman, a diplomat from Sicily. He would be useful in an exchange, but much less so than if he were from one of the countries that regularly used the isthmus. From previous experience, Rafael knew that the value of diplomats decreased and their smell increased the longer they were kept hostage, particularly if the "sponsors" they represented were contenders in an unstable political climate. He had heard that the carved-up Italian peninsula had changed governments as frequently as did the most unstable of the South American countries. He knew he would need to find a disposition for the man quickly.

He didn't know yet what he would do with the young American woman, although she had aroused him when he saw her on the train and he had felt that again when he watched her standing in her bloomers outside the train cars. He had observed her talking with, listening mostly, to the other women hostages before Nick Deacy had claimed them but noted that she hadn't said a word since Deacy's boats had moved out at the fork and on up the Gatuncillo. She kept her eyes fixed forward, avoiding responding to his attempts at eye contact. She ignored the Italian, who periodically tried to converse with her. She was shapely, and he wondered what she might feel like under him. He didn't have time to think about that right now, but he knew he would get back to that.

By torchlight, he moved his boats and rafts upriver in the darkness and only rested when they came to another fork. The crocs were big but would stay away if they kept in the boats, took care where they beached. His men knew to avoid the brush that hung low. The protection from discovery wasn't necessary, but during the day, the snakes basked in the branches of the bigger trees, hunted in them for monkeys and bats at night. And he didn't want any surprises. He positioned himself so that he could see upriver. Anyone pursuing would poke along using torches, and he wanted to see them long before they would see him. He would make them rue their pursuit.

CHAPTER THIRTY-FOUR

◇◇◇◇◇◇◇◇◇◇◇◇◇◇◇◇◇◇

RUNNELS

He fretted. No sleep. Pondered. The bastards would have almost a full day's lead with a jungle to hide them, and the thought of losing them worried him worse than what he might find if and when he caught up with them. He thought about the days ahead and wondered if this pursuit would be as brutally painful as the Oklahoma and Texas hunts he had been on when he had pursued the Comanche war parties. Long rides. Deadly. Always.

He had just turned sixteen back then, he remembered, on that first hunt. It was a coming-of-age event for him; hadn't even shaved for the first time, when he set out in the early fall morning of '44 with twelve other rangers. He had been selected, deputized with the others, no one younger than him, all carrying out a grim, sacred, practical mission. A righteous hunt, some of the others called it, though he really hadn't needed to think of it that way back then—because it was also good sport, and he liked good sport, always was up for a funning game like tracking the coyotes at home, the mangy dogs that would creep in through the sage at night and pick off the herd's strays and slower calves. He had learned that cold play as a young boy, tracking them, then taking them down and letting them rot out there for the other mutts to see. Always best if he got a bitch with a hidden, young litter that would starve without her nipples. One shot killed seven. Funning by the leverage of a .44 caliber slug.

What made it so much better on that particular morning was that he was riding in the company of commissioned men, had been given the opportunity by none other than Captain Jack Coffee Hays himself, who had become famous fighting none other than Buffalo Hump himself four years earlier at Plum Creek. The captain had increased his formidable reputation six months later, when he killed eight Comanche, all by himself at Uvalde Canyon. And then he increased it even more two years later, when he helped keep the Mexicans out of Texas. Repelled 'em back across the river. The man was widespread famous, and Runnels was riding with him! His first introduction to glory days, he remembered.

On that hunt, they had stayed out an entire fortnight tracking, trying to intercept a fast, mean bunch who had raided several farmsteads, small towns, and haciendas along a two-hundred-mile stretch. These particular Comanches were really nasty sons of bitches. They had tortured and killed some eighty people, including tamed Apaches and Kiowa; men, women, and kids; keeping their hostages for a short while but discarding them after they had their fun. So, as Ran thought about it, after he had seen some of the remains, he had agreed with the other men. It was a righteous hunt after all. Purposeful and dangerous "retributional" murder. Righteous, he thought.

By the time they arrived at the first burn-out and started tracking, they knew they were outnumbered by, and likely far behind, the Comanche fast-horse pony soldiers. They kept on, however, because unless the killers had changed mounts within the last few days, their ponies were tired. Had to be. And Captain Hays had equipped his men with the improved Colt five-shot pistols and rifled carbines. So Hays told them, as they started to get nervous over the estimates of the number of warriors they might encounter, that if they caught up with them, he figured the odds were evened up. And he said that these Comanches were greedy bastards, had slowed themselves down carting away a lot of loot—silver bullion, rifles, cloth, and sugar that they wouldn't give up. Greedy. Hays had predicted the Comanches would hold on to their pack animals, not let 'em go, and keep heading back to Colorado, assuming the size of their party would discourage pursuit. So they wouldn't be thinking right, encumbered with greed as they were. The odds were evened up, the captain said. And the Comanches would be shooting single-shot muskets and would need to get in close to win a skirmish. The odds were evened up, he said.

And the boys were reassured because Hays always knew how to figure the best ways to even up the odds, to stand his ground, keep them all calm. To even it up all the more, on this occasion, Hays had brought along a fifty-inch, long-barreled, needle gun, German-made and rifled, that he had been given by Sam Houston himself. The captain let him practice with it. It had a telescope mounted on it, set high above the rifle's sights so he could see what was coming and estimate the distance better. Plan his shots better.

Over that next week on that hunt, by setting up iron clinkers at three hundred, four hundred, and even six hundred yards, he realized he could hit a small target almost every time, hear the dull plunk without ever having to see the hole in a piece of paper. He knew that each hit likely meant a kill no matter where it hit on the body because of that caliber, even with a nearly spent bullet. He hunted buffalo, which were easy because the herd just continued grazing as their bulls and cows fell next to them, and antelope with their devil eyes, skittish, had to be hit with one shot or they would be a mile away in a few seconds. But just one shot.

He thought about that, how he had practiced, how he had hunted them and then killed them all—the buffalo, the antelope, and then the Comanches—one by one from as far off as a thousand yards. Killed their horses first if they didn't have another mount and were by themselves, and then let the other rangers run 'em down. He learned to like that advantage, he remembered. And for the big bunch, the captain asked him to pick off the chiefs. One by one. As he did so, when they finally caught up with the main group, the rest of the Comanches just lost their will to fight. They left their pack animals and scattered. And Captain Hays didn't lose one man on that hunt. Twelve Comanches, four chiefs. He had taken down five of them with the captain's German rifle. And he'd been just sixteen.

He fell asleep for a few minutes but awoke when he heard more Isthmus Guard posse riders arrive in the night. Making a lot of noise. As he lay there, he thought back about Henry Black Rattle. Didn't want to, but knew it would be useful to pull that out and think about it before tomorrow because maybe, he thought, it would help him prepare himself to find this Bocamalo, steel himself and scrape his wits to a sharp hone. First time in years he had thought about it. Mean, angry bastard of a gutter puke, that Henry.

Runnels had been on his own on that one twelve years ago. No commission on this hunt. The captain had moved on to the gold fields in San Francisco, and now, Ran was on his own. Folks were coming to him now because of his own reputation. He was an Indian killer. So they came to him. And he did it, killed them, he told himself, for no other reason than that it had to be done. As he lay there looking up at the Panama stars, thinking about all of that so many years ago, he tried to refind the sting of it as he had on that particular occasion, the grief, but couldn't. He pushed on it anyway, see if he could make himself feel anything again. All he could remember now was that he went on that hunt because it had to be done—it was a righteous hunt—because of what had happened at the Key Ranch, where he'd buried the family, his friends, his lover, and her husband. A righteous hunt. He had to find Black Rattle, he remembered. Find him; persecute and kill him with the greatest prejudice he had ever mustered. Do it alone. Just the two of them.

He had tracked Black Rattle for two weeks by himself back then . . .

He closed his eyes for a few minutes and tried to forget the heat. This was hotter than Texas, not dry, and even in the cooler breezes of the evening, his shirt and pants were wet with the air's moisture.

He drifted a bit, dozed . . . and he was back in Texas, north of the Brazos and White Rivers again. He was on a fast mount and was running lean with her . . . a sturdy paint mare, quiet even when running at full gallop. She was patient with him. A smart, sure-footed partner. Good legs and big hindquarters. And Henry Black Rattle was running fat, with pack animals carrying his booty.

He had to find Black Rattle before he made it into the San Cristobal Mountain foothills, where his people stayed in the summer, or Ran knew he would lose him or have to turn back. Henry didn't know he was being followed yet. Thought he had gotten away again, clean and smug lucky. By the looks of the tracks, Black Rattle had found himself a shoed animal and was trading off with his two pack animals, a mule and another horse, unshod with a wide frog on its left rear hoof.

Ran tracked him at a slow walk for what seemed like one hundred and twenty miles over eight days and got within telescope range by the ninth day. Henry looked ridiculous without his war paint, Ran thought. Was wearing a tall, beaver stovepipe hat with pink and yellow ribbons coiled around it and trailing down his back. Ran observed him patiently for two days, logging Henry's routine in the small ledger he always kept, compared his notes with what he had learned over the preceding week from examining the Indian's camp ashes. He saw where the bastard liked to piss; what he ate; how long he took to feed, crap, and clean himself; how close he slept to his animals; how he was armed; what he carried with him in his morning constitutional; and what he kept by his blanket at night. Saw where he kept the scalps on his saddle. Noted that one of them had blonde hair, still tied with a bloody blue bow. Lorena's. He made a note of that. Broke the pencil tip. A righteous hunt.

He concluded he would have to come in on Henry at night or wait for him to take his crap in the morning. Long shot on him there in the brush wouldn't do. Couldn't afford to miss him. Neither would shooting at his horse while he was mounting. Henry would just discard the dead one and run with his other mount before Ran could get off another shot, and then he would have to track and fight him without the benefit of surprise. And the son of a bitch would likely win in that case because he was a sneaky, deadly snake of a bitch.

He knew about Henry. He had been adopted at the age of three by Buffalo Hump after the warrior killed the boy's Osage father and white mother. Was raised Comanche. They called him "Black Rattle" for a reason. Wearing black face paint and tattooed over his entire body with small diamond-back snake patterns, he scored numerous coups on his opponents before making his final, always deadly strike, which had earned him the approval of the Comanche old ones. By the age of

nineteen, Henry had proven himself repeatedly as a murderous warrior in battles against the Mexicans, Apache, and then
later against Captain Hays's Texas Rangers at Bandera Pass. At
the famous battle of Walker's Creek, riding with Yellow Wolf
and facing Captain Hays again, he put lances through two
rangers, Bob Gillespie and Sam Walker, and killed Joe Ginny
with a single blow to the head. Rattle had split with Buffalo
Hump in '46, when his father decided to accept the whites'
treaty offer, moving the Comanche south of the Brazos. Said
he didn't want to stay, "didn't want to rot away, get fat with
the old ones." Still had too much juice in him to give in. Too
many new fancy things to steal. "Too much seed to spread,"
they had all said about him. And over the two years that he
had been on his own, keeping a family in the mountains of
New Mexico, his raids and attacks into Texas and Oklahoma
were always efficient. As a marauder, he was swift and always
vicious, acting mostly alone in all the murders he had perpe-
trated. He would strike and be long gone so that no one had
ever been able to catch him. Sneaky son of a bitch; imperturb-
able, big viper with twelve heads. Black Rattle. And now he
was within Ran's reach.

On the eleventh morning one hour before sunup, after
saying his make-peace prayers, oiling his Colts, checking the
primer caps, rotating the cylinders for the twentieth time,
swigging several gulps of water, pissing, and then saying a
different set of prayers asking Providence for forgiveness for
the hatred he was about to vent, Ran tied one pistol lanyard
around his neck and the other around his right wrist. He led his
horse one hundred yards downwind to where he had watched
Black Rattle bed down that night. He threw his hat off to the

side, mounted, put the reins in his teeth, and spurred his horse hard. Twenty yards out at a full gallop on his way to the tree where Henry had bedded, he pulled his carbine and fired one shot into Henry Black Rattle's shoed horse, pulled his right pistol from its holster and fired one shot into the mule, and then another into the second horse. Three shots left in that pistol. He reared up and then made right for Black Rattle's bed to kill the uncircumcised dog whom he expected to be pulling himself up.

The stovepipe hat was there, but the bed was empty. Turning, Ran looked to the right and caught a glint of metal, thought he saw the shadow of the man disappearing over the top of a ridge thirty yards away. Knife was drawn or had retrieved his rifle, he thought. He spurred his pinto and ran up the razor back—he would have to go one direction or the other, and he guessed left, but as he came around the ridge, it fell abruptly into a steep arroyo and he saw nothing. Then the sun broke over to the east on mountains off to his right and blinded him. That's when the first shot hit his pony in the neck. She just shook, dropped to her front knees, and rolled over.

The second shot hit Ran in the left shoulder as he was pulling himself off of the saddle and retrieving his carbine. He dropped behind the paint and listened to her die slowly, quietly, while he lay hunkered down against the saddle trying to remember what his position had been when the bullets hit. Both had come from the left side. He looked in that direction, drew his second pistol with his left hand, the right was burning all the way down to his middle finger. Waited. The pony's breathing just got quieter and then stopped altogether; she was gone, and when the morning black flies began landing on her open eye, she didn't blink. He waited. Thought about why he had pushed himself so into this match. Thought about Lorena Carson. Fresh Lorena. Blushing Lorena. His lover. At least that was how he had thought of her, although she had only kissed him that one time and then told him she couldn't see him. Ever. Because she had feelings for him, and it wasn't right. So he had been noble and kept watch over her homestead, and from miles away, he had always believed he was her protector. And then she was gone, and somewhere back down on the other side of that ridge was all that was really left of her that had any color to it. And that thought kept him alive, he realized, even in the pain of the slightest movement. And that thought kept him resolute that he would fight this son of a bitch and cut his balls off.

Ran waited for what must have been over two hours, until he couldn't take it anymore. He had reloaded the pistol and realized he could still move his right arm, bone had to be bruised but not broken. He crawled on his back away from his paint, looking to stay in the shadows. Both Colts were cocked. He could pump two shots and then a third and fourth within a few seconds as long as Rattle didn't come up behind him. He found a high point on the crest with a perch view, scanned the arroyo and the gully that led down to the place where he had shot the mounts. The two horses lay dead within a few feet of where he had hit them, but he could see that the mule had run off into the brush to die in its ornery way. The packs lay untouched. He waited for another hour. Then another. No Henry-Bastard-Son-of-a-Bitch Black Rattle.

He never saw Black Rattle again or heard anything about

him either. Maybe he died in the mountains walking home. Or maybe not. After all, Ran didn't die in the two weeks it took him to find a mount and get himself back to Texas.

As Runnels lay inside his tent thinking about those days, two hours before sunup, he wondered if he was on his own on this hunt as well, even with all the angry men preparing for the morning's chase. More riders came into the camp. Loud talk. He heard a voice he didn't like. Foil.

CHAPTER THIRTY-FIVE

◇◇◇◇◇◇◇◇◇◇◇◇◇◇◇◇◇◇◇◇◇◇◇

FOIL

When he crawled out of the train mess, and walked over the scattered debris of the disaster, bypassing the struggling wounded and the dismembered, he sat down and said his favorite little prayer. It wasn't to God, really, but a brief sigh to the luck of owning his own personal star. The two business partners he had invited to ride in Winfield Scott's car had perished along with eighteen other passengers, yet he, J. Abbot Foil, had walked away shaken but free, another sign that he was fast-witted and blessed, the skillful navigator of any and all turns that fate might throw in his way. Sitting down under a small summer plum tree, he uncorked a flask of brandy he had retrieved from the remains and, before he took his first swig, poured the libation to the gods he had dismissed at the beginning of the train ride.

Looking over the wreckage, and biting into one of the plums, he surmised, not with any modesty or regret but rather with a swell, that a few hasty judges might perceive his actions that immediately preceded the derailment as self-ish or cowardly. But those would be out-of-context judgments, he assured himself, short-sighted and pious interpretations by unfortunate fools who in their simplistic ways of conduct could never appreciate the benefits of cleverness. After all, he alone had analyzed the situation, and when he realized that the train might be in the process of being accosted by bandits, he had prudently moved himself out of view into the luxuri-ous parlor car's privy, where he had remained, even after the resumption of the train's motion, which he assumed meant that the danger had been averted. Just in case. By the grace of his star, because of the sturdy construction of the specially designed head, including its reinforced walls and floor, it had withstood the shearing disintegration of the rest of the car, when it subsequently fell onto its side and scraped on down the embankment. Although he might have been criticized for locking out his two compatriots to fend for themselves, he had seen immediately that there really was not enough room in the privy to accommodate more than one person. It was the type of action any clever person would have taken in similar circumstances, he concluded. And then, no one had seen the events or heard their curses, in any case. After the crash, when Foil unlatched the toilet's door and pulled himself free, his associates were nowhere to be found. He ignored the fecal stink that covered his tweeds and focused his attentions on that which mattered most. He had his business to recover. And he always packed a change of clothing handy when traveling in Panama. So he would attend to that in due time.

His calm relief dissipated immediately, however, when he realized that the rest of the train, with the gold shipment he had personally insured, was not piled up in this mess. Within an hour, as telegraph lines were repaired and messages flew up and down the line and into the disaster site, he learned about the rest of the events at Puente Espiritu that had preceded the wreck. The derailment had been an intentional, vicious distraction. At that moment, the full gravity and implications of the entire event overwhelmed him. For the next several hours, in an anxious, angry rage, he shouted off messages to associates and officials in a constant stream, for he knew he would be bankrupt and ruined forever unless he found a way to recover as much of the shipment as possible. From the relief station at the scene, he telegraphed his most influential partner, Nelson, the American counsel, who told him they were fortunate that none other than Ran Runnels himself was supposed to be somewhere near Aspinwall, traveling on Nicaraguan business with his father-in-law.

Late that night, upon his arrival at the site of the massacre at the bridge, Foil immediately began giving orders and sent for Runnels, whom he presumed would be jumping to his command, given the sizable additional financial obligation which he had incurred in bringing the famous Indian-killing, bandit-hanging Texas Ranger out of retirement. He was stunned when Runnels sent a message back to him that Foil was to come to *his* camp to receive instructions. Puffing and loudly pouting angrily, Foil almost ran down to Runnel's river camp and bullied his way into his tent, full bent on commandeering, as was his right. Runnels shut him up.

Foil could not contain himself and boiled over into a raging rant that embarrassed his sycophants who had followed him into the tent. Runnels, who was a slightly built man, simply put up his hand, waited for Foil to stop swearing, and then calmly told Foil that he, Runnels, was in charge and would immediately resign the commission if Foil had any other thoughts on the matter. Foil fell into a perspiring, red-flushed silence. Runnels dismissed everyone else from his tent. Then he elaborated simply, "Let's get this straight. One boss. That's me. Every other soul I allow to come along is a follower."

Foil started to protest again, and Runnels continued, "A difficult situation here, Mr. Big Shot. Pretty smart, mean, sons of a bitches. Got a good lead on us. And you've tried to saddle me with a bunch of idiots with guns just itching for a fight. And, you know, most of them have not even one poke of an idea what that really means." Foil started to speak. Runnels put up his hand again, stopping him. "No arguments. No playing off any of the men I select, and no disputes about who I bring and who I choose to leave behind. They're mine. You got that, Junior?"

Foil, red-faced and clenching his fists, barely contained himself. "It's Mr. Foil to you," he said. Runnels did not respond. "Almost three million in raw gold here, Runnels. Each cargo box is worth thirty thousand!" Runnels still ignored him. After a long, silent pause, Foil turned and exited. Feigning control, he lit a cigar and then turned to his company's secretary and asked him for a summary of the plans as he knew them and was told that Runnels had already selected his contingent for the posse. He had chosen twenty-five men, almost all Isthmus Guard, and had already sent men up both sides of the river on trails to pursue and report. He had selected one of the victims, an Italian valet who had lost his wife and children in the holdup, but Runnels had refused to bring anyone else from the train. He flatly had refused to bring any of the miners who had demanded to accompany the posse.

"He told us he needed to lead an organized company, not follow a mob," said the secretary, who noted that several of the miners, a few in pairs and the rest by themselves, had already purchased horses and set off in the afternoon in pursuit along the jungle's river trails. "Runnels said he was waiting for more mules and boats. Said the horses would be of no use in the jungle. Sent his own men on the trails by foot."

A few hours later, half-way through the loading of the mules onto rafts and the posse onto the bungos and piraguas, the first report came back from upriver. The miners had gotten into it at Las Cruces.

CHAPTER THIRTY-SIX

<><><><><><><><><><><><><><>

GATTOPARDI

Over the course of that horrible, devastating day, despite a headache that seemed to intensify with each minute, he had reached several conclusions. First and foremost, he decided he needed to devote all of his remaining energy to preserve himself. They, the other hostages, would have to fend for themselves, unfortunately. And that only made sense. It would be much less likely that their captors would release all of them at once, and it was only logical that, given his diplomatic stature, they should trade him initially. He certainly was the most valuable person who had been taken. By trading him first, his captors would obtain a handsome reward from the Colombian government on behalf of his aristocratic Sicilian Bourbon connections and perhaps might also negotiate additional bonuses . . . . amnesty or at least safe passage away from the mess they had created. He would assure his captors that he would personally advocate for that on their behalf. He also decided that when he was released, assuming he still had any strength remaining, he would then advocate, with all of his diplomatic prowess, for the release of the other hostages—or at least put in a plea with their captors that they be treated well. It would be the decent thing to do. It was "noblesse oblige," he told himself with some degree of reassurance.

He began practicing silently in Spanish what he would say to his captors when the right opportunity presented itself. He turned his thoughts away from the brutal acts he had witnessed, and tried instead to converse quietly with each of the boatmen as they pushed the flotilla up the river. When they landed, he helped them lift the padlocked containers off the rafts, wrenching his neck in the process. He helped pull the canoes out of the water. He helped feed the mules. For a short while, he believed he was making some headway into securing the goodwill of his captors. They gave him back his britches.

By the end of the first day, however, after he realized he had been traded like a farm animal, and the brigands split up, Emilio started fearing that he might not be given any opportunity to negotiate at all. The further they traveled upstream without any signs of being pursued, the more he realized that no one was really listening to his charming overtures. That made him feel even sicker than he already knew he was. As darkness enveloped them all, he started breathing quickly and then felt faint, then wished he had eaten and drunk more water during the day. The gnats, mosquitoes, and flies had bitten every exposed part of his body, the aching in his neck and back that had started after he helped unload the containers had intensified, and it felt like his head might explode at any moment with each pounding heartbeat. He imagined his brains popping out through his eye sockets in the evening's relentless heat. Anticipating his captors' responses to his negotiations, he found that he could not think through solutions. He started debating with himself, and when he looked down at some of the papers in his valise, he realized he couldn't understand most of the words on the documents either, especially his own writing. By sundown, laying by himself off to the side and away from the rest, he fell into a limp heap and vomited vehemently. His retching continued intermittently all night, but he continued talking, hoping that someone might listen. In the deep blackness of the night, as his voice weakened, the jungle and river sounds intensified, as if loudly hollering back at him to drown out his coarse supplications. It was then that he realized he might not be able to talk his way out of this mess at all. And with that, suddenly he missed his Italy and the reassurance of its gentle sun, the rolling verdant hills that he might never see again.

CHAPTER THIRTY-SEVEN

LITA AND GABI

They had been tied down during the defilement. Six hours further up the Gatuncillo beyond the Chagres fork, in the waning light and drain of the evening, after Deacy had sent his men away to secure the boats, in an abandoned mining camp and next to a stagnant slag pond at Cobre Agua, he violated the two of them in front of each other, slapping, punching, and kicking them both if either of them protested or cried. All the way up the river beforehand, they had listened to him sing, laughing and working himself up, predicting what he would do to them when they finally landed.

While Deacy was pulling up his breeches, turning to walk

back to the men guarding the boats, Gabi pulled herself up and looked over at Lita Scarpello who was silently weeping, bleeding through eyes swollen shut from the beating. When he was out of sight, she apologized for hollering at Lita during the rape, for telling her to shut up. She had been with violent men long ago. She knew what they could do—that he did not kill them told her that Deacy intended to keep them longer, perhaps for other purposes. She told Lita that she had heard the men in the boat talking about the whorehouse at the copper smelter camp further up the river and thought he might sell them there. She knew what it was to be sold as chattel. She had stood exposed as a young girl on the auction block, right next to the cattle and sheep pens in Bahia. She had learned to endure the repeated indignities of rape and beatings from men and not a few women, all of whom shared the notion that somehow wealth and luck gave them the prerogative to be cruel. She had no intention of repeating the suffering she had endured before Tomas Bossman Gonsalves had found her and she had somehow turned his head. She had gotten away from it all. Tomas was crude, but who was she to judge? she said. And he never had beaten her like the others had. Rather than descending back into hell, Gabi would kill herself first, she said.

Her salvation by Gonsalves, she told Lita, had come when she was indentured in a small whorehouse that catered to rich men in Sao Paulo. "Shouting Tomas," the name many called Gonsalves, had come in looking for companionship and, after servicing him, she noticed that he was silent. He seemed morose. This was unusual for any of the men, but especially for this sturdy, little one, whom she and the others had heard from their rooms as soon as he had stepped into the parlor down-stairs. He had talked and bragged continuously, quieted only during his selection of her, then resumed his boasting all the way up the stairs and all through their encounter. Afterwards, he had sat down on the floor, paused in pulling on his boots, beautiful, ostrich-skin boots, she recalled, and stared at her. She had stopped preening and decided to take a moment to look back. "Que?" she remembered she had said. He blurted out that she looked like his wife, long dead after childbirth, and that he had been alone in his mind since then. He had a nine-year-old son by his wife. He had loved her, he said he now realized at just this moment, for the first time since she had passed.

Gabi had listened quietly. Then, she didn't know why she had done this—she sat down on the floor and helped him put on his other boot. She kissed him on the forehead. He left without another word. Three days later, he came back, and she departed with him that night. She took the name "LaFleur" later that year after a visit with him to Baton Rouge in Norte America. She had all the finery she wanted after that, she said. She knew she was fortunate to be a light-skinned black and attractive, a beautiful "maroon" is what they called her type, she told Lita. She said she knew her looks would fade eventually, and she could be discarded if she didn't manage Gonsalves right. Men were like that, she said. She said she never could have babies—the pregnancies never lasted. After a long pause, she repeated herself: She knew how to run; that's how she had made her way from the slave markets in Bahia down along the Brazilian coastal forests to Sao Paulo. She would never go back to that.

Lita Perdellaño-Scarpello listened. She didn't want to, but did. Deacy had beaten them both, and during his abuse, she had turned her head away, held her breath as his heavy weight pressed down on her, and endured the mixed dirty sour smell of his body and dead breath stink, the burning pain of his entry. She held her tears because he slapped and bit her neck and yanked her hair so hard every time she started to cry that he had pulled out tufts of it. When would he stop? When would he stop? She tried to put her mind elsewhere, anywhere, con-centrate on the flies and mosquitoes that bit into her legs and neck as he grunted and pushed; prayed over and over again to the Virgin, tried to remember the prayers, the one she and her fellow students had disdained as rhymes to a fairy-tale mother. She turned to the right looking over the filthy red pond, out toward the river while Deacy was behind her, hoping that she would see Ari's red shirt, him landing, pulling her away from this monster. The babies were in the boat, and she and Ari and the babies were back upriver on their way again. They were at her breasts suckling hungrily, relieving the aching swelling. He was kissing the bruises of her cheek away, his strong arms holding her up. "*Esta bien. Esta bien.*"

And when she was slapped again and Deacy rolled off of her to take the other woman, she fled to the place where she knew she would have to go. She didn't want to go there because she had disavowed violence long ago, and that renunciation had caused conflict with those associates in school and a few of the younger Jesuits who had said that armed revolt was the only way to effect meaningful change in a corrupted society, beset by rules that benefited only the rule makers and those who wrote of forgiveness in the fairy tales of religion. She felt the welts on the back of her neck from the bites of his filthy, rotten teeth. Although she did not want to go there, she began thinking about how, before they ran, they would kill Deacy.

MAP THREE: BOCAMALO'S ESCAPE

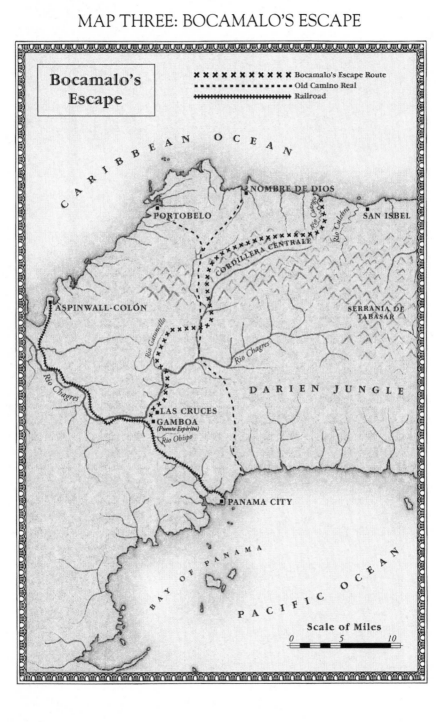

Bocamalo's Escape

× × × × × × × × × × × Bocamalo's Escape Route
▪▪▪▪▪▪▪▪▪▪▪▪▪▪▪▪ Old Camino Real
✚✚✚✚✚✚✚✚✚✚✚✚✚✚ Railroad

CARIBBEAN OCEAN

NOMBRE DE DIOS

PORTOBELO

Rio Cupiro

Rio Culebra

SAN ISBEL

CORDILLERA CENTRALE

ASPINWALL-COLÓN

SERRANIA DE
TABASAR

Rio Gatuncillo

Rio Chagres

Rio Chagres

DARIEN JUNGLE

LAS CRUCES
GAMBOA
(Puente Espíritu)
Rio Obispo

PANAMA CITY

BAY OF PANAMA

PACIFIC OCEAN

Scale of Miles

0   5   10

PART THREE

◇◇◇◇◇◇◇◇◇◇◇◇◇◇◇◇◇

INTO THE DARIÉN

The Darién Gap, a jungle known intimately by few, is an impenetrable, living house, seething with life, fed from relentless unpredictable torrents, ancient and sudden rivers, and the deciduae and detritus that forms its black-red earth.

Dominated by no one, its spirit never tranquil, transformed incessantly by the survival struggles on every inch of its soil, in every drop of its waters, the Darién quickly buries every vestige of man's attempts of permanency. It permits small territorial leases only to those who respect it, like the aborigines who work its woods and river banks. It permits but transient incursions, such as those granted to arrogant entrepreneurs, like the conquistadors who enslaved so many to transport, insecurely, their plunder across their "Camino Real."

CHAPTER THIRTY-EIGHT

EMMY

Upon beaching, as the sun went down, the bearded one, the one Deacy had called "Bocamalo," had tossed her some papayas and coconut. After hesitating for a few minutes, she devoured them. It was the first food she had eaten since the small breakfast at the hotel the day before. She hated herself for accepting it, for behaving that way, gorging herself in front of him, letting him see her weakness. But she forgave herself, anxious that he might take the fruit away, knew that the burning in her stomach would only increase if she had declined. He then handed her half of a ripe mango. He had cut it in a pattern so that its skin turned inward and the pulp pushed outward. Although she was satiated from the other fruit, she accepted it. It was incredibly sweet in a way she had never experienced. She drank more fresh cool coconut juice.

Emmy tried not to look at him directly but, from the corner of her eye, saw him smear paste from a small jar over the exposed areas of his face and hands. She was curious about what he was doing. When he saw her watching, he handed the jar to her, so she did the same, taking a small portion and carefully applying it to the back of her left hand. The paste was thick and pungent. The smell from the small amount she applied penetrated her clothing, and she noticed that the flies and mosquitoes stopped landing on her after that. She saw that he did not extend the same courtesy to Gattopardi. And all the time they had been on the boat together since separating from the other boats, when Deacy had taken Lita and Gabi and moved off to the left up the smaller river, the bearded one, Bocamalo, had been silent. As had she.

He had covertly watched her, she noticed, and paid much less attention to Gattopardi, who repeatedly had tried to make conversation with their captors. Bocamalo took off their manacles on landing for the second time and did not put them back on. It was an interesting shyness, she thought. Was there an advantage in that she might exploit somehow? In different circumstances, a man like this, with command wherewithal and similar organizational skills, might very well flourish, she thought. When she first saw him on the train, she thought that he was handsome and his eyes were sharp, clear, and beautiful. He carried himself with a certain confidence and boldness, but without the swagger she frequently saw in men with the same sturdy physique. She wondered whether his facial deformity, apparent only when he smiled and showed his broadly spaced teeth, made him less prone to call attention to himself. What did that say about him? And what did he gain by the bargain he had made with the man with the yellow hat, that Deacy? What was he looking for?

At a certain point, she realized he was watching her closely, and she felt his stare when she turned her back, when she drank water, when she straightened her disheveled hair and clothing. He watched her and said nothing. This continued all afternoon, and by late afternoon, she sensed that his stares were obsessed. They sent shivers up her back and made her hair tingle down to its roots all through her scalp. Was he planning something? She decided she had no choice—she had to run, before the sun came up.

Lying there that night, listening to the howls and roaring from the jungle, the hissing sounds coming from the caymans in the river, before she had crept away from the river where one of the men stared out guarding, she had kept it all in and tried not to think about Jacob or Sarah or any of the events from the disaster. Instead, she pushed herself to worry for both of the other women, especially Lita who had cried uncontrollably all the way up the river, holding her chest, rocking back and forth, moist stains weeping into her blouse from her engorged breasts. Lita had said that she normally didn't ever cry. Ever. Had prided herself on that. Said she wasn't weeping really, said she wouldn't let go like that. But the tears just poured out. Said she wouldn't think about her babies or her husband, who she said was called "Ari" which meant "lion" in the language of the Old Testament. Lita said she knew he would take care of their children somehow, he would find them, or find her, didn't have time to mourn right now or worry if they were hungry. The mulatto woman, Gabi, had remained silent when Lita went on like that, Emmy noticed. But both she and Emmy had cried while Lita cried. Neither of them could stop it, and for a moment, Emmy remembered what it had been like to be alone when she was pregnant or when her husband Isaac had been away for almost a full year.

Emmy kept it in as best she could. She turned herself away from the events of the past year, the ordeals she and her children had each survived. Somehow, that gave her hope that she would survive all that lay in store because she knew that her God would never be so cruel as to take her through all that—all that she had endured up north—to simply perish in this terrible dilemma. God was not cruel, she had told Lita. He didn't play tricks. And men were not cruel any more than were the animals that preyed on weaker ones. They simply moved in a rationalized survival way of doing what they did, she had always taught Jacob and Sarah. This was an anomaly, this train heist, just as the events on Whidbey with the aborigines up north had been. This was just another anomaly, another disruption of order. God was not like that. He would balance the grief with some good, and she had faith that she would be part of that, somehow. But she wept all the more until the men drew lots for them, and she was separated from the other women into this part of the journey up a different river. And then she stopped crying after that. Her lips felt parched. She didn't sleep. Waited. Wondered if she had cried out all of the water in her body.

Before she ran, just as Gabi, the mulatto woman had told her to do, she had broken the heels off her shoes to avoid twisting her ankles on the exposed twisted roots in the groves of mango trees that lined the banks of the river. But then the bearded one, Bocamalo, had taken their shoes away—to stop them from running. But she would run, barefoot as necessary, as soon as she was certain that everyone was asleep and enough time had passed that the sun would be up.

When she ran, she tried to stay close to the river. The mangrove bog was soft so it didn't hurt her feet as much as she had feared. The moss was moist, and mud squished up through and over her toes. In some spots, she tread in ankle deep folds of black muck. It was too dark to see her feet, and she wondered what she might be stepping into. It was warm, and if she stopped for a moment, she thought she felt it move underneath her feet so she kept on moving. The rotting detritus from the river left a decayed, sulfurous stink, and she could only faintly detect the putrid poultice that she had been given to apply the previous day by Bocamalo. After what seemed like fifteen or twenty minutes, as her eyes became accustomed to the morning darkness, she started to make out details of the forest. She tried to move along in a direction to parallel the river off to her left. No animal trails gave a hint of prior passage, and she entered a long bog grove dominated by huge trees and thick sinuous roots pushing out of the moist warm mess, bigger round than the cedars in the Pacific Northwest, but each one draped with long trailing vines wrapping up the trunks and then hanging down from limbs fifty and sixty feet above, reaching down into the bogs. When she pushed on them, she realized that the vines were rooted. In places the foliage and tree trunks created a solid curtain with an overhang that was impenetrable to light from above or to her right. She moved along the wall and realized after what seemed like an hour, that she could no longer hear the river off to her left. She knew she would have to find it again, if she had any hope of being rescued, but she didn't want to backtrack, even if she could, because she was afraid that she was being followed and sensed that she wouldn't find her way back in any case. She thought she heard something from the direction she had come. And then she felt a burning thirst and, despite the darkness, the humidity overwhelmed her and she had to sit down, to listen and catch her breath. Then the forest chatter suddenly ceased, and a few moments later she heard the sound of a man's voice. It was getting louder and coming toward her. She leaned back pulling herself into the cover of the large palms that surrounded her, holding her breath and waited—watched as the Italian, the nobleman Gattopardi, passed by within thirty yards. He was barefoot and filthy, had likely fallen into the slime. With both arms, he was tightly holding onto his valise and was talking in two voices, carrying on an angry, crazed, vehement conversation with himself in Italian and Spanish. He looked directly at her and snarled, as if warning her to stay away. She waited until he moved on and disappeared, but she could hear him for several minutes afterwards.

It began to rain again. A tentative patter, a few drops striking the broad leaves around her, turned to a rushing loud torrent that bent all the foliage and washed the mud away from her body. Then it stopped. As the light seeped in up ahead, she looked down at her feet and legs. They were covered with black, swollen, shiny leeches, bigger than the ones she had seen the Boston doctors use to bleed her grandmother each time the dropsy illness overwhelmed her. Some of the leeches moved, and when she tore them off, they curled. She bled from the wounds. Still she kept quiet. Puffed. Looked about. Waited. She realized she was really lost. She started to cry. Jacob and Sarah. She had not had the chance to say good-bye. They might never know what happened to her. She was thirsty and felt like she would pass out into the ooze below. Disappear. Could she let that happen? The unremitting heat and stink pushed her down further, and when she tried to lift her foot out of the mud, she couldn't. She tried to lift her right arm and realized that she couldn't do that either, as if it, too, was mired and sucked firm. She fell into the mud onto her bottom and couldn't pick herself up.

A few minutes passed, and she felt a weight on her chest that was like the one she had felt one year ago, when she had realized that she had lost her husband, child, and pregnancy in one brutal savage evening. And just as she started to feel that she could not control it and her survival was no longer a matter of her determination and will, and she might just have to let go, it started to rain again. She stuck her tongue out and felt the patter of large drops splashing onto her face and the cupped hands in her lap. Then it poured and washed her face, and even as warm as the rain was, she felt refreshed. It stopped as suddenly as it started. She picked herself up and began walking again. She had to get out of this mangrove bog somehow, get to higher ground and perhaps see the river. Find some clean water.

After walking for what seemed like hours, the ground firmed up, and she was on an ascent up away from the bog and the putrid smell of slime and mud fell away, and she caught a brief wisp of sweetness from a warm breeze. The trees became smaller the higher she ascended, and light poured in direct, dusty beams at several places ahead. She found what appeared to be a trail, overgrown but wider than the brown soupy animal paths she had tried to follow unsuccessfully several times. At the end of the trail, she saw the rotting stump covered with moss that had been clean-cut at some time in the past, then walking further over broken debris, she saw another stump that was intact and then others that looked as if they had been cut more recently, maybe within a few weeks. Looking ahead, she tried to see if anything moved—nothing but an occasional bird flying high, crossing the path ahead. She felt biting and, looking down, saw huge brown flies crawling on her feet and legs, realized that she was bleeding from where the leeches had suckered. When she slapped at the biggest and slowest of the biters, she saw blood and her skin immediately formed an itching welt. She picked up mud and moss from the trail, pressed it into patties, and coated the exposed parts of her neck, legs, arms, and face. Her feet were bleeding from several small cuts and small black thistles that had stuck between her toes. Every step hurt.

She crossed over a small ridge, and when it dipped down again, pushing through the brambles, she found a small clearing, less than a hundred feet in width, free of the dense foliage and most of the underbrush. She pulled down a branch from a green bamboo and broke it, the way that Gabi had instructed her to do the day before. The water inside it was warm but clean and eased the burning thirst in her throat. At the end of the clear patch stood a small shack with a broken roof and no windows; it was surrounded by an overgrown grove of plantains and plum trees. From the edge of the woods, she stopped, and before entering the area, she watched for a while to see if anything moved in or around it. She could see no signs of recent habitation, so she limped over the stubble to inspect the shack. It was empty. She moved to the nearest tree and picked several ripe plums and sat down near the trunk, careful to keep hidden in case she was being followed. The black plums were dripping with sweet clear sugary nectar, and after brushing away the ants that gathered when she broke the first one open, she bit into the deep red flesh that fell into a sticky lush pulp and knew she had never tasted anything quite like it. She ate four, stems and all, and picked several more, dropping them into the folds of her scarf. She saw one huge plum, larger than her fist, just beyond her reach . . . it looked so fat and ripe, draped over itself, its crimson cracking through the black moist skin, beckoning her so she stretched for it and then, forgetting about the pain in her torn and blistered feet, she began jumping to see if she could catch a leaf to pull down on the branch that held it. She caught a leaf's tip and carefully pulled down at the overhang so that the plum was just inches away. Just as she was about to grasp the prize, she heard it. Men's voices. Laughing. She let go of the leaf and the branch flew up, slingshotting the ripe plum several feet away. Rescue?

Turning in the direction of the voices, she held her breath as she watched the black-bearded Bocamalo, riding on his big white mule, heading right for her. He stopped in front of her, three feet away. He was smiling wryly, and she could see his yellow jack-o-lantern teeth clearly, widely spaced. It was a shy, evil smile. He paused, looked her over from her head down to her swollen, torn feet, then reached back and retrieved the small carpetbag he had taken from the black Brazilian man.

He pushed aside some garments in it, then pulled out Emmy's shoes and tossed them down to her. "I think you will need these for the rest of our journey, Señora," he said.

CHAPTER THIRTY-NINE

RUNNELS

By the time his flotilla reached Las Cruces, the shooting had stopped. Nine of the miners, well armed and emboldened by their collective indignation, had ridden at full gallop into a town that belonged to Haut's men and the families who loved them. Their blind, agitated pursuit of their gold was further impassioned by the other thing that they all had in common—anticipating a war between the states over the slavery question, they all had chosen to transport their gold to mints in New Orleans and Charlotte. Every one of them hated blacks, both Haut's and Bocamalo's gangs had several, and the thought that their gold had been taken by "darkies" collectively enraged them all the more. The fight, marked by sporadic bursts of gunfire, lasted more than two hours and awakened a normally sleepy nest of thieves and cutthroats. The miners didn't know the streets and didn't anticipate the ferocity of the response to their uncoordinated assault.

The first one to go down had been a hardy, stubborn, exceptionally pious Lutheran German named Otto Schwerhart from Baltimore. Twelve years before, he had trekked with the Donner Party over the Sierras via the Hastings Cutoff to California and had survived that infamous tragedy, frequently boasting that he had done so without succumbing to eating the flesh of his fellow travelers. When he walked out of the Sierras, he weighed fifty pounds less than when he had started the journey up the pass. After striking out as a panhandler in the gold fields, he had moved north to the Fraser River in British Columbia, where he did succeed in finding a rich claim after fourteen months of starvation and toil. He had taken as a sign from God that his rich find was a reward to him for his years of patient, honorable forbearance and durable faith. He never saw the man who shot him on the crumbling Las Cruces street, ironically named Via Dolorosa. The bullet that tore into his left flank burst his spleen and colon, and, surrounded by barking dogs, he bled out within a few painful minutes, bewildered by his newly found vulnerability.

The second and third miners to die that afternoon were brothers from Alabama named Abel and Perce Fellows. They had fought against Santa Anna in Mexico, then made their way, unscathed somehow, through the Comanche badlands and up into San Francisco in '49. They had panned unsuccessfully for over three years, nearly exhausting their grubstake, and had given up, moving to Bellingham in the Washington Territory. With what remained of their family's funds, they sought opportunity in the lumber trade. When the Fraser River strike in '58 set off another national gold fever, they caught the disease again and quit their faltering efforts to make a fortune with a sawmill. They panned on numerous creeks and streams for nine months before seeing the flash of their first flecks and then waited on their claim through a full, frozen-ground winter before confirming their find. The tiny golden sparkles turned out to be the wash-cast from a rich set of veins running through a cliff side embedded with white quartz. The dust and nuggets they had accumulated in less than one year was piled in pouches in two sealed Foil cargo boxes numbered 452 and 453. The gold assayer had said their cargo was worth at least two hundred and fifty thousand. Leaving their claims in the care of their two young wives, they were traveling back to Mobile via the Charlotte mint to raise more investment money from their families for an expanded cliff-side mining operation. Perce died first when he burst headlong into a saloon owned by one of Haut's sergeants. His brother, Abel, was gunned down while trying to pull him out through the swinging double doors.

The fourth to die was a big, amiable Swede named Lars Bjornsen from Fredricksburg. Teased often for his inept clumsiness and fear of horses, he had travelled with a trapper team over the Rockies in 1843 and into the Northwest by way of the Columbia River, walking the entire way. So severe was his equinophobia that when he had finally secured a substantial claim on a tributary to the Coquihalla River, he created an elaborate and ingenious rig that used water wheels rather than horses or mules to move his ore, and walked for miles to the small station that many used for store supply. The four containers of gold nuggets and dust that he had entrusted to Foil Cargo represented his entire fortune, accumulated over two years, working twelve hours a day. When the robbery occurred, he forced himself to overcome his fears of riding in order to join the pursuit and recover what he could. But he could not read, and he spoke not one word of Spanish. He broke his neck when his borrowed shod horse slipped on the cobblestones under a makeshift sign that read *"Pasear a su caballo."* "Walk your horse."

The fifth miner, a Finn named Horst "Lucky" Heldt, had also lived for much of his early life in Mississippi before shipping around the tip of South America up to the Pacific Northwest. He knew himself to be a self-sufficient man and was extremely proud of it. More than once, he had successfully driven off claim jumpers, and his daring resourcefulness had helped him avoid certain beheading by marauding Kwakiutl when he jumped off of a seventy-foot cliff into the cold Fraser River. He had broken both ankles in the fall, but the pursuing aborigines who had seen him do that had left him alone after that, assuming that he was a protected spirit. He believed that, too, and took great pride in repeating that story often. His reputation in Vancouver as an intrepid, lucky man was as important to him as were the riches he had acquired by his mining. On the day that he rode onto the Las Cruces docks looking for the robbers, he intended to add to his personal legend. Recognizing some of the train robbers off-loading some of the heavy chests from the train heist, without waiting for the other miners to catch up, he began firing into the crowd and took down three of the highwaymen with his double-barreled scattergun. He spoke enough Spanish to ask one of the dying bandits about where he would find the cargo and Pallino Haut. On his way to his mount, a twelve-year-old girl, the daughter of one of the three he had killed, rushed up behind him, reached up and pulled a razor across his neck. Attempting to stanch his hemorrhage while guiding his horse, he rode out of town after telling the remaining four miners about the cantina across town where he had been told Pallino Haut and their gold likely would be found.

The remaining foursome—three from Vancouver and the fourth a Peruvian broker representing a Peruvian mining collective's gold—rushed into the fight without much forethought and surprised Pallino Haut in a small cantina, shooting him, his wife, and two of his children. Unfortunately, the Deriéni survivors of the gunfire returned with others. The four miners thus found themselves trapped inside the small building surrounded by an enraged crowd that shot hundreds of bullets into the adobe walls and through the shuttered windows and doors. When the miners refused to come out on the offer of an amnesty guaranteed by the town's bishop, the mob outside pushed the priest aside and set fire to the building. The four miners' burnt bodies were dragged through the streets and hanged on the docks. They remained there until a large troop of New Grenada soldiers entered town to restore order two days later.

None of Haut's share of the gold was ever recovered.

The escalating fiasco disgusted Runnels, who had immediately set off upon hearing about the gunfight. He knew his own pursuit now would be more visible, and the town's agitated population would likely attempt to prevent his pursuit. Dismissing Foil's protests, he ordered a bypass of the distraction of Las Cruces altogether, pushing upriver to gain on the main group of raiders. His boats and rafts were followed on riverbank trails for several miles upstream by angry natives and friends of Haut, but his flotilla of men and mules was far enough away from the docks and the town's riverbanks that the shots fired at them from the town fell short. He sent word to his contacts to request that Las Cruces be secured by the New Grenada military, which fortunately had not yet tried to interfere with his efforts.

Foil trailed behind in the last boats. Without consulting Runnels, he sent his own messengers back downriver to convey far along both coasts his offer of rewards, of unspecified "but substantial" amounts, for Deacy and the man known as Bocamalo. He also called for more volunteers and bounty hunters to join in the pursuit. By the end of the second day, more than one hundred other men and women, some experienced and disciplined but many others just amateurs, were on the river and trails up and down the Chagres, looking for bounty and booty, whichever happened to cross their way.

CHAPTER FORTY

<><><><><><><><><><><><><><><><>

BRETT

Ever been in a fight?" was all Runnels said, turning his head sideways.

Brett nodded. "Apaches. Mexicans."

"And just why do you want to go with us on this?" When Brett responded that he thought his skills would be of use to the posse, and he knew one of the hostages, Emmy Evers, Runnels stared at him, then smirked knowingly. "Fine, Doc. You can come. Likely'll be some patchin' up to do in a day or three." Then he looked Brett directly in the eyes. "Keep out of my way, and do as I say." Brett was surprised at the confident command this young, slight-shouldered man exhibited.

Earlier in the day, Brett had found the streets leading to the

Panama City rail terminal jammed with traffic—frustrated, delayed travelers; railroad workers; and Isthmus Guard hires. He had to resort to a lie to get himself and his mule on the one transport leaving that afternoon, telling one railroad official after another that he was a physician assigned by the US Army to investigate the disaster. All equestrian and foot traffic had been blocked by Isthmus Guard, and after discussing the terrain and the hazards of the old trails outside of the railroad thoroughfare, Brett decided against riding through the countryside or in jungle parallel paths.

The ten-mile ride to the site of the holdup took much longer than he expected. It took several hours to replace the rails that had been destroyed by the bandits. By the time the transport reached the Puente Espiritu bridge in the early evening, the area was crowded with an array of railroad and New Grenada officials attempting to sort through the mess and police the opportunists, scavengers, and curious native onlookers. No one was being allowed to cross the span to the site of the derailment several miles downline, for although the fire set by Bocamalo's men had been extinguished by intermittent rain, the railroad's engineers had not confirmed the bridge's soundness. And there were bodies that still needed to be retrieved from the deep gully one hundred and fifty feet below.

After securing his mount, Brett had pushed forward and eventually found his way to the line of covered corpses of the victims. Again invoking his credentials as a physician, he inspected the remains, one by one, eleven bodies in all, pulling the canvas back with mounting apprehension at each body, now bloated and putrid in the afternoon heat. They had been executed in the same manner he had seen used by assassins in New York and San Francisco: shot behind the head. Neither Emmy Evers nor her children were among them. He then spoke with several of the weary passengers and heard a confusing array of stories about the heist. He met an Italian man named Scarpello. The fellow looked able and fit and spoke some English. He conveyed that his wife and children had been abducted by the desperadoes. He also said that he was certain that a woman matching the description of Emmy had also been taken hostage. "She wore black, bella signora, ferocious brown eyes. A sad fire smoldering there, I think," he said. Brett knew that had to be Emmy. Accompanied by Scarpello, he had made his way to the tent of Ran Runnels, "El Verdugo," who, they were told, was arranging a rescue effort. He and Scarpello volunteered their services.

Bret watched Runnels look over the Italian and ask him the same questions he had been asked. As he listened to the exchange between Runnels and Scarpello, he also understood that the Italian was likely the only one of the entire group of survivors who could reliably identify Deacy and Bocamalo. So it didn't surprise Brett that Runnels agreed to bring the Italian with him as well.

As Brett thought about it, he realized that the men in Runnel's twenty-five man posse likely had different purposes for this chase. The volunteers from the Isthmus Guard would be bent on revenge, Runnels was looking to hang bandits, Scarpello was hoping to rescue his wife and children, and he, himself, was on a quest to find a woman he hardly knew, but whom he instinctively understood might be the most important person in his life. He didn't know how he had reached that conclusion, had so little to go on, one lengthy intelligent conversation and a brief encounter that morning that had left him dumbfounded, but he knew he had to continue on and try to find Emmy.

They pushed off before first light after word came about the firefight in Las Cruces. It was scorching hot by nine o'clock as they bypassed the town. Most of the men had shed their shirts by then and were crouching down bare-chested on the boats to avoid the town's gunfire, bullets plinking in the water near them. Upriver, when the shooting finally stopped, Brett tried to have a conversation with Runnels, who responded in terse sentences but did open up a bit when Brett mentioned the Apaches. Runnels had fought them in lower Texas and also had rescued quite a few of them from the Comanches, who had obliterated many of the smaller tribes in their dominance of the territory. Brett had mostly been on police actions and a few pursuits but had experienced very few direct encounters in which he had to use his side arm. But he had repaired many wounds and, like Runnels, had buried many men, women, and children. Both men became silent after that.

Later on that morning, he spoke at length with Scarpello and learned that he was a follower of the internationally famous Italian revolutionary, Giuseppe Garibaldi, and had been assigned by him to be the valet, protector, and covert observer of a diplomat who purportedly was trying to arrange for the hero's reintroduction into South American political causes. Scarpello told him his children and Emmy's boy and girl had disappeared at the same time that his wife, Emmy, and his employer, Emilio Gattopardi, had been taken. He presumed that they all were now hostage, but he couldn't be certain. He was pursuing the only option he had to recover his family. He said his little boys were named Giovanni "Jonny" and Falco. Brett saw the anguish on the man's visage and heard the pain in his voice. As for Gattopardi, he would have to fend for himself, Scarpello said.

It took seven hours to move upstream after bypassing Las Cruces, and by the time they reached the first big fork, the shadows were running long on the river. During their rest, Brett watched Runnels's scouts reconnoitering upstream on both the Chagres and Gatuncillo. Five hundred yards up the Gatuncillo, they found debris that appeared to be from the survivors. Among the objects scattered on the bank of the Gatuncillo was the shawl that Scarpello's wife, Lita, had been wearing when she had been abducted. Thirty minutes later, the other scouts from the Chagres returned with a black veil that had been tied in a knot to an overhanging tree branch that had been stripped of its leaves at the tip so that the veil could not be missed by travelers moving upstream, but would have been shielded from view by those looking back downstream. Brett distinctly remembered that Emmy Evers had worn it on the train and in the hotel restaurant in San Francisco. It was a deliberate sign.

He listened to Runnels discuss with his lieutenants the significance of the findings. Were they being purposely confused, or was someone sending signals? He asked Brett about the black veil—was Emmy Evers the sort of person who might take a chance like that? Brett thought about his conversation with her in San Francisco, her intelligence, and her purposeful determination. "I expect she is," he said. Runnels shook his head and threw the stick he had been whittling into the river, spitting after it in apparent disgust. He told his posse's lieutenants he couldn't ignore either sign, and thus, he reluctantly was forced to split his posse in half. "Odds might be evened up after all," Brett heard Runnels say under his breath.

Ari Scarpello joined the group moving up the Gatuncillo, and Brett stayed with the group that would be led by Runnels on up the Chagres. They said good-bye to each other, understanding that they might not ever see each other again. Foil trailed behind and then, after discussing his options with his assistant, chose to follow Runnels. He sent his assistant with the other group.

Moving up the Chagres, Brett reflected on the dimensions of this vicious heist. Counting the deaths of the miners, thirty-eight people had been killed in the Puente Espiritu holdup. He had been told that another forty-four had been killed or injured in the derailment that most certainly was related to this outrage. It was rumored that almost two and half million in gold had been stolen, and ten or more people were missing or taken hostage for unknown reasons. Several women had been raped, and all the passengers who had survived had been robbed. The brutality of it all was like that he had seen in Mexico and in Texas during the Comanche wars.

He had heard that the isthmus crossing was notorious for such atrocities. In the days before the railroad, before the Isthmus Guard had begun patrolling the railroad pathway cut through the jungle, robberies of pack trains had been a common occurrence. Murder took as many hapless travelers' lives as did the dysentery, malaria, typhus, dengue, typhoid, and yellow fever that was endemic to this tropical area. But the rapid railroad passage had reduced the disease deaths and morbidity almost completely, at least for those who did not linger in either Panama City or Aspinwall. He learned from one of the English-speaking men in the entourage that none other than Ran Runnels, the laconic, determined, small-boned little man who led this group had been responsible for the cleanup of the Deriéni.

Brett had certainly seen depredation. He had heard that in the Mexican war, the American volunteers and some of the troops under both Winfield Scott and Zachary Taylor had been responsible for multiple instances of wanton murder. He knew that the Veracruz assault, in which Scott had bombarded the city prior to marching in, had resulted in the deaths of hundreds of innocent civilians, and the Mexican people perceived the American hero to be a villainous monster. In his twelve years with the United States military, in Mexico and in Colorado and California fighting various indigenous aboriginal tribes, he had seen firing squads and had tried to manage the aftermath of massacres. The cruelty of it all was always dispiriting, even for one trained as was he, in the dispassionate comportment of one's duty in the face of armed conflict.

But this instance was overwhelmingly disturbing, and he wondered whether the kidnapping of Emmy Evers was responsible for the difficulty he was having with it. He didn't really know her. But from his observations and reflections over the past month, he had made several assumptions about who and what she was. Was that fair to her? he wondered. If she survived this ordeal would his perceptions about her be changed? If she had been violated, would that matter to him? He knew many men would banish women so despoiled from the privilege of decent respect, irrespective of the circumstances of their victimization. He had heard that the Turks stoned such women to death. And American society would punish such stigmatization with a condemnatory quarantine, at least in the Richmond and Philadelphia societies in which he had been a member. The gossip would be vicious. He wanted to rescue Emmy Evers from that ruin if he could. Protect her. He wondered if it was too late.

He asked Runnels for a pistol.

CHAPTER FORTY-ONE

◇◇◇◇◇◇◇◇◇◇◇◇◇◇◇◇◇◇◇◇

EMMY AND
BOCAMALO

He had told her that his name was "Rafael." He said that he had grown up in Cartegena and was the orphan-descendant of impoverished royalty. He claimed he had once been a priest and had taken a vow to redistribute the wealth of the rich to the poor of the earth and protect the innocent. He said that he had once seen a vision of the Virgin Mother of Christ, and she had given him dispensation to do what was necessary to save mankind from itself. The Virgin had called him by his first name.

Emmy listened quietly as she rode directly behind his mount

on a smaller, gray, fourteen-hand molly. Three of the men had broken off from the train earlier in the day, each taking a pack mule with their share of cargo boxes and supplies. Five of his men and one woman, tending ten heavily weighted jack mules, trailed behind, strung out over almost a hundred yards. The woman and all of the men, including Rafael, had taken off their shirts and were sweating heavily in the afternoon's humid air. All of them wore various forms of tattoos, but Rafael's back, chest, and arms were completely covered with them, and the patterns—strange, intricate, and sinuous symbols mostly—stood out under the glistening from his perspiration. It was his tattoos that distinguished him from the other men, all of whom, white and black, had black beards like him. She noticed that each of the men also had at least one form of deformity: One man had a prominent dark red, raised birthmark that covered the right side of his head and face. Another had an empty socket instead of a left eye. A third man, a black man, was club-footed. The lead vaquero had scarred nubs for ears, so that his hat, cinched tightly to his chin, rode low on his head.

The heat grew worse as the day progressed. Emmy had torn off her sleeves and taken off her skirt down to her bloomers. She didn't care for modesty and paid no attention to what was on his or any of the other bodies. She was exhausted and just wanted to stop the melting. She needed to sleep.

They rode upwards through a dense thicket of underbrush until they came to another area, a plateau almost barren of vegetation as if it had been permanently scorched. It was covered instead with large and small rough stones that looked like the dull black pumice with which her family's maid had scrubbed Emmy's face when she had been a child in Boston. At one corner of the plateau stood the remains of what looked to Emmy like an altar with blocks of stone surrounding it that might have been seating or benches at one time. She pulled aside briefly to look at them while the others passed. They had to be ancient, she thought. Block carvings on the face of the largest stone, almost six feet high and canted on its side, had vestiges of human figures—all were in the grips of a large sinuous reptile with three long, pointed heads.

The pack train passed the huge stones on the plateau without stopping and at the farthest edge turned down onto what appeared to be a worn path leading into a steep, dusty gully. It then crossed through a thicket of thorny bushes and moved on up further into the hills, which, from down below, looked to Emmy like they were dotted with caves. The mules kicked as they passed through the bushes, and Emmy felt bites from the long brown spikes as they whipped back from the passing animals in front of her. Black clouds rolled quickly covering the sun, but it did not rain. Rafael gestured for the rest of his gang to proceed past him, and as they did so, he pulled up alongside of Emmy's molly.

"This is 'Montaña de los Lagartos.' You should be careful here." She saw that he watched for her reaction, but Emmy gave none. He pointed up at the cliffs off to the right. "Cuevas de los lagartos, where they say the Old Ones lived before the conquistadors came and exterminated them all." Emmy looked up in the direction he was pointing but did not respond. She saw that he was staring intently at the caves, like they held some meaning for him.

"Who will be coming for you?" he asked after a long pause,

looking at her sitting in her filthy pantaloons astride her mount. He looked down at her bleeding feet—she had been unable to put on her shoes because of the swelling and pain. She did not respond to that question either, but she knew that something on her face must have told him what she suspected he already knew. She was losing hope.

"They would be fools to not try to get you back," he laughed, looking her over and then at her eyes for a reaction. He was taunting her, she knew. And then his eyes narrowed. "And bigger fools to try to follow."

When she did not react, he spit, then stuck a dirty finger into his mouth and held it up to feel for the wind's direction. There wasn't much of a breeze that she could feel.

"They are fumbling around right now, fighting with their insurers and creditors," he said. "They don't know where to start." He laughed again. Emmy maintained her silence as they rode on, and they quickly caught up, moving to the middle of the pack. Rafael then left her and pushed his mule back up closer to the front of the line. "Watch her. She may run again," she heard him say in Spanish to the mute Mestizo woman of his lead vaquero. She saw the woman turn and look at with her a knowing stare and smirk. Emmy didn't like the woman. She had seen her during the holdup, rifling through the pants, purses, and the bodies of the victims. She had dead eyes.

They rode for another four hours upwards into the hills until the darkness made the footing impossible to see more than a few feet ahead. They dismounted, and Rafael's men prepared a camp in a huge empty cave he had selected on the hillside. There they built a small fire for the first time since they had begun their escape on the river. On the fire they threw big pieces of termite nest, which kept the flying insects away.

In the dim light of the fire, Emmy saw on the wall what looked like crude drawings of men and women standing in a circle. They were fornicating. The male figures were large and had huge members, and the smaller women seemed suspended on the phalluses. Surrounding all of the characters in the circle were sinuous forms with designs resembling the ones she had seen carved on the stone on the plateau. She was too tired to study them and started to fall asleep.

She awoke when the quiet woman and one of the men returned from the brush below carrying two pig-like animals that looked like very large rodents and the fresh, limp carcasses of large green, red, and black lizards, two in each hand. She watched the woman gut the dead animals and peel their skins away as neatly as if she were opening a pile of plantains. She tossed the entrails and skins into the fire. The fire popped and sizzled, and the smoke smelled sweet. They threw the large rodents onto the fire, and one man sharpened mesquite branches and then skewered the skinned lizards and propped them one by one onto the fire as the three other men laid out their bed rolls. Sitting on a rock near the edge of the circle, Emmy didn't know whether the nausea she felt was from a ravenous hunger, the spectacle of the lizards, or her plight. She felt very hot and then chilled.

She fell asleep for a few minutes, and when she opened her eyes and looked up, she saw that Rafael was watching her again as he and one of his men carried in the cargo boxes. When he was finished, he walked over and sat down next to her, reached into his pocket, and handed her the foul-smelling poultice. "Put this on—on your feet, arms, and neck. It will keep the scorpions away, too."

The men kept up a coarse banter for over an hour. Emmy listened but understood very little, even though she had learned some Spanish from a few workers on her farm when she lived in the Oregon Territory. The vaquero's woman said nothing but uttered a few grunts and tried to talk. The men seemed to understand her, laughed at her comment, and as Emmy listened, she was able to make out a few words, realizing the woman wasn't mute after all, but tongue-tied, or . . . watching her closely, Emmy realized the woman had only part of a tongue. The woman recognized Emmy's surprised look at the moment of that realization and shot back a hateful glance. Emmy looked away, but she could feel the woman glowering at her.

They were high above the jungle now so that its constant din from chirping, whistling, and howling seemed far away. The Mestizo woman watched Emmy the rest of the night. Eventually, the conversations stopped, and only the fire made noise, occasional pops and the settling of the logs as they burned through.

When the two men who had been standing guard came in to eat, Rafael left to position their replacements. Emmy laid down on a blanket, but it was too hot to cover herself, and she stared out the mouth of the cave at a black sky partially covered by clouds that hid most of the stars. It hurt to keep her eyes open. Her back and legs and shoulders ached for her to rest. She dozed intermittently but could not sleep.

She wondered what would happen next. She knew she needed to run again, but she also knew she would never survive now if she did so. They had traveled so far from the river, and she no longer had any bearings. She doubted that she could find her way back along the trail they had followed. She had left pieces of her skirt tied to branches back on the trail when she was certain no one was watching but had heard nothing. It hadn't rained, but when it did, likely all traces of their passing would be washed away, she realized.

Was this how it would end? Just three days before, she had been anticipating with some mild apprehension, returning to the comforts of her family in Boston. It seemed so far away now. Unreachable.

For some reason she thought about the black men and women she had seen in chains getting onto the flatcar in Panama City. She wondered if they had all been stolen as she had been, wrenched away violently, or whether they had been born into their condition as she had heard so many of the slaves in the southern states had been. She wondered what type of hope each of them might have had, and understood suddenly the bewilderment she saw in them when they had been set free by this Rafael. She thought of Jacob and the damage his abduction had caused him. She wondered if it was irreparable, or if he survived yet another ordeal, whether the wounds would turn to scars that would shrink over time then turn into insensitive places that would prevent him from being stable and productive, that would preclude him from happiness or satisfaction with life. She thought about the gravity of sinful acts that evil men do—purposefully or unintentionally. In her opinion, its horror was measured less by the number of wounds it opened than by the quantity of scars it left. She would rather have open wounds than scars, she thought, because at least with open wounds the pain and rawness were awakeners.

After a half-hour, Rafael came in from his rounds and again sat down next to her. The others, including the mute woman, had laid down to sleep. He watched the fire for a few minutes. "You have a little boy who is wounded," he said. "You worry for him, but you cannot reach him for some reason. He is hiding inside of himself. He will die inside there. I saw that on the train." For the first time since being taken captive, Emmy turned to look directly at Rafael. As much as she despised him, he was speaking the truth, she knew.

"I was intending to put you on the river, give you a chance to be found, you know. But you ran away." He laughed. "Now you get to be with me. Maybe you will become my woman," he said, without looking at her. He laughed again, then he stood up and walked over to some bedding next to the mules and laid down there. Emmy's heart was pounding, and the nausea she had felt earlier returned. In the fire's flickering light, she noticed the design of the tattoos on his muscular arms for the first time. As he flexed his muscles, she thought she saw the patterns on the tattoos writhing. Predatory beings.

Rafael knew they all called him "Bocamalo" behind his back. When he was a young boy, it had been the worst of insults, one that always provoked a violent retribution that he easily justified to himself. But now he understood it to be a famous name that frightened men, so he was proud of it when he saw it on posters or heard people use it when they were unaware that he was listening. He didn't know why he had told the widow woman his real name, one that he hadn't used for years. Normally, he had simply responded only to "*Capitán*." Perhaps it was that she had smiled at him on the train and something about her had drawn him to think of her since then, to look at her. He didn't know why he had told her all of the lies about himself.

As he stared up at the big blue-black sky outside of the cave, he knew he was looking at the very same stars as did others, but somehow he knew that he saw them much differently, and each one of them said something much different to him than they would have said to anyone else. It had always been that way, since he had been a small child. He wondered why he was so unique, in a way that went far beyond the things that he thought must have made others feel both alone and special at the same time. Perhaps it was somehow related to the protection his mother, Ava gave to him while she, at the same time ignored him for everything else, especially when she was working on men. He didn't know, and the memories of Ava were fading now anyway. He still could feel her face, see the flush and color of her cheeks when she was angry— which was often—see her soft small hands and tiny feet, her freckled legs. But he couldn't see her face anymore, and that made him sad. He longed to hear her voice but only heard it once in a while, in his dreams that were always the same. She was sending him away again.

When he was small and lived with her in Cartegena and then later, with her and the Greek man in Turbo and San Blas, he had learned that he was smarter and stronger than the rest of the children, whether they had visible defects or not. But

Ava told him that being clever was much more important than being stronger than others, and he knew he was clever. Very clever. He learned from the Greek man about a man called Ulysses and about another warrior named Ajax and how Ulysses had outsmarted everyone and how a man named Hector had died because he was noble and brave but was not clever. He was a dead hero. Not clever. He had failed.

Rafael turned on his side and looked over at the fire that was dying out, and could see the young American woman who had worn black on the train and was now outlined against the darkness behind her in the big cave. He didn't know her name. But he was a patient man. She would tell him eventually, he knew. This wasn't the first time he had a quiet captive.

He wondered what she was like, if he kept her, if she would turn to him—behave, but lie and reveal herself in the way all the rest had. When he was younger, he had taken them, sometimes in groups, sometimes by themselves. Many women and a few men, too. Priests, soldiers, rich. Not the poor, unless they deserved it. He had seen through them as they tried their stupid ploys and pathetic pleadings. Some, the most foolish, had thrown themselves at him. Some had fought for a while and then gave up when they saw that giving up was not something he would ever do. Some, the men especially, the ones who had always gotten their way by being bullies, tried to provoke him into swiftly finishing them off, but he had always seen through that as well.

They all gave up, whether they prayed or used words, spit or stayed silent. He saw it in their eyes, always at the last moment, when they gave up their fight and their souls. They always looked away, only a flick sometimes, as he stared at them, unwavering and intense in a way he had learned very early on, watching their spirit dwindle in their pain and misery. And he had seen it over and over again. The men, especially the privileged and the arrogant ones, were weaker than most of the women he had found. He had noticed that the ones with calloused hands held on the longest. And he was stronger than them all.

He knew he was supposed to feel some guilt for what he had done to them, for the fun he had watching them and the anger he had taken out on them. He had been told when he was a little boy and when he lived in Portobelo with the priests that he should seek penance for the evil things that he did, that he knew all men did. But he never felt guilt. Why should he? None of them ever felt guilt in their actions when they pushed him and everyone else aside. They just took what they wanted and justified it in so many ways and then placed jewels on the walls of the churches beneath the pictures of the saints or draped them on the Virgin, who he knew now had never existed. They bought their way out of the guilt they were told they had to carry. It was such a big joke, and he had seen it when he was just a little boy, while he was watching his mother with every type of man wearing every type of uniform and vestment. They were all alike when they were intimate, and they all died in the same way as cowards. He had confirmed it.

He hadn't taken a captive for himself, for his own pleasure, to satisfy his curiosity, in a long, long time. He remembered the first ones and the memories from his first explorations with them, unobserved and quiet, still gave him arousal at times. But that was many years ago. And he had felt no desire to take a woman, to be with one, for at least three years, he realized. After all of them, after all of these years, maybe he was a burnt-out case, like some of the old lepers he had seen, whose disease had just stopped the melting away of their flesh, its rotting job complete. Was that how a soul, no longer fettered by the temptations of the flesh, found its way into redemption? he wondered.

And, even though he found himself watching her, stimulated for the first time in a long time for some odd reason, he still wasn't certain he would keep this particular woman, this widow who had worn black. She did seem different from the rest, and that piqued his curiosity. He felt some sadness for the boy who was her son, as if he knew him somehow but did not know why. Did the boy need this woman? He would ask her when he had the chance.

If he did decide to peel her back, the way he had all the others when he was younger, would she disappoint him—and turn out to be a coward, too? Would she turn out to be a whore, like all the rest, all of them, the women and men? And if so, how long would it take for her to reveal what type of coward she was before he had to make that final decision. If she dismissed him, as she tried to do when they had first bound her, if she kept that up, he would break her down quickly. If she dared to judge him, as had some of the others, she would regret that, and he would make certain she understood her foolishness. If she was an innocent, like a child, he might let her go. It didn't really matter. She would die one way or another out here—with or without his help.

CHAPTER FORTY-TWO

<><><><><><><><><><><><><><><>

RUNNELS AND BRETT

Runnels's posse caught up with one of the Deriéni while he was transferring some of the cargo from one of his mules that had gone lame less than a mile from where he and two others had split off from Bocamalo's mule train at its disembarkation place from the Chagres. The man had tarried, they learned, because he thought it was safe to do so. He told them he had been on Deriéni gold train raids in the past, and he never thought that anyone would have been able to follow their trail. When Runnels told the Deriéni that it was he, El Verdugo himself, who had caught him, the dying man shook his head. He should have known better, he said. It hadn't rained in two days, and the mule scat and other signs were fresh enough. He should have known better.

Runnels was furious. Despite the advantage of surprise, the bandit was well armed and he got off the first shots, blasting down two of Runnels's men who had blundered onto him, and then had retreated into the cover of a shale pile that provided a protective stone overhang. He refused to come out despite Runnels's offer of a civil, swift execution. It took two precious hours to dislodge the bandit, and Runnels had to kill him in a sloppy way to do it.

While Brett was attempting to doctor the dying man, Runnels pushed on his belly and was able to elicit from him the confirmation of his guess that Bocamalo's group had split into two parties. The man told him that he thought Bocamalo, his *Capitán*, was headed for the Caribbean coast, because most of the men who had continued on with him had been with him for a long time, and were from that area. The *Capitán* still had most of the contraband, "*gran parte de carga*" and a female captive, he said. He said that both the woman and the man from Italy had escaped two nights before, but they had recaptured the woman. "*Mujer reserva privada del capitán.*" He said that two other women captives had been taken by Nick Deacy up the Gatuncillo branch.

Foil then interrupted Runnels and started pushing the dying man for more details about the number of cargo boxes that Bocamalo was carrying, but, as if making a silent comment to the tone in Foil's voice, the man stopped talking. His eyes rolled back, and he stopped breathing.

Runnels fumed and turned inward in silence. He was angry

with Brett for not keeping the man alive longer because he needed to know more. How many men were left in Bocamalo's party? Did others split off? How many mules and what supplies did they have? Were they well armed? What did he really look like? Did he fit the description Scarpello and the other heist victims had given him?

Runnels kicked dirt onto the dead man. Two of his men were dead, four mules had been disabled, and he would need to send at least one of his men back with a mule to transport the one box of gold they had recovered. He tried to send Foil, who was useless, privately opined and second-guessed his every decision, but the prig refused to go, stating that the one box of gold wouldn't cover even a fraction of his own potential personal losses. Foil said he intended to see this through. As Runnels thought about it, he knew it would have been stupid to give Foil that responsibility anyway. He would just get himself lost, although Runnels really didn't care if Foil were to disappear. So he had to send one of the younger riders back.

He was frustrated. The odds were turning against him even more. They would have to backtrack a bit to pick up the trail of the larger party, and he was now down three competent men. He looked up at the sky and wondered how long the weather would stay with him and keep the signs from washing away.

He looked at the bodies of the two men he had lost in the fight. He knew both of them from the early days, before either of them had married, and although neither of them had ridden with him, he knew they were reliable, hardy fellas. Chileans, he remembered, with pretty good common sense. They were experienced. So he wondered how they had let themselves be shot at close range like that. Should have known better. He remembered that each of them had brothers who had been killed in the train heist. So they were angry and had underestimated. He had seen that deadly combination, anger and impulsiveness, so many times before. Damned foolish behavior, when anyone with a gun, professional or amateur, calculating or desperate, was likely use it to take a shot at you in a determined way. He wondered which was more valuable in a fight between equally armed foes—the need for survival, like Bocamalo's man had when he was surprised by the two vaqueros, or the Chileans' desire for retribution. Better to be desperate than angry, he knew. As sobered as his men were by this gunfight, he would have to hold the reins even tighter, he realized. Maybe he would let Foil, the calculating headstrong little prick, charge into the next gunfight. He laughed, picturing that.

From what Runnels could tell by his own maps, Bocamalo was heading northwest toward the mountains, but seemed to be moving east of the old Camino Real trail that led down the coast to Portobelo. He couldn't be headed for the abandoned town of Nombre de Dios, because the paved road of the Camino Real that led there had been destroyed over a hundred years previously by the Spanish to prevent pirates and the Brits from using it to attack their gold convoys. The hills that Bocamalo was crossing were on a more eastward trek of the Cordillera Centrale and were much higher than those for the old Spanish gold trails, which, although they were mostly abandoned now since the railroad had opened, likely might still be functional. Why would he be moving in that direction? Was Bocamalo headed east to make his way to Colombia? How would Bocamalo find his way through that almost impenetrable terrain? Runnels didn't know that region well enough, he realized, to answer that. There was a river there, but he couldn't remember its name.

He instructed the young rider he was sending back down the Chagres to convey to his patron, Nelson, to send a well-armed posse of Isthmus Guards out of Colón to Portobelo in case Bocamalo's party emerged there or a few miles east at Nombre de Dios. He fretted that it would take the messenger at least two days to get the information to Nelson and at least one more day to get a posse to Portobelo, but he told the kid to tell Nelson that if they caught Bocamalo to hold him there because he intended to be the one who hanged the bastard. And if they killed him in a gunfight, they were to hold his body—so he could hang it and display it from Colón to Panama City for anyone who would ever think of attempting a heist of their railroad.

The more he thought about it, the more he knew he didn't know how much of a lead Bocamalo had on them, how close they were. Three hours until darkness, and they needed to push on, couldn't spend much time on a burial. He did say a hasty little prayer over the bodies of his men and had them covered with stones, but it was foolish to pretend that it made any real difference. The men were now departed, and, one way or another, the jungle would finish that disposition very quickly.

Brett knew that both of Runnels's men likely had died almost immediately from the ten-gauge shotgun blasts, so he didn't really feel any guilt for not going to them during the fight.

He and everyone else had been pinned down for almost two hours by the well-concealed man who was shooting from under a rocky overhang. His position, overlooking a narrow draw, couldn't be flanked. While he watched Ran Runnels's reactions to their predicament, Brett had listened for sounds from the downed men, but one of the dying mules was braying loudly, and neither man had made any noise as far as Brett could tell. So he had just stayed put. After the mule died, there was little sound at all. The forest was watching. Sensible thing to do, to stay put, he knew, and by this time in his career, he was beyond guilt in any case.

He thought about how he had changed over time and how he had arrived at that practical way of looking at things. In the Mexican War, as a newly graduated volunteer physician in the US Army, he recalled how he had berated himself repeatedly for not intervening quickly or appropriately enough in what seemed to be salvageable injuries—for not amputating a leg early enough to prevent gangrene from setting in, for not providing immobilization when he should have suspected a fracture of the spine, for not telling a dying man the right words to put his spirit at rest before he died.

Brett remembered it had taken him a long time to get over the revulsion he felt when he had to take off a man's arm or leg. He hated seeing the men in agony, hearing their pleadings and bargaining, and wondered if he had lost some of his own hearing as a result of their screaming. But over time, in Texas and then in California, he had learned to say just the right comforting words, whether he believed them or not, and to make better choices and quicker decisions. He had forgiven himself, he realized, for his mistakes and for his own youthful ignorance. He also, finally, had established what he considered the right modicum of emotional distance between himself and his patients, rather than comparing and likening them to himself as he had done in the cases he treated right out of medical school. He finally had understood that the distance he now maintained was a practical measure—bringing him close enough so that he could retain some of his empathetic abilities, which is what he believed every ill or wounded person really wanted from a physician—but keeping him far enough away that he could get on with the business at hand. He had come to accept that as necessary for him to be a competent, productive healer.

Competency was what was important, he knew, not the other things of pride—the prestige and power—that set a man apart from others, which helped give a man the notion that he was somehow superior to others. Those prideful things, he admitted, may have prompted him to become a sawbones in the first place. But it was his sense of competency that kept him engaged in the practice, despite its many burdens. Certainly he still took pride in his profession and was fascinated by the social aspects of the human interactions it provided. He had stories—lots of stories, all physicians did—but he seldom told them anymore because he had concluded it didn't really matter and doing so just upset people or ruined dinner parties.

He also had come to realize that he couldn't really relate well to other physicians he knew in private practice as well as in the military, particularly those who had decided that doctoring people was a convenient way to get rich quickly. For example, when Brett was a very young man and was considering a profession, he had looked up to his uncle, a distinguished osteopath back at home in Virginia who had become quite influential and important. He was "sagacious," everyone said, "and someone to emulate." But, as Brett had watched over time, he knew that his uncle had changed over the years; he had become overtly greedy. He observed that his uncle was now dismissive to his poorer patients and had eventually stopped treating anyone who couldn't pay, and pay well. Brett was disillusioned and felt betrayed and wondered whether people really respected his uncle because he was effective as a physician or rather because he had used his skills primarily to become a wealthy land- and slave-owner. He wondered whether people equated one's wealth with competency. Brett hated witnessing that transformation in his uncle, but as he reflected back on it and what he remembered from the early days, he wasn't certain that hadn't been a part of his uncle's character all along.

In response to this disillusionment, and what he saw as repeated manifestations of avarice by the actions of many of the prominent physicians in Richmond, two years into his own studies, he reaffirmed his commitment to the Hippocratic principles and the notion of selflessness in the performance of his duties. To the great disappointment of his family, he turned down a prestigious assistantship with a prominent Charlotte doctor, who had a large clientele. Thinking he might be doing some real good by treating the wounded of war instead of the routine cases found in a civilian practice, Brett instead chose to enlist in the military, just as the fight with the Mexicans began in '46. He was just twenty-three years old. In retrospect, he realized that he had been enticed by the promise of a grand, patriotic adventure as well, fresh out of his studies at the Virginia Medical

College in Richmond. Hadn't *that* been a miscalculation on his part? he reflected. As an assistant surgeon in the US Army, his duties were mostly taken up with the management of minor infirmities and the manipulations of malingerers.

And here he was, again being shot at, thousands of miles away from his home on the Chicahominy, riding with Runnels—such a strange man—and a posse of angry men looking to catch a murderer and retrieve a fortune in gold. Here he was, pursuing the rescue of a woman with whom he had spent less than four hours. Had his father still been alive he would have been chastised for this impulsiveness, Brett realized.

That made him think about Emmy Evers again and why he was so attracted to her: the way she carried herself, her poise and dignified, quiet demeanor. He had watched and listened carefully when she sat with Letterman and the group of other soldiers a few weeks back in San Francisco, noticed how she answered questions and conversed, how she handled the exchanges. She was a good listener and exhibited the skill of a trained diplomat, neatly parrying every thrust, even when the forays by the officers could have been taken as forward or offensive. He had seen the firm but gentle way she spoke to her two children and to the aborigine whom she had committed to enroll in an institution of higher learning. He had watched her eyes as she recounted a few of the events of what must have been a terrible ordeal, and when she spoke about her slain husband. Brett was impressed that she showed neither self-pity nor anger. And she was lovely and sturdy, a beautiful, well-educated, and level-headed woman, uncommonly so in comparison to the many women he had met over the years.

That thought, the comparison to other women to whom Brett had been attracted in the past, made him wonder again about himself, why he had not previously really pursued any woman. There had been one disappointing foray into a romance with a classmate, the first and only woman who had been admitted to the medical college. Was it that he really had difficulty communicating his feelings to anyone? He had been warned to keep his feelings to himself were he ever to be a successful physician. Or had he, very simply, set his standards unrealistically high? Perhaps. As he thought about that, he sensed Emmy Evers seemed to meet whatever it was he wanted in a mate. Whatever it was.

He weighed the risks and rewards of his being successful in saving Emmy. Would she turn her head in his direction, accept his advances as a result? Most women would swoon over such heroism, he believed. Or might it take even more effort? Could he support her and her family? Would that be important to her? Would she abide by a marriage oath, stay by his side, richer or poorer, ill or healthy? He knew he would, and sensed that she would as well, for the right person. For someone she loved. He wondered what a civilian practitioner's life might be like now in these modern times. His widowed father had left him a bankrupted estate, and, with the salary of a military surgeon, he had accumulated little wealth. He would have to establish a practice, assuming he survived this most interesting of episodes in his life. He decided Emmy was worth it, this venture. He had done much more foolish things in the past, and the best of outcomes in this one promised a relationship that, deep down, he believed was meant to be. And although he had come to serious doubt about the existence of a supreme being, he accepted that what will be, will be.

Brett thought about all of that for the first half-hour while they were pinned down. Funny how his thoughts ran, he mused.

When a piece of lead whizzed over his head and split a tree limb three feet behind him, he stopped his introspection and looked over at the other men in the posse. Runnels was sitting calmly behind a stump five feet away, studying a map while he fiddled with his ammunition. Some of the other men were dispersed behind a variety of barriers, including two of the dead mules. Foil, lying prone on his belly with his arms covering his head, hadn't moved from that position for over twenty minutes since discharging one unaimed shot in the direction of the bandit.

Runnels did the shooting that finally ended the match. Brett watched him unpack a waxed tin box and carefully select cartridges, one by one, load them into the breach of his long-barreled rifle, turn, aim, and place shots into the overhang of the shale carve-out where the man had hidden. They heard a high pitched yelp on the sixth and a loud groan on the eleventh shot. Runnels then turned and said with a little laugh, "*That* got 'em."

After a quiet half-hour, Runnels told him, "He's up there dyin', Doc. Let's get on up 'n see what we kin learn." Then Brett watched Runnels stand up straight, pull and cock his pistol, walk past the bodies of his dead deputies and the mules, and move sixty yards directly up to the stone hole where they had cornered the Derién bandit. After returning his pistol to its holster, Runnels waved Brett up to the covered perch where he found the writhing, dying man. The man had been hit twice, likely first in his shoulder and then in mid-abdomen. Bile and brown blood covered his shirt, and when Brett cut the garment away, he knew from the entrance wound and swollen belly that the ricochet slug had likely penetrated the man's colon and liver. He was surprised that the man had lasted as long as he had. The belly was filled with blood, he knew. He was more surprised that the man complained only of the wound in his shattered shoulder. Runnels did all of the questioning, and the man died quickly. The woman captive was Emmy Evers, Brett hoped, but he had been able to elicit no description. All he had to affirm that hope was the one other sign they had found on the trail, another piece of black veil discretely tied to a tree five miles back.

While two of Runnels's men quickly butchered one of the dead mules and packed its hindquarters and back straps, scouts rode out in four directions, hoping to pick up signs of Bocamalo's larger party. Within an hour, one of the scouts came back. He had found the trail of a large group of iron-shod mules emerging from a shallow stream about three miles away. By the signs, he estimated it to be fresh, perhaps less than four or five hours old. For the first time, Brett saw that Runnels was excited. He quickly mounted, and Brett followed with the eight men who still remained in his party. Then Runnels seemed to catch himself. He held up his hand and stopped. "Three hours 'til we can't see. Slow down, now. No more blunders. There's viper pits all along here, and I don't want any falling in one of 'em."

They rode for the better part of two hours. The trail left by the bandits skirted waterfalls and deep drops leading to a place on a high plateau covered with gray-black pumice and very little vegetation. Bocamalo had camped there. They pitched their camp there as well. Brett sat on the first watch looking over the treetops of a dense forest below and, from his perch, what appeared to be entrance and exit trails from the plateau. He didn't know how high up they were. They had to be far above the river, he reasoned, because the mosquitoes and gnats had disappeared. But there were lots of flies still, brown, black, and green, large and tiny, and they all gave painful bites that made him scratch every exposed surface, including his face and nose, and he had nasty chigger bites all over both of his legs, despite tucking his pant legs into his boots. He listened to the howling and heard a big cat roaring in the distance far below. Puma? Jaguar? Did they have tigers in this part of the world? He couldn't remember. Later, just before being relieved from his watch, he heard more roaring and the squealing of what sounded like a wild boar. It didn't go on for very long.

Runnels didn't let them build a fire to cook so they ate a ration of jerky and tack and went to sleep quickly. When Brett woke up in the morning, he was able to see the plateau better and realized that they had been sleeping in an area that had some history. The early morning sun had spread out across the barren, rocky area. Walking back from relieving himself, he realized that he had slept at the foot of some enormous stone blocks with crude images carved into them. Two had a bit of color, chalky blue and red, on their surface. Walking around the stones, he saw that the carvings on most them had been worn away, likely by years of rain. On the biggest stone's surface, however, was a moderately intact bas-relief sculpture—an icon of some sort, he realized—not the type of Mexican Aztec or Chilean Inca art forms he had seen while on leave in London in '51, in an extensive display at the Hyde Park Grand Exhibit. The figures on this relief, a serpent or dragon with three heads entwined with men, were crude by comparison to the Aztec works. The heads of the humans were more block-like angular in form than he remembered seeing in the Inca sculptures. The serpent held the embattled men by their necks in its front and hind legs and was rearing backwards to a large, disembodied foot stepping down on its arched back. Brett walked around the block and several meters away found a second massive stone, lying on its side, which must have been at one time, he deduced, stacked on top of the larger one, because the carvings on that stone were an obvious continuation of the first. He realized that the huge foot stepping down on the back of the serpent belonged to that of a large-chested woman with four breasts. There was enough detail on the rearing serpent that he could read its expressions. One face was angry, another was leering, and the third seemed to show pain or agony. He asked Runnels if he had ever seen anything quite like it, but Runnels didn't respond. Brett made a sketch of it and tucked it away so he could show it to a professor he knew in Charleston. The image frightened him a bit.

All through the day, despite a few quick downpours that obscured the tracks, they continued to see the trail of Boca-malo's entourage. It was hard going, and they labored to cover even seven miles up and down the steep, slippery ground of the forest during the daylight. By the late afternoon of the third day, they found a large cave in which the bandits had camped the evening before. After inspecting it and sifting through the cool ashes and garbage, Runnels told them they were somewhat closer to catching up with them and estimated they were now about three hours behind.

Runnels told them that he had finally figured out where Bocamalo might be headed. Somehow the bandit was making his way eastward along the spine of the mountains, on to the Serrania de Tabasar, past Nombre de Dios, via the old abandoned and destroyed part of the Camino Real, which they would cross at some point. He likely was en route to one of the small rivers like the Rio Cuango or the Culebra that led to small villages on the Gulf of San Blas.

Runnels told Brett that he had never traveled there, and it might take two days to get down the mountainside from there and find a navigable part of the river. If they got lost, they might get lost completely, let alone ever find Bocamalo. If they did indeed come to a waterway like the Cuango, which led north to the Caribbean, and if they could find Embera aborigines, they would negotiate with them for their bungo craft and also quickly build rafts for the mules.

He said that wouldn't be an easy task. The three centuries of well-known cruelty by the Spaniards had made the Embera as well as the Kuna shy and very resistant to trade. And if, indeed, Bocamalo was headed for one of the rivers, Runnels said they would have to move faster going down the mountain if they were to catch him—before he had time to make his own rafts and get boats to make his way downstream to the ship that Runnels suspected was waiting at the mouth of the river.

While Runnels was looking over his maps, Brett found another piece of Emmy's black skirt, rolled into a ball at the base of the drawings on the cave's wall. As Brett inspected the drawings, he saw what looked like fresh markings off to the right, scratched into the cave wall below the figures. He looked closer. It was Emmy Evers's initials with a date and a word that looked to him like "dying."

CHAPTER FORTY-THREE

◇◇◇◇◇◇◇◇◇◇◇◇◇◇◇◇◇◇◇◇

SCARPELLO

Even wretched-tired as he was, Ari Scarpello had been unable to sleep for more than a few hours at a stretch. Knowing he couldn't afford to miss anything, he had pushed himself into a raw alertness, watching, sniffing, tugging at his ears for any sound or sign that might provide a dram of hope. Despite the relentless, humid heat on the water, the swarms of mosquitoes, gnats, and flies that plagued the posse, he pursued every slight, out-of-the-ordinary movement; every ill-fitting pattern or color with an extraordinary forceful will. By the afternoon of the second day, he was spent. He thought he might be seeing spirits with each turn up the languid, slowly moving river. More than once, he thought he saw Lita or glimpsed his son running through underbrush. He called out several times, but no human voices responded out of the cacophony on shore.

He understood distorted hopes in the midst of peril. He had been in danger himself many times during his life, especially over the past twelve years during his travels with Garibaldi, who was described by some critics as reckless for his own safety and that of his followers. He had watched comrades fall. He had been with Garibaldi when they had narrowly escaped from Italy. He saw Anita, Garibaldi's wife, die during that flight. Over the years, he had marched in numerous protests and had been fired upon. He had been wounded in Rome in '48 when they attempted to overthrow the pope. But he had never been wounded quite like this. Each of those episodes were adventures, and as a young man, he was as immortal as were all young men who believed that their lives were attached to a charismatic spirit that would endure long beyond their ashes were dispersed to the winds of time.

This, however, was not an adventure. There was no romance in the brutality of this rescue, he knew. This ordeal struck at the nest of his heart.

When he first had met Lita Perdellaño in Quito six years before, he had been a different person. He knew he had been an arrogant young man back then, attached as a trusted lieutenant to Garibaldi, an internationally famous man who repeatedly had achieved phenomenal victories against overwhelmingly large, uniformed forces. He had observed how Garibaldi had succeeded—by riding with his irregulars into battles without a strategy; carrying the field with bold, headlong charges that always energized his troops and unnerved the enemy. It was that energy that gave Ari Scarpello the sense that he, too, by mere affinity and proximity, was protected and immortal.

But there was something about Lita Perdellaño that upset that hubris. She was more than his equal, he had concluded. She rode as well as he did and shot from a horse better than any dragoon. She held her ground in the impassioned arguments over little things that fierce lovers sometimes have. As he had prepared to leave with Garibaldi, he knew he would be back to find her someday, for he doubted that he would ever find anyone again who would ever be as passionate and bold, or hold in tiny hands the command over as much of his heart as she did. And when he learned she would bear his child—he was overthrown forever. When he met his little boy, Jonny, his commitment to his family was sealed in steel, and with the birth of his second child, that steel was tempered hard. From then on, he understood that he would need to meld that commitment somehow, with his aspirations to be part of a revolution's historical change. He decided he would teach his children to be honest citizens of a decent and just new world order. They would carry on, one way or another, with a vision to redistribute wealth and privilege. They would wear red and spill blood if necessary. And if he had any legacy, it would be that he and his progeny had helped make an enduring difference to the betterment of mankind, without the need for religions or the help of their fairy tales. But the revolution would have to wait. He needed to rescue that which he had now built into the core of his vision. He had to find his family.

At first he thought the caymans were nipping at a small wounded deer, and it was only when she raised her arm vertically that he had looked again at the scene, fortunately for her. He was the first one to see Gabi, and had he not, she would have been taken by the caymans that had moved onto the bank close to her and were starting to become aggressive. She barely moved at their tentative little bites. Her tattered undergarments covered in dried blood, she lay by the river's edge and was delirious when they retrieved her. After almost a half-hour, she began responding more coherently to the questions from Ari and the others. Ari, who spoke a little Portuguese, was able to make enough sense of her words and to put together a disjointed description of the events from the previous day. She had been with his wife, Lita. The first word she spoke was "*morte,*" which made Ari's heart drop, but then he realized that she was speaking about someone else—Deacy.

Gabi then collapsed and was unable to continue for another hour. When she recovered, this time with more strength, she said she thought she and Lita had killed Deacy while he was attempting to rape them again.

She told them that after he had assaulted them the evening before, Deacy had come to them early the next morning very drunk. He was chewing on a large piece of pork shank, loudly snorting a song. Lita had feigned sleep, so he had turned to Gabi. He was still holding the shank of pork as he pulled his britches down and knelt down on top of her. Gabi said Lita had waited until he was fully in the act and was making grunting noises, then she pulled Deacy's knife from his belt and cut across his neck. Clutching his bleeding throat, he had rolled off Gabi and then attempted to stand up. Lita then stabbed him in the chest. Deacy crawled away into the bushes, "still holding the pork shank," she said. Gabi said she wasn't sure he was dead, but he had made no noise—either because he was dead or couldn't speak because his windpipe had been cut. She remembered hearing his throat gurgle and whistle.

She and Lita then ran, avoiding the camp at the landing, stumbling through the underbrush in the direction they thought they had come the day before. It was still dark. They were separated almost immediately when Lita stepped on something sharp and cried out. Gabi said she didn't turn, was afraid to stop because she didn't know if she was being pursued, so she kept running and running. Ari asked her how long she had run, and Gabi said she knew how to run. It had been all day until she couldn't run anymore.

She told Ari there had been no children on any of the boats.

The other men listening to Gabi's tale looked at Ari when she said that. They all knew what that meant. He had told them he thought his wife and children had been taken. But now he didn't know where any of them were, and they were not together.

Over the objections of Foil's man, who wanted to rush forward upriver to the copper mining site to surprise Deacy's gang, Runnels's lieutenant commanded the group to quietly move on up. They put Gabi in the rear boat, left the muzzled mules, and tethered the rafts behind, then moved cautiously upstream in the bungo boats, weapons primed and ready. The Kuna pole men signaled when they were around a bend within a few hundred yards of the camp's docks. There they beached and moved quietly through the riverbank's underbrush until they were within fifty yards of the old mine's broken-down landing. Boats and rafts were moored without cargo. The camp appeared to be deserted. After a half-hour, the lieutenant signaled for his two advance men to move ahead into the camp. They all watched for another fifteen minutes and then, on signal, followed. They found that the camp had been vacated. The fire's ashes were cold. Deep tracks, of heavily burdened animals, moved into the jungle in different directions. It appeared that the gang had disbursed, fanned out on three different paths. An early morning rain had obliterated the tracks into the brown soup of the forest's floor so that it was difficult to determine how many mules were in each pack.

They found Deacy in the underbrush near where Gabi said they had been kept the night before. His body was sitting up, embedded against the long sharp spines of a black Chunga palm tree. The swarming beetles and ants had already taken much of him, but they were able to identify him by the yellow conductor's hat, which lay off to the side.

When Ari learned from Gabi that no children had been taken hostage, and Lita had run but might have been hurt or could have been retaken, he broke down and wept for the first time in his life. The men in the posse who observed his keening wail looked away, moving to their business of landing their mules in preparation to follow the trails of the Derién marauders.

Ari quieted after a bit, and after a short pause, he stood up and walked over to the posse's lieutenant. He asked him for permission to take a mule and commandeer one of the Derién's bungo boats, and said that Gabi had agreed to help him search the jungle's area between the camp and the place where he had found her on the riverbank. If he could not find Lita there, he would bring Gabi back downriver to safety and then travel to the site of the robbery to see if he could find his children. If he found them, when he found them, he said, he would then come back upriver to search for Lita again. He then asked the lieutenant that if they found Lita, or if they found her remains, that they tell her that he would be back. He put Deacy's pistol into his sash and headed into the forest.

As he and Gabi headed into the jungle to retrace her steps from the day before, he reminded himself that he didn't believe in God. But he knew he was praying to Him for the first time in his life.

CHAPTER FORTY-FOUR

EMMY, BOCAMALO, AND BRETT

She believed she was dying. By the time they reached the navigable part of the Cuango and met the Embera waiting for them with their boats, Emmy had fallen from her mount three times, the first time almost dropping off the edge of a steep embankment that she knew likely would have killed her had she not held, somehow, onto the reins. Less than an hour into their descent on the twisting trail, she had found a raised, irregular, grainy rash that covered her chest and arms all the way down to her wrists. It felt like a coarse, gritty sandpaper embedded under her skin. She was burning up with a fever, and although the morning air had been mercifully cooled by several short cloudbursts, she tore away at her blouse to find some relief. After the second fall, the mute woman who had been watching, lashed her mule to Emmy's and threw a rope around her waist, giving slack at times when the path was too narrow for tandem riding, so that Emmy's mount could trail behind safely.

After her third fall, she heard Rafael tell them all to stop to rest and water their animals. The brief respite, she didn't know how long it had lasted, didn't help much. They finally stopped, almost five hours later at the part of the Cuango that looked wide enough to navigate. Emmy could not stand up. Her skin and bones ached, and she began vomiting as soon as she dismounted.

In the swirling all around her, she thought she heard Rafael barking out commands and saw the men unloading their mules, taking off the saddles and cargo boxes, and placing them into awaiting boats. His voice was impatient and rough, not smooth and silky, as it had been before when he had spoken to her. She looked up. Other men whom she hadn't seen before, blacks mostly, had tethered the mules and were leading them away. They were all laughing. She fell into a deep sleep that carried her into a dark place with no boundaries. Its quiet terrain seemed to go on and on.

She didn't know if she was awake or sleeping, alive or dead. She had moved away from a place that was hidden and now she was floating, visible to all of the men who had taken her and everyone else she had met over the years—Rafael, her brother and father, and everyone she had left behind in Boston and on Whidbey Island where she had buried Isaac's remains. She looked down to see if she could stand anymore but could not find her legs. Then she saw them again; they were swollen and angry red and covered with sores. She saw her children, Jacob and Sarah, on the train, but they were grown adults now and they had children with them. Jacob was pointing outside of the window, and he was handsome, tall like his father. He was sad. She wanted to come down next to him and put her arm around him, pull him close, and he seemed to want that, too, but then he pulled away, stiffened, and turned squarely to the window. He told the little boy next to him, "Look out there. Your grandmother is out there. She is following this train."

And then Emmy was outside looking in. She wanted to get in, but the train car was moving too fast and the tall grass on the plain was holding her back. The car sped on and away. She had to catch it! She couldn't let it get away. She needed to get into that car and get away from the outside that was so cold and so hot all at once, and the tepid wind, transformed into a smiling specter, quietly stared at her foolishly standing outside.

She pushed her way past it onto the train but found herself in another compartment, and she didn't recognize anyone as she floated down the aisle, her painful feet mercifully not touching the ground. Then she was sitting behind two young boys. They had notes pinned to the lapels of their coats. She knew them somehow. Where were they going?

She felt several arms lifting her up. They were placing her . . . into a boat on a river. She was drifting off again into a confused haze when she heard shouting and gunshots.

Rafael, who had been standing up in his vessel watching the last of the four piragua craft move away from the bank, saw three of his men, including his lead vaquero, fall into the water before he heard any of the shots. The force of the slug that hit Rafael in the right chest, twisted him down, throwing him backwards onto the edge of one of the cargo boxes and nearly capsizing the boat. He felt the wind knocked out of him, and it hurt to take even a slight breath. But the piragua was moving swiftly downstream now, and the rest of the shots coming from the woods behind them were falling short.

As his boat moved downstream, Rafael pulled himself up onto his left elbow and watched the mute woman struggling to pull her husband's body back into the boat. An intense gunfight had erupted on shore between the Cimaroon mule skinners, struggling to restrain their pack animals, and his pursuers who were shooting at them from the woods. It would be a drawn-out fight, he knew, because the Cimaroon, hardened descendants of slaves escaped from the Spanish, were fierce, angry men. For centuries, until the railroad had been built, they had made life hell for all travelers of the Camino Real and all across the isthmus. Now, with that trail all but abandoned and the rail lines patrolled by Isthmus Guards, their best chieftains hanged or hunted, the Cimaroons scratched out a mean meager existence, robbing anyone foolhardy enough to travel the ancient Spanish gold trail. They always had trusted him as an ally, but they had never buried their hatred for rich whites. These ones were all relatives of two of his gang members and would be protecting their share of the gold as well as the mules he had left with them as payment for acting as a rear guard for their retreat.

He had no idea if his pursuers were indeed Isthmus Guard or undisciplined bounty hunters. But it didn't matter, for he had told the blacks that he would be pursued by the Isthmus Guard, and they hated the railroad's henchmen almost as much as they hated the cruel Spanish whose forefathers had enslaved the Cimaroon ancestors generations ago. He knew their stubborn, ferocious firefight would give him a good amount of time to escape down to San Isbel.

As much as it hurt for him to breath, he knew he would not die today. The bullet's force had been diminished as it struck the pack of playing cards he had been carrying in his shirt pocket. The slug had penetrated most of the cards before deflecting off. Although he was in pain, he knew he would survive. He had been shot more seriously in the past and had recovered from those wounds, he told himself. The gunshot and the fall onto the cargo box had broken some bones, he was certain, but he wasn't bleeding heavily and could feel the big bullet, lodged under the skin right over his sixth rib, grating and rubbing every time he took a breath. He could get it out later.

He had not thought anyone would have been able to follow him, especially with the care he had taken to move along pathways that only he and the Cimaroon knew on the remnants of the old Camino Real leg that once had led to Nombre de Dios. But he knew he had caused enough havoc that there would be determined pursuit by many. He was relieved at his luck in this development. His pursuers, whoever they were, would have to find a way to take their own mounts down the snake-like curves in the stream, because, unlike him, they would have no transport waiting for them when they completed the trek to the mouth of the Rio Cuango. So they would need to build rafts to carry their mules, which would take hours, or find their way along the Cuango's banks which would take almost another full day if they didn't get lost in the Darién.

He stood up in the boat and waved shoreward at whoever had taken a shot at him to let the man know that he had missed his chance. Even if his pursuers survived their fight with the mule skinners, they would never catch him.

He looked for the carpetbag that had been on his saddle for something to dress his wound. It was filled with fine silk shirts that he could tear up for bandages. The bleeding from his wound was increasing.

Brett had glassed ahead. He had climbed with Runnels at least ninety feet up, to the thick branch of a tall tonka bean tree, to view the river downstream. He could see where Bocamalo's party had stopped. He saw a man in a serape directing other men, who were wearing loincloths. They were carrying the limp body of a woman over to one of the boats. It was Emmy. He strained to see if she showed any signs of life, but they were too far away.

He had to get to her. He started climbing down, and as he was doing so, he heard Runnels who had climbed even higher up above shout down to his men, telling them to get ready to ride. Then he saw Foil, his rifle unsheathed, jump on his mount and take off, followed by three of the other men.

Runnels saw this, too and started swearing. "Son-of-a-bitch-bastard's gonna stick his little knob right in it for us after all, ain't he?" By the time he and Runnels reached ground and pulled themselves onto their mounts, they heard shots from up ahead. Then more shots, followed by several clusters of shots from pistols, shotguns, and rifles. About one hundred yards away from the embarkation point, they found Foil and the others hiding behind the trees, shooting downstream at the blacks hiding behind the big boulders by the river. In the foreground, a few blacks and several mules lay motionless. One of Runnels's posse lay sprawled on the ground, still holding the reins of his mule, which was calmly chewing at a shrub.

The firefight dragged out well over an hour, and by the time the shooting stopped, more men on both sides had been wounded or killed. Neither of the two from Bocamalo's party who had been shot and fallen into the river from their boats had survived. The Derién blacks had melted away, taking their wounded men and surviving mules with them. In the aftermath, as Brett looked after the three wounded Isthmus Guards, he looked over at Foil crowing that his shots had killed at least two of the bandits, and then over at Runnels, who was silently looking downstream as his men began chopping up balsa logs to fashion rafts to carry them down the river. By the time they finished strapping the rafts together, it would be too dark to go very far. But they all knew it would be unwise to stay there because they knew that the Deriéni would return with more men and guns. Brett estimated they were at least four hours behind Bocamalo now as a result of the fiasco precipitated by Foil. He had been so close, again. He could see that Emmy was ill. She needed him, and that gave him some hope.

CHAPTER FORTY-FIVE

◇◇◇◇◇◇◇◇◇◇◇◇◇◇◇◇◇◇◇

JOJO

He saw himself flying for several moments, without the pleasure he felt when he dreamt of being a swallow that commands the air when it swoops. This flight was uncontrolled, and he remembered the dread he felt in the uncertainty of how it would end as he was thrown like a child's floppy toy into the air. As he was flying above it, he remembered how the twisted derailed car looked, its top popped off like the lid on one of the tin cans the whites used for their tobacco.

He had been thrown clear, but he was certain his left arm must be broken at the elbow and it also hurt to move his wrist and shoulder, left knee, and both ankles. Considering the mayhem of the train wreck, all of the injuries and suffering, he had been fortunate, he knew.

He did his best to help the injured survivors from the other cars extricate themselves from the wreckage, but when the railroad people arrived, they took over and pushed him aside. No one had bothered to help him, however, but he figured that it was because he was not one of them. So he fashioned a sling from the sprawled debris of luggage that lay by the side of the track. He couldn't find his own belongings or his knife. When he regained his wits, he searched, but Emmy, Jacob, and Sarah weren't there among the injured or dead.

A few hours later, in the noise and confusion of the aftermath, a locomotive pulling four flatcars with men, mules, and boats chugged past the wreckage, southward in the direction of the bridge on which they had stopped that morning. It was then he overheard people talking about a holdup and massacre. That's what had happened! Their car had been detached on the trestle! He had to get back there! When a second locomotive came up the tracks, he tried to get on board but was told by armed men to stay clear. So, in great pain, he followed on foot. It took almost five hours for him to walk what he estimated would ordinarily be an easy two-mile trek along a gradual grade of cleared road.

When he arrived, he found a melee of sober, officious men in linen suits, soldiers, and angry men in shirtsleeves, black and white, doing various tasks, clearing wreckage and moving remains. Many onlookers and natives stood outside the roped-off area surrounding the train cars. He passed men standing on the trestle hollering back and forth to other men in the river gully below. Jojo could see what appeared to be a wrapped body at the end of a rope; four men were pulling the body up from the deep gully. People he recalled seeing on the car where he had left Jacob were sitting in the shade and were being questioned by other people who were writing things down. When he approached the area off to the right of cars, a sentry pointed a shotgun at him and told him that he could not enter the site of the holdup. He tried explaining, but that did no good. So he sat down and waited for things to change.

After another hour, watching the change of guard, Jojo used the opportunity to approach the new man, who he noted, spoke English with a strong Irish accent. He mimicked the lilt and inflection in the man's speech and told him he had been a robbery victim and had to go back to finish his description of events to the official men and then retrieve his belongings. That worked. The man let him pass.

Jojo found the car where he had left Jacob with Emmy. Its windows were all cracked. He found Emmy's suitcases, lying open along the track. Her family's belongings and some of his own were strewn about, mixed in with that of all the other passengers. A few neatly folded expensive men's dress shirts lay on the car's steps next to a wealthy woman's long white gown. The gown had shiny gold and silver beads all over it. It had been carefully draped over one of the rails of the car by someone.

He saw no signs of Emmy or the children. He wandered down line and saw several men examining a line of bodies partially covered under oilskin tarps. He approached one of the men, the Italian fellow in the red shirt whom he had seen in the car in which he had left Jacob that morning. From him, he learned that he and his wife had hidden his children and Sarah and Jacob under the passenger car's wheels, but he believed they all had been taken by the robbers along with the man's wife and a woman who fit Emmy's description. The man was very distraught. But he seemed resolute and said he was volunteering to be part of the rescue posse.

Jojo knew it was hopeless for him to ask to be included in the posse. He could not turn his wrist or hand without feeling a sharp pain in his elbow. Despite his tracking skills and experience, as a stranger to the whites he would be considered useless and a hindrance. He was not angry about what he knew they would think. He would slow them down, and the grinding pain would distract him. He remembered the pain when he had broken a wrist bone and an ankle bone five years ago on a hunt when an angry moose cow charged him and pinned him against a tree. The huge beast, protecting her two calves, which Jojo had stumbled upon in the brush of a high hill on Vancouver Island, had kicked him repeatedly and knocked him out. He remembered the treatment his father insisted he follow as he limped home. "Wear the splints and walk slowly," his father had said. They had been fifty miles from their home and far away from any nearby river. That had been a painful journey, but his bone had mended. He would have to keep his elbow in its sling and let itself heal. In the waning light of the early evening, as the railroad men coupled a big locomotive from Panama City to the cars, Jojo found a quiet place to sit, observe, and think about things. He was very tired so he laid back onto the grass.

He awoke early in the morning during a very light rain and realized he had slept during the evening and all through the commotion and noise during the night. The rail cars had been taken away. The bodies by the flatcars were gone. The guards were gone. All of the passengers who had been sitting near him were gone as well. People—natives and others—rummaged about collecting the clothing and remnants of possessions that were left by the track. He walked over to the place where Emmy, Sarah, and Jacob's car had rested. Stooping low and looking at the tracks from a low angle, he tried to imagine the children hiding under the train car and wondered how they might have been discovered by the bandits. Stepping up to the tracks, he saw a marking in the dust that looked like the shoe print from the dress boots Emmy had purchased for Jacob in San Francisco. It was next to prints made by two other children's shoes. He found more on the other side of the track. Running tracks, three children's markings running into the woods, followed by the deep boot tracks of one man that stopped about forty feet short of the woods, then turned back toward the train.

The children hadn't been taken. They had escaped. He turned to tell someone about this, but no official men were there, just a mean-looking bunch of scavengers. Jojo turned back and limped into the woods, following the children's tracks.

CHAPTER FORTY-SIX

◇◇◇◇◇◇◇◇◇◇◇◇◇◇◇◇◇◇◇◇

BOCAMALO

Rafael stopped his piragua at a low bank landing, where the mates of two of his vaqueros were waiting. Although his chest and back were aching with every breath, he helped his men quickly unload the cargo boxes with their share of the gold and reposition the loads on the boats. Before shoving off, with the help of the mute Mestizo woman, he changed the dressings, which by now had soaked through with blood. She was holding back her grief, he saw. He put his arm around her and held her for a moment before getting into the boat where they had placed the American woman. As he pushed off from the bank, he watched the Mestizo woman in the boat behind, standing over the body of her slain husband, weeping as she poled the craft downstream. He couldn't understand what she was saying. The river's current increased, and they struggled to keep the boats from foundering.

Was this unanticipated, close pursuit the result of a betrayal by someone close? he wondered. The preparation for the train robbery had taken months, and he had kept almost all of it in his head—everything, the persons, the places, the timing of events, everything. He had contracted only with those who he dependably knew would keep quiet. He regretted that, in order to bring more men to the grand plan, he'd had to rely on Deacy and Pallino Haut. But he had given them little detail about his own plans, and he was certain they quickly would destroy themselves without any help. He would be long gone and out of the country before anyone conceivably could know where to start to look for him. He knew that his most trusted old cronies would keep quiet, even if they were caught. And even if they were tortured, they really knew very little about him. No, he felt safe, at least as it related to betrayal, he reassured himself.

His dressings were starting to soak through again.

He thought about the Mestizo woman and her wailing over her dead, earless husband. Rafael wondered whether it had made any difference to her that he himself had held her. In the past, he never would have tried to comfort anyone. He wondered why he had done that. Since the time when he was a small boy in Cartegena, he had been alone, and even when he had led his gangs in Colón, he had kept his distance from the men and women he had organized. It was him against the world. He speculated that, because he was considered a fair person and so very much more organized and clever than all the rest, his alliances had been very durable. But he had never really had a close bond with anyone. He thought the respect he had acquired, the following from those he had attracted to achieve the purposes he wanted, was simply a good bargain for all. When he called for their help, they came because it almost always led to a good return for them when they simply did what he asked them to do. He didn't need friendships. Never had needed them. But the grunted keening by the vaquero's Mestizo woman disturbed him. He wondered whether the dead were given comfort from any of that sorrow.

A few hours later, the river widened and slowed. In the waning light of the sun, dropping quickly over the hills to the west, Rafael could see the river's mouth pouring slowly into the ocean a half-mile away. He strained to see over the breakers near the mouth of the river. Then he saw three ships on the horizon and realized that the schooner that he was to have met in a few days would likely stand off to avoid Yankee search vessels. They had never done that in the past that he could recall. He cursed himself for not anticipating that.

After beaching the craft, he scanned the shore with his glass and saw that mules were tethered and waiting on the western bank of the river just as he had arranged. But there were only five instead of the six he had purchased. He turned and looked back in the direction of the rugged jungle lowland hills he had just traversed and estimated how long it would be before his pursuers caught up, if they succeeded in beating back the Cimaroon. He looked at the gold in his piragua boats. Then he looked at the young American woman. If he moved quickly, he and the mute woman could load his eight sealed cargo boxes, and she could depart with hers. But if he did so, he would have to leave the young American woman behind. She would die out here in her condition. There was unfinished business with her that he didn't understand yet. He realized he was lusting for her but would not entertain that in these circumstances. He looked upriver again.

He reached into the pants pocket where he had put the lucky deck of cards that had saved his life. When he played the game of *Solitario*, he had learned that it was always best to be consistent, to always take the same course with the draw and turn of the cards, always right to left, always taking from the largest column of face-down cards, so that the odds of uncovering a hidden key were better than if he simply took the closest one available—at least that was his method. When he did that, he almost always won and did so quickly. It was not luckiness. What did that tell him? It was best to be consistent and methodical in assessing the options and determining the odds of succeeding. Consistency.

But what did these particular cards tell him the last time he had used this deck, stacked in the way he had last played the game? Before he had been shot and almost killed. He looked at the cards. They were covered in blood, and all but a few had been pierced by the bullet, which must have slipped sideways off the ones on the bottom, the final ones, the survivors, he mused, and penetrated his chest. He turned over the first of the three cards at the very bottom of the deck that hadn't been pierced. It was a queen of spades. It was a sign, perhaps God, that he knew he could not ignore.

He looked upstream again. There was no time to play Patience now. He would have to find a place to safely hide the gold and then come back for it when the pursuit was over.

And he knew where to go to hide himself and take the young American woman.

CHAPTER FORTY-SEVEN

◇◇◇◇◇◇◇◇◇◇◇◇◇◇◇◇◇◇◇

EMMY AND BOCAMALO

There was no music, ever, in her dreams. And for that reason, as well as for other reasons, she knew she was dreaming again, because her dreams always came like this—color, but no music. Telling events, they were, with movement and that brought thoughts that she otherwise might not allow herself to entertain, little epiphanies she might not otherwise discover, when she was awake. So the dreams, they were useful, and for that reason, she always tried to remember them and think about what they said. This type of dream never came when she was feeling well, at least not that she could recollect. And she knew she was ill because she was boiling hot, so very hot. She tried to pull the covers off but couldn't find them.

She knew she was drifting down and wondered if she was drifting away. She could feel the water around her, and at times she heard weeping, in and out and in, over the water and the tapping and chirping and calls from the jungle as she passed through it. It was muffled, this weeping. A woman's sound that she, as another grieving woman, understood very well. And then she felt the swaying stop and the heat and glare of the sun waning and she was laying on moist sand, forming itself around her like a cool, soft pillow, all the way down to her heels. And then the shrill sounds of beach birds, they had to be beach birds, not the Northwest seagulls but more sharp and narrow. Piercing. Piping. But no music.

She heard coarse laughter, a man's deep rumble. She looked over and saw Rafael walking past her. He was grinning loudly, carrying two big, bulging, canvas bags with his left hand, his arm extended, and a large curved red stick in his right. He was laughing, and the bags were alive, moving with spirits that didn't want to be contained. He threw the canvas bags into the piragua then sat down, his back leaning against the beached boat, next to the mute woman who was carving a sharp stick. The woman turned her knife to Rafael. She cut his bloody dressings, then pushed the tip of her knife into the wound on his chest. Rafael grimaced and laughed out a shrill, wobbled song.

Emmy closed her eyes. She fell asleep again.

No music. She was with Jacob again, and he was so much like his father, she thought, as she watched him run his fingers across the soft, blond stubble of his chin's first-time beard. He walked from the room, and she started to follow, but the plump silk cushions of her mother's divan blocked her. When she tried to go around them, she found more cushions just like the divan's blocking, forcing her to go sideways several steps. She looked up again but found that Jacob had left the house and she was outside again.

She felt big arms lifting her into a saddle. She looked. They were the strong tattooed arms of a man. They wrapped around her waist, pulling her close. It wasn't Isaac or George Pickett or her father. She smelled the musk in the man's sweat. She felt the rise and fall of him breathing, her back to his firm, wet chest. She smelled his perfumed breath with each movement. It was tinted with mint and rosemary. It barely covered a base layer that hinted of decay.

A few feet away, riding alongside, she saw the mute woman, the one without a tongue who couldn't cluck like her. The woman was riding behind a man with no ears, and he was slumped forward. She was holding him up, and he was dead. Emmy understood. She reached out to the woman with a look that told her something, that she understood. Was she still dreaming?

They were riding away from the beach toward the forest again. The next time the woman turned Emmy saw that the woman's eyes were alive now. Ashes that had covered them had been washed away. And by her brief glance back, Emmy knew she had seen her heart and they shared a deep pain that went from way back in the darkness into this light. Sisters in black, carrying their dead.

Emmy didn't remember being laid down. She woke for a

short time and was in a dark, cool place. She felt cool water trickling on to her back, arms, and legs. She turned and saw the mute woman attending to her, humming quietly by her side, holding each arm and hand, stroking them one by one. Then her feet. Then her face. Touching her. Emmy no longer was chilled or hot, but she was very tired. She slept deeply.

When Emmy awoke, she was now alone in the cool, quiet, dark place, and as her eyes became accustomed to its darkness, she knew she was again in a cave, but smaller than the one she had been in before. She knew she was better. After laying there for a long time, she turned and pulled herself up, lightheaded, crawled to the opening, and found herself on a broad ledge overlooking a river that cut through a forest and disappeared into it. The evening wind was warm. Beyond the forest lay a broad expanse of water. The ocean? she wondered. She looked down. The ledge had to be a hundred feet up above the trees below. Somehow she felt secure while kneeling there, looking out.

The mute woman was sitting on one side of the ledge, humming a doleful repetitive chant to herself and rocking back and forth. Twenty feet below, off to her left, she saw Rafael sitting, watching the river. She looked down at her right hand and noticed an angular pattern faintly etched on her palm and fingers, encircling her forearm and moving all the way up to her shoulder. She looked at her left arm and saw the same pattern down to her wrist, thin, parallel lines ending in whorls. The same design was on both of her feet and moved up her legs into her thighs and over the front of her pelvis and up onto her belly and chest. It was similar to the pattern she had seen on the mute woman's arms and back, the ones that emerged when the mute woman's husband had painted her with the juice of a green fruit she had seen him crush to a pulp. She smelled the pungent odor of the poultice that Rafael had given her to apply a few days before. She wondered if this was a form of baptism. Or marking for ownership.

They made no fire that evening. Rafael stayed below on the ledge all night, watching the forest below.

In the morning, Emmy saw that the mute woman was not there. The tattoos the woman had etched on her arms had darkened to a red-umber brown. She wondered if she had patterns on her back and face. Because of the heat, she decided to stay in the cave until the shadows lengthened on the trees below. It did not rain.

As she lay there in the cool darkness, she thought again about Jacob and Sarah and what they had been through with her over the past year. Were they safe? They had been separated from her, and she had let them be separated from Jojo on the morning of the attack. He had been a surrogate father of sorts, in many ways, despite his young age, much more competent than their own father had been. She had trusted that but had taken his services and all the security it provided for granted, she realized. She had not appreciated the danger and should have, with all that she had seen. She had thought she might simply endure this horror and then, when it was over, get on with her life with them. But events had worsened. She had little hope for herself now. She might never see them again. Was it her love for her children that kept her going? If *they* had already perished, what was left for her?

Death was closer than ever before, she knew. In the quiet of the cave, she wondered about the right way she should live the ending to her life's story.

She wondered how it would end, if Rafael would kill her or, worse, attempt to destroy her soul. That made her again think about the slaves she had seen in Panama City in the station, waiting on the flatcars of the train. Most of them had given up and already must be mostly dead inside, she had surmised. If not, how much of themselves, of their spirits, had they been able to preserve and how had they managed it? What kept those people going? What small things had they preserved during *their* ordeals, something treasured they kept to sustain them through their days, day in and day out? If it weren't a treasured hope, was there an ember of something else—hatred or an abiding revulsion for their captors perhaps? Was such an ember visible enough that it would keep their captors wary? And if it were well suppressed and hidden, a tiny smoldering fragment of hatred, a bitter piece of coal, would it be enough to rekindle their spirits, if an opportunity for freedom arose? And would there be a residue from that fuel that forever tainted that spirit?

She fought the powerful urge to resort to that way of persevering because she knew those feelings could not be hidden successfully. And Emmy understood that those feelings, used as fuel for survival, ultimately burned through the walls of the vessels that contained them.

She wondered, could hatred and contempt for one's captors be replaced with something else, something that sustained oneself but did not corrupt or corrode? Thinking about the right ending for her soul, she wondered, should she—could she—surmount such feelings to find an understanding, some empathy for the devils themselves, that could be kept inside as an alternative means of survival? Forgiving them?

She closed her eyes, said a quiet prayer to Providence, and slept again.

That evening, Rafael moved up to the ledge where Emmy was sitting and sat down next to her. Emmy noticed that his dressing was fresh, and there was no blood staining it.

"Where did the mute woman go?" she asked.

"She left to be with her people," he said. "They are many miles away, in Nombre de Dios."

"What did she do with her man?" Emmy inquired.

"She will take him there to be burned on a pyre at his home. So the forest or river does not claim him," he said.

Emmy listened. His words made her spirit sink even lower. The Mestizo woman had been the only one whom she might have been able to reach, and now she was gone. She was here alone with Rafael. Emmy felt deeply sad about this, but even more so, after he told her about the mute woman's journey and her story.

As a little girl, Rafael said, thirty-five years before, the Mestizo woman had been branded by the Spanish just before they abandoned Nombre de Dios and their other colonies. One of the soldiers had cut off her tongue for daring to speak back to him. Afterwards, she had hidden in the Darién, where the Mestizo man, the one who had been his lead vaquero, had found her. Both of his ears had been cut off by the same Spanish man who had hurt her. The Spanish man had called himself and his friends "conquistadors."

"I then killed that Spanish man," Rafael said proudly and watched for Emmy's reaction. She gave none.

After a long pause, he asked, "What happened to your son?"

"He was taken by evil people. Evil people who did not know

they were evil. He suffered, as much I believe from his belief that he was abandoned, as he was from all that happened to him up there. I was able to find him again." As she said that, she thought about not ever being able to see her Jacob again. "I do not know what will happen to him now." Emmy told Rafael the story about what had happened up north. As sad as she felt about all of that, she heard herself speak without bitterness.

There was another long silence. Emmy looked down at her tattoos, then looked out over the forest. She thought about all of the events that had transpired over the past week, and what he had said about killing the Spanish man in Nombre de Dios.

"You have murdered many people, Rafael."

Rafael stared out over the jungle and was quiet for the rest of the night.

Rafael did not sleep that night. He had to watch out below for his pursuers, and his chest still ached. But at least the raw grating pain from the bullet was no longer present. He had given the bullet to the Mestizo's mute woman after she had removed it. It would be a lucky talisman for her and might protect her in her mournful journey to her home in Nombre de Dios.

He looked at the vista from the cave's ledge. It hadn't changed in all these years since he had left many years before. He had been surprised that he had not forgotten the way to the cave. But he was not surprised that the home he had taken for himself when he was a child had been reclaimed by the fruit bats and small animals; all of his cave's hoard, even the books he had stolen from the Greek man, eaten or destroyed by them. He would give their home back to them when he was certain that the gringos had given up their search.

He wondered about the American woman. He hadn't lain with her yet. He wondered what it would be like, her finally giving in. He lusted for it, to take her, and he had imagined the feeling and the sounds and the movements she would make, him teaching her about pleasures she couldn't possibly know about, her submitting and needing him. But he held back . . . because it had to be right if it were to happen. If it were to endure. He didn't want to steal her or take her by force. That had never been satisfying when he had done that, and he realized, he had never been satisfied by any of the many women he had taken. It always ended the wrong way. And then he had to bury them. It had to be right. And it wasn't right yet.

He thought about the options for truly winning someone like her—he was strong. People admired him. He knew he was a hero to many, although he knew his admirers were all simple fools, and now he had enough wealth to never ever work again. Or need to run. He could leave the isthmus and live sumptuously and safely with her wherever he wanted, privately and above judgment, anywhere in the entire world. He closed his eyes thinking about it . . . perhaps Greece, in a castle on an island like the ones that he had been told had beaches of golden sand, with a sun that rose every morning revealing the clear turquoise water lapping onto an ancient land of heroes he had read about; or perhaps North America in their California; or southern France for the wine and food, where Ava had once said she longed to visit. He never wanted to see Spain. He could buy the American woman things. Many things.

But the story of what the woman's son had endured moved him somehow, and then the words she had chosen—that he was a murderer—had disturbed him, pushed him back from what he wanted to say, to bring the American woman to his side. He knew he had killed men and women and, by bad timing, some unfortunate ones, old and young who were in the wrong place at the wrong time. But he had never really thought of himself as a coward, a *sociopata*, a "*dolofónos*" as he had heard the Greek man call some people. He was just doing his job, acting as an angel of God. Couldn't she understand that? Didn't anyone understand? At the heart of it all, he was a good man after all, someone to be admired. She just did not understand.

In the morning, he brought the American woman some salted pork broth and more fresh water. She had recovered from the shaking fever. That proved that she was strong. Many men and women had died with that form of illness, but she never had the black vomit or yellowing of her gills that usually preceded such deaths. He didn't know what illness had overcome her, but she was recovered. She could keep up with him.

He waited, but she did not speak all that morning. He could not wait any longer. He sat beside her again.

"I was never a priest," he confessed.

"I never met my father."

"My mother married a man, a drunkard, who killed her."

He saw that the woman listened. He had separated each sentence with a long pause, waiting for some response. She gave none. He showed her the pack of cards that had saved his life. He tried to tell her about his past, about Ava, about Cartegena and Colón—and all the pain—but as he did so he started to stutter badly while trying to find the words, and then, knowing that he was slipping back, failing, and sensing that he was not breaking through, that he would be judged harshly, he concluded, saying perfectly, "We survive by winning the wars we do not start, Señora."

The din of the forest below seemed to increase in its diversity, an array of beings calling to each other, challenging, beckoning with cries that pierced through the steady treble of the cicadas, which had been especially loud over the past few days. Then it quieted back down. He held his breath waiting for her response.

Measuring her words carefully, she said, "Wars, and all the hatred that comes with them, are started for reasons that always seem justified at the beginning, I believe. We survive, Señor, by walking away from the wars that we cannot win." Looking over the tattoos on her right arm, she continued, "And that is true for all, in all wars, because no one wins *any* war." She was quiet and firm in her response. She turned and looked, first in his eyes, then at his scarred, deformed upper lip, then back into his eyes.

"Self-hatred condemns even a good man's soul to desperation and despair, does it not? . . . to do desperate things. That one has suffered, no matter how horribly, does not have to condemn one to make others suffer. We are all flawed. When I remember that, it helps me forgive others for theirs." She looked down, then back at him.

"But you, Señor, will test me on that for a lifetime. "

After another long pause, she said, "You have much to put to rest, Rafael."

She turned away and said no more.

Her words and the kind, gentle firmness of the stare she had given him as she said those last words cut right into his chest and made him take in a short breath. As much as he thought he wanted her, needed her, Rafael sensed right then and there that he likely might not ever win her love. The old ache, one that had never really left, came alive again. It was a sadness that had always made him sick. After a long pause, he stood up and walked to the edge of the shelf on which they sat.

He sighed, looked at the jungle below, saw birds flying in some haste, flustered and moving in a random pattern that then coalesced into a wave that lilted over the tops of the trees far below. They were telling him something, and he wondered whether they were reacting to something traveling in the forest below or somehow had sensed and were reacting to the feelings he had from her words.

When the birds settled back down onto different trees, he smiled and was calm. The night before, when he had turned the small carpetbag upside down and shaken it to pour out the silk shirts to wrap new dressings around his chest, he had discovered why the Brazilian slaver had guarded the bag so carefully. It had a false bottom. And what he discovered told him he did not have to worry about retrieving the gold he had hidden.

But the old ache was there, for what she had said was conveyed with a compassionate sadness that, deep down, he knew could not be surmounted. And that was more important at this moment than any of the other riches he might have won.

CHAPTER FORTY-EIGHT

RUNNELS AND BRETT

He glassed two riders on one mule, leading a second animal carrying cargo, moving west in the distance. They looked like two of the gang they had shot at in the afternoon, the day before yesterday. One of the riders, a man, was slumped over. Dead or dying, likely, Runnels thought, and it wasn't the woman that the doc was seeking. Where was she? Where was Bocamalo?

It had taken them much longer than he had anticipated to get down the Cuango because the river had been obstructed by so many fallen trees, a few of which had been cut by Bocamalo.

They gave up trying to transport their mules by raft. To save time, Runnels had again decided to divide his posse in half with himself, Foil, and the young doc in the first group on a raft, and his three remaining Isthmus Guards driving all the mules, parallel to the river in the second. Within an hour, the riders had fallen behind out of sight, and he wasn't certain where they were now.

By the time they got to the mouth of the river and beached their float, the pair on the mule was no longer visible. But they had left an easy trail to follow back to the river. By the depth of the hoof marks, both mules were carrying heavy loads.

They followed their trail backwards to where it had emerged from the forest and then to a shallow river about eight feet wide that ran eastward toward the coast and joined as a downstream tributary to the Cuango. That's where he lost their trail. Neither Foil nor the doc were trackers, so it would be up to him and it was getting dark. He looked up at the sky. If it rained, they would lose their chance to find where the mule tracks entered the stream.

He walked up and down the small tributary for over two hours, and just as he was about to give up in the failing light, he saw it—several hundred yards from where the river entered the forest's canopy. It wasn't tracks that he saw; it was a cut in the rocks and clay. The moss on the rocks had been disturbed, sliced across. The sign was faint. He almost missed it after passing it three times because he had allowed himself to be irritated and had lost focus. No mule tracks. He followed the direction of the cut into the tall grass and found a few leaves bent backwards. It appeared that some tall leaves had been carefully broken off at the ground. Subtle. If there was something behind the wall of grass, it had been hidden skill-fully. He drew his pistol and carefully stepped in, pushing the reeds aside. Four feet past the wall of tall reed grass, he saw the marks of a boat's flat bottom. Five feet past those marks, he found two piraguas, bottoms up and covered with mud and grass so that they almost blended into the background and wouldn't have been visible to anyone climbing one of the tall trees along the riverbank. He looked around. No one. He tilted the boats and saw underneath each four boxes with markings: "FT." Foil Transport.

Brett couldn't sleep that night, not because of the movement on the river he heard, crocs likely, but because he sensed he was close to her again. Runnels had assigned Foil and him to alternate the watch and told them he intended to sleep soundly so that he would be fresh for the tracking at first light. They had to set out early because Runnels was afraid it would rain later in the morning.

What would he find when they finally caught up with them? He had no doubt that Runnels was a match for most opponents, but he didn't really know much about Bocamalo other than that he had been skillful at eluding capture. Why had he left the gold? He had hidden it well and in a way that would fool most searchers, but did he know he was being pursued by Runnels himself? Or was he simply a coward, leav-ing his spoils to distract his pursuers, to dissuade them from chasing him further?

He thought about Emmy again. If she had perished already,

would they ever find her body? If she was dying, why was this Bocamalo, if it was Bocamalo who was her captor, keeping her? If she was recovered, what would this Bocamalo do with her? Did she know help was on its way? If she didn't and had recovered—and had been with Bocamalo for long—would she resist or give in to the life of a captive, fall in love with her captor, the way he had seen it happen with a few of the women taken by the Comanche and Apache in Texas? It had disturbed him to see her limp body in the arms of the men they were pursuing. Somehow, the thought that she was desired by someone else made her all the more attractive to him, he realized.

He thought about how he must now look, with five days of beard growth and the stink of the jungle reeking from every pore. He rehearsed what he would say if and when they found Emmy so that he would not be clumsy as he had been when he had met her previously in San Francisco and on the train. Then he thought about how foolish a thought that was. She would be exhausted and half-crazy, as would be anyone so beset. His words and appearance would not matter. But he decided he would risk disrobing and cleaning himself in the morning, when he could see what might be lurking in the water.

In the morning, however, Brett was awakened by Runnels, carrying his long-barreled rifle slung over his back. He had found the tracks of mules leaving the stream moving up toward the cliffs about a mile and a half upriver from where he had found the boats. They left Foil, perched high above them in a Naked Indian tree with a clear north and south view of the stream below, to guard the boats. Runnels had told Brett that he had a good feeling they were about to find their man. Brett understood that meant he would soon see Emmy again. They left immediately, and he forgot about how he looked or what he would say. He would have a chance to fight for her head on.

CHAPTER FORTY-NINE

◇◇◇◇◇◇◇◇◇◇◇◇◇◇◇◇◇◇◇◇

FOIL

oil waited for over five hours without seeing any movement below, except for occasional pig-like animals with their young wandering down to the water's edge to drink. The animals always watched the stream for many minutes before stepping down onto the rocks, he noted. The adults likely had survived because of their caution, watching for predators. He stood up and peed off of his perch and estimated the distance of the trajectory of his stream. He was fifty-two years old and hadn't lost an inch.

The bungo boats below were well concealed, he had to admit, and more than once he had forgotten just where they were. It made him anxious, angry even, thinking about losing them. He had decided immediately when Runnels found them that these were really his own personal property. The eight cargo boxes contained just enough to cover his own personal potential losses—and then some, perhaps.

He wondered when Runnels and that Brett fellow would return, or when the Isthmus Guards they had left behind to bring the mules would find their way out of the Darién. He wondered whether any of them would return at all. Certainly the Isthmus Guards were capable chaps, but they were trekking through the Darién, trying to follow a river that had many twists and turns. And there were Cimaroons to contend with. They might not make it at all.

He knew Runnels was competent, wouldn't have hired him if he weren't, although he doubted any man deserved a reputation like the one that followed around the brassy, impudent fellow. But he was going up against someone who seemed unkillable. Foil had seen one of his companions take a shot at the man with a .54 caliber long rifle, knock him over, and watched him stand right back up and then wave defiantly at them! He saw the bullet hit the man right in the chest. It had to have been a killing shot! Was the man a ghost or a god? The more he thought about it, Runnels might not come back at all. That worried him. If he didn't return, then Bocamalo most certainly would. And if Runnels couldn't kill him, what were Foil's own chances? He played out the scene: He could try to be quiet and watch impotently as this ghost retrieved and left with the gold, HIS gold, or he could take a shot at the man's back while he was distracted, risking missing him or, worse, angering him by wounding him. He had heard that wounded animals, like bears and jaguars, were vicious and tore humans to bits.

He looked up at the break in the canopy, no rain clouds, then down at his pocket watch. Almost noon. It was hot. He had maybe six or seven hours left before it started to cool. He needed water.

By one o'clock, he couldn't stand it anymore. Despite what Runnels had insisted, he knew he was right. He had to take over, the way it should have been all along. He climbed down, slipping only once when the bark peeled off in his descent from the tall, loose-skinned madrona. At the bottom he cocked his pistol and moved to the stream. Remembering what he saw the pigs do, he watched the stream for several minutes, looking for anything that might hint of a croc or cat. He dropped his canteen into the running water and pulled it up when he felt it fill up. He watched again for several minutes and then finally stepped into and carefully forded the stream to the bank on the other side. He pushed his way into the grass and saw the boats. They weren't as big as he had thought they might be, easily moveable. He turned the first one over, then the second. He dragged them to the river's edge and tied their bow ropes to the reeds then, one by one, dragged the cargo boxes to the boats and placed them in the boats, carefully balancing them, leaving enough room so that he could sit in the bow of the first boat.

The stream led to the Cuango, which led to the ocean. It looked placid enough, and he had seen only a few breakers at its mouth. He was certain that by avoiding the breakers and moving west, close to shore, he could find someone at one of

the little coastal beach villages to get him and his boxes back
to a safe place, twenty miles away in Aspinwall. Someplace
safe and private.

CHAPTER FIFTY

◇◇◇◇◇◇◇◇◇◇◇◇◇◇◇◇◇◇

BOCAMALO

He returned to the cave in the morning and looked in. The American woman was still asleep. He watched her for a while. He moved closer and studied her face. The jagua fruit tattoos painted on her face, arms, and legs by the mute Mestizo woman had darkened even more, and he thought the American woman's face seemed even more beautiful now with them than when he had first seen her on the train. She had long eyelashes and high cheekbones that reminded him of Ava when he would watch her sleeping. He remembered climbing into Ava's bed, before he got older and she met the Greek man who kept Rafael out of her bedroom. Rafael would watch her breathing slowly, peacefully. Dreaming, like this one did when she slept. He remembered pushing the hair away from Ava's face so he could see her soft skin. It had been good to see her at rest. At peace.

During the night, he had moved down a deer trail to the river below to see who it was that was moving through the forest in their direction. He found three men hidden there, not far from where he had placed his boats. The one who was on guard had revealed his position in the darkness by lighting a cigar while the other two had slept. It was that twit, Foil! He shook his head at the man's stupidity.

The second man he had seen on the train. He didn't know who the other sleeping one was because his back was to him. He could have killed them there, but he didn't. He knew they were watching to see if he would come back for the gold. He didn't know how many more might be in the forest, or were on their way. If he killed these ones, it would make a mess that would be difficult to hide. It was better to let them wait for a few days. Maybe they would give up—just take the gold and go away. That would be the best thing, he thought. And they would be so perplexed and amazed at his cleverness.

Why was he laboring over this woman? He would have to decide what to do with her. He could see she was a tough being, tenacious inside of the softness of her body, bruised as it was. That was a texture he loved, he realized. He longed to bite into her essence and dwelled on coming back to it over and over again, reawakening the joy of discovering its fragrance and renewable durability. He longed to own it, wrap it up, and keep it safe; open it up in private and cherish it. He had tried that with other women he had taken and kept, but they never had lasted for very long.

But what good would it be if she kept herself from him? He still didn't even know her name. It made him angry, her statements, her judgment. But, unlike what he had done to others, ones who had been presumptuous enough to judge, he knew that would not be the right thing to do in her case. He didn't know why he felt that way.

Was it that she resembled Ava? Or was it that she had spoken the truth to him and he could not run away from it any more, the way he knew he had in the past when others had spoken similar things? The others whose bones he had buried in the forest, justifying his actions because he knew he was superior to those who dared to pronounce such judgments when they themselves were flawed.

Did he really need this woman? he asked himself. He had never really needed anyone else. It had always been him against the world. Was she worth it? With her, had he chanced upon one of those rare, uncommon hard stones, far more valuable than gold? Or was that notion something he was fabricating, a speculative portrait of her that he wished to keep for himself for reasons he did not yet understand? Was she a soul with imagined symmetries that were, in reality, immeasurable because she kept to herself and might not ever let him in? Was it that she had a son who reminded him of himself somehow? Damaged? What if what she had said to him were true—that he, Rafael, was not as composed as he thought, that he was the main victim of his own self-hatred? He laughed at himself for thinking that. Or did she possess some key that he needed to free himself? Was he fooling himself and acting the fool? Setting his own trap?

He thought about the cost of persisting with someone like

her, perhaps seducing her by wearing her down, taking away any hope for her until she realized that he was her *only* hope and then bring her to need him. Should he make what he knew would be a most painful effort to try to keep her in order to discern the truth about her and to teach her the truth about himself? Could he afford that expensive gamble? To let her see inside? If she continued to resist him, could he hold on to her long enough to turn her, to make it right? And what if, after taking that risk, it turned out that he was wrong about her, that she was not what he hoped she would be—or worse, what if his measurement and use of her ultimately dulled her edge and color, wore down her veneer? He had discarded others, he knew, for that very reason. That would be a waste, would it not? A waste of effort and of yet one more captive who, if left alone, might have been pleasing to a lesser man than he, with less discerning tastes than he. He hated wasting anything.

She stirred, then stretched her arm. She opened her eyes and saw him watching her. She had been dreaming again, he saw. He smiled grimly, knowing that he had never had a dream that he could remember. That, he realized, had separated him from Ava as well.

"There are men in the forest," he said. "One of them is a young soldier who spoke to you twice on the train. One is a well-known arrogant fool. I did not see who the third one was." He saw that her eyes were wide open now.

He handed her some soft plantains and mangos and kept his feelings inside. He watched her peel the sweet fruit. After a pause he said, "We will wait here to give them time to give up and clear out. They should have what they want. If they do not, I will have to cut them down."

CHAPTER FIFTY-ONE

◇◇◇◇◇◇◇◇◇◇◇◇◇◇◇◇◇◇

BRETT AND
RUNNELS

unnels saw movement on the north face of the
hill closest to the river. When he directed his
telescope to it, he saw it wasn't deer. It was Bocamalo and Emmy sitting on a ledge in front of what looked like
a cave, similar to others that dotted the cliffs overlooking the
Cuango's course. He studied them for quite a long time before
saying anything to Brett.

"Afraid she's turned, Doc." He saw the words strike Brett
hard. He didn't want to hear that, but that was exactly what
it looked like. Emmy sat calmly at the side of the man. Both

of them were wearing few clothes, he was in a loincloth, barechested. Emmy wasn't exactly naked, her breasts were covered and she appeared to be wearing the remains of bloomers, but both she and Bocamalo were covered with tattoos. It appeared that Emmy had them on her face as well. Runnels knew that the painted tattoos helped keep mosquitoes and flies away, but why would she have them on her belly?

Runnels knew what it would mean if it were true—if she had turned, if she had given in to her captor in order to survive. It would mean that he would need to take both of them down. This was worse than a simple rape, not that there was anything simple about that, he reflected, as if that weren't bad enough. From what young Brett had told him, this Emmy could survive that type of outrage as well as the vicious rumors that would start and would take a long time, maybe a lifetime, to outlive. But she wore tattoos and was unfettered. She was sitting by the side of an almost naked man. She was conversing with him almost as if he were her best friend! It was very possible that she was no longer a captive, but an accomplice. He'd have to take her down.

Runnels knew Brett would eventually understand, for he knew he had seen similar situations with women and children captives of the Comanche, as had he. He would know that the ones who hadn't given in to their captors immediately, the ones who hadn't been smart enough to quickly choose one warrior as a protector, were repeatedly raped by all the men and abused by all the women. They were then cast out, killed, or enslaved to the entire tribe or to any man who simply wanted the convenience of broken chattel and didn't mind that no prestige came with it.

"That's just what it looks like to me, Doc. Sorry."

From what he could see, she would never be able to be brought back intact. It was best to kill her, to spare her further pain and humiliation. The young man would get over it.

Brett looked through the glass and felt a stabbing pain in his chest as he thought about Runnels's observation. He certainly had seen co-opted captives defend their captors. He had seen it with both the Apache captives as well as the Comanches, and on some of the farms and plantations at home in Virginia as well. The subservience of a slave. Loyalty to coercive power. Co-opted, confused "love." He thought about the crude, transient nature of power achieved by bullies like this Bocamalo monster. The power was a derived currency, dependent on the ongoing presence of force, whether it be brutal physical torture, the promise of absence from it, or something indirect and seductive, like the promise of reward or pleasure. The masters of manipulation, he knew, were adept at working on the soul and heart of their captives. And he knew that if the captivity went on for too long, the captives never could be brought back. They would be diminished, wouldn't accept the norms of society, any civil form of it, and society would never accept them back.

But something didn't make sense. It was what he had perceived about Emmy when he had met her, oh so long ago, it seemed, in San Francisco. She was fierce and smart. She was more than a survivor. Even without hope, he had a sense that she would quickly learn to be in control of any situation and ultimately do the right thing. And she had planted signs that led them to her, hadn't she? Somehow, she would be in control. Wouldn't she? And if she had been broken, even if she were damaged, he knew there would be enough left within her—and he had enough skill—that he could take care of her, bring her back. Bring her back.

CHAPTER FIFTY-TWO

◇◇◇◇◇◇◇◇◇◇◇◇◇◇◇◇◇◇◇◇

EMMY

She had a vague recollection of the gunfight that had occurred a few days before, when she had been ill and delirious. When Rafael told her about the men in the forest below, she was able to put together why the mute woman's husband had died and Rafael was bleeding from a wound on his chest. She found some hope for the first time since she had been taken—a relief and a new worry.

Rafael had promised that he would kill the pursuers if they didn't leave. But Emmy knew they wouldn't leave because she knew it could only be Lieutenant Brett that Rafael had described. She had seen it when she met him—the young man was a romantic, like the way Captain George Pickett had been with her up on the beach on San Juan Island, like her husband Isaac had been once upon a time before he had lost his hope and purpose. Before he had been murdered. Brett had traipsed all across the Darién in a posse, looking for her; he would have no other reason to join the posse. Gallant, she thought. Foolhardy, she realized, because he wouldn't care about the gold, and thus wouldn't give up if they found it. He wouldn't give up until he found her, got himself killed, or got both of them killed. Driven entirely by a notion he had formed about her from a brief encounter in San Francisco, he was walking into a competition with an experienced murderer, a man who was driven by other needs that she didn't understand just yet. This was a young man's infatuation versus a seasoned, tortured man's desperation at a minimum. Not good odds for the young or naive.

She came out onto the ledge and saw that Rafael had departed again. She looked out at the river winding itself into the forest below and strained to see if anyone was on it, but she could not make out much. The birds that she had seen flying in patterns the day before, however, were moving randomly above the trees. Could she be seen? She moved back into the cave and found the bloody silk dressings that Rafael had worn the day before and crawled back out to the ledge, stood up, and began waving them above her head. She looked out for any flash or movement that might indicate that she had been seen. Could she be seen? Could she be seen? If Rafael happened to come back, he would kill her, she knew, but at least she wouldn't be kept. She knew if she were kept, it would eventually lead to torture, and that would lead to a painful death. Because she would never give in to this monster.

Could she be seen? Nothing from below. After a half-hour, her arms were aching, and she couldn't signal any longer, so she scrambled up the side of the cave's entrance to a small bent scrub brush of a tree that held tenuously to the side of the hill. She tied the bloody tatters of the silk shirt to the scrub's sturdiest branch and felt the afternoon's light breeze pick the bloody flag up and flap it. If anyone was looking up . . . she held her breath and moved back down to the cave. And then she wondered where Rafael was.

If she tried to escape to find the river, to warn Brett and the others, she almost certainly would get lost in the jungle going down if she didn't find a path. And she didn't know which direction to travel, even if she did find the river.

But it was time to run.

CHAPTER FIFTY-THREE

◇◇◇◇◇◇◇◇◇◇◇◇◇◇◇◇◇◇◇◇◇

BRETT

They had watched the pair talking for over an hour. Then they saw Bocamalo stand up and leave Emmy sitting by herself on the ledge.

Over the next hour, Brett and Runnels moved up the river, closer to the cliff, trying to keep the cave in view, but a dense foliage on the umbrella of trees lining the river kept it out of sight for almost forty-five minutes until they found another clearing from which to observe.

They marked the direction again and crossed back over the river to the high bank and started climbing straight up through the scrub brush to find a better vantage point. Runnels told him that there had to be a pathway up there, or at least some place where they could observe the area around the cave's mouth without exposing themselves to discovery, a spot from which to take a careful, unobstructed shot if the opportunity presented itself. And they had to get closer, Runnels said, because the range of his Sharps, even with his specially fitted forty-six-inch barrel, was less than a thousand yards. To make a certain kill, he would need to be much closer, within half that distance if possible, because it would be at an uphill target shooting into a side wind. Runnels said that even with the wind and cicadas masking the sounds, he would get only one or two shots for range—the sound would carry enough to alert his target—and even a mild breeze could push the bullet sideways unpredictably. He might miss his target by several yards. When he took the real shot, it had to be on the mark. So they kept moving up the hill to get closer.

They found their perch less than six hundred yards from the peak on the next hill, roughly at the same elevation. It wasn't a perfect spot, but they could see the cave's entrance clearly enough. Runnels said he could make the adjustments.

Brett watched Runnels lie down on his belly behind a large boulder and put cotton plugs in his ears. Runnels unsheathed the rifle then opened his side satchel and unwrapped a long telescope, which he mounted onto the barrel of the Sharps. He then stared through the scope for five minutes, twisting dials and fussing with the elevation.

Brett hoped they hadn't been spotted. He moved up to look for a higher perch to spot for Runnels. He didn't know that Runnels intended to take down Emmy as well.

CHAPTER FIFTY-FOUR

◇◇◇◇◇◇◇◇◇◇◇◇◇◇◇◇◇◇◇◇◇

BOCAMALO

Rafael moved swiftly down to the river on the paths he remembered from his childhood. He carefully skirted the edge of the stream, keeping his head and shoulders low so that he couldn't be seen by anyone on the other side or from the river below. He knew how to move without noise, using the pampas grass as a screen. He was a jaguar, after all.

When he reached the place from which he had observed the trio the night before, he was relieved to see that they were no longer there and no others from the posse had arrived. He could see that the two piraguas had been pushed out onto the stream, which meant that the gold was gone. However, when he moved to the place where he had hidden the boats, he saw that only one person's tracks marked the bank. He picked up a cigar stub. Foil had taken the boats and the gold, just as he had hoped, but the tracks of the two other men led away from the hiding place in the opposite direction toward the cliffs and his hideaway—and the young American woman he had hidden there. Rafael moved back in that direction. He could recover the piraguas in another way; he knew the tides and bet that it wouldn't be difficult to find the fool.

He followed the tracks of the two men heading for the cliffs. If they were trackers, they would find the cave. He unsheathed his knife and started running now. He had to get to the cave before they did.

Three-quarters up the trail, he saw movement, someone coming right toward him, pushing through the bushes. He lay down on ground and moved to the far edge of a break in the scrub and waited. He cocked his rifle and held his breath. He could take both of the men down in seconds.

And then he saw it was the American woman trying to get through the hillside scrub to the river. She was running away from him. He moved quickly and jumped her, pushing her to the ground. He held her by the hair, put his hand over her mouth to keep her quiet, and pulled her head back and looked into her eyes. She was calm and resolute. There was no hatred in her. It was a kind, sad, unassailable pity he read in the look she gave him. The old ache cut into him.

He pulled her up by the hair, twisted her arm behind her back, and began moving up back to the cave. He had something to retrieve there, and then he would get them to the mules he had hidden on the other side of the hill.

CHAPTER FIFTY-FIVE

◇◇◇◇◇◇◇◇◇◇◇◇◇◇◇◇◇◇◇◇◇◇

RUNNELS

R unnels saw movement and then spotted the pair of them for a brief moment. They were walking together, moving back up toward the cave. The foliage prevented a clean shot, and within less than ten seconds, his view was obscured by the trees as they progressed. He estimated that it would take them another five minutes before they reached the ledge and the mouth of the cave, enough time to fire two shots to establish his range. The noise of the cicadas would mask some of the sound, and the wind blowing in his direction would reduce the noise as well. It would be impossible for them to know from which direction the report was coming. They would think that they were secure for a moment. And then they would be dead.

When Runnels had achieved a steady hold, with the barrel cushioned between his hand and the fork of a thick tree trunk, he brought the vertical and horizontal lines of his telescope to line up with the center of a rock on the ledge. He estimated the target was six hundred yards away. He knew from thousands of practice shots over the years that the mass of the .52 caliber bullet would make it drop between fourteen and sixteen feet at that range, so he made his adjustments to give him enough elevation on the shot to compensate. At that distance, the bullet's velocity would drop as well, so he would have to aim for a mid-body shot. He took several deep breaths rapidly to give himself enough air that he wouldn't have to breath in and out as deeply. He saw that the scrub grass near the rock was bending to the right about ten degrees from twelve o'clock on the vertical—so he figured the wind was moving at about five miles per hour. He moved his vertical so that it lined up one foot to the left from the center of the rock. He squeezed the trigger, careful to not jerk the pull.

He didn't hear the boom of the discharge. He never did. But he felt the jolt of the recoil as the Sharps exploded and threw its projectile forward. He kept his eye on the target rock. The dust on the ledge blew up four feet short of the boulder but centered exactly. He had estimated the distance and the wind's velocity perfectly. He smiled because he wouldn't need a second bracket shot for distance. He simply had to adjust slightly the vertical and wait for the two of them to appear. If he was lucky, he could take them both down, "retributional" and mercy killings with one shot, if they were lined up right. Holding each other. Desperate lovers. He let out his breath and waited.

CHAPTER FIFTY-SIX

BRETT

He had moved up to spot for Runnels and scout for movement from a different vantage. Brett settled in and extended his brass telescope. Even though now he could not see the cave or the ledge very well, he had a good view of the hill leading up to it. Off to the side on the left, he saw three mules tethered. Two were saddled. As he moved his scope upwards, he saw it, just below the peak of the easternmost hill overlooking the river, a long white flag flapping in his direction in the western wind blowing across the hilltops. It was a signal from Emmy. Unmistakable.

It was then that Brett saw Bocamalo with Emmy in tow. She didn't appear to be moving cooperatively. He was taking her away. Then he heard a loud boom from below. Runnels was gauging his distance and elevation. He saw them stop, and he knew that the report had alerted Bocamalo, so he put down his scope to be certain that no reflection from his glass gave away his position. He watched without his scope until he saw them start moving again and resume their ascent.

He had to get down to Runnels to let him know about the flag and the mules. He needed to take down Bocamalo when he got up to the cave, to stop him from escaping with Emmy.

He couldn't lose her again.

CHAPTER FIFTY-SEVEN

◇◇◇◇◇◇◇◇◇◇◇◇◇◇◇◇◇◇◇

BOCAMALO

They were clever, he realized, and they were after more than the gold. Although he didn't know where they were, he had heard the rifle shot. They were closing in, he knew, and they either wanted to kill him, rescue the woman, or accomplish both. Why was the young soldier pursuing them? Was it possible that he had more than a happenstance acquaintance with the woman? Rafael didn't know what to do about her. She was running away from him, after all. He still wanted her, but now he didn't know whether to take her or to kill her. She was afraid of him and was running. What should he do? If he killed her, cut her throat, would that end the chase or, instead, increase their resolve to find him and lynch him? It would take just a few minutes to gather his weapons and the carpetbag and get to the mules. He knew where the next hiding place would be. He had taken other women there, preserved the artifacts of his encounters with them, the detailed story of each of those disappointments listed in a diary he hadn't visited for a few years—all locked away where no one would ever find them. He just needed to get to his mules and get out of there.

But should he keep this one or kill her? Add her to his list or let her go?

When they reached the ledge over the cave entrance, he ducked down and pulled her in. He picked up his rifle and the carpetbag, then grabbed her face and looked into her eyes. He felt the ache in his gut as he stared into her.

"Tell me your name," he said.

"It is Emily Evers," she replied.

"What is your son's name?" he asked.

"Jacob. It is Jacob," she said.

As he dragged her out of the cave and stood on the ledge, he pulled a blob of gold, a melted locket on a chain from the carpetbag and put it into her hand. He held his knife in his other hand.

"I have let you get into my head and my heart," he said. "Can you understand that? You must understand that!" Then he put the knife to her neck, wrapped his other arm around her waist, and pulled her to him, squeezing her tightly and kissed her on the mouth, searching for her response.

Runnels's heavy bullet passed through both of them, throwing them off the ledge and down into the brush below.

CHAPTER FIFTY-EIGHT

◇◇◇◇◇◇◇◇◇◇◇◇◇◇◇◇◇◇◇◇◇

RUNNELS AND BRETT

They found Emmy unconscious and lying on a bank of loose rocks and gravel. She had hit her head. The bullet had passed through her upper right shoulder but hadn't broken any bones. An inch lower or a few inches to the left would have burst her lungs or heart, Brett had told him. She might have some damage to the nerves in her arm, but Brett couldn't be certain until he could test her when she wakened. If she did. The doc said he was worried about blood on her brain, but he had only done what he called a "trephination surgery"—boring a hole in the skull to release the blood off the brain, one time before and it didn't work, so he was going to take a chance and just watch and wait.

Runnels found a lot of blood on the ledge and a spent, almost intact piece of lead off to the right of the cave's entrance. The projectile was flattened slightly but had no bone or gristle in its ridges. All three of the mules were gone. The mule tracks and blood led down to the river below, but he couldn't find any exit marks so he assumed Bocamalo had traveled all the way down the river that led out to the Cuango. Runnels couldn't see how Bocamalo or anyone else would have been able to survive a wound like that. If he fell off his mount and into the river, unless they found him within a day, his body would likely never be found.

They were stunned when they saw that the boats and the gold cargo boxes were gone. No marks indicated that anyone other than Foil had pulled them out. He would turn up soon enough, Runnels said.

"Ain't my business, anyway," he said. "Hired to get Bocamalo. Done that."

Brett spent the next seven days with Emmy, helping shuttle her on a pallet westward along the beach and forest past San Isbel and Nombre de Dios. He was relieved that his decision to wait and observe rather than intervene with a makeshift surgical procedure had been right. Four days later, by the time they arrived in Portobelo, Emmy was fully awake and recovering. Her arm was numb all along the shoulder into her elbow, but she could move it. The juice tattoos all over her body had darkened but then had started to fade by the time they reached the hospital that had been built for the Americans in Aspinwall-Colón. The first thing Emmy asked when she came awake was about Jacob, Sarah, and Jojo. But he had no answer.

He stayed by her side night and day, resting only for brief naps, except for the one day when he left to avoid arrest by US Army marshals for alleged desertion. During his vigil, he heard Emmy crying out several times. She had repeated the same thing on the first two nights—something to do with a curse on her son.

Even when she had been comatose, even when she was sleeping, she was beautiful, Brett thought. His time with her had confirmed all that he believed about her. He knew he was in love with her.

When they found her, she had had a melted gold locket and chain clutched in her hand. He knew it must have been important to her, so he put that into her pocket while she slept.

CHAPTER FIFTY-NINE

◇◇◇◇◇◇◇◇◇◇◇◇◇◇◇◇◇◇◇◇◇

FOIL

It seemed easy enough. He had been right about the breakers at the mouth of the Cuango. They were small, and the receding tide pulled both of the boats past them easily. The drift was moving westward, and he had to pole-push very little to steer his boats, tethered together, in that direction. Mostly, it was the current that he knew he had to watch so that he could keep the boats close enough to shore to find placement of his long pole on the coral reef below.

The ocean breeze was cooling, wafting away the stink of the jungle, replacing it with the salty, fresh evaporation from the sea spray. He could see a village in the distance. It was small, but he knew from what Runnels had told him that larger villages and towns were not far. It wouldn't be long.

Foil looked over his craft and their cargo. He had done it again. Such an accomplished man. Based on his calculations, the content of his cargo boxes was at least worth three hundred thousand or more. He would even make a profit on this. The insurance retainer he had purchased would cover some of the losses of the others, and he figured he was also due some of that as well, given the difficult task he had undertaken to track down the thieves. He had decided he needn't disclose to anyone that he had recovered these cargo boxes. He expected he should be able to buy off Runnels and the doctor, if necessary, if either of them survived. And nine of the miners had succumbed as a result of their own rash stupidity, so there likely wouldn't be claims coming any time soon for their shares anyway. If there were, he knew of a hundred reasons for denying, delaying, and confusing the petitioners for recompense. That was how insurance worked, wasn't it? He smiled. He had a fat-bottomed, accommodating little woman waiting for him. She had many tricks, and he knew just what he would do first thing when he got back. He dwelled on that as he pushed the long pole through the water onto the blue and black reef below.

After an hour on the coast, he realized that his boats were moving well enough in the current without his attention, so he sat down to rest and looked at his boxes. Three were intact, but he noticed that the two at the front of the boat were different. He was curious. Holding his pole for balance, he moved carefully up to the front of the boat and examined the boxes. He saw that although they were bolted, their seals were cracked in the middle and their padlocks were broken. The boxes had been heavy like the rest—had the gold been replaced by rocks? He knew that trick. He knelt down, removed the padlock on the closest box, unbolted the latch, and lifted the lid.

The snake that bit into his right arm above the elbow was as thick as his forearm, and its fangs were so long and it had bitten so deeply that it took him almost a half-minute to dislodge it. When he threw it into the water, one of its fangs broke off in his arm. While he was fighting the big snake wrapped around his arm, he saw a second one slip out of the cargo box and then coil itself by the pole he had dropped. Both of the vipers had gray, brown, and black triangles on their backs— the *Fer de Lance*—the ones Runnels had told him to be wary of when they slept or walked near rotten logs. Aggressive, deadly snakes. After hearing that, he had always slept with a horsehair lariat circled around him, which he had been told by one of the vaqueros would keep out the vipers. He looked at the broken off fang embedded deeply under the skin in the middle of the blue sailing vessel tattooed on his bicep. The swelling distorted the ship's outline. Its masts were leaning forward, and the puncture lifted the image as if a torpedo had blown its way into the stern.

He felt dizzy so he moved back to the other side of the boat. Where was the other snake? He looked to see where the village was. It was smaller, and he realized he was drifting away from the shore in the current. No ships in sight. He was drifting away. He couldn't swim. He felt nauseated, had a metallic taste in his mouth, and his tongue was numb. He threw up over the edge of the boat. It just wasn't fair.

CHAPTER SIXTY

◇◇◇◇◇◇◇◇◇◇◇◇◇◇◇◇◇◇◇◇◇◇

JOJO

Their trail had not been difficult to follow. The children had been running so they had broken branches and bent the grass. Despite the pain in both ankles, Jojo took only a half-hour to find the place where they had stopped to hide and rest. Moving in a widening circle around that spot, he picked up the next part of their flight. Their markings were joined by that of two others, barefoot, small. Their trail moved almost entirely downhill, through a muddy ravine, over a fallen moss-covered log that crossed over a small stream. It dropped through a well-worn path under a tall waterfall and down to the six-foot-wide stream below. Their trail then moved downstream northwest along the water's edge where it joined a large river. He could see the Puente Espiritu bridge in the distance. One hour later, he found the Embera village.

Jojo kept himself hidden as best he could, lying in the crook of a smooth-barked tree, watching the thatched huts set on stilts by the water. From his hiding place, he could see into a large hut with no walls that was at least three times as wide as the ones that surrounded it. To keep hidden, he had covered his shirt with broad palm leaves, stuffing them into his belt and over his shoulders, and smeared river mud on his face and hands. The day before, he had shed the stiff clothing he had worn on the train, trading them for some cloth breeches and a loosely fitting linen shirt he had found in the debris strewn around the train cars. He had thrown away his shoes and tossed the silly derby hat Mrs. Evers had insisted he wear for the trip off the bridge when he had crossed it. He had expected it to sail a bit like a swallow, but it had dropped like a dead crow.

He watched the village for half of the day and into the night, searching for Sarah, Jacob, and the boy he had seen on the train, but saw nothing and after darkness the village was quiet. He wasn't afraid of the night or the new sounds of this forest, although he wondered whether there were grizzly or mountain lions. He had seen snakes, vipers, but they were slower than the rattlers at home and he knew how to spot them and avoid them. And he was fairly comfortable. He just didn't like the insects and the heat.

Early the next morning, he saw movement. A group of men, all of them naked, arrived in two long boats that were like the dugouts his people used in the Northwest, except they seemed much lighter and did not have any ornamentation on them.

The men were very short and had fat tub bellies and thin legs, just like the old ones from the tribes he knew. All of them wore tattoos and paint on their faces, arms and bellies in patterns that were more ornate than the markings he knew from the coastal and inland tribes of Vancouver. They moved to the big hut, sat down, and started talking with men who came out of some of the smaller huts. He was too far away to hear their talking very well, and he could not recognize any of the words they used. Their discussion was loud at times, as if they were arguing over something important, but eventually, they quieted down. Then all the men began clapping their hands on their knees. Jojo recognized that pattern from when he had observed the arguments of the elders of the tribes with which he had grown up in the Northwest. It seemed as if they had arrived at some common agreement.

After sharing some food and drink, one of the younger men from the village left and went to the third hut, returning a few minutes later with a woman. She held a young white infant at her breast. The young man left again and returned with two more women who were leading three children: Jacob, Sarah, and the other boy. They wore loincloths but nothing else and were covered in tattoos. Two of the oldest men started talking loudly, and then all the men began clapping their hands on their thighs. Two women brought mangos, plantains, and shells filled with some kind of drink to the children. All three of the children ate and drank. Then two young men with spears, the woman with the white baby at her breast, and three of the men who had arrived in the long dugout stood up and took Sarah, Jacob, and the other boy by the hand and led them out and down a path away from the village. They passed closely enough to where Jojo hid that he could see the children's faces. He could tell they were frightened, and Jacob was hugging close to his sister. He let them pass and waited until the men in the large hut started talking and laughing again.

Jojo slipped from the tree and moved into the woods on a course parallel to the path taken by the group with the children. A dog started barking so he kept low and moved as quickly as he could, his swollen ankles aching with every step. He wasn't keeping up with them. He wondered where they were being led. Had the children been sold? Would these people simply abandon them in the forest as he had seen some clans do with diseased members? Were these people cannibals, as he had been told?

He found himself back down on the river and looked downstream, where the entire group was getting into a long dugout at the water's edge. They shoved off in the direction of the Puente Espiritu. He was too far away, and even if had been close enough to intervene, he would have been of no use in a fight with his arm broken as it was. There was no craft close enough for him to commandeer and follow, and with his arm immobilized in a makeshift splint, he knew he could not navigate one in any case. He was helpless. He hollered out after them, maybe he could find a way to negotiate with them, but they were too far away to hear him.

They were out of sight in less than five minutes.

The dog barking was getting closer.

PART FOUR

◇◇◇◇◇◇◇◇◇◇◇◇◇◇◇◇◇◇◇

IN ROME, IN BOSTON, IN NOMBRE DE DIOS

Nations, states, and towns come and go; cities and cultures rise and fall invariably and inevitably for curious reasons, but none so strange or understandable as that of the revolution. Cutting through the Gordian knots that bind cultures to encrusted protocol, undermining arrogant notions of enduring control and permanency, rejecting the tired reds scrubbed from rusted machines, adorning itself instead with the disturbing crimsons lifted from courtyard walls, revolution—always the fierce lurker—is both purposeful and impatient.

The Papal States in 1860, directed from Rome by the Vatican, still bisected the Italian peninsula and helped divide its people as it had for over eleven hundred years. By the mid-nineteenth century, however, recurrent domestic revolt, political compromises, and repeated incursions by foreign powers substantially diminished the broad expanse of that domain. The Vatican's strategists, as well as the Bourbon aristocratic and absentee landholders of Sicily and southern Italy, had great interest in seeing inspirational troublemakers like Giuseppe Garibaldi distracted from their revolutionary activities and dispatched, one way or another. By the end of 1860, as the Western world watched, the Vatican found itself besieged and in disarray because of the successful activities of Garibaldi in southern Italy and the "Risorgimento" movement.

Boston in 1860, like many mid-nineteenth-century cities of the northern states, was the home of many ardent proponents of sweeping liberal upheaval in the young American nation, including aggressive reforms that might hasten universal emancipation. After Abraham Lincoln's partisan election in November of that year, the fervor for dramatic action increased, manifested by rallies and marches by abolitionists. Boston lost many sons in the upcoming war that its liberal citizens so righteously helped provoke.

Nombre de Dios in 1960 was a forgotten town. Its busy port once sheltered ships and protected the imports and exports of Spain's colonial empire, but the Spanish abandoned it to the "Mestizos" early in 1625 in favor of the natural protection and more easily fortified harbors of Portobelo and Colón. In that year, the colonial governor also ordered destruction of the road connecting Nombre de Dios to the Camino Real, so that British and French privateers could not use it in the future as a back-door route to attack the Spanish gold trains. The Spanish further reduced their risk from English piracy by diversifying the transport of their gold from other cities like Veracruz and Cartegena. When widespread revolution expelled the Spanish from their Central and South American colonies two hundred years later in 1821, the defeated colonists left towns like Nombre de Dios in ruins and without infrastructure to support the remaining communities. The town's economy, so dependent on slave labor, devolved into dilapidation. Its impoverished population survived in spirit by syncretic ceremony and superstition.

CHAPTER SIXTY-ONE

◇◇◇◇◇◇◇◇◇◇◇◇◇◇◇◇◇◇◇◇

GATTOPARDI

He was conducted to a room a few steps away from the *Segnatura*, the most famous study in Rome, and as he passed it, he was able to glimpse the frescos inside. The solemnity with which this session was conducted, hosted in such lavish surroundings, reminded him of his importance, as he knew was his due.

The interview lasted several hours. It was thorough, and both the monsignor and the two other men assigned to this case took several pages of notes. Although they were disappointed that he had no documents to verify his testimonial, which was discursive and disjointed at times, what he said about his covert mission in South America was corroborated by the accounts of others as well as by the letters he had previously sent off from Brazil, Ecuador, Paraguay, and Chile.

During a break in the session when his interviewers excused themselves for a few hours, he reflected on the events and wondered whether he should be happy that he was still alive and now back in Rome in the Vatican itself, or should be grieving over the loss of so much.

Sitting in the room alone, looking out the window at the manicured topiaries in the garden below, Gattopardi realized that he must have appeared to them to be a broken man. He had regained only a few of the many kilos he had lost during his escape from the bandits who had robbed the train in Panama. Despite his purchase of new clothing, he was emaciated and he realized that his handsome figure was now gone. His skin was hanging, his cheeks sunken and tinged with yellow. Even his shoes felt too large. The concoctions that had been administered to him for the intestinal worms seemed to have only made things worse. He had tried to convey to the interviewers what his ordeal had been like, but they seemed disinterested and kept bringing him back to discuss his diplomatic interactions that had preceded the terrible events. Didn't they understand that the outrage he had survived, the ordeal itself, was germane to the very mission he was sent on? They needed to understand. He was an honest man, he told himself.

In Panama, he had been found almost two weeks after he had been last seen and had been presumed lost. When the three bounty hunters discovered him, he was starving, his clothing shred to rags. He babbled nonsense in Italian and Spanish and was covered with dried feces from howler monkeys that had followed him and then attacked him on the day of his escape from Bocamalo. He was still faithfully carrying the tattered remains of a teal-blue portfolio. But it was empty. When the mercenaries forced him to bathe, half-inch red, pointing boils under his skin started moving again, painfully, in several places. In Las Cruces, the barber who cut down on them found large brown scaly worms, the larvae of botflies, the barber said. Emilio knew he had been fortunate that the Dominican priest in Las Cruces was Italian. The priest told him no one had been looking for him.

When his interviewers returned, he started the conversation by imploring them to listen to what he had heard from God Himself in the jungle. The Darién was there to test man, He had said. It will abide briefly to the incursions of the arrogant, but it will prevail as a testimony to its fertile power. Mankind must concede, leave its conceits behind, for such vanities—and he pointed to the paintings on the walls and the ceiling, the tapestries, and rich marble beneath their feet—are ephemeral and will not endure. God had told him that his ordeal was a warning and a punishment for his co-opted, duplicitous behavior and that he should never have agreed to stand in the way of a just transformation of human society.

After his long, rambling discourse, there was silence, a long pause.

The monsignor leading the interview had listened carefully, and the other two men had stopped writing. They looked at each other, nodded, closed their journals, then thanked Emilio for his time and service. They told him he would be called upon again for further discussion. But they did not specify

when. He was conducted down to the piazza outside the basil-
ica. It was quiet and deserted in the hot sun of the afternoon.

CHAPTER SIXTY-TWO

◇◇◇◇◇◇◇◇◇◇◇◇◇◇◇◇◇◇◇◇◇◇

EMMY

From the window in her bedroom, she was able to look out onto the south end of the Boston Commons, but with the trees now barren in the coldest part of an exceptionally cold winter, she could see the cemetery off to the right as well. It was covered by yet another heavy snow, and she observed that no funerals had been conducted for over a week. It was too cold, and the ground was frozen likely. No visitors had crossed Boylston over to the graveyard either during that time. She wondered whether the dead really cared. Perhaps they did not, as long as they had such a thick white blanket to cover them. Neither Sarah nor Jacob seemed concerned that they were unable to take walks and had been kept inside the small brownstone for the better part of a week. They hadn't seen snow for over a year, and the cold, such a dramatic contrast to the isthmus' swelter, helped suppress the memories from their family's ordeal five months before in Panama. Both of the children had said that, somehow, the snow reminded them of JoJo. They all missed him. They had heard nothing about him since the events.

The headlines of the Boston newspapers on her lap brought on feelings that she hadn't had time to process for a while. Both the *Courier* and the *Post* reported that a historic meeting between the King of Sardinia and General Giuseppe Garibaldi was likely to lead to the unification of the Italian peninsula. The Italian peninsula would become a nation united under a shared language after centuries of control by other countries. Both papers also gave fresh accounts of the actions of Major Anderson who had moved his command to Fort Sumter in Charleston and was refusing to abandon that post. That prompted her to put the papers down and reach for one of the letters she had received several days before from Rory Brett. She needed to read it again.

Rory had written at least two to three times every week since they had parted in New Orleans and he had returned to Virginia to settle his estate. He had been worried that the recent very partisan election of Abraham Lincoln would provoke rash actions by hotheads on both sides of the troublesome issue of slave ownership. It did. Less than a few weeks after the November election, South Carolina's legislature had voted to separate from the Union. All of the southern slaveholding states were in a fervent state of agitation, as were the northern states that opposed slavery and had unanimously supported Lincoln in the election. Until last week, when the snow had reached six inches, massive demonstrations by black-clad followers of the Wide-Awake Movement had marched by torchlight down the streets of Boston, New York, and Philadelphia, clamoring for an immediate change. Abolitionists were crowing, and as loudly as they shouted, she knew that the southerners were screaming back. Some of them, like her sister's husband, an ardent Republican abolitionist, were arguing for a military solution to force a solution.

In his letters to her, Rory wrote that many of his associates in the Shenandoah were arming and the ranks of the local militias were swelling. Some of his neighbors were hoarding. He was concerned that hostile actions might precipitate bloodshed and hoped Virginia's elected officials would keep their heads to be certain their state stayed out of conflict, to keep their homes safe and avoid destructive, irreversible actions. Because of its proximity to Washington, he believed Virginia would be hard hit if violence escalated, and he didn't want that. He said he had seen enough of war. Emmy understood that very well. As much as she detested the stubborn stupidity with which the southern states were defending their perceived right to own the bodies and souls of other human beings, she was dismayed at the inflammatory rhetoric she read in all of the opinion articles, letters, and editorials. The passionate fervor she sensed all about her was making sensible civil solutions more difficult, she thought.

But it also was the report of the Italian situation that made her go back to this particular letter, for in it Rory mentioned Ari Scarpello, the brave mustachioed man who had saved his children and hers during the heist by hiding them in the train's undercarriage. Rory said that Scarpello had not gone to Italy to join Garibaldi. Instead, after all four of the children had turned up safe, he had sent his own two on to New York to be in the safekeeping of some relatives. Rory said Ari was returning to the Darién jungle to look for his wife, Lita.

She thought about Lita and Gabi, the two women who had been abducted with her by the Deriéni. They were fierce and brave, much more than she, she reflected. Gabi's advice had saved Emmy's life, likely. Emmy was incensed that the Panama Rail Company had reluctantly only given Gabi a paltry two hundred dollars and a refund of the ticket price as recompense for what she had endured. Emmy subsequently had learned that Gabi had left for Brazil to find her companion's adult son, who had survived the holdup. But she had heard nothing else. Nothing more about Ari Scarpello either. She believed she owed a great deal to that man and his wife.

She started to write to Rory but put the pen down.

She picked up the top newspaper on her desk and searched the page for something she had glanced at earlier, wondering if it was related. It said that Miss Jenny Lind, "The Swedish Nightingale," had agreed to perform in a concert featuring arias from the grand operas *Rigoletto* and *Tosca* by the popular composer, Verdi. The concert was a memorial benefit for the families of four opera singers, all friends of hers, who had perished in a recent train accident in Panama. No other details. Grand opera, indeed, she thought. These composers and their dramatists who wrote the librettos had no idea. Nothing she had seen or heard on their stages, no matter how beautiful the music or theatrically wondrous the spectacle—nothing could ever capture what she and her family knew about the world now.

Their arrival in Boston had settled a few things. Her family had provided a bit of comfort, but Emmy's father was too self-absorbed in his newly elected position to be of much help. Her sister seemed to be as domineering and competitive as she had been when she and Sarah were in their teens. And their mother, the only one who Emmy knew would provide a kind ear to her confidences, was "dwindling irreversibly and fast" from her sugar disease, according to the family's physician.

Emmy took a deep breath. She was penniless as a result of the events, and her children had changed. Jacob was worse now, it seemed. He was talking to himself more, occasionally mumbling in brief sentences. He still suffered night terrors; they had worsened since the events, compounded, she feared, by everything he had witnessed. And he had started a fire in his grandfather's office a few days ago. It was the second time he had done so since they had arrived in Boston. She didn't know what that meant—and JoJo was gone. She had no real help with Jacob.

Sarah now was withdrawn and seemed a bit more tentative than in the past. She had said they hadn't been abused by the aborigines who had found them; the natives, whoever they were, had simply taken them in, kept them for several days, and then deposited them by the bridge on the railroad tracks. They had disappeared into the forest. No one knew who they were.

Emmy started to write to Rory Brett again. She needed to reassure him somehow, tell him that she had faith that men with temperance and wisdom ultimately would prevail, but also to respond to his request that he visit her in Washington if she accompanied her father there when he was sworn in with

Senator Butler and the Massachusetts delegation. She wanted to tell him she wasn't ready, but she didn't really know how to say it without hurting him because he was so very earnest and had done so much for her. He had said he would care for her. She put the pen down again. Using her right hand was painful and she was clumsy and slow with it now, so she had to be careful about committing a pen to paper. She would have been in this case anyway.

Would he, could he, wait? To let her recompose?

So much depended on what might happen in the next few months, she realized. She had two young children who had seen horrible events while living, traveling, and suffering along with her on the ungovernable peripheries of civilization. She hoped that their fortunes might change and that she was wrong about what she was beginning to perceive from her experiencing firsthand the erratic behaviors of passionate but unbridled men and women. She knew very well what an individual could justify to himself or herself over public or personal causes.

Despite what she sensed, she hoped that she was wrong, and the worst was behind her now. As fortunate as she believed she was in so many ways to have survived yet another ordeal, she hoped that, in the future, the luck she would be given by Providence, rather than rescuing her from danger, preempted it in the first place.

"A dull, but secure peace, Dear God," she said to herself, quietly.

She had children to raise. She had to start up her life again.

CHAPTER SIXTY-THREE

<><><><><><><><><><><><><><><><>

SARAH

Few would have noticed, but she did, while preening in the luxury of her grandmother's big mirror. The white hairs were back, fine ones, and there were six of them now. She knew that plucking them likely would not stop them from returning again. But she would pluck them out anyway to keep her disguise intact, to make people think she was still only an eleven-year-old.

She had a name for her game of predicting who people were and then matching that with what she guessed was in store for them. She had decided she should call the exercise "Wisdom." By continuing to play it, practicing it on every encounter with others, she would hone her skills of observation, she wagered, thus justifying the distinction she had claimed for herself—that she possessed an "old soul." She had decided such a characteristic made her very special, indeed. She planned to keep that way of looking at herself until her body actually *did* grow old. She would have to find a different word to describe herself when that finally occurred in *this* life. That word, "old," applied to an aging body and carried with it so many other things that she didn't want for herself, particularly the prominence of decay, like what she saw in both of her grandparents. But for now, being an "old one," and having the ability to predict destinies because of what she had seen—probably from previous existences—was a wonderful badge that set her apart; exotic, almost. Thinking of herself being that way made her privately very proud.

And why should she not be proud of that? It wasn't that she had been perfect in her guesses at the destiny of each soul that she had met on the train. She had been wrong about the man with the bushy black beard who had played Solitaire, the one she had thought was a lonely soul. He was that and more, her mother had said. Emmy said she would explain in greater detail later on, when Sarah was old enough to understand such things.

Sarah continued to try to make sense of their brief captivity, when she, Jacob, Jonny Scarpello, and his baby brother had been brought by the aborigine boy and his father back to their Embera village. They had played by themselves, mostly. They had watched the aborigines, and the aborigines had watched them.

From what she could tell, in the end, the tribal elders had decided that they just didn't want anything to do with her or the other white children. They decided to take her and the others back to the iron rails and leave them there to be rediscovered by their own tribe. She thought that was interesting. Would they have presented too much trouble for the aborigines? She remembered that her mother had said that the whites had exterminated the isthmus aborigines. Or was it something else? Her brother's behavior?

What should she do about Jacob, now that Jojo had gone missing? Her brother kept to himself, and she had not been able to really reach him as she had earlier on, before this latest turn of bad luck. In the village of the Embera, he had moved himself into a corner and stared at the door, even when it was dark, as if he were expecting someone to enter. When the woman had come in carrying Jonny's baby brother and he was painted in brown and black markings, Jacob had started to rock back and forth and scream. He had pushed himself further into the corner. When the other aborigine women entered, fed them all again, and put a juice-paint over their own tattoos and took Jonny and her and applied the brown juice in patterns over their arms, they left Jacob alone in his corner. He would only let Sarah come close. Finally, the women gave her the juice-paint, which kept the bugs away. She was the only one who could get Jacob to bare his arms and chest so she could paint him, too. She told him she would make a plaid pattern, like the one they both knew from a tartan blanket at home, and he let her do it. But he really hadn't said very much to her or to anyone else since then. Even now in Boston, he cried every night, all night long. He wet his bed.

He was still a lost boy, she realized. She would keep working on it. But with all of her wisdom, she didn't know how he would end up.

CHAPTER SIXTY-FOUR

◇◇◇◇◇◇◇◇◇◇◇◇◇◇◇◇◇◇◇◇◇◇

EMMY

When the post arrived that afternoon, her sister brought her two letters and a parcel. One letter was from Rory Brett. The second was posted from Bellingham, Washington. It was from Captain George Pickett. She opened the letter from Pickett first. It was written in the same ornate calligraphy as the first letter he had written to her when she lived on Whidbey Island. He said he was resigning his commission from the army and would be traveling back east. He said that he thought of her often, their night-long walk on the beach on San Juan Island, and hoped that he might see her again, someday soon in the future. But that was all. She remembered her feelings from that experience. It was less than a year ago but seemed like so much longer. "Pickett George." Gallant, handsome George Pickett. Where was he headed? Would he be in Virginia when she traveled to Washington with her father?

She turned to the parcel. It was addressed to her son, "Master Jacob Evers, care of Mrs. Emily Evers." It had no return address, but the red and green postal stamps told her that it had passed through stations in New Orleans and Charlotte. Something else from Rory?

Emmy opened it and found a small silk pouch. Rolled inside the pouch was a playing card, a two of hearts flecked with blood stains, and an unsigned note addressed to Jacob, written in Greek and in English. The note said:

"Jacob: This card was on the bottom of the deck. Your mother will know what that means.

"What is wrapped inside of this card is for you, Señor. Please tell your mother that, like you and me, it has its flaws. But do accept it as a gift. This is a short life, after all. Is it not?"

Emmy shook the pouch and a large polished, cut diamond fell into her hand. It was as big as her thumbnail.

EPILOGUE

∞∞∞∞∞∞∞∞∞∞∞∞∞∞∞∞

DIA DEL DIABLO

On this day each year, in the streets, the devils fight with the children of the Cimaroons. The blacks and Mestizos will tell you that these devils—red, green, and blue, with sharp teeth and wooden faces that split open to become human—are the slavers who took them and beat them and killed them and maimed them for centuries. The fight goes on all day and all night in this sacred time, down the alleys of Portobelo and Nombre de Dios, the purging contests moving aside only for the passing procession of the velvet-robed Black Christ who cannot be put back into his sanctuary until midnight and all the devils have been transformed back into human beings, blessed and saved by holy water of the christening.

On that day, in the year of the Lord 1860, the mute Mestizo woman carried her husband, whose ears had been cut away when he was a boy, to the pyre she had built near the old fort from the wood of abandoned houses where men had died in pain and no one returned because their ghosts stayed on. It was a grand fire that she tended all night. She knew he deserved it because he was the only one who had ever heard her, the only one who really listened. And when the ashes were picked up by the morning's incoming tide, they spread him along the long shore that belonged to everyone who was free on the earth.

AUTHOR'S NOTES

◇◇◇◇◇◇◇◇◇◇◇◇◇◇◇◇◇◇◇◇◇

Ran Runnels, famously known throughout Panama then and now as "El Verdugo" or "The Hangman," was recruited in 1852 by Ambassador William Nelson on behalf of the Panama Railroad Company, to rid the Isthmus of Panama of the many thieves and killers who preyed on the passengers and cargo traversing the company's new highway. Runnels, a former Texas Ranger and mule skinner who rode with the famous Colonel Jack "Coffee" Hays during the Comanche wars and the Mexican-American war, took on the railroad job reluctantly. Initially, the railroad company attempted to hire Hays himself, but by then, he was well established as the sheriff of San Francisco. Hays recommended Runnels for the job.

While the railroad was still under construction, Runnels ran his operation quietly for over a year—under his cover as the director of the "Runnels Express Services", a mule transportation company. He visited the taverns and whorehouses, listening for gossip, and keeping a list of names of perpetrators and underwriters of the numerous heists and outrages in a private journal. Then, on one night, he and his men, who later became known famously as the secret "Isthmus Guard," visited the known whereabouts of thirty seven men, many of whom were prominent citizens, captured them, and lynched them on the parapets of Panama City. No trials were ever conducted. When the railroad began operating in 1855, the gold robberies and murderous plundering began again. In response, Runnels repeated his executions. On one day, he lynched thirty-five men and a few women in Aspinwall-Colón. The robberies stopped. A few years later, his intervention in the famous "Watermelon War" in Panama City resulted in the rescue of scores of travelers who were trapped by an angry ghetto mob in the train terminal. Little is known about Runnels after his "retirement" other than that he married the niece of the Panamanian governor. Some say that he was later involved in mercenary incidents in Nicaragua, where he briefly held the post of US consul. He died of tuberculosis in 1877 and is buried in Rivas, Nicaragua.

General Giuseppe Garibaldi and the Risorgimento dominated the headlines of newspapers throughout the Western world in the mid-nineteenth century. Garibaldi inspired young idealists internationally with his revolutionary exploits in South America and Italy, and his victories in 1860 that ended the Bourbon reign in southern Italy and Sicily and led to the unification of the Italian peninsula under King Victor Emanuel II. Garibaldi was a passionate abolitionist and an ardent proponent for universal suffrage and the emancipation of women. During the American Civil War, he was offered a major general's commission in the United States Army through a letter from Secretary of State William H. Seward to H.S. Sanford, the US minister in Brussels. According to Italian historian Petacco,

"Garibaldi was ready to accept Lincoln's 1862 offer but on one condition: that the war's objective be declared as the abolition of slavery. But at that stage, Lincoln was unwilling to make such a statement lest he worsen an agricultural crisis." On August 6, 1863, after the Emancipation Proclamation had been issued, Garibaldi wrote to Lincoln: "Posterity will call you the great emancipator, a more enviable title

General Giuseppe Garibaldi

than any crown could be, and greater than any merely mundane treasure."

General Winfield Scott was, before the American Civil War, the most famous and celebrated military commander since Andrew Jackson, having achieved fame as the result of his leadership and prominent victories in both the War of 1812 and the Mexican-American War. He ran unsuccessfully for the office of president twice, running as the Whig Party's candidate in 1852 and losing in that election by three hundred thousand votes. Considered a brilliant tactician and strategist by admirers, but also arrogant and pompous by many detractors, he was

General Winfield Scott and entourage

known by his own staff as "Old Fuss and Feathers" because of his insistence on disciplined decorum and grandiose displays of protocol.

He was a very big man and, by his later years, weighed more than three hundred and eighty pounds, necessitating pulleys and ropes to hoist him onto his horse. He is reputed to have frequently fallen asleep during meetings, likely due in part to a pathology that is now called "Pickwickian syndrome" or "obesity hypoventilation syndrome," a condition in which severely overweight people fail to breath rapidly or deeply enough resulting in low blood oxygen levels and high blood carbon dioxide (CO_2) levels. Some detractors said he was cat-napping again while sitting at the telegraph desk as reports came in from the Union defeat at the First Battle of Bull Run. His nickname by that time had become "Old Fat and Feeble."

In 1859, Scott traveled by way of the Isthmus of Panama to the San Juan Islands of the Pacific Northwest to intervene in a confrontation and prevent a dispute over territory from escalating into a full-scale war between the United States and Great Britain. (Captain George Pickett, as you will remember from *Widow Walk*, had been assigned there to prevent the British from seizing the island.) After that successful intercession, Scott's entourage traveled to San Francisco where he was honored in numerous lavish celebrations by the citizenry, militia, and the military. His party traveled back via the isthmus to the East Coast as tensions increased over the prospects of war that might result if the southern states seceded from the Union.

Scott predicted that a military conflict would be potentially ruinous for the country. He knew that the Union was unprepared for such a terrible event, for under President James Buchanan, Scott's US Army and Navy had been reduced in number to less than sixteen thousand active military personnel scattered all across the vast US territory. When war did begin after the firing on Fort Sumter in South Carolina, Scott was asked to command a newly formed seventy-five-thousand-man army composed mostly of inexperienced volunteers. Almost half of the experienced and trained officers had resigned their commissions, including Robert E. Lee, Thomas "Stonewall" Jackson, Albert Sydney Johnston, Joseph Johnston, and George Pickett, to join the Confederate Army.

There were rumors at the beginning of the war that Scott himself, a Virginian, might leave the Union to join his home state's newly formed army. However, he was an ardent proponent and defender of the Union, and the rumors had no merit. War always presents great temptation for the ambitious and the opportunists. Despite his extensive battle experience and repeated diplomatic successes, Scott was criticized and ridiculed as being a dysfunctional and useless relic of the past. There was also enormous pressure on Lincoln from numerous factions to end the war by marching the new army onto Richmond. Over Scott's objections, Lincoln approved a plan to take the Confederate capitol with an inexperienced army. After the disastrous US military's defeat at the battle of Bull Run, Scott, then seventy-three years old, was forced to resign and was replaced and retired by President Abraham Lincoln.

However, it was Scott's "Anaconda Plan," a strategy named perhaps by what he saw on his travels across the Isthmus of Panama, that Lincoln followed and which ultimately resulted in the defeat of the Confederacy's secession. The strategy entailed a naval blockade along the entire southern and Gulf of Mexico coastline, the capture of New Orleans and the seizure of important ports along the Mississippi, and the destruction of rail lines and supply sources.

Captain Jonathan Letterman, MD, surgeon, US Army, traveled across the Isthmus of Panama in early 1860 to fight the Ute Indians. He was ordered to join the Army of the Potomac later that year. Letterman distinguished himself prominently in the American Civil War as the Union Army's surgeon general, devising revised and well-organized field methods for the evacuation and treatment of wounded Union soldiers.

Senator Benjamin Butler established himself as an influential politician in Massachusetts and became one of many "political generals" of the US Army during the American Civil War. Always controversial and aggressive, accused of corruption and opportunistic enrichment, he achieved the epithet "Beast Butler" as the result of his actions as the commander of New Orleans during its occupation.

Diseases. The primary causes of death of isthmus travelers before the 1855 with the opening of the railroad were disease and murder. Dengue fever—also known as "Breakbones Fever" (the illness that besets Emmy Evers), malaria, and yellow fever were endemic in Panama until the early twentieth century when US military medical researchers identified the mosquito as their vector. Cholera was controlled in most Panamanian cities by governmental efforts to improve sanitation.

The Panama Railroad Company completed the forty-seven-mile, sea-to-sea run from Aspinwall-Colón to Panama City in 1855 at the cost of seven million dollars. Its investors recouped their investment within the first year, charging exorbitant fees for passenger and cargo. Until the Panama Canal was completed years later, the Panama Railroad was one of the most profitable enterprises in the world.

The Camino Real of Panama, a paved four-foot-wide road, was built over a path that for thousands of years had been one of the most important trade routes in Central America. The trail, likely originally created by pre-Colombian isthmus aboriginal Cueva, Conejo, and Culebra peoples, traversed one hundred kilometers across the Isthmus of Panama from the Pacific Ocean to the Caribbean and Atlantic Oceans.

The Spanish, utilizing enslaved aboriginal and African labor, paved the road with perpendicularly placed limestone and volcanic flagstones and maintained it for three hundred years until 1821 when Spain was forced to give up most of its Central and South American colonies. When the Panama Canal was created in 1911, a good portion of the southern road from Panama City into the Darién was submerged under what is now an artificial lake and reservoir for the canals.

A second alternatively used trail, the Camino Las Cruces, still exists in many places and spans a shorter distance from Panama City to the ancient town of Las Cruces on the Chagres River. To this day, the Las Cruces pathway is considered very dangerous because of the predatory bandits in the area.

The Embera, Kuna, and Wounaan are aboriginal peoples of the Panamanian isthmus whom the Spanish colonists called "Cuevas" (Cave), "Conejo" (Rabbit), and "Culebra" (Snake) people. After the Cuevas and other aboriginal peoples were exterminated or enslaved by the Spanish beginning in 1510, the semi-nomadic Embera-Wounaan and Kuna peoples moved into the Darién from Colombia. The Embera-Wounaan were formerly and widely known by the name Chocó, and they speak the Embera and Wounaan languages, part of the Chocoan language family.

Slavery and the Cimaroons. The Cimaroons were African slaves who escaped from the Spanish and lived in the forests of the Darién. For hundreds of years, they and their decedents preyed on the travelers of the Camino Real and the Rio Chagres, allying themselves on numerous occasions with English buccaneers and French pirates in order to plunder Spanish gold trains. The "Festival Congo de Diablos" is an annual Panamanian-Caribbean celebration of the escape from Spanish slavery.

Slavery and Poverty. In 1888, Brazil became the last new-world country in the southern hemisphere to ban slavery. Panama granted freedom to its indigenous and imported enslaved people in 1852. Many slaves imported from the Barbados and other countries had been granted emancipation by the Panama Railroad Company in return for work on the railroad. After the railroad was completed and became the main method of transport, much of the work that had previously allowed gainful employment to a good portion of the Panamanian population, especially within the diverse trades serving the transportation of travelers and supplies on the old roads and rivers, simply was no longer necessary. Poverty in isthmus increased dramatically, and displaced, unemployed people moved into the ghettos of Colón and the notorious Mingello of Panama City. There were frequent riots by disenfranchised, discontented, and impoverished people, including some that led to massacres, like the one that occurred in the disastrous "Watermelon War," noted in chapter 18.

ACKNOWLEDGMENTS

◇◇◇◇◇◇◇◇◇◇◇◇◇◇◇◇◇◇

To: Allen Hurt and Barbara Bourdeau,
for their consistent, constructive inspiration

To: Kelsye Nelson, Sherry Roberts, Randy Mott, Neil
Gonzalez, Hobbs Allison, Miae Aramori, John Aylward,
Melody Bish, Rose Ambrosio Bradley, Patti Cage, Shawn
Comerford, S.P. Hays, Christopher Landess, Francesca
LaSalle, Angela LaSalle, Jonathan Louie, Mike McAuliffe,
Tom McGurk, Patty Campbell McKillop, Brian McKillop,
Harvey Meislin, David McClinton, Tina Minnick, Archana
Murthy, P.J. O'Malley, Carey Pelto, Mike Phillips, Sonya
Pease, Shannon Polson, Paul Racey, Tony Roberts, Teresa
Stahnke, Maureen Matthiesen Weber, and Wendi Wills for
their production assistance, encouragement and comments

To: Alcy Aguilar, Christian Strassnig, and the Embera
people of the Darién for research assistance on Panama and
the Camino Real

ABOUT THE AUTHOR

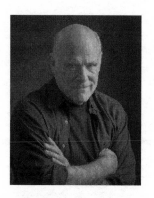

A former emergency medicine company CEO and co-founder and chief medical officer for a national multi-specialty healthcare organization, Gerard LaSalle MD currently teaches physicians about leadership and the business of medicine at several universities, including Cornell, Columbia, UCLA, and the University of Washington. In his nonmedical pursuits, he is an award-winning documentary and animation filmmaker, sculptor, poet, and historical fiction writer. LaSalle writes from his home in Seattle and works on his metal, wood, ceramic, and stone sculpture from his studio on Maury Island, Washington.

Isthmus is the author's second book in the historical series that began with *Widow Walk*, which earned the 2014 eLit Silver Medal for Multicultural Historical Fiction, a 2013 USA Best Book Award, and was a finalist for the 2013 Indie Excellence Book Award. It is available at Amazon, Audibles, and Barnes & Noble or www.widow-walk.com.

ISTHMUS
BOOK GUIDE

◇◇◇◇◇◇◇◇◇◇◇◇◇◇◇◇◇◇◇◇◇◇◇◇◇

1. The 1849 discovery of gold in California dramatically increased the travel across the Panamanian isthmus. For several years, the local economy flourished with the increase of coast-to-coast travelers and cargo. What was the impact on the local economy of the region when the railroad was completed? What was the impact of the high tariffs imposed by the railroad on travelers and natives of Panama?

2. Why did "The Watermelon War" erupt and what is its significance to the North American white and ex-slave cultures that were involved in it?

3. What is the "Dia del Diablo" and why is it celebrated in Portobelo and Nombre de Dios? What is its relationship to colonialism and slavery?

4. What do you think the caves of the "Old Ones" represent to Bocamalo?

5. What were the mid-nineteenth-century medical theories about causes and therapy for the diseases that killed so many railroad construction workers and travelers in the isthmus?

6. Who was Garibaldi and why was the Italian "Risorgimento" so fascinating to the world in 1860? How is it related to slavery and women's rights?

7. The character of Emmy in *Widow Walk* has been compared to that of Scarlett O'Hara in *Gone with the Wind*. Emmy faces different challenges in *Isthmus*. How is her response to the events in *Isthmus* consistent or different than in *Widow Walk*?

8. Do you think there is justification for the actions of Runnels? Of Bocamalo?

9. Describe the characters of Runnels, Brett, and Foil.

10. Imagine yourself as one of the captives of a killer such as Deacy or Bocamalo. How would you plan to survive?

Note: Additional questions for this book guide are available on www.widow-walk.com.

Read the award-winning prequel to *Isthmus*
WIDOW WALK

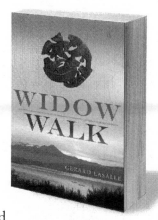

WIDOW WALK is based on the real events surrounding the revenge murder of Isaac Ebey, a prominent citizen who lived on Whidbey Island in the mid-1800s.

Author Gerard LaSalle combines his love of history with a compelling story of a woman's determination to find her kidnapped son. The novel vividly depicts those turbulent times, when the United States and Britain both attempted to control vast, fertile new lands in the Pacific Northwest and contain its native "aboriginal" populations.

In *Widow Walk*, brave people fight to survive predation and the violent confrontations that inevitably accompany ambition and expansionism. This is a story of courage, character, and the emergence of those who endured.

"*Widow Walk* is American Historical Fiction in the finest tradition, a direct descendent of Last of the Mohicans and Cold Mountain. LaSalle recounts the brutal, poignant clash between Native American Indian tribes and white settlers in the Pacific Northwest with economy and beauty, writing clean, devastating prose that clutches at your heart. This lean, unsparing narrative will make you look away in sorrow—before raising your fist in triumph. A quintessential rendering of the American Experience."

—Richard Barager, author of *Altamont Augie*
Silver Medal winner 2011 Book of the Year Awards

Available on Amazon and at
www.GerardLaSalle.com

65624178R00251

Made in the USA
Lexington, KY
18 July 2017